Passionate Calanettis

CARA COLTER
SCARLET WILSON
TERESA CARPENTER

MILLS & BOON

SOLDIER, HERO... HUSBAND?

CARA COLTER

To the team of editors and writers
who worked so tirelessly on this series:
I am proud to have been a part of it.
I stand in awe of your creative brilliance.

CHAPTER ONE

CONNOR BENSON AWOKE with a start. It was dark. And it was hot. Where was he? Somalia? Iraq? Afghanistan? Wherever he was, it was so secret, even his mother didn't know.

That feeling tickled along his spine, a sense of imminent danger. It brought him to red alert. Still not knowing exactly where he was, he was suddenly extremely focused, on nothing and everything. Each of his senses was so wide-open it was almost painful.

The tick of a clock somewhere in the room seemed explosively loud. Connor could feel the faint prickliness of the bedclothes against his naked skin, and he could feel a single bead of sweat slide down his temple. He could smell the residue of his own sweat and aftershave, and farther away, coffee.

Another sound rose above the ticking of the clock and the deliberate steadiness of his own breathing. It was a whispery noise just beyond this room, and as unobtrusive as it was, Connor knew it was that sound that had woken him. It was the sneaky sound of someone trying to be very quiet.

Connor tossed off the thin blanket and was out of the bed in one smooth movement, from dead asleep to warrior alert in the time it took to draw a single breath. The floor was stone under his bare feet and he moved across it soundlessly. His nickname on his SEAL team had been "the Cat."

At six foot five, every inch of that honed muscle, his comrades didn't mean a friendly house cat, either.

They meant the kind of cat that lived like a shadow on the edge of the mountains, or in the deepest forests and the darkest jungles, where men were afraid to go. They meant the kind of cat that was big and strong and silent. They meant the kind of cat that could go from relaxed to ready to pounce in the blink of an eye. They meant the kind of cat that had deadly and killing instincts.

Those instincts guided Connor across the room on silent feet to the door that had a faint sliver of light slipping under it. His movement was seemingly unhurried, but his muscles were tensing with lethal purpose.

Though most people would have detected no scent at all, when he paused on his side of the door, just under the aroma of coffee, Connor could taste the air. He *knew* someone was on the other side of that door. He also knew they were not directly in front of it—a hint of a shadow told him someone was to the left of the door. It was not a guess. His muscles tautened even more. His heart began to pick up the tempo. Not with fear. No, there was no fear at all. What he felt was anticipation.

Adrenaline coursed through his veins as Connor flung open the door.

He was nearly blinded by sunlight in the hallway, but it didn't stop his momentum. He hurled himself left, at the figure, back to him, rising from a crouch beside his door well. His hands closed around slender shoulders.

Slender?

A scent he had not noticed before tickled his nostrils. *Perfume?*

His mind screamed, *Abort!* It was too late not to touch, but not too late to temper his considerable strength. Instead of taking the culprit to the ground, he used the existing momentum to spin the person skulking outside his door toward him. The force of the spin caused a stumble, and as luscious curves came in full contact with him, Connor recognized the truth.

Her.

Connor stared down into the eyes of the woman he had just attacked, stunned. It wasn't that women couldn't be bad guys, but this woman so obviously was not. He cursed under his breath, and her eyes, already wide, widened more.

She seemed to realize she was still pressed, full length, against him, and she pushed herself away.

"Ma sei pazzo!" she said. Her voice was gorgeous, husky and rich, a note of astonishment in it that matched the astonishment in her huge, wide eyes. She definitely had the most beautiful eyes he had ever seen.

Eyes that, at the moment, were wide with shock. Now that she had pushed away from him, her hand went to the sweet swell of her breast, and he could see where her pulse beat wildly in the delicate column of her throat.

Connor, ever the soldier, and still in that place of heightened awareness, took in every exquisite detail of her. She had long, dark hair, luxuriously thick and straight, that was capturing the incredible morning light that poured in through the arched windows of the hallway they were in. Her hair fell in a shimmering waterfall of dark chocolate past slender bare shoulders.

At least a foot shorter than he was, the woman had on a bright, flower-patterned dress. It was sleeveless and accentuated the lovely litheness of her figure. The dress was pinched by a narrow belt at a tiny waist and then the skirt flared out in a way that made him able to picture her dancing, that skirt flying around her. She had sandals on her delicate feet, her toenails painted a soft shade of pink.

Her coloring looked as if it was naturally pale, but golden from the sun. Her skin was flawless. *Ma sei pazzo.* It occurred to Connor he was not in Iraq. Or Somalia. Not Afghanistan, either.

He cringed inwardly at his mistake. "Jeez," he said, out loud. "I'm in Italy."

It all came back to him. He was in a small town in Tuscany on a puffball mission for Itus Security, the company he and his friend Justin had started after Justin's injury had made them both leave the US Navy SEALs, though for different reasons.

"Sì, Italia."

Yes, he was in Italy. And it was not a secret. Everyone in his world, including his mother, knew exactly where he was. In fact, his mother had been thrilled for him when he had told her the Tuscan village of Monte Calanetti was on his itinerary.

Italy? she had said breathlessly. She had looked at him with ridiculously hope-filled eyes and said softly, *The land of amore.*

If anybody had a right to be soured by love, it was his mom, who'd had him when she was barely sixteen and had suffered through all it meant to be a single mother at that age.

In addition, Connor knew exactly what his years of service in the world's trouble spots and danger zones had made him. He knew only a mother could look at a battle-hardened and emotionally bereft specimen like Connor and hope love was in his future.

"Do you speak English?" he asked the young woman. He kept his voice deliberately quiet, threading it with calm. The woman was still watching him silently, with those doe-like eyes, and just like a doe, was ready to bolt at one more wrong move from him.

She nodded warily.

He deserved her wariness. "Sorry, ma'am," he muttered. "I seem to have a bit of jet lag. I was disoriented."

"You came out of that room as if you expected an assassin!" she said accusingly, finding her voice.

No point sharing with her that was exactly what he had been expecting. There was something sweetly angelic in her face that suggested that would be entirely foreign to her world.

Looking at her, it did occur to Connor that if a man was not completely hardened to life, the woman in front of him—beautiful and angelic, yet still sensual in an understated way—might have made his thoughts go to *amore*.

"I said I was sorry. I hope I didn't hurt you." Connor had tempered his strength, but even so, she was right. He had come out of that room expecting trouble of one variety or another, and his force had been substantial.

"No. No, I'm not hurt," she insisted hastily, but then she folded her hands over her shoulders and rubbed them.

He stepped in close to her again, aware of her scent

intensifying. He carefully pried her hands off her shoulders. She stopped breathing, staring up at him, her hands drifting to her sides.

If he was not mistaken, he stopped breathing, too, as he leaned in close and inspected the golden surface of her shoulders for damage. He stepped back and started to breathe again.

"There are no marks on your shoulders," he said quietly. "You won't be bruised."

"I told you I was fine."

He shrugged, looked away from her, ran a hand through his hair and then looked back. "I just thought I should make sure. What does that mean? What you said to me? *Ma sei pazzo?*"

"It's an exclamation of surprise," she said.

It was her eyes sliding away from him that alerted him to the fact there might be more to it than that, so he lifted an eyebrow at her, waiting.

"Specifically," she said, looking back at him, "it means *are you crazy?*" She was unrepentant, tilting her chin at him.

"Ah. Well. I can't really argue with that, or blame you for thinking it."

His senses were beginning to stand down, but even so, the woman's scent tickled his nostrils. Her perfume was very distinctive—it had an exotic, spicy scent that was headier than any perfume he had ever smelled. He looked once more into the liquid pools of green and gold that were her eyes and recognized a weak inclination to fall toward those pools of light and grace, calm and decency.

Instead, he reminded himself who he really was. He let his thoughts travel away from her and down the road to the sense of failure that traveled with him these days, around the globe, like a shadow.

What had just happened was precisely why he'd had to leave the only world he had known for nearly two decades. He'd started making mistakes. It was why he had left the SEALs when Justin had. In his line of work, mistakes demanded a price be paid. Often it was a huge price. Sometimes it was an irrevocable one.

And he knew, from firsthand experience, it was even harder when it was someone other than yourself who paid the price for your mistakes.

"It's all right," she stammered, and he realized she had seen something in his face that he would have preferred she hadn't seen.

And of course it was not all right to be attacking innocent civilians. Now that the initial shock had worn off, Connor could see she was trembling slightly, like a leaf in a breeze, and her eyes were wide on him. Her gaze flitted down the length of him, and then flew back to his face, shocked.

He glanced down at himself.

"Sheesh," he muttered. "Would that be adding insult to injury?"

"I told you I wasn't injured," she stammered. "And I'm not sure what you mean by insulted."

"It's an expression," he clarified, "just like your *ma sei pazzo*. It means on top of giving you a good scare, I've embarrassed you with my state of undress."

Her eyes flew to his state of undress, again, and then back up to his face. She confirmed that she was indeed embarrassed when her blush deepened to crimson.

He would probably be blushing himself if he had any scrap of modesty remaining in himself, but he did not. He'd lived in the rough company of men his entire adult life and guys had a tendency to be very comfortable in their underwear.

Still, he was very aware that he was standing in this beautiful woman's presence outfitted only in army-green boxer briefs that covered only the essential parts of himself.

Despite the circumstances he found himself in, he was reluctantly charmed that she was blushing so profusely it looked as if she had been standing with her face too close to a robust fire.

"Sorry, I'm disoriented," he said again, by way of explanation. "I've been on an insane schedule. I was in—" he had to think about it for a second "—Azerbaijan yesterday putting a security team in place for the World Food Conference. And the day before that…ah, never mind."

She struggled to regain her composure. "You're Signor Benson, of course."

"Connor, please."

"I'm sorry I was not here to greet you last night. Nico told me you would arrive late." Her English, he noted, was perfect, the accent lilting and lovely in the background of the precisely formed words. Her voice itself was enchanting, husky and unconsciously sensual. Or maybe it was that accent that just made everything she said seem insanely pleasing. Connor was willing to bet she could read a grocery list and sound sexy. He felt, crazily, as if he could listen to her all day.

"I think it was close to three in the morning when I arrived."

She nodded. "Nico told me your arrival would be very late. That's why I closed the shutters when I pre-

pared your room. To block out the light so you could
sleep in. I was just leaving you something to eat this
morning. I have to be at work in a few minutes."

"Schoolteacher?" he guessed.

She frowned at him. "Nico told you that?"

"No, I guessed."

"But how?"

"You just have that look about you."

"Is this a good thing or a bad thing to have this look
about me?"

He shrugged, realizing he shouldn't have said anything. It was part of what he did. He was very, very
good at reading people. He could almost always tell,
within seconds, what kind of lifestyle someone had,
the general direction of their career paths and pursuits,
if not the specifics. Sometimes his life and the lives of
others depended on that ability to accurately read and
sort details. This was something she, living here in her
sheltered little village in Italy, did not have to know.

"I still do not understand if it is a good thing or a
bad thing to have this schoolteacher look about me,"
she pressed.

"A good thing," he assured her.

She looked skeptical.

"You're very tidy. And organized." He gestured at
the tray beside his door. "And thoughtful, closing the
shutters so I could sleep in. So, I figured some profession that required compassion. A teacher. Or a nurse.
But the dress made me lean toward teacher. Your students probably like bright colors."

He was talking *way* too much, which he put down
as another aftereffect of jet lag. She was nibbling her
lip, which was plump as a plum, and frowning at him.

"It's like a magician's trick," she said, not approvingly.

"No, really, it's something everyone can do. It's just observing details."

She looked as if she was considering having another long, hard look at all of him, as if he had invited her to play a parlor game. But then, wisely, she decided against it.

Connor glanced at the tray set so carefully by his door, more proof of a tidy, organized, caring personality. It was loaded with a carafe of coffee and rolls still steaming from the oven. There was a small glass jar of homemade preserves and a large orange.

The fact he had guessed right about her being a teacher did not alleviate his annoyance with himself over this other stupid error. He'd heard someone sneaking around, all right—sneaking his breakfast into place so as not to disturb him.

"Thank you," he said, "for taking me in on such short notice. I should have made arrangements for a place to stay before I arrived, but I didn't think it was going to be a problem. When I researched it, there seemed to be lots of accommodations in the village."

"There are many accommodations here, and usually there would be more availability," she offered. "Today looks as if it will be an exception, but it is usually not overly hot in May. That makes it the preferred month for weddings in Tuscany."

Weddings.

"Ah, signor," she said, and the fright had finally melted from her and a tiny bit of playfulness twinkled in her eyes. "You are right! Sometimes you can see things about people that they don't tell you."

"Such as?"

"Even though you are here to help with the royal wedding, you do not like weddings."

What he didn't like was being read as easily as he read other people. Had he actually encouraged this observation? He hoped not.

"What makes you say that?" he asked.

"Just a little flinch," she said, and for a moment he thought she was going to reach over and touch his face, but she thought better of it and touched the line of her own jaw instead. "Right here."

Her fright had brought out his protective instincts, even though he had caused it. Her power of observation, brought out with just the tiniest of suggestions, was somehow far more dangerous to him. He noticed she had ignored his invitation to call him by his first name.

"I'm not exactly here to help with the wedding," he said, just in case she had the absurd notion he was going to be arranging flowers or something. "My company, Itus, will be providing the security. I'm going to do reconnaissance this month so all the pieces will be in place for when we come back at the end of July. Though you are right on one count— weddings are just about my least favorite thing," he admitted gruffly.

"You've experienced many?" She raised an eyebrow at him, and again he felt danger in the air. Was she teasing him, ever so slightly?

"Unfortunately, I have experienced many weddings," Connor said.

"Unfortunately?" she prodded. "Most people would see a wedding as a celebration of all that is good in life. Love. Hope. Happy endings."

"Humph," he said, not trying to hide his cynicism. Over his years in the SEALs, lots of his team members had gotten married. And with predictably disastrous results. The job was too hard on the women who were left behind to fret and worry about their husbands. Or worse, who grew too lonely and sought someone else's company.

He was not about to share his personal revelations about the fickle nature of love with her, though. Around a woman like her—who saw weddings as symbols of love and hope and happy endings—it was important to reveal nothing personal, to keep everything on a professional level.

"My company, Itus Security," Connor said, veering deliberately away from his personal experiences, "has handled security for some very high-profile nuptials. As a security detail, weddings are a nightmare. Too many variables. Locations. Guests. Rehearsals. Photos. Dinners. And that's before you factor in Bridezilla and her entourage."

"Bridezilla?" she asked, baffled.

Some things did not translate. "Bride turned monster over her big day."

His hostess drew in a sharp breath. "I do not think you will find Christina Rose like that," she said sternly. "She is an amazing woman who is sweet and generous and totally committed to her country."

Connor cocked his head at her. He was hopeful for any inside information that might prove useful to the security detail. "You know her?"

She looked embarrassed all over again, but this time there was annoyance in it, too. "Of course not. But her husband-to-be, Prince Antonio de l'Accardi, is a member of a much-loved royal family. That has made her a very famous woman. I have read about her."

"Well, don't believe half of what you read. No, don't believe *any* of what you read."

"So, you don't believe in weddings, and you are a cynic, also."

"Cynic is an understatement. I think you might have picked up I was a bit of a battle-hardened warrior when I treated you like an assassin instead of just saying good morning like a normal person would have," he said.

There. Letting her know, right off the bat, he was not a normal person.

"Well, I choose to believe Christina Rose is everything she appears to be." Her eyes rested on him, and he heard, without her saying a word, *And so are you.*

Connor lifted a shoulder, noting that his hostess had a bit of fire underneath that angelic first impression. It didn't matter to him what the future princess's personality was. It would be her big day, laden with that thing he was most allergic to, emotion. And it didn't matter to him what his hostess's personality was, either.

"Believe me," he muttered, "Christina Rose will find a million ways, intentional or not, to make my life very difficult."

But that was why he was here, nearly two months early, in the Tuscan village of Monte Calanetti. Not to save the world from bad guys, but to do risk assessment, to protect some royals he had never heard of from a country he had also never heard of—Halenica—as they exchanged their vows.

That was his mission. The lady in front of him could fill his life with complications, too, if he was not the disciplined ex-soldier that he was. As it was, he was not going to be sidetracked by a little schoolteacher in a flowered dress, no matter how cute she was.

And she was plenty cute.

But if that proved a problem, he would just keep his ear to the ground for another place to stay. He'd survived some pretty rough living arrangements. He wasn't fussy.

"Thank you for breakfast," he said curtly, moving into emotional lockdown, work mode. "Please thank your mother for providing me with a place to stay on such short notice, signorina."

"My mother?"

"Signora Rossi?"

A tiny smile, pained, played across the beautiful full-ness of her lips.

"No, signor. I am Signora Rossi. Please call me Isa-bella."

So he had made another mistake. A small one, but a mistake, nonetheless. Looking at Isabella, after she made that statement, he could see, despite his finely honed powers of observation, he'd been wrong about her. She was not as young as her slender figure and flawless skin had led him to believe. She might have been in her thirties, not her twenties.

No wonder Justin had him on wedding duty. Connor was just making mistakes all over the place.

And no wonder Justin had said to Connor, when he gave him this assignment, "Hey, when is the last time you had a holiday? Take your time in Monte Calanetti. Enjoy the sights. Soak up some sun. Drink some wine. Fall in love."

Justin really had no more right to believe in love than he himself did, but his friend was as bad as his mother in the optimism department. Justin had even hinted there was a woman friend in his life.

"And for goodness' sake," Justin had said, "take a break from swimming. *What* are you training for, anyway?"

But Justin, his best friend, his comrade in arms, his brother, was part of the reason Connor swam. Justin, whose whole life had been changed forever because of a mistake. One made by Connor.

So giving up swimming was out of the question, but at least, Connor told himself grimly, he wouldn't be falling in love with the woman in front of him. After having felt her pressed against him, and after having been so aware of her in every way this morning, it was a relief to find out she was married.

"*Grazie*, Signora Rossi," he said, trying out clumsy Italian, "for providing me with accommodation on such short notice. You can reassure your husband that I will not begin every morning by attacking you."

His attempt at humor seemed to fall as flat as his Italian. He spoke three languages well, and several more not so well. Connor knew, from his international travels, that most people warmed to someone who attempted to use their language, no matter how clumsy the effort.

But his hostess looked faintly distressed.

And then he realized he had made his worst mistake of the day, and it wasn't that he had accidentally propositioned her by mispronouncing a word.

Because Isabella Rossi said to him, with quiet dignity, "I'm afraid my beloved husband, Giorgio, is gone, signor. I am a widow."

Connor wanted to tell her that she of all people, then,

should not believe a wedding was a symbol of love and hope and happy endings.

But he considered himself a man who was something of an expert in the nature of courage, and he had to admit he reluctantly admired her ability to believe in hope and happy endings when, just like his mother, she had obviously had plenty of evidence to the contrary.

"I'm sorry for your loss," he offered, grudgingly.

"My husband has been gone six years, and I miss him still," she said softly.

Connor felt the funniest stir of something he did not like. Was it envy? Did he envy the man this woman had loved so deeply?

Stupid jet lag. It seemed to have opened up a part of him that normally would have been under close guard, buttoned down tight. Thoroughly annoyed with himself and his wayward thoughts in the land of *amore*, Connor turned from Signora Isabella Rossi, scooped up the tray and went into his room. Just before he shut the door, her voice stopped him.

"I provide a simple dinner at around seven for my guests, when I have them," she said, suddenly all business. "If you could let me know in the mornings if you are requiring this service, I would appreciate it."

Connor, a man who was nothing if not deeply instinctual, knew there was some dangerous physical awareness between them, a primal man-woman thing. Eating her food and sitting across a table from her would not be an option.

On the other hand, he did not know the lay of the land in the village, and he would have to eat somewhere today until he figured that out. Besides, Isabella Rossi had shown she was unusually astute at reading people.

He did not want her to know he perceived her as such a threat that he was willing to go hungry rather than spend more time with her.

"Thank you," he said, keeping his tone carefully neutral. "That would be perfect for tonight. I hope the rest of your day goes better than it began, signora."

CHAPTER TWO

ISABELLA STOOD IN the hallway, feeling frozen to the spot and looking at Connor Benson, balancing the tray of food she had provided for him on the jutting bone of one very sexy, very exposed hip. She felt as if she had been run over by a truck.

Which, in a sense, she had. Not that Connor Benson looked anything like a truck. But she had been virtually run down by him, had felt the full naked strength of him pressed against her own body. It had been a disconcerting encounter in every way.

His scent was still tickling her nostrils, and she was taken aback by how much she liked the exquisitely tangy smell of a man in the morning.

Now she'd gone and offered him dinner. Everyone in town knew she occasionally would take in a lodger for a little extra money. She always offered her guests dinner. Why was it suddenly a big deal?

It was because her guests were usually retired college professors or young travelers on a budget. She not had a guest quite like Connor Benson before. In fact, it would be quite safe to say she had never met a man like Connor Benson before.

"I hope my day goes better, too," she muttered,

and then added in Italian, "but it is not looking hopeful."

This man in her house, who stood before her unselfconscious in his near nakedness, was the antithesis of everything Isabella's husband, Giorgio, had been.

In fact, Isabella had grown up in Florence and walked nearly daily by the Palazzo Vecchio, where the replica of Michelangelo's statue *David* stood. The statue represented a perfection of male physique that had filled the frail Giorgio with envy, and at which she had scoffed.

"Such men do not exist," she had reassured Giorgio. She had swept her hand over the square. "Look. Show me one who looks like this."

And then they would dissolve into giggles at the fact the modern Italian male was quite far removed from Michelangelo's vision.

And yet this nearly naked man standing in the doorway of the room she had let to him made Isabella uncomfortably aware that not only did perfection of male physique exist, it awakened something in her that she had never quite felt before.

That thought made her feel intensely guilty, as if she was being disloyal to her deceased husband, and so she rationalized the way she was feeling.

It was because she had been pulled so unexpectedly against the hard length of him that her awareness was so intense, she told herself.

Her defenses had been completely down. She had just been innocently putting his breakfast beside his door when he had catapulted out of it and turned her around, making her stumble into him.

And now her whole world felt turned around, because she had endured a forced encounter with the heated silk of his skin, stretched taut over those sleek muscles. She had been without the company of a man for a long time. This kind of reaction to a complete stranger did not reflect in any way on her relationship with Giorgio! It was the absence of male companionship that had obviously made her very sensitive to physical contact.

It didn't help that Connor Benson was unbelievably, sinfully gorgeous. Not just the perfection of his male form, but his face was extraordinary. His very short cropped light brown hair only accentuated the fact that he had a face that would make people—especially women people—stop in their tracks.

He had deep blue eyes, a straight nose, high cheekbones, a jutting chin.

He was the epitome of strength. She thought of his warrior response to her outside his door, that terrifying moment when she had been spun around toward him, the look on his face, as if it was all *normal* for him.

There was something exquisitely dangerous about Connor Benson.

The thoughts appalled her. They felt like a betrayal of Giorgio, whom she had loved, yes, with all her heart.

"I've become pathetic," Isabella muttered to herself, again in Italian. A pathetic young widow, whose whole life had become her comfy house and the children she taught. She found love in the mutual adoration she and her students had for each other.

Why did it grate on her that her houseguest had known she was a schoolteacher? What would she have wanted him to think she was?

Something, she realized reluctantly, just a little more exciting.

"I'm sorry?" Connor said.

She realized she had mumbled about her self-diagnosis of being pathetic out loud, though thankfully, in Italian. She realized her face was burning as if the inner hunger he had made her feel was evident to him.

Well, it probably was. Men like this—powerfully built, extraordinarily handsome, oozing self-confidence—were used to using their looks to charm women, to having their wicked way. They were not above using their amazing physical charisma to make conquests.

He'd already told her how he felt about weddings, which translated to an aversion to commitment. Even she, for all that she had married young and lived a sheltered life, knew that a man like this one standing before her, so at ease with near nakedness, spelled trouble, in English or Italian, and all in capital letters, too.

This man could never be sweetly loyal and uncomplicated. Connor Benson had warned her. He was not normal. He was cynical and hard and jaded. She could see that in the deep blue of his eyes, even if he had not admitted it to her, which he had. She would have been able to see it, even before he had challenged her to look for details to know things about people that they were not saying.

"I said be careful of the shower," she blurted out.

That exquisite eyebrow was raised at her, as if she had said something suggestive.

"It isn't working properly," she said in a rush.

"Oh?"

"I'm having it fixed, but the town's only plumber is busy with the renovations at the palazzo. I have to wait for him. Now, I'm late for work," she choked out, looking at her wristwatch to confirm that. Her wrist was naked—she had not put on her watch this morning. She stared at the blank place on her wrist a moment too long, then hazarded another look at Mr. Benson.

The sensuous line of Connor Benson's mouth lifted faintly upward. The hunger that unfurled in her belly made her think of a tiger who had spotted raw meat after being on a steady diet of flower petals.

Isabella turned and fled.

And if she was not mistaken, the soft notes of a faintly wicked chuckle followed her before Connor Benson shut his bedroom door.

Outside her house, Isabella noted the day was showing promise of unusual heat. She told herself that was what was making her face feel as if it was on fire as she hurried along the twisted, cobbled streets of Monte Calanetti to the primary school where she taught.

Yes, it was the heat, not the memory of his slow drawl, the way *ma'am* had slipped off his lips. He sounded like one of the cowboys in those old American Western movies Giorgio had enjoyed so much when he was bedridden.

Really? The way Connor Benson said *ma'am* should have been faintly comical. How come it was anything but? How come his deep voice and his slow drawl had been as soft as a silk handkerchief being trailed with deliberate seduction over the curve of her neck?

She thought of Connor Benson's attempt at Italian when he had tried to assure that her mornings would not begin with an attack. That accent should have made that comical, too, but it hadn't been. She had loved it that he had tried to speak her language.

"*Buongiorno*, Signora Rossi. You look beautiful this morning!"

Isabella smiled at the butcher, who had come out of his shop to unwind his awning, but once she was by him, she frowned. She passed him every morning. He always said good morning. But he had never added that she looked beautiful before.

It was embarrassing. Her encounter with Connor Benson this morning had lasted maybe five minutes. How was it that it had made her feel so uncomfortable, so hungry and so alive? And so much so that she was radiating it for others to see?

"Isabella," she told herself sternly, using her best schoolteacher voice, "that is quite enough."

But it was not, apparently, quite enough.

Because she found herself thinking that she had not told him anything about his accommodations. She could do that over dinner tonight.

Isabella was *never* distracted when she was teaching. She loved her job and her students and always felt totally present and engaged when she was with the children. Her job, really, was what had brought her back from the brink of despair after Giorgio's death.

But today, her mind wandered excessively to what kind of meal she would cook for her guest.

Candles, of course, would be ridiculous, wouldn't they? And they would give the wrong message entirely.

She had not made her mother's recipe of *lasagne verdi al forno* for years. Food, and finally even the smell of cooking, had made Giorgio sick. Isabella was shocked at how much she *wanted* to cook, to prepare a beautiful meal. Yes, lasagna, and a fresh loaf of ciabatta bread, a lovely red wine. School in many places in Italy, including Monte Calanetti, ran for six days instead of five, but the days were short, her workday over at one. That gave her plenty of time to cook the extravagant meal.

So, on the way home from school, she stopped at the grocer's and the bakery and picked up everything she needed. She had several beautiful bottles of wine from Nico's Calanetti vineyard that she had never opened. Wine opened was meant to be drunk. It had seemed silly and wasteful to open a whole bottle for herself.

From the deep silence in the house, Isabella knew that Connor was not there when she arrived home. Already, it occurred to her she knew his scent, and her nose sniffed the air for him.

She began unloading the contents of her grocery bags in her homey little kitchen. She considered putting on a fresh dress. One that would make him rethink his assessment of her as a schoolteacher. It was then that Isabella became aware that it wasn't just the idea of cooking that was filling her with this lovely sense of purpose.

It was the idea of cooking for a man.

She stopped what she was doing and sat down heavily at her kitchen table.

"Isabella," she chided herself, "you are acting as if this is a date. It's very dangerous. You are out of your league. You will only get hurt if you play games with a man like Connor Benson."

She was also aware she felt faintly guilty, as if this intense awareness of another man—okay, she would call a spade a spade, she was attracted to Connor Benson—was a betrayal of the love she had had with Giorgio.

Everyone kept telling her it was time to move on, and

in her head she knew they were right. Six years was a long time for a woman to be alone. If she did not make a move soon, she would probably never have the children she longed for.

But no matter what her head said, her heart said no. Her heart had been hurt enough for this lifetime. Her heart did not want to fall in love ever again.

Slowly, feeling unreasonably dejected, she put everything away instead of leaving it out to cook with. She would bring anything that would spoil to school tomorrow and give it to Luigi Caravetti. He was from a single-parent family, and she knew his mother was struggling right now.

She opened a can of soup, as she would have normally done, and broke the bread into pieces. She would invite Connor to share this humble fare with her when he arrived. She needed to go over things with him, make clear what she did and did not provide.

It wasn't very much later that he came in the front door. She felt she was ready. Or as ready as a woman could ever be for a man like that.

"I have soup if you would like some," she called out formally.

"*Grazie*, that sounds great."

Isabella wished Connor would not try to speak Italian. It made her not want to be formal at all. It made her long to teach him a few words or phrases, to correct his pronunciation. She listened as he went up the stairs. She heard the shower turn on. Her mind went to the memory of touching that perfect body this morning, and something shivered along her spine. It was a warning. If she was smart there would be no language lessons with Connor Benson.

A little while later, he came into the kitchen. Oh, God. He was so big in this tiny room. It was as if he took up all the space. Her eyes felt as if they wanted to go anywhere but to him.

But where else could they go, when he was taking up all the space?

He was freshly showered. He had on a clean shirt. He smelled wonderful. His hair was dark and damp, and towel roughened. He had not shaved, so his whiskers were thick, and she could almost imagine how they would feel scraping across a woman's skin.

"I hope you don't expect homemade," she said. Her voice sounded like a croak.

"I didn't expect anything at all, ma'am."

There was that *ma'am* again, slow and steady, dragging across the back of her neck, drugging her senses.

"Isabella." Her voice sounded like a whisper. "Please, sit."

He took a seat at her table. It made her table seem ridiculous, as if it had been made to go in a dollhouse.

"Isabella," he said, as if he was trying it out. Her name came off his tongue like honey. She wished she had not invited him to call her by it.

"It smells good in here," he said conversationally and then looked around with interest. "It's quaint, exactly what I would expect an Italian kitchen to look like. That stone wall must be original to the house."

She felt tongue-tied but managed to squeak, "Don't be fooled by its charm. This house is three hundred years old. And it can be quite cranky."

"I think I noticed the crankiness in the shower just now," he said.

"I warned you about that." She did not want to be thinking about him in the shower, *again*.

"No big deal. Woke me up, though. The water was pouring out and then stopped, and then poured out again. I'll have a look at it for you, if you want."

"No," she said, proudly and firmly. She did not need to give herself the idea there was a man she could rely on to help her. "You are a guest in this house. I have already called the plumber, but I'm afraid with the renovation at the villa, my house is not a priority for him."

"I don't mind having a look at it."

Some longing shivered along her spine, which she straightened, instantly. "Signor, this house is three hundred years old. If you start looking at all the things wrong with it, I'm afraid you will not have time to do the job you came here to do. So, please, no, I can manage."

He looked faintly skeptical about her ability—or maybe the ability of any woman who was alone—to manage a three-hundred-year-old house, but wisely, he said nothing.

She dished out soup from the stove, gestured to the bread, took a seat across from him. She felt as if she was sitting rigidly upright, like a recent graduate from charm school.

"Relax," he said softly, "I won't bite you."

She was appalled that her discomfort was so transparent.

"Bite me?" she squeaked. She was also appalled at the picture that sprang to mind. And that it involved the cranky shower!

"It's American slang. It means I won't hurt you."

Wouldn't he? It seemed to her Connor Benson was

the kind of man who hurt women without meaning to, and she didn't mean by attacking them outside the bedroom door in the morning, either. He was the kind of man who could make a woman think heated thoughts or dream naive and romantic dreams that he would not stick around to fulfill.

"This morning excepted," he growled.

"You didn't hurt me!"

"Not physically. I can tell you're nervous around me now."

She could feel the color climbing up her face. She wanted to deny that, and couldn't. Instead, she changed the subject. "How was your day?"

"Uneventful," he said. "I met with Nico and had an initial look around. It's a very beautiful village."

"Thank you. I like it very much." Her voice sounded stilted. What was wrong with her? Well, she'd married young. Giorgio had been her only boyfriend. She was not accustomed to this kind of encounter. "Would you like wine?"

"I'm not much of a drinker."

"You might like to try this one. It's one of Nico's best, from his Calanetti vineyard."

"All right," he said. She suspected he had said yes to help her relax, not because he really wanted the wine.

The wine was on the counter. Isabella was glad her back was to him, because she struggled with getting it open. But finally, she was able to turn back and pour him a glass. She could feel a dewy bead of sweat on her forehead. She blew on her bangs in case they were sticking.

He sipped it carefully as she sat back down. "It's really good. What would you say? *Buono?*"

"Yes, *buono*. Nico's vineyard is one of the pride and joys of our region." She took a sip of wine. And then another. It occurred to her neither of them were eating the soup.

Suddenly, it all felt just a little too cozy. Perhaps she should not have insisted on the wine. She took rather too large a gulp and set down her glass.

It was time to get down to business. "I will provide a simple supper like this, Mondays to Saturdays, the same days that I work. On Sunday, I do not. I provide breakfast every day, but I don't usually leave a tray by the bedroom door."

"I wouldn't risk that again, either," he said drily. She had the uncomfortable feeling he was amused by her.

"It's not a hotel," she said sternly, "so I don't make beds."

"Understood." Did he intentionally say that with a military inflection, as if he was a lower rank being addressed by a superior? Was he perceiving her as bossy?

Given how she wanted to keep everything formal between them, wouldn't that be a good thing?

"I also do not provide laundry service." Thank goodness. She could not even imagine touching his intimate things. "I have a washing machine through that door that you are welcome to use. There is a laundry service in the village if you prefer. Except for sheets, which I do once a week. I provide fresh towels every day."

"I can do my own sheets, thanks."

"All right. Yes. That's fine. The common areas of the house are yours to use if you want to watch television or cook your own meals, or put things in the refrigerator."

The thought of him in her space made her take another rather large and fortifying sip of the wine.

"I don't watch television," he told her, "and I'm accustomed to preparing my own meals. I don't want you to feel put out by me. I can tell it is a bit of an imposition for you having a man in your house."

He was toying with the stem of his wineglass. He put it to his lips and took a long sip, watching her.

She tilted her chin at him, took a sip of her own wine. "What would make you say that? It's no imposition at all, Signor Benson."

Her heart was beating hard in her throat. He shrugged and lifted his wineglass to his lips again, watched her over the rim.

She might as well not have bothered denying it was any kind of imposition for her. She could feel her discomfort snaking along her spine, and he was not the kind of man you could hide things from.

"Connor, please," he said. "We're not very formal where I come from."

"Connor," she agreed. He had caught on that she was being too formal. Didn't he know it would protect them both? But she said his name anyway, even though it felt as if she was losing ground fast. She was using his first name. It felt as though she was agreeing, somehow, to dance with the devil.

But the question was, was the devil in him, or was it in her?

"And where are you from?" she asked. This was to prove to him she was not at all formal and stuffy and could hold a polite conversation with the best of them. She hoped it would not appear as if she was desperately eager for details about him, which she was not! She still had not touched her soup. Neither had he.

"I'm from Texas," he said.

"I thought the accent was like that of a cowboy."

He laughed at that. His laughter was deep and engaging, relaxing some of the constant hardness from his face, and she found herself staring at him.

"Ma'am—"

"Isabella," she reminded him.

"Isabella—"

Him saying her name, in that drawl, made her feel the same as if she had drunk a whole bottle of wine from the Calanetti vineyard instead of taken a few sips out of her glass.

Well, actually, her glass was empty, and so was his. He noticed, and tipped the wine out over both their glasses.

"Most people hear that drawl and automatically lower my intelligence by twenty points or so."

"I can tell you are a very intelligent man," she said seriously.

"I was just trying to make the point that regional accents can lead to judgments in the United States. Like you thinking I'm a cowboy. I'm about the farthest thing from a cowboy that you'll ever see."

"Oh! I thought everybody from Texas was a cowboy."

He laughed again. "You and the rest of the world. I grew up in a very poor neighborhood in Corpus Christi, which is a coastal city. I started picking up a bit of work at the shipyards when I was about eleven, and occasionally cattle would come through, but that's the closest I came to any real cowboys."

"Eleven?" she said, horrified. "That is very young to be working."

Something in his expression became guarded. He

lifted a shoulder. "I was big for my age. No one asked how old I was."

"But why were you working at eleven?" she pressed.

For a moment, he looked as though he might not answer. Then he said quietly, "My mom was a single parent. It was pretty hand-to-mouth at times. I did what I could to help."

"Was your mom a widow?" she asked. She and Giorgio had not had children, though she had wanted to, even with Giorgio's prognosis. Now she wondered, from the quickly veiled pain in Connor's face, if that wouldn't have been a selfish thing, indeed, to try and raise a child or children without the benefit of a father.

"No," he said gruffly. "She wasn't a widow. She found herself pregnant at sixteen and abandoned by my father, whom she would never name. Her own family turned their backs on her. They said she brought shame on them by being pregnant."

"Your poor mother. Her own family turned away from her?" She thought of her family's reaction to the news she was going to marry Giorgio.

Life has enough heartbreak, her mother had said. *You have to invite one by marrying a dying man?*

Isabella could have pointed out to her mother that she should be an expert on heartbreak, since Isabella's father, with his constant infidelities, had broken her heart again and again and again. One thing about Giorgio? He was sweetly and strongly loyal. He would *never* be like that.

But it had seemed unnecessarily cruel to point that out to her mother, and so she had said nothing. And even though they were not happy with her choice, Isabella's family had not abandoned her. At least not physically.

Connor lifted a shoulder. "My mother is an amazing woman. She managed to keep me in line and out of jail through my wild youth. That couldn't have been easy."

"I'm sure it was not," Isabella said primly.

He grinned as if he had enjoyed every second of his wild youth. "Then I joined up."

"Joined up?"

"I joined the navy as soon as I was old enough."

"How old is that?"

"Seventeen."

She drew in her breath sharply.

"I served in the regular navy for two years, and then I was drawn to the SEALs."

"SEALs? What is this?"

"It stands for sea, air, land. It's an arm of the navy. Combat divers."

She could tell there was a bit more to it than what he was saying.

"And your mother? Was she heartbroken when you left her to join the military?"

He smiled wryly. "Not at all. Once she didn't have to expend all of her energy keeping me fed and in line, she married a rich guy she cleaned for. She seems deliriously happy and has produced a number of little half siblings for me."

"You adore them," Isabella guessed.

"Guilty."

"I'm glad your mother found happiness."

"Me, too, though her luck at love has made her think everyone should try it."

"And shouldn't they?" Isabella found herself asking softly.

He rolled his shoulders, and something shut down

in his face. "A man who seeks danger with the intensity and trajectory of a heat-seeking missile is not exactly a good bet in the love department. I've seen lots of my buddies go down that road. They come home cold and hard and damaged. Normal life and domestic duties seem unbearably dull after the adrenaline rush of action."

"That sounds very lonely," Isabella offered. *And like a warning.* Which she dutifully noted.

Connor studied her for a moment. Whatever had opened between them closed like a door slamming shut. He pushed back from the table abruptly. "Lonely? Not at all," he insisted coolly. "Thank you for dinner."

But he hadn't eaten dinner. After a moment, she cleared his uneaten soup off the table and cleaned up the kitchen.

Really, he had let her know in every way possible that any interest in him would not be appreciated.

After putting her small kitchen in order, she retreated to her office. She hesitated only a moment before she looked up navy seals on the internet. She felt guilty as sin doing it, but it did not stop her.

It was actually SEALs, she discovered, and they were not just combat divers. Sometimes called Frogmen because they were equally adept in the water or on land, they were one of the most elite, and secretive, commando forces in the world.

Only a very few men, of the hundreds who tried, could make it through their rigorous training program.

Isabella could tell from what she read that Connor had led a life of extreme adventure and excitement. He was, unfortunately, the larger-than-life kind of man who intrigued.

But he had told her with his own words what he was. Cold and hard and damaged. She was all done rescuing men.

Rescuing men? something whispered within her. *But you never felt you were rescuing Giorgio. Never. You did it all for love.*

But suddenly, sickeningly, she just wasn't that sure what her motives had been in marrying a man with such a terrible prognosis.

And fairly or not, looking at her husband and her marriage through a different lens felt as if it was entirely the fault of Connor Benson.

Even knowing she had been quite curious enough for one night, she decided to look up one more thing. She put in the name Itus Security. There was a picture of a very good-looking man named Justin Arnold. He was the CEO of the company. Beside his picture was one of Connor, who was the chief of operations. There was a list of services they offered, and a number of testimonials from very high-profile clients.

Their company was named after the Greek god of protection, Itus, and their mission statement was, "As in legend, Itus is sworn to protect the innocent from those who would do them harm."

Intrigued, she went and read the mythology around Itus. A while later, Isabella shut off the computer and squared her shoulders.

A month. Connor Benson was going to be under her roof for a month. After one day, she was feeling a terrible uneasiness, as if he could, with just his close proximity, change everything about her, even the way she looked at her past.

"I have to avoid him," she whispered to herself. And

it felt as if her very survival depended on that. She went to bed and set her alarm for very early. She could put out his breakfast things and leave the house without even seeing him tomorrow. There were always things to do at school. Right now, she was preparing her class to perform a song and skit at the annual spring fete, and she had props to make, simple costumes to prepare.

She had a feeling with Connor under her roof and her badly needing her schoolroom to hide out in and something to distract from the uncomfortable feelings she was experiencing, she was about to produce the best song and skit the good citizens of Monte Calanetti had ever seen!

CHAPTER THREE

CONNOR RETREATED TO his room, annoyed with himself. He was not generally so chatty. What moment of madness had made him say yes to that wine? And why had so very little of it made him feel so off balance?

Intoxicated.

Maybe it hadn't been the wine, but just sharing a simple meal with a beautiful woman in the quintessential Italian kitchen, with its old stone walls and its deep windows open to the breeze, that had brought his guard down.

He had told Isabella things he had not told people he'd worked with for twenty years. Justin knew about his hardscrabble upbringing on the wrong side of Corpus Christi, but no one else did.

The soft look in Isabella's eyes as he had told her had actually made him feel not that he wanted to tell her less, but as though he wanted to tell her more, as if his every secret would be safe with her.

As if he had carried a burden alone for way too long.

"Stop it," Connor snapped grimly at himself. He acknowledged he was tired beyond reason. You didn't unload on a woman like her. She, cute little schoolteacher that she was, wouldn't be able to handle it, to hold up to it. She'd buried her husband and that had sent her into full retreat. That's why someone so gorgeous was still unmarried six years later.

So there would be no more wine tastings over supper that loosened his tongue. No more suppers, in fact. Tomorrow, rested, his first duty would be to find a nice little place to eat supper every night.

With none of the local wines. That one tonight had seemed to have some beautiful Tuscan enchantment built right into it.

And if avoiding her at dinner proved to be not enough defense, he would go in search of another place to stay.

Not that he wanted to hurt her feelings.

"The Cat does not worry about people's feelings," he said, annoyed with himself. What he needed to do was deal with the exhaustion first. He peeled off his clothes and rolled into bed and slept, but not before grumpily acknowledging how hungry he was.

Connor awoke very early. He knew where he was this time. Again, he could hear the sounds of someone trying to be very quiet. He rolled over and looked at his bedside clock.

Five a.m. What the heck? He had the awful thought Isabella might have gotten up so early to make him breakfast. That made him feel guilty since he knew she had a full day of work to put in. Guilt was as unusual for him as worrying about feelings. Still, he needed to tell her not to bother.

He slipped on a pair of lightweight khakis and pulled a shirt over his head, and went downstairs to the kitchen.

She had her back to him.

"Isabella?"

She shrieked and turned, hand to her throat.

"Sorry," he said, "I've startled you again."

She dropped her hand from her throat. "No, you didn't," she said, even though it was more than obvious she had been very startled.

"Whatever. I think we've got to quit meeting like this."

The expression must have lost something in the translation, because she only looked annoyed as she turned back to the counter. "I just wasn't expecting you to be up so early."

"I wasn't expecting you up this early."

"I'm preparing for the spring festival," she said. "I have extra work to do at school."

"And extra work to do here, because of me?"

She glanced over her shoulder at him, and then looked quickly back at what she was doing, silent.

"I wanted to let you know not to fuss over me. A box of cereal on the table and some milk in the fridge is all I need in the morning. And coffee."

"I'll just show you how to use the coffeemaker then—"

He smiled. "I've made coffee on every continent and in two dozen different countries. I can probably figure it out."

She looked very pretty this morning. Her hair was scraped back in a ponytail. It made her look, again, younger than he knew her to be. The rather severe hairstyle also showed off the flawless lines of her face. She had on a different sleeveless dress, and her lips had a hint of gloss on them that made them look full and faintly pouty.

"All right then," she said, moving away from the coffeemaker. "So, no breakfast?"

"I don't need supper tonight, either. I'm kind of used to fending for myself."

And he did not miss the look of relief on her face.

So he added, "Actually, I probably won't need dinner any night. Instead of letting you know if I won't be here, how about if I let you know if I will?"

The look on her face changed to something else, quickly masked. It only showed him the wisdom of his decision. The little schoolteacher *wanted* someone to look after, and it would be better if she did not get any ideas that it was going to be him!

"I actually like to swim before I eat anything in the morning. This is the perfect time of day for swimming."

"It's not even light out."

"I know. That's what makes it perfect."

Whenever he could, Connor had begun every morning of his life for as long as he could remember with a swim. That affinity for the water had, in part, been what made him such a good fit for the SEALs. But when he left the SEALs, it was the only place he had found where he could outrun—or outswim, as it were—his many demons. Despite Justin's well-meaning advice to take a rest from it, Connor simply could not imagine life without the great stress relief and fitness provided by the water.

"You'll wake people up."

"Actually, Nico invited me to use the pool at his private garden in the villa, but I'd prefer to swim in the river."

"The river? It's very cold at this time of year."

"Perfect."

"And probably dangerous."

"I doubt it, but I already warned you about men like me and danger."

"Yes, you did," she whispered. "There's a place on the river where the boys swim in the summer. Would you like me to show it to you?"

"You aren't trying to protect me from danger, are you, Isabella?" he asked quietly.

"That would be a very foolish undertaking, I'm sure," she said, a little stain that confirmed his suspicions moving up her cheeks. "It's hard to find, the place where the boys swim. That's all."

"Yes, please, then, show it to me," he heard himself saying, though he had no doubt he could find good places to swim all by himself. He didn't want to hurt her pride. "Yes, I'd like that very much."

And so he found himself, with dawn smudging the air, painting the medieval skyline of Monte Calanetti in magnificence, walking down twisting streets not yet touched by the light beside Isabella to the river.

And enjoying the pink-painted splendor of the moment way more than he had a right to.

Isabella contemplated what moment of madness had made the words slip from her mouth that she would show Connor the way to the river. By getting up so early, she'd been trying to avoid him this morning.

Instead, she was walking through the still darkened streets of Monte Calanetti with him by her side.

And despite the pure madness that must have motivated her invitation, she would not have withdrawn it had she been given a chance. Because that moment, of unguarded impulse, had led to this one.

It was unexpectedly magical, the streets still dim, the

brilliance of the dawn that was staining the sky above them not yet reaching into the cracks and crevices of the town. The occasional light was blinking on in the houses and businesses they passed.

Isabella was intensely aware of how it felt to have this man walk beside her. He was so big, his presence commanding. He had gone back up to his room for a moment, and when he came down he carried a small black bag and had a white towel strung around his neck.

He had a way of walking—shoulders back, stride long and confident and calm—that gave a sense that he owned the earth and he knew it. Isabella had never felt unsafe in Monte Calanetti, but she was aware, walking beside him, of feeling immensely protected.

"I can't believe the light," he said. "I've never seen anything like it."

"It's part of what makes Tuscany famous, that quality of light. Artists throng here for that."

"How would you say this in Italian?" he said, making a sweeping gesture that took in everything—the amazing light and the twisting streets, still in shadows, dawn beginning to paint the rooflines in gold.

She thought a moment. Wasn't this exactly what she had longed to do and had decided was dangerous? The morning was too beautiful to fight with herself, to be petty about what she would and wouldn't give. She would give him a few words, nothing more.

"In tutto il suo splendore," Isabella said.

He repeated it, rolling the words off his tongue. Mixed with his drawl and the deepness of his voice, it was very charming.

"And the translation?" he asked her.

"In glory."

"Ah," he said. "Perfect."

After that neither of them attempted conversation, but the quiet was comfortable between them as they moved down the narrow streets. It gave a sense of walking toward the light as they left the last of the buildings behind and followed the road past the neat row of vineyards that followed the undulating green of the hills.

"There it is," she said, finally, pointing at the ribbon of river that had become visible up ahead of them. "When you come to the bridge, turn right and follow the river. You'll see a tire suspended on a rope where the boys swim."

"Thank you. *Grazie*."

"You're welcome." She should have turned back toward the town, but she did not. She recognized a reluctance to leave the simple glory of this moment behind. He must have felt that, too.

"Come with me." His voice was husky.

Come with him? Where?

"Swimming?" she asked. Her voice felt very squeaky. It felt as if he had asked something far graver. To tangle their lives together, to follow the thread of magic that had led them through the town in the enchanted light of early morning.

When he said nothing, she rushed to fill the silence. "I couldn't possibly. I don't know how to swim. The water will be cold. I—I—I don't have proper bathing wear."

"Don't come this far and not at least put your feet in the water."

It felt as if he was saying something else altogether. He was inviting her to wake up instead of sleeping. He was inviting her to really live instead of going through the motions of living.

"I have to tell you a little secret," she confessed. "I've never learned to swim because I am a little bit afraid of the water."

"All the more reason to say yes instead of no," he said.

It occurred to her Connor Benson was that kind of man. Being with him would challenge you to be more than you had been before. She had always been perfectly content with who she was before!

"Maybe another time," she said uneasily.

"Putting your feet in the water is the first step to swimming, to overcoming that fear."

"It's not as if it's a crippling fear—it's not as if it changes my life," she said defensively, already sorry she'd confided in him that she was afraid.

"Fear can be a gift," he said, his voice calm and low. "It can show you that you are in very real danger. But an irrational fear can change your life in ways you don't even understand. If you give in to it, it can expand. So, one day you're afraid of swimming, the next you're afraid of everything."

Did he see her as afraid of everything? And how much truth was there in that? She looked at the safe little world she had created for herself. Maybe, even if it was annoying, maybe he was right. She needed to stretch just a tiny bit out of her comfort zone.

What would it hurt to get her feet wet?

"All right," she whispered, and was rewarded with a tentative smile. The smile put the dawn to shame and warned her exploring new territories and experiences was always going to be fraught with hidden dangers.

That's why she had chosen life as a schoolteacher in a small town. Her choices had given her a life with a reassuring sameness to everything that made her feel safe and secure.

Though in this amazing dawn, she saw things in a new and less flattering light. Had she allowed herself to become utterly boring? Apparently. Apparently she had become the kind of woman who you could tell in a single glance was a schoolteacher.

They came to the bridge and stood on it for a moment. The water was flowing underneath it like liquid gold, stained by the rising sun. They stood there in silence, watching morning mist rise off the vineyards all around them.

"Everyone should know how to swim," he said sternly, as if he was deliberately moving away from the magic of the shared moment, as if he was making sure she was not mistaken about his motivations in asking her to join him.

"Really? Why?"

He frowned at her, as if the question was too silly to deserve an answer.

"Most of the world's population, including you, lives near some sort of body of water. You could be in a boat that capsizes. You could fall in."

"I suppose," she agreed, but looking at him, she recognized what was at his very core. He protected people. It was more than evident that was his vocation and his calling. His shoulders were huge and broad, but broad enough to carry the weight of the whole world?

He broke her gaze, as if he knew she had seen something of him that he did not want her to see. Connor moved off the bridge and found a path worn deep by the feet of hundreds of hot little boys over many, many years.

The path was steep in places, and her footwear—a pair of flimsy sandals, fine for town—was not very good for scrambling over rocks.

"Oh," she gasped at one point, when she nearly fell.

He turned, took it all in in a breath, and his hands found her waist and encircled it. He lifted her easily over the rough spot and set her down. But his hands remained around her waist for just a hair too long, and then he turned away just a hair too quickly.

Her sensation of being with a man who would protect her with his life, if need be, strengthened.

It made her feel exquisitely feminine to be the one being looked after, for a change. Giorgio had never looked after her. It had always been the other way around.

A touch of guilt rippled along the perfect mirrored surface of the morning. But it evaporated like the mist rising all around them as they arrived at the swimming hole. Her awareness of Connor seemed to fill up every crack and crevice in her, just as sunlight would be filling every crack and crevice as it poured into the town.

The river widened here, gurgling on both sides of a pool that was large and placid. A tree leaned over it, and from a sturdy branch, a tire swung on a frayed rope.

Connor kicked off his shoes and shucked his trousers and his shirt and stood before her much as he had yesterday, totally unself-conscious in bathing trunks that were the same cut and style as his underwear had been, and every bit as sexy. He bent over his bag for a moment and fished out something that he held loosely in his left hand.

He stepped to the water's edge.

"Is it cold?" she asked.

"Oh, yeah," he said with deep pleasure. He reached back his right hand for her. "It's a bit slippery."

Crazy to accept that invitation, but really, it was much too late to stop accepting the crazy invitations now. She kicked out of her sandals and reached out. His hand closed around hers, and he tugged her gently to the water's edge. She was not sure anything in her entire life had felt as right as accepting the strength of that hand, feeling it close around her own, with a promise of strength and protection.

"The first step to swimming," he encouraged her.

She stuck a toe in, shrieked and pulled it back out swiftly. She tried to loosen her hand from his, but he just laughed and held tight until she put her toe back in the water.

"Come on," he said, patiently. "Just try it."

And so, her hand held firmly in his, she stepped into the icy cold water and felt her eyes go round. The mud on the bottom oozed up between her toes.

It felt wondrous. She didn't feel the least bit afraid. He tugged her hand and smiled. What could she do? She could say yes to life. Isabella bunched up her skirt in her other hand and lifted it. The morning air on her naked thighs felt exquisite. She saw his eyes move there, to where she had lifted her skirt out of the water, and felt slightly vindicated by the flash of deep masculine heat she saw in them. That was not the look one gave a boring schoolteacher.

He led her deeper into the water—it crept up to her calves and to her knees—and he smiled at her squeal that was part protest and mostly delight. And then she was laughing.

The laughter felt as if it was bubbling up from a hidden stream deep within her; it had been trapped and now it was set free.

Connor was staring at her, and his gaze added to the sense of heightened awareness. She was entering another world, a foreign land of sensation, his hand so warm and strong guiding her, the cold water tugging on her feet and her bare calves, licking at her knees, storming her senses. She was not sure she had ever felt so exquisitely and fully alive.

Something sizzled in the air between them, as real as getting a jolt from a loose wire. Connor Benson was looking at her lips. She allowed herself to look at his.

A knife-edged awareness surged through her. If she took one tiny step toward him, she knew he would kiss her.

Was this what she had given up when she had chosen Giorgio? Was this what her mother had tried to tell her she would miss? The thought was an unexpected dark spot in the brightness of her unleashed spirit.

She felt the laughter dry up within her, and Isabella let go of Connor's hand and took a step back instead of toward him.

"What?" he asked.

She backed away from his touch, from the exquisite intoxication of his closeness. It was clouding her judgment. It was making her crazy.

Ma sei pazzo, she chided herself inside her own head, backing away from the delicious craziness that beckoned to her.

But he did not allow her to escape. For every step

back she took, he took one forward, until she was up against the slippery bank and could not move for fear of falling in the water. He came to her and lifted her chin, looked deeply into her eyes. "What?" he asked again, softly.

She could feel the strength in his hands, the calm in his eyes. She could smell the scents of him and of the morning mingling. She could lean toward all of this...

But she didn't.

"Nothing," she said. "I have to go. I can't—"

Can't what? she asked herself. Enjoy life? Be open to new experiences? She broke away from his gaze—a gaze that seemed to know all her secrets, to strip her of everything she had regarded as truth before. She gathered her skirt, shoved by him, waded up the river to where it was easy to find the bank and left the water.

"You can use my towel to dry off your feet," he called.

She did that. She grabbed his towel and her shoes and found a dry place on the bank to sit and towel off her feet.

She dared to glance at him. He stood, watching her. He was so extraordinarily attractive, those strong legs set in the water, the morning light playing with the features of his face, so comfortable in his own skin. Italians had an expression about men like this.

Sa il fatto suo.

He knows what he is about. He knows himself.

And then this man who knew himself so well, who knew his every strength and his every weakness, lifted a shoulder, dismissing her. He dipped the mask and snorkel he held in his left hand into the water. He slipped them on, resting them on his forehead. Then he casually saluted her, adjusted the mask and snorkel, and dived neatly into the water and disappeared.

She held her breath. Where on earth had he gone? It seemed as if he could not possibly be down there for that long without something having happened. Was he tangled in a branch under the water? Had he hit his head on a rock?

But then the water broke, at the far edge of the pool, where faster water fed it. He broke the surface, and without looking back began to swim against the current.

It would always be like this if you were with a man like him, Isabella told herself sternly. *You would always wonder what danger he had managed to find.*

And still, she could not tear her eyes away from him. She watched in utter amazement as Connor propelled himself through the water. His strength and his grace were utterly awe-inspiring. It was as if there was no current at all, his body cutting through the water at high speed. If she didn't know better, she would think he had flippers on, but no flippers had come out of that bag. She watched him swim until he reached a bend in the river, swam around it and disappeared.

She finished drying her feet and put her shoes on. It was harder navigating the tricky path back to the bridge without him.

But it was what she had to do. She had to navigate without him—she had to go back to the way her life had been before they took that walk into a world of enchantment, this world where fears evaporated like the morning mist was evaporating under the Tuscan sun.

Isabella had to be who she was before.

A few minutes did not alter the course of an entire life. But she of all people should know that was not true, because the entire course of her life had been altered the second she had said *I do* to Giorgio.

And it felt like the worst kind of sin that these few minutes this morning had filled her with regret, for the first time, at what the choice to say those words had made her miss in life.

But one thing about saying that to Giorgio? If she ever did say those words to a man again—and that was a big, big *if*—it would be to one who would grow old with her.

And there would never, ever be a guarantee of that with a man like Connor Benson.

The river was amazing to swim in, and Connor quickly made morning swims a part of his Monte Calanetti routine. His time in the military had made him move toward a structured approach to life. He loved routine and order. From firsthand experience, Connor knew when the world turned to chaos—which it could do in the blink of an eye—that was when an investment in discipline paid dividends.

And so now he developed a schedule for his days. He rose early, before Isabella was up, walked to the river and swam against the current in the cold water until his muscles ached but his mind was sharply clear and focused.

It was all working out quite nicely. By the time he returned, Isabella had left for work.

Isabella. The clear mind made Connor uncomfortably aware, especially after that magical morning together, that this time Isabella could well be the chaos waiting to unfold in his life.

And that kind of chaos was way more dangerous than

the sudden crack of a sniper's rifle, or a bomb going off on the side of the road.

Oh, she seemed innocent enough, the last place a man would expect chaos to come from, but that would be a man who had not felt her hand close around his, who had not heard her unexpected shriek of delighted laughter split the silence of the morning as her toes touched ice-cold water. That would be a man who had not, for one crazy, glorious moment, looked at her lips and wanted to taste the promise of them, wanted to see if they tasted like the nectar of life itself.

The answer was simple. No more dawn encounters. No more walking through streets so quiet he could hear her dress swishing against her bare legs, no more putting his hands around her narrow waist to lift her over the rocky parts of the trail. No more wading in icy cold water with her. No more encouraging her to explore the world of sensation.

And especially no more looking at the sweet plumpness of her lips!

A man—one not as disciplined as Connor knew himself to be—could live to see the light that had come on in Isabella's face that morning by the river.

And so, he was avoiding her. And his avoidance had helped him develop a routine that he was comfortable with. There were no more tongue-loosening little chats over wine, and no more shocking morning encounters in the hallway or kitchen, and most of all, no more morning strolls through a predawn town.

Isabella seemed to enjoy routine as much as he himself did, and so it was proving easy to avoid her. He, an expert on figuring out people's habits, had her routine down pat in no time. It fit perfectly with his lifestyle.

By the time he returned from his early morning swims, Isabella was gone. He used the kitchen and did his laundry when she was at school. A lot of his work could be done on his computer, and he took advantage of her absence and the coolness on the lower floors of her house to do that when she was not there.

When she was at home in the evenings, he went out to eat and did reconnaissance. It was cooler then, anyway, and he made sure never to be back until her house lights—and her bedroom light, which he could see from the street—were out.

Even with all that effort, it was hard to ignore the fact he was sharing a house with a woman. No, it seemed his avoidance strategy had made *more* awareness, not less, tingle along his spine. Her little touches were everywhere in that house: an exquisite painting, a fresh vase of flowers, the smell of toast and coffee in the morning. Her scent was in the air.

And by now it had become apparent to him that all the while he was congratulating himself on his avoidance strategy, the truth was it was so successful because she was avoiding him!

By the fifth day of living under her roof, after succeeding with zero encounters of the Isabella-in-person kind, Connor was not at all sure what his success meant, because he was fairly certain he had never been more aware of another person.

Connor came into the house. It was much earlier than he usually arrived in the afternoon, but he felt a need to change clothes before he went and found a place to eat tonight. It had been another scorching day in Monte Calanetti and he thought he might head to the river for the second time that day.

He paused and listened. Had he managed to get in before she got home from school?

Today, for the first time, he realized he had not been successful in avoiding sharing the house with his appealing roommate. He could hear the one and only shower running upstairs.

Well, that was okay. He would nip into his room and get his swim things and a change of clothes. Isabella wouldn't even know he'd been in the space. The thought of bumping into her in the hallway, fresh out of the shower, made him hurriedly gather his swim things from his room.

His escape was nearly complete when the sound of an explosion, followed by a woman's shriek of terror, came from the bathroom. There was a loud *thunk*.

And then there was the worst thing of all.

Complete and utter silence.

CHAPTER FOUR

WITHOUT EVEN THINKING, doing what came as naturally to him as breathing, Connor threw down his things and ran into the hallway, straight toward the now silent bathroom.

"Isabella? Are you okay?"

There was no answer. He pounded on the door. There was still no answer. He tried the door. It was locked.

"Isabella?"

When there was still no answer, he put his shoulder to the door. The old wood cracked with ease and the door fell open.

He was hit in the face by water. He threw his hands up over his face and peered out between two fingers. Water was spewing out of the pipe where the showerhead had been, going in every direction, drenching the walls in water. The showerhead was on the floor under the sink.

Isabella was on the floor, soaked. The shower curtain had been ripped from its rod, and it was draped across her naked body. Turning his back to the spraying water to protect her from the worst of it, he crouched down beside her. Her head was bleeding and a lump was already rising.

"Isabella," he said, touching her wet arm.

She opened her eyes, dazed. Her brows knit as she looked at him in confusion.

"I—I—I don't know what happened."

"I think the showerhead blew off and hit you." He rose quickly, turned off the water at the handle, and then crouched back beside her.

"Please don't tell me, 'I told you so.'" Her eyes were wide on his face, all those greens and golds mixed together like the shades of an exotic flower.

"I won't."

"I should have let you fix it when the plumber wouldn't come. Didn't want to be dependent." Her voice was slightly slurred. It sounded like a bit of a confession. Her eyes suddenly widened even more. "Are you in my bathroom?"

"Yes, I'm afraid so."

She went very still. If it was possible, she grew whiter. "Am I naked?" she whispered.

"Ah, I'm afraid so."

"I have never been so mortified." She clenched her eyes shut as if she was hoping when she opened them this would all go away.

"Now we're even," he said, trying valiantly to put her at ease. "Though I think I've mentioned before that we should stop meeting like this."

She groaned weakly—at his attempt at humor or because of pain and humiliation, he wasn't so certain.

"We're not even," she decided. "We'd be even if you had ever been embarrassed about being unclothed, which I suspect you never have been."

He didn't say anything.

"In your whole life."

He still didn't say anything.

"Have you?" she demanded.

"Uh, well, you're not exactly unclothed. You must have pulled down the shower curtain when you came out of the shower enclosure. You're decent."

"My shower curtain is transparent," she said through clenched teeth.

"I'm not looking."

Of course her eyes flew open just as he looked. "Just for injuries!"

She clenched her eyes tightly shut again.

"I'm going to help you get up."

"No, you aren't!" She tried to tuck the transparent shower curtain tighter around her. It had the unfortunate result of becoming even more transparent.

"Ah, yes, I am," he said, keeping his eyes on her face. Chaos had struck. And all that discipline was paying off, after all. He could look just at her face. Couldn't he?

"I can get up myself." She wiggled ineffectually this way and that, trying to figure out how to get up on the slippery floor and keep the small protection of the shower curtain around her at the same time. She gave up with a sigh.

He reached out to help her.

"Don't touch me." She slapped at his hand, but it was halfhearted.

"You can trust me." His hand closed around hers, and this time she surrendered. "I have pretty extensive first-aid training."

"Yes, I know."

He lifted an eyebrow at her.

"I read about it. On the internet. The SEALs."

"Oh." She had read about what he'd done for a living. He contemplated that.

"Not that I was spying."

"No, of course not."

"Just intrigued."

"Ah."

"It seems like you have done very dangerous things."

"Yes."

Her voice suddenly went very soft. "Things that make a man very lonely."

Her eyes felt as if they were looking deep within him, as if she could see his soul, as if she could see the vast emptiness that was there. Her hand tightened marginally on his.

"Maybe," he said, telling himself he was only agreeing because he didn't want her to get riled up.

"I feel lonely, too, sometimes." And then, just like that, she was crying.

"Hey." He patted her shoulder clumsily, realized how very naked she was and pulled his hand away. He stared at it as if it was burning.

She seemed to realize how awkward this situation really was. "You need to leave me alone," she sobbed. "I'm not even dressed."

What *wasn't* happening? He wasn't leaving her alone. What *was* happening? He was going to try and make her okay with this.

"Don't worry about it," he said, pulling his attention away from his hand and ordering himself to buck up. "You've had a bit of a shock. People say and do things they wouldn't normally say or do. I'm a trained professional. I deal with stuff like this all the time."

Even as she scrubbed furiously at her tearstained

face, she looked dubious. She slid a look down at her thin covering of a shower curtain. "Like a doctor?"

"Sort of," he agreed.

"And you deal with unclothed, crying, lonely women who have been assaulted by exploding showers? All the time?"

"I just meant I deal with the unexpected." He tried for a soothing note in the face of her voice rising a bit shrilly. "It's what I'm trained to do. Let's get you up off the floor."

He reached for the nearest towel rack and tugged a towel off it, and then, as an afterthought, another one. He put both of them on top of her, trying to fasten them, without much success, around the sopping, slippery, transparent shower curtain.

Tucking the thick white terry towels around her as best he could, he slipped his arm under her shoulder and lifted her to a little dressing table bench. It was the first time he had touched her since he had held her hand at the pool in the river. Awareness quivered along his spine, but he could not give in to that. He needed to be professional right now, as he never had been before.

Connor guided Isabella to sitting and tucked the towels a little tighter around her.

Professional, he told himself grimly.

"Let's just have a look at that bump on your head." *That was good*, he told himself of his neutral tone.

"Why are you lonely?" he heard himself growl as he parted her hair and dabbed at the bump with a wet cloth.

What was professional about that? *Distracting her*, Connor told himself. He turned from her for a moment and opened the medicine chest over her sink. He found iodine and cotton balls.

"I suppose you find me pathetic," she said.

Distracting her would have been talking about any-thing—the upcoming royal wedding, the grape crops—not probing her personal tragedies.

She grimaced as he found the cut on her head and dabbed it.

"I don't find you pathetic," he told her. "You were married. Your husband died. It seems to me you would be lonely."

"Thank you," she said softly.

Leave it, he ordered himself. "I mean, of course I've wondered why such a beautiful woman would stay alone."

"You wondered about me?"

Just as she had wondered about him, going online to find out about the SEALs. All this curiosity between them was just normal, wasn't it? They were two strang-ers sharing a house. Naturally they would have ques-tions.

"Did you love your husband that much?" Connor asked. "That you are prepared to stay lonely forever? To grieve him forever?"

"Yes," she said. It came out sounding like a hiccup. "Where there is deep grief, there was deep love."

And something about the way she said that made his radar go up. He realized he didn't believe her. It was none of his business. He ordered himself not to probe. He was, at heart, a soldier. He would always be a sol-dier. That's what he did. He obeyed orders.

So, why did he hear his own voice saying, in direct defiance of the command he had just given it, "Tell me about your husband."

It was not, as he would have liked himself to believe, to provide a distraction for her while he doctored her head.

"No one, least of all not my very traditional family, understood my decision to marry him," she said, sticking her chin up as if daring him to reach the same conclusion.

"Why's that?" he asked, keeping his voice carefully noncommittal.

"He was very ill when we married. We knew he was going to die."

He had to work to keep his face schooled.

"My mother was begging me, on the eve of my wedding, not to do it. She said, *Life has enough heartbreak—you have to invite one by marrying a dying man?*"

It seemed to Connor her mother had a point, but he didn't say anything. He pretended intense concentration on the small bump on her head.

"Giorgio was part of the fabric of my life from the first day I started school."

Connor could just picture her starting school: little dark pigtails, a pinafore dress, knee socks and a scraped knee.

Something that had never happened to him happened—he wondered what Isabella's daughter would look like, if she had one someday. He felt it was a tragedy that she had said no to her own little girl somewhere along the line.

"Giorgio was never good-looking." Isabella looked at Connor critically. He was pretty sure she found *him* good-looking, but not nearly as sure if she saw that as a good thing or a bad thing.

"He wasn't even good-looking as a child, though his

eyes held such depths of beauty they took my breath away from the first moment I looked in their liquid dark depths."

He had to bite his tongue from saying cynically, *How very poetic.*

"He was always sickly—perhaps seeds of the illness that killed him had been growing since we were children."

Connor did not like the picture she was painting of the man she had married. Good grief. What had she been thinking?

She seemed to sense his judgment, because she tilted her chin at him. "He took the fact he was different from all the other boys and made that his greatest strength."

"Oh," he said flatly, not a question. But she took it as a question.

"Giorgio was able to use such a simple thing as a word to spin entire worlds, enchanted kingdoms. He could see what others missed—the pure magic in a ladybug's flight, the whole universe residing in the center of an opening flower. While other boys were crass and full of frightening energy, Giorgio was sensitive and sweetly contemplative."

Connor hoped he wasn't scowling. He himself had been one of those crass boys, full of frightening energy.

"When he asked me to marry him, I didn't even have to think about it, I just said yes."

What kind of man, knowing his prognosis was fatal, would ask someone he supposedly loved to share that with him?

"I've never even been on a real date. Giorgio was not well enough to go out for dinner, or to the movies. Certainly not dancing."

She'd never been on a date? That last— certainly not dancing — seemed to have been offered with a bit of wistfulness.

"I still have the poems he wrote for me, and the splendor of them is still wrenching enough to make me weep."

Connor looked at her lips. If she hadn't dated any other men, she probably hadn't kissed any other men, either. He had the irreverent feeling he could make her forget the splendor of those poems in about twenty seconds flat. He made himself focus on the small cut on her head.

"At sixteen I declared my love for him. At twenty I married him, over the protests of my entire family. He had already been diagnosed with his illness. At twenty-six I laid him to rest. In my heart is nothing but gratitude for the amazing time we had."

She seemed to be expecting him to say something, so he said, "Uh-huh," when what he really wanted to do was take her by those slender, very naked shoulders and shake some sense into her.

"Now in me is an empty place that nothing—and no one—can ever fill."

Her tale made Connor want to kiss the living daylights out of her, to wake her up from her trance, to show her maybe that empty place inside her could be filled. But he recognized he was treading on dangerous and unfamiliar ground if he thought he would be the one who was up to the challenge of filling her empty places. Isabella apparently liked the sensitive type. Which, if the way he felt about her husband was any indication, Connor most definitely was not. The man had been sick. That wasn't his fault. And yet Connor felt aggravated, as if Giorgio had taken advantage of Isabella's soft heart to give her a life of looking after him.

"You think I felt sorry for him," she gasped. "You think I didn't love him at all."

"Hey! I didn't say that."

"You didn't have to. I saw it in your face. You think I don't have a clue what love is."

He was the one who had told her to be observant, but he hadn't been expecting this. "I don't know what you think you saw in my face, but it wasn't that. You did not see that in *my* face, because you are looking at a person who truly does not have a clue what love is."

"Humph." She seemed unconvinced. She seemed unfairly angry at him.

"Maybe," he suggested carefully, "you said out loud the doubt you've been nursing inside since the day you married him."

With speed that took him by surprise, she smacked him hard, open-handed, across his face, hard enough to turn his head. He looked slowly back at her as she stood up. The towel fell to the ground, leaving only the shower curtain around her. Gathering her shower curtain, regal as Christina Rose could ever hope to be, as confident as the emperor with no clothes, Isabella got up and walked by him and out of the bathroom. He watched as she walked down the hallway to her bedroom, entered it, sent one damning look back at him and slammed the door.

Connor Benson stood frozen to the spot, absolutely stunned. He touched his face where her palm had met his cheek.

Jeez, for a little bit of a thing she packed a better wallop than a lot of men he'd known.

* * *

Isabella lay, wrapped in her shower curtain, on her bed in a pool of dampness and self-loathing. She could not believe she had struck Connor. She was going to have to apologize. It was so unlike her!

It was only because she had hit her head. He'd said it himself. She'd had a bit of a shock—people did and said things they wouldn't normally say under those circumstances.

Isabella would not normally confess all kinds of things to him. She had told him she was lonely in a moment of dazed weakness. It was also in a moment of dazed weakness that she had given in to his encouragement to talk about Giorgio.

What a mistake that had been. She had seen in Connor's face that he thought her marriage had been a sham.

Or was what he said more accurate? That bump on the head had removed a filter she had been trying desperately to keep in place, and her own doubts, not Connor's, had spilled out of her.

She got up off the bed. Enough of the self-pity and introspection. Yes, she was lonely, but why had she confessed that to him instead of just looking after it herself?

People had to be responsible for themselves!

Tonight was a case in point. She had been invited to the sixteenth birthday party of one of her former students. As a teacher, she was often invited to her pupils' family events, but she rarely attended. So, who did she have to blame but herself if she was lonely?

It wasn't Connor's fault that he had made her aware of the loneliness as if it was a sharp shard of glass inside her.

She went to her closet and threw open the door. She

wasn't going to the party as a demure little school-teacher, either. She wasn't wearing a dress that would label her prim and tidy for all the world to see.

She was not dressing in a way that sent the message she was safe and boring, and not quite alive somehow.

Way at the back of the closet was a dress she had bought a long time ago, on a holiday she had forced herself to take a year or two after Giorgio died. The purchase had really been the fault of one of those pushy salesclerks who had brought her the dress, saying she had never seen a dress so perfect for someone.

It was the salesclerk's gushing that had made Isabella purchase the dress, which had been way more expensive than what she could afford. When she brought it home, she had had buyer's remorse, and dismissed it as not right for her. Still, it hung in her closet, all these years later. Why had she never given it away?

She took it out and laid it on the bed, eyed it critically. Not right for the old her. Perfect for the new her.

The dress was red as blood and had a low V on both the front and back, which meant she couldn't wear it with any bra that she owned.

It was the dress of a woman who was not filled with unreasonable fears.

Feeling ridiculously racy for the fact she had on no bra, she slipped the dress over her head, then looked at herself in her full-length mirror. She remembered why she had purchased the dress, and it wasn't strictly because of the salesclerk gushing over it.

The dress gave Isabella a glimpse of who she could be. It was as if it took her from mouse to siren in the blink of an eye. She looked confident and sexy and like a woman who was uninhibited and knew how to have fun and let go. It was the dress of a woman who had the satisfying knowledge she could have any man she wanted.

Isabella put makeup on the bump on her head and then arranged her hair over it. She dabbed mascara on her lashes and blush on her cheeks. She glossed her lips and put on a little spray of perfume.

She found her highest heels, and a tiny clutch handbag, and a little silver bracelet. Taking a deep breath, she marched out of her room. Connor's bedroom door was closed. Summoning all her courage, she knocked on the door.

After a long moment, long enough for her heart to pound in her throat as if it planned to jump out of her, the door opened. He stood there looking down at her. He was wet, still, from the water from the broken shower spewing all over him, from helping her. Awareness of him tingled along her spine.

She was so glad she had put on the red dress when Connor's mouth fell open before he snapped it shut. Something flashed in his eyes before he quickly veiled it. But even if she had led a sheltered life, Isabella knew desire when she saw it.

He folded his arms over his chest.

"My, my," he growled.

She tossed her head, pleased with the way his eyes followed the motion of her hair. "I'm going to a birthday party. I wanted to apologize before I left. I have never hit a person in my whole life. I'm deeply ashamed."

"Really?" he growled doubtfully.

"Really," she said, lifting her chin.

"That's kind of not the dress of someone who is deeply ashamed."

"The dress has nothing to do with this!"

"I think it does."

"Explain yourself."

He lifted a shoulder. "All right. I think you're a boiling cauldron of repressed passion."

"Maybe it's not repressed," she snapped.

His eyes went to her lips and stayed there long enough to make the point that they could find out how repressed or unrepressed she was right this second if she wanted. Her eyes skittered to his lips. She blinked first and looked away. When she looked back, his gaze was unflinching.

"In a dress like that, lots of people are going to want to find out, *is she, or isn't she?* You aren't going be lonely for very long at all."

Since the whole idea of putting on the dress had been to look passionate, why did she want to smack him again? And badly. She could tell this apology was premature. She had to grip her clutch extra tightly to keep her hand from flying free and hitting him across his handsome, smug face.

No, she didn't want to smack him. That wasn't the truth at all. The truth was exactly as he had said. She was a boiling cauldron of repressed passion, and she wanted to throw herself at Connor and let all that repressed passion boil out.

Isabella was absolutely appalled with herself. She took a step back from him and turned away. "Have a good evening, signor," she said formally, the prim little schoolteacher after all, a child playing dress-up in her red finery.

"Yeah. You, too."

She turned and walked away. And just because she

knew he was watching her, or maybe to prove to herself she wasn't just playing dress-up, she put a little extra swing in her step and felt the red dress swirl around her.

She glanced over her shoulder and caught him still watching her, his eyes narrowed with unconcealed masculine appreciation.

Surprisingly, given that unsettling encounter with Connor, Isabella did have a good evening. Sixteenth birthday parties for young women were a huge event in Monte Calanetti. It was a coming-of-age celebration, probably very much like a debutante ball in the southern US. The party signified the transition from being a child to being a woman.

While looking at the giggling young woman, Valerie, flushed with excitement in her finery, Isabella was struck by how extremely young and innocent she was. She was no more an adult that Isabella was an astronaut.

And yet Isabella had been sixteen herself when she had first declared her undying love for Giorgio. And how adult and sophisticated and sure of herself she had felt at that time. Now, watching this young woman, it seemed it would be laughable to make a lifelong declaration of love at that age, and then to feel bound by it.

The pensive thoughts did not last long, though. Isabella had been seated with some of her coworkers, and the talk turned to preparations for the spring fete and anticipation of the royal wedding being held in Monte Calanetti.

Then there was harmless gossip about who was getting married and divorced and who was burying parents. And, of course, in an Italian village, what was loved more than a pregnancy?

Nothing. But with each pregnancy revealed, Isabella

felt happy and yet crushed, too. She did not think envy was an admirable emotion, and yet the thought of someone holding that beautiful, wiggling, warm bundle of life filled her with a terrible sense of longing for the life she did not have. And would probably never have. Not now.

"Have you heard? Marianna is pregnant."

Again Isabella's happiness for Marianna was laced with her own sense of loss. She listened halfheartedly as the circumstances around Marianna's pregnancy were placed under the microscope of the small, close-knit village. They were not ideal.

Italy was still mostly Catholic, and small towns like Monte Calanetti were very traditional. A pregnancy without the benefit of marriage still raised eyebrows. There was some conjecture around the table about how Marianna's brothers, the staunchly conservative Angelo and Nico, might have reacted to news of a pregnancy.

After it had been discussed to death, it was all put aside and a decision was made.

"We will have to have a baby shower."

This was announced with a sigh of pure happiness and murmurs of delight from the other women. A baby in Italy was always seen as a blessing.

For some reason that made Isabella think of Connor talking about the abandonment of his mother by his father. Marianna's beau looked like the kind of man who would stand by her no matter what. Angelo and Nico, while they might rage and wring their hands, would never turn their backs on their own blood. Never.

Isabella wondered if that was the root of Connor wanting to protect the whole world—a little boy wanting to protect his mother. The thought made her heart ache for him. Not that she wanted to spoil this evening with one single thought about her houseguest!

Though Isabella was careful with the wine, some others were not, and the jokes became quite ribald and the laughter loud. The gathering was around a torch-lit courtyard, and after the dinner the tables were cleared away for dancing, and a live band came out.

The dress made Isabella feel different, less repressed and more carefree. To her astonishment, men she'd known for years were lining up to ask her to dance, and she soon felt as if she was flushed with as much excitement as the young Valerie.

It was after one in the morning before she realized how late it was.

"I have to work in the morning!"

She refused an offer to be walked home, and instead went down the darkened streets by herself. Partway home, she realized her feet ached from all the dancing, and she slipped off her shoes and went barefoot.

A little ways from her house, she saw a figure coming toward her. She knew from his size and the way he carried himself exactly who it was, and she felt her heart begin to race.

But his walk was different, purposeful, the strides long and hard, like a gladiator entering the arena, like a warrior entering the battlefield.

He stopped in front of her and gazed down at her. His eyes were flashing with cold anger.

"Where the hell have you been?"

"Scusi?"

"You heard me."

"I told you I was at a birthday party," she said.

"Well, I assumed a child's birthday party, and I thought it would be over at a decent time."

"What's it to you?" she snapped, angry at his high-handed manner, angry that he thought he could treat her like a child on the night she felt sexy and adult.

Her tone was louder than she intended. In fact, both their tones might have been louder than they thought. A light came on in a window above the street.

Connor stepped back from her, ran a hand through his hair and looked away. "You're waking the neighbors," he said, glancing up at that window.

"Me?" she said, unrepentant.

"Us," he conceded.

"Well, I have an excuse—boiling cauldron of repressed passion that I am, I am now shrieking like a fishwife in the streets. What's yours?"

"Good question," he said.

"You rescued me this afternoon. That does not put you in charge of my life!"

"You're right," Connor said. The anger had faded from his face. Instead, he looked faintly confused. Her own annoyance at him ebbed away a little bit.

"Are you out here looking for me?" she asked, astounded.

He could barely look at her, but he nodded.

What remained of her anger drained away. "But why?" She remembered thinking earlier tonight, with the news of Marianna's pregnancy, of the burden he had placed on himself of looking after the whole world. She remembered wondering if the first person he had felt protective of was his mother.

Almost against her will, something in her softened toward him.

"Hell, I started thinking about you bumping your head. It can be such a tricky injury. I should have checked more for signs of concussion."

"You were worried about me," she said. It was not a question.

"It's just that you'd had quite a bang on the head, and you were dressed like that, and I started thinking you might not be making the best decisions."

"I'm thirty-three years old!"

"But you'd had a head injury. And you said you were lonely… I thought you might be…" His voice trailed away uncomfortably.

She looked at him silently. She should be insulted. He thought she might be what? Getting carried away with the first man who looked at her with avarice? But poor Connor looked tormented. His expression stole her indignation away from her.

"Vulnerable," he continued.

That was so true. She did feel very vulnerable. But it seemed he felt vulnerable, too.

"It's not that you wouldn't make good decisions under normal conditions," he said hastily. "But a bump on the head can cause confusion. Alter judgment slightly. I'm sorry. Am I making a fool of myself?"

"No," she said softly, "you are not. I am quite touched by your concern for me."

"I'm not sure it's rational," he said. "It's just that, unfortunately, I've just seen a lot of people get themselves in trouble before they know what's happened to them."

"I wasn't in trouble. But the party wasn't for a child. Not really. For a sixteen-year-old. It's a big deal in Monte Calanetti. Almost like a wedding. A meal and dancing. The party could go on all night."

"I hate it when I act from emotion," he said gruffly.

"Do you?"

He stepped one step closer to her. He lifted her hair off her shoulder with his hand. "What are you doing to me?" he asked huskily. "I feel as if I'm not thinking straight."

"Ah."

"I find you very beautiful. It's hard for a man to think straight around that."

"It's just the dress," she said.

"No, Isabella, it's not."

"It's not?"

"There's something about you that makes me think with my heart instead of my head."

"Oh, dear," she said, and her tone was playfully mocking.

"Here's what I think," he said firmly, as if he had it all figured out.

"Yes?"

"I should take you on a date."

CHAPTER FIVE

ISABELLA STARED AT CONNOR. He should take her on a date? But was that his head or his heart talking? Because the way he said it, it was almost as though he hoped to get her out of his system.

"You should?" she asked.

"Sure. I mean, if you'd like to."

There was something very endearing about seeing this big, self-assured, superconfident Texan looking so unsure of himself.

"I'd like to," she said softly. "I'd like to, very much."

And then it seemed slightly and wonderfully ridiculous that they turned and walked home together.

Only it didn't seem ridiculous when his hand found hers.

It felt not as if she was going to go on a real date for the first time in her life, but as if she was coming home.

"I've gone and done something really stupid," Connor whispered into his phone.

"Huh? Who is this?"

"Justin, it's me."

"Connor?"

"Yeah."

"What the hell is going on?"

"There's this girl."

Something relaxed in Justin's tone. "This better be good—it's two o'clock in the morning here."

Connor contemplated that. Was there one rational thing left in him? No, that's why he was consulting his friend. That's what SEALs did when they were in a pickle, they relied on each other.

"She's not really a girl. A woman."

"Uh-huh?"

"I asked her out."

"That sounds like it's worthy of a two a.m. phone call."

"The thing is, I didn't really ask her out for me. I asked her out for her. She's a widow. She married really young. She's missed a lot. She's never been on a real date before."

Silence.

Connor sighed. "I'm the wrong guy for this, aren't I?"

Silence.

"I mean, I'm just the wrong guy to try and show her how it can be."

"How what can be?"

"You know."

"You'll have to spell it out for me. I'm having that two-o'clock-in-the-morning brain fart."

"How it can be, uh, when two people like each other. A lot."

"You mean falling in love?" Justin asked. He sounded wide-awake now.

"No!" Connor had to backtrack. He was sorry he had admitted liking her. A lot. His mission was one of altruism, and he wanted to make Justin understand that.

"I mean maybe falling in love," Connor said carefully, "just not with me. I just want to show her life can be fun. I want to show her she's missed something, and not to be afraid to embrace it. That it is not too late for her."

"From the embracer of all things romantic," Justin said wryly.

"You're not helping! I guess I want to show her what she should be looking for in a guy. Not me. I mean, I'm leaving. I'm here for the short term only. But if I could just give her an idea how a date should feel."

"Very altruistic."

"Are you being sarcastic?"

Justin sighed. "Okay. Ask me a specific question, and I will try to help you with it."

"What should I do with her on a date? I was thinking dinner and a movie."

"So, basically the same thing you've done on every single date you've ever been on?"

"Yes."

"Hmm."

"What does that mean?" Connor demanded. "I hate it when you say *hmm* like that."

"It just seems to me if you're trying to show her life is good, and trying to encourage her to embrace the great adventure, and trying to show her what a good date would feel like, you should put a bit more thought into it."

"I've been thinking of nothing else!"

"Just a sec." Connor could hear Justin talking to someone, the sound muffled as if he had stuck the phone under his pillow. Connor was pretty sure the other voice was feminine. He strained his ears. Justin came back on a moment later.

"Be original. A picnic in the moonlight. Something like that."

"That is the hokiest thing I've ever heard."

"Well, then, don't ask."

"Okay, I won't." And Connor contemplated the fact that Justin was with someone. Justin really was getting on with his life. It occurred to Connor that the wheelchair Justin used was holding Connor back more than it was his friend.

"Don't hang up, Connor. The red line is going off."

The red line. That was the dedicated line for emergencies for their company.

Justin came back on the phone. His voice was completely different, the sleep stripped from it. This voice, crisp, take-charge and take-no-prisoners, was a voice Connor recognized. He was a warrior now, and Connor shifted into that role easily, aware he was far more at ease with this than the places of the heart that he had very nearly gone to.

"How long would it take you to get back to Azerbaijan?"

Connor was already opening a different screen on his phone, looking up flights. "I could be in Baku in under six hours if I can make the connections."

"A vulture has landed. Go."

A vulture had landed. It was their code for a bad guy, known to them. In a similar code, Justin and whoever was on the ground in Azerbaijan would text the details to Connor's phone as they had them. Connor was aware as he threw things in his bag that he felt a sense of purpose and mission. This was the world he moved in with absolute ease. This was where he belonged.

He scrawled a note for Isabella, sent a quick text to

Nico and slipped out the door, back into the comfort of all that was familiar.

It was ironic just how safe danger made Connor Benson feel.

Isabella was aware, as soon as she woke up the next morning, that Connor was gone. She could feel his absence in the house, as if some energy that was necessary to life was gone.

She found his note on the kitchen table but was not comforted by it. Was it convenient that he was suddenly called away at the same time things were taking a turn between them? Was he deliberately cooling things off?

Isabella nursed the hope that he would call, and it increased her tension when he did not. He *was* cooling things off.

Still, she could not believe it was possible to miss Connor so much. In the short time he had been part of her life, his presence had made a big impact on her household without her really realizing it at the time. There was something about having a man in her house—even though they had mostly avoided each other—that made her feel safe. That in itself was not really rational—he had attacked her the very first day.

So, no, her acute sense of missing him had very little to do with a sense of safety. Maybe even the opposite. There was a sense that very *unsafe* things could unfold between them. And that made each day have a delicious sense of anticipation.

She looked at his note, over and over, trying to glean any emotion from it, trying to discern which way the compass was swinging. His handwriting was no surprise, strong and bold. The message was to the point:

"Called away on business. Will pay for my room for days I am not here. Please hold for my return."

Given their middle-of-the-street conversation of the night before he had written that note—given his invitation to go on a date—it seemed very impersonal and businesslike. He had signed it only with his first name, no term of endearment.

What would she expect? *Love, Connor.* No, definitely not that. *Hugs?* That was laughable. How about *best wishes?* Or *can't wait to see you again?*

Despite all her misgivings, Isabella could feel herself anticipating his return like a child anticipating Christmas, even though she chided herself not to.

He had asked her on a date. If he followed through, she wondered what he had in mind. She felt excited about it, when really, that was the most unsafe thing of all.

Or maybe she really did not know the first thing about safety. Because she turned on the news one night, and it was focused on Azerbaijan. Normally, Isabella did not watch the news, and she would have flipped by the station. But tonight, she recalled that first morning Connor had said that was where he was coming from. Was that where his business had called him back to?

And indeed, the story was about an incident that had happened at the World Food Conference. Members of an unnamed private security organization had apprehended someone who had made threats against one of the delegates. Details were sketchy, and there was no footage. Had Connor's company been involved? Her gut said it had been.

When the story was over, Isabella shut off the TV,

but she sat there until the room grew dark, thinking about what she had seen.

She was aware her stomach was in a knot. She was aware that *this* would be the reality of tangling your life with a man like Connor Benson.

Six days after he departed, a knock came on her front door. It was dinnertime, and Isabella was not sure who would come calling at that hour.

She swung open the door to see Connor standing there.

He looked so wondrously familiar. Her heart began to pound unreasonably. Her anxiety about the kind of work he did left her in a rush of warm relief to see him standing there, so obviously unharmed.

"Oh!" she said. She could feel herself blushing as she stepped back from the door. "You didn't have to knock. You live here."

He cocked his head at her, lifted a brow.

"I mean, you're a guest here. I want you to feel you can come and go as you please."

"I know that, but I also knew you didn't know when I would be back. I didn't want to startle you. Again."

She regarded him. His face was deeply etched with exhaustion. But there was something else there, too. It was as she had suspected when she read his curt note—he had bought himself some time and now he seemed remote, as if they wanted different things. It was as if he had thought about that late-night meeting in the street and decided he wanted something different than what she wanted. He wanted them to be strangers. She wanted them to be friends.

Or more than friends?

Her anxieties were realized. Isabella could feel the

excitement that had been building about his return leaving her like air hissing out of a pricked balloon.

"Come in," she said. "It's hot outside. Are you hungry?"

He hesitated. Isabella had the feeling they were not back at square one, they were somewhere even before square one. Was he going to pretend he had never even asked her on a date?

"Come eat," she said, more forcefully than she intended. She felt as if she did not want to give him room to retreat, physically, to his room, or emotionally, away from her.

She suspected it was because Connor was a soldier, and he responded to the command in her voice. He dropped his bag inside the door and followed her into the kitchen. He took a chair at the table, and she moved to get him some of the pasta she had made for her own dinner. Now, passing it to him, she could see even more clearly the exhaustion in the lines of his face. His mouth had a stern set to it, as if smiling was foreign to him.

She felt guilty. Whatever he had just come from, it had been hard, and it had taken a very obvious toll on him. What was she thinking, making this all about her?

"Where have you been?" she asked, lowering herself in the seat across from him.

"Just a job."

"Ah. Azerbaijan?"

He frowned at her.

"The World Food Conference?"

"The conference is over now. Everything went fine." He dug into the pasta like a starving man. It did her heart good to see him eat like that, even if he was doing it to avoid her.

"I saw something about it on television one night. Was there some kind of threat made against some of the delegates?"

His voice was cool, it didn't invite probing. "Everything went fine," he repeated.

"Someone was apprehended."

"Really?"

"Really. By the private firm that looked after security for the event."

He lifted his eyebrows at her. *So what?*

"Were you in danger?" she asked him softly.

He lifted a shoulder. "Not particularly."

She knew then that he *had* been in danger, and that he shouldered the dangers of his job with the ease of long practice. This was not a man you could be timid with. This was not a man you could beg not to go to his world because it would soothe something in you. She found she had more courage than she ever would have believed. Because she felt proud of him, and in awe of his strength.

"Ah, Itus," she said. "Ever humble."

He looked up from his plate, lifted a brow at her. "What do you know about Itus?"

"I know in Greek mythology, he is the god of protection."

"It's just a name," he said. "My business partner, Justin, named the company. He picked that name. I am not a Greek mythology kind of guy."

"I wonder if your business partner was thinking of you when he chose that name."

Connor frowned, uninviting, but she went on anyway.

"Because Itus was very like you," she said quietly.

"Me?" He snorted, self-deprecating.

"Yes, you."

"In what way?" Connor had a bemused look on his face.

"He was a mortal boy, only seventeen when he was chosen to protect the god Apollo. He was given two swords, and he became so good with them that he beat the god Ares in a sword fight, though he would not boast about it. Apollo wanted to make him a god, and Zeus agreed, possibly because he did not want any more of his gods beaten in sword fights with mere mortals. Itus refused the honor. He did not feel he was worthy, but Apollo insisted and made him eat the food that would make him immortal."

Connor actually cast a wary glance down at his pasta.

"Then Apollo released him from his duties, and Itus now spends his days protecting the innocent from those who would do them harm."

"Look—" he set down his utensils, very deliberately "—Isabella, there is no use thinking there is anything the least romantic about me. Or what I do. It's hard, dirty, dangerous work—"

"You forgot lonely," she said quietly.

"—and it makes me a poor choice for a companion. No, not a poor choice. The worst choice. I should have never asked you out on a date. It was stupid and frivolous."

She felt the sharp bite of disappointment, but she was not totally unprepared for it. The crispness of his note had hinted this might be coming. At the same time, she could see it was the result of the events he had just come from that made something so simple as going on a date seem frivolous to him.

"I've decided," he said, his voice curt, "a date between us is out of the question. I mean, we are living together under the same roof for two more weeks. It's just way too awkward."

"I agree," she said soothingly.

That seemed to pull him up short. He regarded her suspiciously and then continued, "I mean, if I'm going to spend time with you, I should make it count. I should teach you something useful."

She found herself gazing at his lips, thinking she had an idea or two what she'd like Connor Benson to teach her. "What would that be?"

"I should teach you how to swim."

"Instead of a date," she clarified.

He nodded vigorously. "It's not good to go through life with fears."

"Ah." It seemed ironic that he would say that when it was more than apparent he might have a fear or two about the date he had asked her on. She decided now might not be the best time to point that out to him.

"Once you know how to swim," Connor said seriously, "it gives you confidence and courage in dealing with all kinds of things that come up in life."

But not dates. Again, Isabella bit her tongue to keep herself from saying it out loud. So, her Itus did not want to date her, but he still wanted to protect her, or give her some tools to protect herself.

"Someday I believe you will have children," he continued sternly. "You can give them no greater gift than comfort in the water."

She could argue with him, of course. It seemed unlikely she would ever have children. But if she did, it seemed to Isabella there were all kinds of gifts parents gave their children, and that the greatest of those was love, not swimming lessons.

But he was in full retreat, and she had a feeling that the mention of the word *love* would probably push him right out her door and out of her life, so she bit her tongue again. It was probably good to learn this tongue-biting skill. You would need it a great deal around a man like him.

"I would be deeply appreciative if you would teach me how to swim," Isabella said.

He looked at her, wary of her demure tone.

She smiled back at him, though she had to bite her tongue, yet again, to keep from laughing out loud. She could so clearly see he was terrified of going on a date with her. His terror made her feel powerful and attractive and sexy. She had never really felt those things before. It was worth facing her own terror of the water dead-on.

A swimming lesson? He didn't know what he was letting himself in for. In fact, Connor Benson had no idea that he was teaching her already, all about the nature of confidence and courage.

"When should we start?" she asked, sweetly. "And where?"

"I'll arrange with Nico to use his pool," Connor said. "An hour, every afternoon from tomorrow, Monday to Friday, should give you the basics."

"I can learn to swim in five days?"

"Well, you won't be trying out for the Italian swim team, but you'll have some basic skills you can practice."

"Thank you," she said, lowering her eyes from his so he would not see the glee dancing in hers. When she looked back up, Connor was eyeing her suspiciously. Then he pushed back from the table and left the room.

"Things are improving between us," she said softly to herself. "I managed to feed him something before he ran away this time."

He probably hadn't considered that little detail when he was planning swimming lessons. No, Connor had probably not given a single thought to how hard it was going to be to run away from her in a swimming pool, especially since she had no love of the water. She'd be clinging to him like a barnacle to the bottom of a boat.

But there was another problem. Where, in a tiny place like Monte Calanetti, on such short notice, was she going to find the right bathing suit for this? Obviously she would have to make do with what she could find for tomorrow.

But he'd said it would take a week.

It was so much better than a date! A whole week.

She went into her office and shut the door. She flipped on her computer and typed the words she wanted into the search engine. Then she narrowed the search by putting in the necessary delivery dates.

By the time Isabella was done, she felt extremely naughty. The way she had felt in the red dress should have been fair warning to her, and to Connor, both.

Isabella Rossi *liked* feeling naughty.

As Connor was waiting in the water of Nico's beautiful pool, Isabella came through the back gate and gave him a quick wave before ducking into the cabana beside the pool.

He was pleased to note she looked particularly understated today in a longish skirt in a dull shade of beige and a baggy blouse in the same color. Her glossy hair was pulled back tightly, and she was carrying a large book bag that she was hugging to her chest. Really? She looked more like a nerdy student than the teacher.

He surveyed the pool while he waited for her. It was nestled in the garden grotto behind the house, and the pool had been made to look like a pond. Ferns trailed fronds in the water, and there was a small waterfall at one end of it.

Lovely as it was aesthetically, it was not really a pool for serious swimming, but it was large enough to do a few strokes, plus it had a deep end. It was about the furthest thing from the pools he had done SEAL training in, but it would do for an introduction to swimming basics.

Connor was feeling enormously pleased with himself. Teaching Isabella how to swim—instead of going on a date—had been a brainstorm. Swimming, after all, was useful. Tackling an irrational fear was useful. When he left this place, he would leave her with a skill that would be practical to her for her whole life. He would leave her with a sense of herself that was different than what it had been before. That sounded quite a bit better than leaving her with the heartache that a date promised.

She was staying here in this idyllic little village in Tuscany, and he was leaving, so what was the sense of exploring the sparks that were flying between them?

Isabella came out of the cabana. She had taken her hair out of the elastic when it would have been more sensible to leave it in. She had on an enormous poncho-like caftan that covered her from her head to her toes. It had hideous wide stripes in a crazy array of colors.

It reminded him of pictures he had seen of what people wore to music festivals in the '60s.

When she stood on the deck he was at eye level with her feet. Her toenails were painted lime green, and as odd a choice as that was, he had to admit it was adorable, and a little less nerdy than the rest of her ensemble.

"What's that thing?" he asked her. He noticed that her face had been scrubbed free of makeup, probably in preparation for her swim.

"What thing?"

"That thing you're wearing."

She looked down at herself. "Oh. My swim cover."

He had to bite back a smile. She had to wear a swim cover to get from the cabana to the pool? The walk might have been twenty yards.

"Well, how about if you take it off and get in the water."

She hesitated. He could see the pulse beating in her throat. She looked past him at the water and gulped.

"Believe me, you can't swim with it on."

"Oh," she said, as if he was breaking world news to her. Isabella reached for the zipper, and closed her eyes. Because she was afraid of the water? Or was she sweetly shy about being seen in her swimming suit?

She bent over to get the zipper undone. Her swim cover was still doing its job. Covering. The zipper stuck partway down, and she tugged and tugged, but nothing happened. Suddenly, in frustration, she gave up on the zipper and pulled the caftan from her shoulders. As she was freed from the bulky covering, it slid down and settled in a lump at her waist.

Connor stared helplessly.

Her eyes locked on his. He looked away, focusing

on those little green toenails, not sure he wanted her to see what he was thinking. She pushed the caftan away from her waist and it floated to the ground, at his eye level, creating a puddle that looked like a burlap bag around her little monster-toed feet.

He was left looking at the length of her lovely legs. Then she stepped out of the fabric puddle and kicked the covering aside.

Connor reminded himself he had seen her in a transparent shower curtain. And a red dress that had made his mouth go dry. Whatever this was, it could not be any worse than that. Isabella was a practical schoolteacher. She would know how to pick a good bathing suit.

Having thus reassured himself, Connor cocked his head upward to see more than her feet and her legs. His mouth fell open. He gulped. He snapped his mouth shut so that the practical schoolteacher would not guess how much she was rattling his world.

A swimming lesson? Whose dumb idea had this been?

She was wearing one of the tiniest swimsuits he had ever seen, if you could call that scrap of fabric—three scraps of fabric—a swimsuit. Isabella was wearing a string bikini in an amazing shade of lime green that made her skin look as golden as the sand at a beach in New Zealand, Kaiteriteri, that he had visited once. Her dark hair spilled over that golden expanse of skin, shiny and beautiful.

"Is something wrong?" she asked. Her tone was all innocence, but he wasn't fooled. No woman put on a bathing suit like that without knowing exactly what she was doing!

Suck it up, he ordered himself. He'd seen her in a

shower curtain. Nothing could be worse than that. Except this was worse than that. It was worse, even, than the red dress.

Isabella Rossi, village schoolteacher, nerdy girl, was smoking hot!

"Wrong?" he choked out, not willing to give her the victory. "What could possibly be wrong?"

"I don't know. You have a look on your face."

"A look on my face?" he demanded.

"Mmm. Like you've been smacked with a frozen fish."

He wiped whatever look he had on his face off. He felt as though he'd been smacked, all right, and not with a frozen fish. Smacked with awareness of her. He had the ugly feeling she wasn't as innocent as she appeared. In fact, Connor had the ugly feeling that she might be toying with him.

He forced himself to find his voice. It had to be addressed. "You really should have left your hair up."

"Oh? Why's that?"

What was he doing talking about her hair? He needed to tell her the bathing suit wasn't going to work. At all. "You don't want to get it in your face."

"I'm not planning on getting my face wet."

"You have to get your face wet. To swim."

She didn't look the least convinced. She dismissed him with a little wave of her hand. "Oh, well, maybe next time I'll get my face wet."

Address it, he ordered himself. "Uh, that bathing suit—"

"Yes?" Her voice was husky.

"—is really nice."

Now, *that* he had not meant to say. At all. Isabella was beaming at him.

"—but, it isn't, er, really made for swimming."

Unless he was mistaken, and he was pretty sure he was not, the little minx was lapping up his discomfort.

"It's called a bathing suit," she said stubbornly.

"Maybe it's for *sun*bathing. I mean, if you were to dive in the water with that thing..."

His voice trailed away.

"I'm not planning on diving today, either," she informed him primly.

Wait a minute. Who was in charge here? He suspected, in that bathing suit, she was. "Well, I wasn't planning on that, either, but—"

"The bathing suit will have to suffice," she said. The schoolteacher voice was very at odds with the drop-dead gorgeous woman standing in front of him. "Selection—"

Seduction? No, no, she'd said *selection*, not *seduction*.

"—is very limited in Monte Calanetti at this time of year. I ordered some other things on the internet. They should arrive soon."

How soon was soon, he wanted to demand. Maybe they could postpone.

"I'm sure it will be fine," Isabella said, "You already said it's not as if I'm training for the national swim team."

She had him there. He wanted to teach her enough to hold her own if she fell out of a boat. Or in the river. Or got carried away unexpectedly by a current. He wanted to teach her enough that being around water did not make that pulse go crazy in her throat, like a rabbit being chased by dogs. The way it was now.

Was that because she was about to get wet? Or was it because she was trying out her bold new self on him?

Connor considered, again, postponing. He glanced at her face. A tiny little smile was playing across her lips before she doused it. She *was* toying with him!

"Get in the water," he snapped. The sooner she was covered up with anything, including water, the better. If the bathing suit fell off, or melted, they'd deal with that when it happened. Just as they had dealt with the shower catastrophe.

But really, how much could one man take?

Isabella stuck her toe in and yanked it back out. She made a face. She hugged herself, either not as confident in the skimpy suit as she wanted him to believe or suddenly aware that she was tackling something she was afraid of.

"I can't just jump in," she decided.

She could sit on the edge of the pool, reach out and put her hands around his neck... Connor gave himself a shake. This was going to be quite hard enough! "There are stairs at that end."

She looked where he was pointing and saw the stairs entering the pool at the shallow end. She eyed her dropped caftan for a second, as if she was considering putting it back on for the short walk to the stairs. Or putting it back on and fleeing.

Instead, she tilted her chin up and went over there, wiggling her hips self-consciously the whole way. It gave Connor plenty of opportunity to study how much of her was not covered by those skimpy green scraps of fabric. It also gave him plenty of opportunity to set his face into a mask of indifference.

At the top of the stairs, she repeated the put-one-toe-in-and-withdraw-it procedure. Still in the water, he slogged his way over to that end of the pool and stood close to the bottom of the stairs.

"At this rate we are still going to be here tomorrow," he groused out loud, instead of saying what he really wanted, which was *get in the water, dammit*.

She held up a hand, a very Italian gesture that warned him not to hurry her, and then Isabella proceeded to get into the water with painful slowness.

CHAPTER SIX

AS CONNOR WATCHED, Isabella got on the first stair leading into the pool. She was acting as if the world was tilting and her life depended on her hanging on to the handrail.

The world was tilting, and Connor felt as if his life depended on her getting in the water. With the water at her ankles, she paused there, allowing him to wallow in the full impact of that bathing suit. Was that a piercing, right below her belly button? Was his jaw clenched?

"The easiest way is just to jump in," he told her. Yes, definitely clenched. He deliberately relaxed it.

"Never let it be said I'm easy."

He contemplated her. Her command of English and all its nuances and slang was not good enough for her to have meant that the way it sounded. Though the beautiful young widow was probably about the furthest thing from easy that he had ever met.

She went down one more step. Now she was up to her knees. She had both hands on the handrail. Her knuckles were white.

"I thought the water would be warmer," she said.

"It's perfect." His jaw was clenching again.

She wrinkled her nose, letting him know their ideas

of perfect were different, which would be a very good thing for him to keep in mind, because a bathing suit like that made a man think he could make anything work out, even against impossible odds.

And the odds were impossible. Everything about them was different. He was large, she was tiny. He was powerful, she was fragile. He was cynical, she was innocent. They were culturally a million miles apart. He's seen colleagues fall for the seemingly exotic girls of foreign lands. It never worked.

He tried to hold those thoughts as, finally, Isabella was at the bottom of the steps, up to her cute little belly button in water. It was a little dark mole under her belly button, not a piercing. He was not sure which was sexier.

Isabella was still holding onto the handrail as if her life depended on it. He tried to remember why he had thought getting her in the water would be easier on him. It was not.

"Let go of the handrail and walk over to me," he said.

"Not yet." Her voice had a little quaver to it.

And that changed everything. Because it reminded him this wasn't about him. It wasn't about recalculating impossible odds. It was about her, giving her a few tools to deal with the harsh realities of life. And he could not let her scanty little bathing suit distract him from that. That's one of the things he was trained to do. Sift through information very quickly, ignore the distractions, focus on the mission.

So he crossed the distance that remained between them and pried her hand, ever so gently, off the handrail. He placed himself right in front of her and held out his other hand. She hesitated and then placed her hand in his.

Their hands joined as they faced each other, they were like two dance partners who had never danced together sizing each other up. It occurred to him this was going to be like no swimming lesson he had ever given before.

"Don't even look at the water," he said softly. "Just look at me."

Her eyes fastened on his face as if she was drowning and he was the lifeline. Her gaze was as disconcerting as the bikini. Maybe more so. It made the mission waver a little more.

"See?" he said, forcing himself to speak, keeping his voice soft, and taking a step back, "No danger. No crocodiles. No chance of falling over a ledge. No current to sweep you away."

No danger. Ha-ha. Her hand, small but strong in his, felt like one of the gravest dangers he had ever encountered. Had he really thought getting her in the water was going to be better than watching her on the deck?

Now, added to his physical awareness of her hands in his, she was so close to him he could smell that spicy perfume that was hers and hers alone. It felt as if he was being swept away by the absolute trust in her eyes fastened on his, the way she was holding his hands. She took her first tiny step through the water toward him.

He backed up. She took one more. He backed up two. And then they were doing a slow waltz through the water. He was careful to stay in the shallows, even though it wasn't nearly deep enough to help him deal with the worst of the distractions. Was that tiny bathing suit top sliding sideways just a touch?

Connor repeated his command to himself.

Suck it up.

"See?" he said softly. "It's not so bad, is it? Just stay in the moment. Don't think one thought about what could happen."

She actually closed her eyes. A tiny smile touched her lips. He ordered himself not to look at her lips and definitely not to think about what could happen. Connor felt the purity of the moment—water on his skin, her hair shining in the sun, her small hands in his, the rapturous look on her face—seducing him.

Somehow, he'd had this utterly foolish idea that he was going to pretend she was a raw recruit and be able to keep professional distance from her as he taught her the basics of swimming. He was not sure how he had deluded himself. He had never had that much imagination. He'd always prided himself on being such a realist.

"The water does feel amazing on my skin," she breathed. Her eyes remained closed in wonder.

Connor cleared his throat. "So now you've seen the water in this end of the swimming pool holds no danger to you," he said, trying desperately to stick to the business at hand and not think one single thought about her skin. "So, let's try the next step."

Her eyes flew open and that pulse in her throat picked up tempo. "What is the next step?"

"I'd like you to learn the water will support you. Human beings are buoyant. They float."

She looked doubtful about that—the pulse in her throat went crazy.

"Isabella, you will float."

"I'm scared."

"I know."

His life's work had presented him with this situation, again and again. He'd had plenty of encounters with people, civilians, who found themselves in difficult situations. Families who, through no fault of their own, found themselves in war zones. Hostages, in the wrong place at the wrong time, who didn't know the rule book, who had spent their entire lives blissfully oblivious to the fact there was a rule book.

Connor had led people from burning buildings, evacuated the terrified, navigated the fear of others in a thousand different ways. He'd dealt with people who were scared. He did it all the time.

He excelled at this: at infusing his abundance of confidence and calm into panicky people through his voice and his actions.

It felt different this time, way too personal, as if that enemy called fear was hovering at the edges of his own awareness. But that was his fault, not hers, bikini notwithstanding. He took a deep breath, gathered himself, formed a plan.

"I'm going to stand beside you," he said quietly, "with my hands like this. You are going to lie down in the water, on your back, and let my hands support you."

"Oh, God," she said in Italian. "I don't think I can. Could we just walk around some more? I was getting the hang of that. Walking in water. I think it's biblical."

"I think that may be walking *on* water."

"It's good enough for me. For today."

"Swimming lessons, heavy emphasis on the swimming."

"My hair isn't right. And the bathing suit won't work. You already said that."

"We'll figure it out. Together."

Together. He did not excel at figuring things out *together.* It had been his greatest weakness with the

SEALs. He was not a good team player. He had a tendency to go maverick. The last time he had done it, against orders, Justin had followed him...

"Are you all right?" Her hand, wet, warm, was on his cheek.

He shook his head. How was it she could see what no one else ever saw? "Yeah. I'm fine."

She didn't move her hand. He didn't move it, either. He had to stop this craziness. He shook his head again, trying to be all business. But droplets of water flew off his hair and rained down on her face, emphasizing the compassion there.

"Lie down in the water." His voice had a snap to it, like a flag caught in the wind.

Isabella's hand dropped to her side, but Connor could feel the warmth of it on his face as if it still rested there.

"No, I—" She twisted and looked at the stairs.

"Trust me," he said in *that* voice, firm, the voice of a man who was used to being in charge of everything, including the safety of others.

She dragged her eyes back from the staircase and looked at him for a long moment. Her eyes, with the water reflecting in them, looked more green than gold.

"Okay," she whispered.

"So just lean back," he coaxed her.

She leaned back an inch.

"Maybe a little more."

She leaned back another inch, so stiff-spined she looked like a tree bending over. He sighed and moved into her swiftly, before she could guess what he was going to do. Maybe he didn't even know what he was going to do himself until he had done it.

He scooped Isabella up and held her against his chest.

"Oh," she sighed with surprise. She would have weighed about as much as a feather under normal circumstances. With the water taking most of her weight, it was like holding a puff of air.

Except that her skin was warm and sensual, like silk. She blinked up at him and then twined her arms around his neck.

What part of the Swimming 101 manual was this in? he demanded of himself. He pried her fingers from around his neck and put her away from his chest, supporting her body on his hands, at right angles from his own.

"Okay," he said. His voice was faintly hoarse, not completely his talking-a-hostage-away-from-the-bad-guy voice. "Just relax. That's it. Now straighten out your legs. I've got you."

Tentatively, she did as he asked, her forehead wrinkled with anxiety as she gave herself over to the water. Her hair floated out in the water around her face, like dark silk ribbons. The small of her back was resting securely on his hands. Her skin was warmer than the water, and he felt a primal awareness of her that he did not want to feel.

At all.

"You're a bit tense," he told her. He heard the tension in his own voice and took a deep, steadying breath. "Relax. I won't bite."

"Yes," she said. "So you've said."

"Focus on your breathing. Put your hands on your tummy—no, you don't need them, I've got you—and breathe until you feel your tummy rising instead of your chest."

Shoot. Did he have to mention her chest just as his voice was returning to normal?

"This is quite amazing," she said after a moment.

"Amazing," he agreed. His jaw was starting to hurt from clenching his teeth so tightly. "So, just try moving your legs a bit. Kick."

She did a little kick.

"Very good," he encouraged her. "Harder, both of them."

She kicked tentatively. And then harder. The splash hit him in the face, which seemed to motivate more strenuous kicking on her part. She giggled.

That giggle helped him turn a page. Connor pretended to be worried about getting wet, ducking the worst of the splash while never letting her go. She giggled some more.

"Now straighten your legs out. Think of a pair of scissors opening and closing and kick like that. That's perfect. That's why it's called a scissor kick. Now, instead of just standing here, I'm going to let the kick propel you. I'll move with you, though. You see how it works? Your legs are amazingly strong."

What he meant was that everyone's legs were amazingly strong, that this particular movement used the gluteus maximus, the largest muscle in the human body, but he didn't clarify, since she looked so pleased. And there was no denying her legs were amazing!

He supported her and guided her until she had kicked around the pool in a large circle.

"Now," he said, "my hands are still here, but I'm moving them away from you, so you can see it's the water supporting you, not me."

"No."

"Yes."

She glared up at him.

"Don't be nervous. The water's only three feet deep here. You can stand up at any time. Just relax. I'm going to—"

"No! Don't let go of me. I'm not ready."

He'd heard it again and again, looking into the eyes of a terrified civilian who was being asked to do something that required more of them than had ever been required before.

"Yes, you are," he said, "you are ready."

Slowly, he slid his hands out from underneath her. Her eyes grew wide, and then she got nervous, and her body folded at the center, legs and head going up, abdomen and torso going down, under the water.

"Ahh," she yelped.

His hands were floating inches below her, and so he supported her again, very quickly.

"Try and keep your body stiff."

"I thought I was supposed to relax!"

"Well, relaxed stiffness."

"There is no such thing."

"Maybe not in Italian. There is in English." He managed to say it with a straight face.

She smiled in spite of herself, and then he let her go, and she tried again. Again, she got nervous and began to fold; again he used his hands to steady her. The third time, she got it. She kicked on her own and he shadowed her.

"Am I swimming?" she demanded. "Am I swimming all by myself?"

He smiled at her enthusiasm, and she seemed to realize she was swimming, unaided, on her back. The realization ruined it, of course. This time he wasn't quite quick enough, and her head went under the water. She came up sputtering, her hair spilling rivulets of water down her golden skin. She grabbed for him and clung to him.

He realized he was enjoying that way too much and put her away from his chest, though he allowed her to hang on to his forearms.

"That wasn't so bad, was it?" he asked her.

She shook water from her hair. "No," she said, surprised and then delighted. "No, it was fine. I just held my breath when I went under."

There was a moment when people reached deep inside and found out who they really were that was awe-inspiring. It could happen as you sneaked them across a border or pushed them out of a plane, or it happened in those moments, large and small, when people required just a tiny bit more of themselves.

And so it could happen just like this, a woman in a swimming pool on a warm spring day when everything seemed suddenly infused with a light that was not the sun.

It was always an amazing thing to be a part of this moment. She was grinning ear to ear, which increased Connor's sensation of basking in the light. He had to force himself to move away from that moment and back on task.

"And that brings us to part two," Connor said. "For some reason, people have a natural aversion to getting their faces wet."

"I told you not today," she said. The grin disappeared.

"Let's just ride this wave of discovery," he suggested.

For a moment, she looked as if she intended to argue, but then, reluctantly, she smiled again. "All right. Let's ride this wave."

Both of them had said it—let's. Let *us*. Us. A duo. A team. Sheesh.

"So, before you dunk again, we're going to work on getting your face wet," Connor said. There it was again, slipping off his tongue naturally. *We.* "Lie on my hands again, this time on your stomach."

She flopped down on her stomach, and he supported her, his hands on the firm flesh of her belly. "Good. Now put your face in the water and blow air out of your mouth. Make bubbles. The more the better. Think of yourself as a motorboat."

Whatever reservations she might have had up until this point now disappeared. Isabella gave herself over to learning to swim with unreserved enthusiasm. With Connor supporting her stomach, she blew bubbles and then they added a scissor kick. She managed a few kicks without any support before she went under and came up laughing.

Isabella laughing.

Isabella soaking wet, in the world's skimpiest bathing suit, laughing.

It was probably one of the most dangerous moments of Connor's entire life, and he had had a life fraught with danger.

It wasn't dangerous because she was so beautiful, or even because she had lost her self-consciousness and she was so sexy in her teeny bathing suit. It wasn't dangerous because she was finding her inner resources of courage and strength.

No, what made the moment beautiful was her joy.

What made the moment astounding was the serious expression gone from her face and the sorrow completely erased from her eyes. No matter what the danger to himself, Connor was glad he had given her this moment.

"I think that's probably enough for today," he said gruffly. "We'll start some basic arm work tomorrow, moving toward a front crawl. And we'll do work on your legs with a kickboard. By the end of the week, you'll be swimming across this pool by yourself."

"Really?"

"You are a complete natural."

"I am?" she asked, so pleased.

"Absolutely."

"What an amazing afternoon." She cocked her head at him. "What do the American teenagers say? Awesome!"

She was standing facing him. She leaned a bit closer. He had plenty of time to move away from her. But somehow he didn't, frozen to the spot, like a deer in headlights, not able to back away from where *awesome* could take them.

She stood on tippy toes. Her body, slippery and lithe, came in contact with his in a far different way than it had when he was using his arms to buoy her up in the water. She kissed him, a tiny brushing of their lips.

He, of all people, knew how little time it took to change everything. A millisecond. The time for a bullet to find its way from rifle to target, the time for tires to crunch across the trigger device on an explosive, the time for a school to go from rooms of laughing children to completely engulfed in flames. He, of all people, knew how quickly everything could change.

But maybe he hadn't known this: as quickly as you

could be sucked into darkness and everything could shatter around you, just as quickly you could be thrust toward the light, propelled into a world that promised love was stronger.

Love? He felt furious with himself, and not too happy with Isabella, either. But then she was backed away from him, still laughing, that delightful, carefree, water-over-rocks laughter, as if she had no awareness at all how badly she had just disrupted his well-ordered world.

"Thank you, Connor. I can't wait for tomorrow."

And then she walked away from him, through the water, by herself, the woman she had been an hour ago—clinging to the handrail and then to him—gone forever.

Isabella got out of the pool without the benefit of the stairs. She put her hands on the deck and levered herself out, wiggling her bottom at him in the process. And then, free of the pool, she gathered up that voluminous caftan but didn't put it on. She scampered across the deck to the cabana, not once looking back.

Thank goodness she did not look back. Because she would have seen him, still standing in the water, stunned by the power of that one tiny little brush of lips. To change everything.

The man he had been an hour ago might have been gone forever, too. Because the thing about a kiss like that? It opened a door. It opened a door that was pretty darned difficult to wrestle shut again once it had been opened. It changed everything in subtle ways.

Connor sucked in a deep breath. He said a word under his breath that he would never say in Isabella's presence. He dived under the surface of the water. His momentum carried him to one end of the pool. Though there was hardly room to get going, he began to do furious laps, butterfly stroke.

But by the time Isabella emerged from the cabana, he was aware that swimming had not defused what he was feeling. Even that most challenging stroke did not begin to burn off the fire that brush of her lips against his had stoked within him.

CHAPTER SEVEN

ISABELLA CONTEMPLATED THE fact that she had kissed Connor Benson. Really, as far as kisses went, it had been nothing. A peck. A thank-you.

But even in Italy, where people were passionate, a thank-you kiss might normally be placed on the cheek, not the lips.

Connor's lips looked so firm. And yet, giving under the pressure of hers, they had felt soft and pliable. His lips had tasted of something, but she wasn't sure what. It had been pure, like holding out your tongue to catch raindrops.

Heaven. That's what they had tasted of. The problem was, after tasting something like that, a person could spend her life in pursuit of it. It had really been a foolish thing to do, reckless, especially with them living under her roof together.

But in that moment, after the lesson, she had just felt so bold, so ready to do just as he suggested, to ride the wave of discovery instead of fighting it. It had been wonderful tackling the water, doing something she had always been afraid of. It had made her feel free in a way she never had before.

From the moment she had chosen that bathing suit

over the far more conservative ones available, even with the limited selection in Monte Calanetti at this time of year, Isabella had felt she was saying yes to life.

The swimming lesson itself had made her feel so alive and so bold and as if the world and this day were plump with possibilities instead of just one day following the next, safe and routine.

Isabella came out of the cabana and saw that Connor was swimming like a man possessed. The stroke he was using was amazing, his powerful arms and shoulders lifting his torso and propelling him out of the water as if he had been shot out of a cannon.

He noticed her, she was not sure how, and he stopped and stood up. He folded his arms over the lines of his chest. Her awareness of him rippled through her like a current that could sweep her away.

"I forgot to tell you, I found another place to stay," he said.

She knew instantly he was lying. He hadn't found another place to stay. He had tasted the reckless danger, too, as soon as her lips had touched his, and decided to find different accommodations.

He was acknowledging something was going on between them. Something more powerful than he could control. And even though he had told her to ride the wave of discovery, he was not prepared to do that himself.

She held her breath. Was he going to cancel swimming?

"I'll see you tomorrow. And I'll pay you for your place for the agreed dates." he said. He dived back under the water before she could let him know she was not going to help him assuage his guilt by allowing him to pay her for a room he wasn't going to occupy.

Isabella had never really felt this before: an acute awareness of her feminine power.

She walked home by herself, aware that the buoyancy of the water seemed to have infused her. Even though Connor had said he was moving out, her steps were light, and she felt as if she was walking on air.

She got home to discover a parcel had been delivered. It was one of the bathing suits she had ordered online, from Milan. She was pleased it had been delivered so quickly, that overnight delivery had meant just that.

And she was even more pleased when she opened the parcel and slipped the fabric from the tissue paper. So tiny! How could it possibly have cost so much money? Still, she hugged the scraps of fabric to her and went to try the new suit on. It was no more a *swim*suit than the lime-green bikini today had been.

But she had given herself permission, with that first bold choice of a bathing suit, to start exploring a different side of herself. More feminine. More sexy. Deeply alive within her own body. Deeply appreciative of herself as a woman, and of the power that came with acknowledging this new side of herself.

Isabella was choosing the bathing suits of a woman who wanted a man to be very aware she was a woman. Not to just tease him, but to let him know he was not going to be able to shunt her aside so easily, just because he'd switched from a date to swimming lessons.

She thought of the way Connor had been swimming when she left Nico's garden area—like a man possessed, or at the very least, like a man trying to clear his head—and allowed herself the satisfied chuckle of someone who had succeeded beyond their wildest dreams.

Still, when she heard him come in later, pack his

bags and leave, she avoided him. Already her house felt empty without him. If she went and saw him, she was not at all certain she could trust herself not to beg him to stay.

She would not beg him to stay, but she was not above making him sorry he had left.

The next day at the pool, she wore the same over-size caftan out onto the deck. Connor was in the pool tossing a blue flutter board into the air and catching it, pretending he'd barely registered her arrival.

But when she dropped the caftan, he registered her arrival—he missed his catch on the kickboard.

If it was possible, her new bathing suit, black and shiny, was even skimpier than the one she had worn yesterday. She really took her time getting into the water, savoring the scowl on his face.

When she reached the bottom stair, he shoved the kickboard at her and snapped some instructions.

"Aren't you even going to say hello?" she asked, petulant.

"Hello," he snapped.

"Your new accommodations must not be very nice."

"What would make you say that?"

"You seem like you haven't slept well or something. You have grumpy lines." She touched the sides of her own mouth to show him where. He stared at her mouth. His grumpy lines deepened.

"We're going to work on your kick today." And so they did. There was a lot less touching this second day of instruction. It was shameful how disappointed she was by that. He announced the session was over from the opposite end of the pool. Isabella was fairly certain this was to discourage thank-you kisses.

Though, even without the kiss, his swimming seemed even more furious when she left than it had the day before.

The third day, another bathing suit had arrived. It was not a bikini. It was a leopard-patterned one-piece with a plunging neckline and the legs cut very high. It was so racy—and not the competitive swimming kind of racy—that Isabella actually debated not wearing it at all.

But she was so glad she had when they sat side by side on the pool deck, legs dangling in the water for lesson number three. His mouth set in a grim line, Connor demonstrated the arm movements for the front crawl. Really? Him showing off his arm muscles like that was no more fair than her showing off in her bikini!

They ended the lesson in the water. With him at her side she managed to swim across the width of the shallow end of the pool, once on her back and then once on her front.

The only reason he touched her at all was because she swallowed some water and came up choking. He slammed her on the back a few times before ordering her back to work.

When she emerged from the cabana, she noticed that Connor was churning up enough water to create a tidal wave.

The fourth day, not wanting it to be too obvious she was enjoying driving him crazy, she put the lime-green bikini from the first day back on. He got her into the deep end. He taught her to tread water, arms doing huge swooping circles, legs bicycling.

"You don't work hard at it," he warned her. "You relax. It's something you should be able to do for a long, long time."

And then he made her do it for half an hour, treading water right beside her without ever touching her. Once again, when she left he was covering the pool in length-eating strokes.

The fifth day, she arrived at the pool in her newest bathing suit. It was too bad he'd left her house and she'd refused his money. It would have helped her afford all these suits.

This one was a simple black one-piece, a tank style. The most suitable for swimming, it made the light come on in his eyes just as the others had done.

"Today," he announced, "we'll do a quick review of everything we have learned, and then we're done."

Done. Isabella thought of that. No more seeing him every day, unless she caught glimpses of him in the village, going about his business. Her life would be as empty as her house.

And then the wedding would come and go, and he would be gone from Monte Calanetti for good. Forever.

She got in the water and stood at the bottom of the stairs.

"Don't stand there gripping the rail like that," he snapped. "You've come farther than that."

The tone! As bossy as if she was some green recruit he had authority over. A beach ball, rolling around on the deck, pushed by the wind, plopped in the water beside her. On an impulse, she picked it up and hurled it at his head.

He caught it easily and squinted at her. For a moment she thought he was going to ignore her protest of his high-handed ways. But then he tossed the ball high in the air and spiked it at her. She swiveled out of the way with a little squeal. The ball missed her, and then she grabbed it. She threw. He dived under the water.

Connor resurfaced and grabbed the ball. He threw it hard. She, who a week ago had been afraid to get her face wet, ducked under the water. She came up and grabbed the ball. He was swimming away from her. She waded in after him, threw the ball when he stopped. It bounced off his head.

"Ha-ha, one for me," she cried.

He grabbed the ball and tossed it. It hit her arm. "Even. One for me, too." He swam right up to her, his powerful strokes bringing him to her in a breath. He grabbed the ball and let her have it from close range. "Two for me."

"Oh!"

Just like that, all the tension that had been building between them for a week dissolved into laughter. They were playing. The last lesson was forgotten, and they were like children chasing each other around the pool, shrieking and laughing and calling taunts at each other.

And then she missed a throw and the ball bounced onto the deck. Neither of them bothered to get it, and now they were just playing tag without the ball between them. The air filled with their hoots of laughter. She tagged him with a shove and swam away. He came after her hard and splashed her, then tagged her and was off. She knew she couldn't possibly catch him, and so he was letting her shove him and splash him.

An hour went by. They were breathless, the air shimmering with their awareness of each other.

Reluctant for it ever to end, Isabella finally gave in first and hauled herself up on the deck and lay there on her tummy, panting, exhausted. A shadow passed over her. He was standing above her.

Isabella was aware she was holding her breath. He had moved out of her house to avoid her. But then, after a moment, he lowered himself to the deck, on his stomach, right beside her. He wasn't touching her, but he was so close she could feel a wave of warmth coming off the outer part of his arm.

He closed his eyes, and she unabashedly studied him. She could see how the water was beading on his skin, droplets tangled in his eyelashes, sunlight turning them to diamonds. She could see the smooth perfection of his skin, the lines of his muscles, the swimmer's broadness of his shoulders and back.

She had never, ever been more aware of another human being than she was of Connor, lying beside her. She sighed with something that sounded very much like surrender, and closed her eyes.

Lying there on the pool deck beside Isabella, Connor felt as if the whole world came to a standstill. When danger was near, he always felt this—his senses heightened until they were almost painful. And he felt it again right now, as he had never felt it before.

He could feel the gentle Tuscan sun on his back and the heat rising up through the pool deck and warming every cell of his skin. He could hear the birds singing, but more, he could separate their songs, so he could hear each one individually. She sighed—a contented sound like a kitten's mew—and he could feel the puff of air from that sigh touch his lips, as life-altering as her kiss had been.

He could smell the flowers that bloomed in abundance around the pool, the faint tang of chlorine and most of all Isabella. The spicy scent had been washed away and replaced by an aroma that was dizzying in its feminine purity.

He had only one sense left to explore. He opened his eyes and gazed at Isabella stretched out on the pool deck. Her hair hung thick and wet and luxurious down the narrowness of her back. Her black bathing suit clung to her like a second skin, caressing the curve of her back and the swell of her firm buttock. Her skin was as flawless as porcelain. The roundness of her cheek was pressed into the deck, and her lashes were so thick and long they cast a faint shadow there. Her lips had not a hint of lipstick on them, and yet they naturally called to him, full and plump and sensuous.

As if she sensed him studying her, she opened her eyes. He unabashedly threw himself into the color of them—it felt as if he was swimming in cool pools of sun-filtered greens and golds and browns.

A few days ago, he had gone to the chapel at the palazzo. It had been strictly work. If he was a bad guy, where would he hide? What were the weak places both in the chapel and around it? He'd taken some pictures and made some notes of the exterior and then moved inside.

Logan Cascini, the project manager for the whole restoration, had come up to him. Connor had been touching base with Logan on and off since he arrived, and there was an affinity between the two men.

"You have to see what has complicated my life today," Logan had said wryly.

"That's gotta be a woman," Connor had muttered.

"That sounds like the voice of experience," Logan said, raising a quizzical eyebrow.

"Show me your complication," Connor said, not following Logan's implied invitation to elaborate.

"This is the final wall we're working on. We're just pulling off that old wood paneling."

Connor followed Logan over to a side wall of the church. The workmen were absolutely silent, their normal chatter gone.

As they uncovered it, Connor, who considered himself no kind of art lover, had stood there, frozen by the beauty of what he was seeing revealed.

"It's a fresco," Logan supplied, "probably centuries old, and probably by one of the lesser Renaissance painters."

"I've never seen anything so beautiful," Connor said when he could find his voice. The fresco was the Madonna and child. The expression on the Madonna's face was so infused with love that Connor could feel an uncomfortable emotion closing his throat.

"And like all beautiful women," Logan said, "she is complicated."

"Now *you* sound like the voice of experience."

For a moment something pained appeared in Logan's eyes, but then he rolled his shoulders and ran a hand through his hair. "You don't find something like this and just keep on as if it's normal. I'll have to notify the authorities. Depending what they decide, the wedding could be delayed."

Connor had let out a long, low whistle, loaded with the sympathy of a man who knew firsthand how the unexpected could mess with a guy's plans.

Then, taking one more look at the fresco, he had said goodbye to Logan and left the chapel.

Now, days later, lying side by side at the pool with Isabella, with the sun warming their backs, he was feeling that again.

Paralyzed by almost incomprehensible beauty. When Isabella saw how intently he was looking at her, she smiled and didn't look away. Neither did he.

The danger he was in came to him slowly. He'd tried to fight this attraction every way that he knew how. He'd tried to create distance. He'd tried to nip it in the bud. He'd even moved out of her house.

But still, he was falling in love with Isabella Rossi. Or maybe he already had. That was why he had felt such an urgent need to cancel that date, to get out from under the same roof as her. It was why he was in this state of heightened awareness and had been for days. The fact that he could see beauty so intensely was connected to what he was experiencing with this woman.

She reached out and touched his shoulder, and again, because of his heightened awareness, he felt that touch as though he had never been touched before, had never felt so exquisitely connected to another human being before.

"I've gone from being terrified of the water to loving it," she said huskily.

"I know, you have been a great student." He was the wrong man for a woman to love. He had always known that. His childhood had left him wary of relationships, and his choice of work had suited that perfectly. He had told himself he was protecting women from the potential for loss, but in fact he had been protecting himself.

Because he'd always known only the bravest of women could handle what he was dishing out.

True, he wasn't in active service anymore. But what had just gone down in Azerbaijan was plenty of evidence he still had his knack for finding danger.

It seemed to him this little slip of a woman lying on the deck beside him was the bravest of women.

"Connor?"

"Huh?"

"I've never had that before, what I had just now."

"What?"

"Just fun," she said. "Just good old-fashioned fun. Even when I was a child, Giorgio was my best friend. He couldn't run and play like everyone else, and so I stayed with him. We read and drew pictures, but I've never really had this. Just to let go of everything, to play until I'm so out of breath I feel as if I can't breathe.

"I mean, I do it with my students. I have fun with them, but it's not the same. I have to be the adult. I have to maintain a modicum of control. I don't ever get to be this carefree."

His awareness of her deepened yet again. Her beautiful eyes were sparkling with tears.

"So, thank you," she said. "I'm never going to be able to thank you enough. Never."

His awareness of himself deepened, too, but not in a good way. An unexpected element inserted itself into the pure and sizzling awareness of the moment. Connor suddenly felt ashamed of himself. He'd backed out of that date out of pure terror of what she was doing to him. He'd left her house because he couldn't trust himself around her without wanting to taste her lips again.

But when he'd challenged her to embrace what terrified her, she had done it in a heartbeat. She had shown incredible bravery.

And now she was telling him she'd never had fun. That fooling around in the swimming pool was the most fun she'd ever had. She'd given her whole life to looking after others. Her husband, and then the kids at school.

It seemed to Connor he was being given an opportunity to do something good. Maybe the best thing he'd ever done. It wasn't about whether or not he was comfortable. It wasn't about that at all. That feeling that maybe he was falling for her deepened in him. Didn't that call him to be a better man? Didn't it ask him to be more than he had ever been before. Braver? Stronger? More compassionate?

"You know that date I canceled?" His voice was so low it came out sounding like a whisper.

She went very still.

"You want to give me another chance?"

"Yes," she said, her voice low, too, as if they were in a church. "Yes, I do."

"What about tomorrow night?"

"That would be perfect."

Isabella looked at her bed. It was covered with every single item of clothing that she owned. She had tried on the red dress and then taken it off. He'd already seen it. It wasn't the message she wanted to give. Nothing was the message she wanted to give.

Suddenly, frustrated, exhausted from trying things on and ripping them back off, she threw herself down on the bed, falling backward into the heap of clothes. Isabella lay there, staring at the ceiling.

She thought back over their week of swimming lessons. There had been the most delicious sense of getting to know Connor, of connecting with him. There had been the most delicious awareness of him physically, a yearning to touch him and taste him that was astonishingly powerful. That small kiss had shown her what was going on between them was like riding a wild horse. It wasn't going to be controlled.

She had never felt that for Giorgio.

A stab of guilt pierced her heart. And she had a terrible moment of self-awareness. Giorgio, despite the fact he was dying, had been the safest choice she could make. He had been her friend, and she had loved him as a friend.

But that other kind of love? The kind that was filled with passion and excitement? Hadn't she known from the time she was a little girl that that kind was unpredictable and hurtful and destructive?

Connor would never be unfaithful. After you knew him for ten minutes, you knew that of him. That he was a man of complete honor.

But he had pitted his formidable strength against the wrongs of the world. He had warned her that he sought out danger, and that he found it. She had seen that for herself when she had caught the tail end of that news clip out of Azerbaijan.

To allow herself to love Connor Benson would be to open herself up to pain such as she had never felt, not even when she was a little girl and had seen her father in a café with a woman who was not her mother.

From the second she had spotted him, Isabella had begun working on an elaborate story: it was someone from work. It was a friend. It was a cousin. And then her father had leaned forward and kissed that woman on the mouth with unmistakable passion.

Then there had been the different pain: watching Giorgio die, every day a series of losses for him, and for them, until she was feeding the man she married baby food from a spoon.

And so, this week Isabella had tackled one of her fears. She had learned to swim. And she had deliberately fanned the fire she had seen in Connor's eyes.

But without considering the consequences. In a way, she had won. He had given in. He had asked her out again after canceling the first time. But was she really ready to open herself to more pain?

Isabella realized, sadly, she had used up all her bravery. She did not have any left. She certainly did not have the kind left that you would need to go on the wild ride that was love.

Not with a man like Connor Benson.

The next morning, she caught up with him on the edge of town. She had known he would be there, heading out for his early morning swim.

"Connor."

He swung around and looked at her. His smile held as much promise as the sun that was just beginning to touch the rooftops of Monte Calanetti.

"I'm sorry. About tonight?"

His smile faded.

"I can't. I realized I have a previous obligation."

He cocked his head at her.

She should have thought of the previous obligation before now! She blurted out the first thing that came to her head. "My students are putting on a skit for the spring fete. I'm not ready. The costumes aren't finished. I haven't started the props."

He was looking at her quietly.

"So, clearly a date is out of the question. For right now."

And in a while, he would be gone, anyway. If she could just hold off for a few more days, she would be what she most liked to be. Safe. She would leave that woman she had been introduced to in Nico's swimming pool behind, a memory that would fade more with each passing day, and then week, and then year.

Besides, neither of them had addressed where a date would be leading—down that dark road to heartbreak? There were so many different routes to get to that destination.

So, if she should be so pleased with herself that she was taking control of a situation that had the potential to get seriously out of control if she let it, why did she feel so annoyed that instead of looking dismayed that she had canceled their date, he looked downright relieved.

"Is it the swimming lessons that put you behind the eight ball?" he asked.

She frowned at him. "What is this? Behind the eight ball?"

"Have you ever played pool?"

"Isn't that what we just did all week?"

He threw back his head and laughed. Oh, of all the things he could have done, that was the worst. It filled her with an ache to live in a state of playful days of hearing him laugh. But of course, given what he did for a living, that was unrealistic.

There would be far more days of waiting for him, of anxiety sitting in her stomach like a pool of acid, of uncertainty and fear.

"In America, we play a variation of billiards called pool. Guys like me who spend ninety-nine percent of our lives bored out of our skulls become very good at it. There's a game in pool called eight ball," he said. "The eight ball is black. You can only touch it when it's the last ball on the table, otherwise you lose. So, if it gets between you and the ball you are aiming at, you are in a very difficult predicament. That's what 'behind the eight ball' means."

"What about the one percent?" she asked. She didn't care about the eight ball.

"Huh?"

"You spend ninety-nine percent of your life bored out of your skull—what about the one percent?"

"Oh, that."

She waited.

He grinned at her, devil-may-care. "It's one percent of all hell breaking loose." He held that smile, but she saw something else in his eyes, as if he held within him shadows of every terrible thing he had ever seen.

"And that's the part you love, and also the part you pay a price for."

He did not like it when the powers of observation that he had encouraged her to hone were turned on him.

"Weren't we talking about you?"

"Yes, we were," she said. "I think that would be an accurate description of how I feel right now, behind this eight ball. I have much to do, and not enough time to do it."

"My fault. Because of the swimming. I'll help you get ready for your skit. I'm winding down on the recon for the wedding anyway. I'll be wrapped up in a couple of days."

And then he would be gone.

CHAPTER EIGHT

"YOU WON'T LIKE IT," Isabella said with all the firmness she could muster. "You won't like helping me. I'm making paper sunshine cutouts."

Connor laughed again, but she could hear a faint edge to it. "Lady, my life has been so full of things I didn't like it would make your head spin."

Again, that hint of the dark places he had been that he carried within him. "What is this, make your head spin?"

"I'll explain it to you over paper sunshines."

Isabella was ashamed of her weakness. She could not give up what he was offering. She could not give up an opportunity to spend time with him. It seemed to her that she had caught a glimpse of his world when they went swimming. Now she had an overwhelming desire to see how he would react to hers.

No doubt with utter boredom. But at least it was not a date, that event that was so loaded with romantic expectation and foolish hopes.

"All right," she said stiffly. "Come after school. Class gets out at one."

"Okay," he said. He sauntered away, into the magic of Monte Calanetti's dawn, whistling. Whistling! It confirmed that he was not the least distressed that she had canceled the date. The exact opposite, in fact.

He was very punctual, and Connor Benson showed up just as her students were swarming out the door of her classroom. He looked like a ship plowing through the sea of bright blue uniforms. Luigi Caravetti, who always had too much energy, was walking backward, catcalling at one of the girls.

Connor sidestepped him easily, but at that very moment, Luigi swung around and smashed into him.

Connor barely moved, but Luigi fell down. With absolute ease, Connor went down on his haunches, helped the little boy up, picked up the homework Luigi wouldn't do anyway and handed it back to him. Luigi said something to him and then wound up and kicked Connor in the shin and ran off before Isabella could reprimand him.

Rubbing his shin, he turned to her and grinned ruefully.

"I'm sorry," she said, "Luigi is a bit of a handful. What did he say to you?"

"I don't know. He said it in Italian. I'm beginning to pick up a few phrases, so I think he told me to watch were I was going. And then he switched to English."

"He doesn't know any English."

"Ah, well, there's a universal word that all little boys—and most big ones—love to use."

"Oh! I will speak to him tomorrow."

"No, that's okay. He kind of reminded me of me at that age. And if I was going to guess something about him? No dad in the picture."

Again, Isabella was taken by Connor's incredible powers of observation. "That's true. In fact, his poor mother had to get a court order to keep the father away from them. He's not, apparently, a very nice man. But still, Luigi is troubled about it all. Children are always troubled about difficulties between their parents."

The last of the children clattered down the stairway to the main floor of the school, and they were cloaked in sudden silence. Then Connor Benson was in her classroom.

"So," he said, putting his hands in his pockets and rocking back on his heels, "this is your world."

"Ninety-nine percent boring," she told him. "One percent all hell breaking loose."

Connor gave her an odd look that she interpreted as *you don't have a clue what all hell breaking loose looks like*. But then he shrugged it off, as if he had given himself a mental order to lighten up. "I'm going to guess that one percent is largely your little Luigi."

"You would be guessing right."

"Nobody asked me what I was doing here when I came in," he said.

"Sorry?"

"When I came in and asked for your classroom, no one at the office asked me what I wanted or what I was doing at the school. They didn't even ask to see identification."

"Obviously we are in need of a security expert!" she said brightly, but he didn't seem amused. She became more serious. "We haven't experienced the kinds of problems here that you have in America."

Did he mutter *yet* under his breath? He removed his hands from his pockets and turned away from her and wandered around her classroom. At first she thought he was looking at drawings and pictures, and she was pleased that he was curious about her world. But then Isabella realized that Connor actually seemed to be looking for something else. She was not sure what.

He stood at the front, taking note of both the doors into the room. Then she saw him go to the windows, open the lock on one. He slid the window open and leaned out, looking at the ground.

He came to the table at the back, where she had the project laid out. He seemed faintly uneasy, but he lifted a sun with the hole in the center and put his head through it, attached the elastic around his chin.

She had planned to be so reserved, professional, accepting his help as a volunteer, but nothing more. Instead, she giggled at the picture this big self-assured man made with his face poking through a hole in a cardboard sunshine. The wall came tumbling down as she joined him at the art table at the back of the room.

How could he wear that silly thing with such aplomb? That's what confidence did, she supposed. "Boys are sunshine," she said.

"And girls?"

She picked up a pink flower and put her head through the center of it and attached the elastic. "Girls are flowers."

He smiled at her, but she still thought she detected faint uneasiness in him. Well, was that so unusual? Many men seemed uneasy in classrooms. The furniture was all in miniature, after all. The spaces were too tiny for most men, and Connor was even larger than most men.

"These are done," Isabella said, resting her hand on one stack, "but we have seven sunshines remaining to cut out and thirteen flowers. The children drew their own, but the cutting part can be quite difficult for little hands. The cardboard is a bit thick." She gave him a pair of scissors.

He sank into one of the little chairs. She actually wondered if it would break under his weight.

"That doesn't look very comfortable."

"I'm used to discomfort." Connor picked up a particularly messy-looking sun drawn on yellow construction paper.

"Luigi's?" he guessed.

She lifted a shoulder—*yes*.

When they had been swimming, that task had occupied them and filled the space between them. There had been no need for conversation on a personal level.

Now, tongue caught slightly between his teeth as he tried to fit his hands in the little scissors, Connor said, "So, tell me everything."

"What?"

"Where you grew up, how many kids are in your family, what your favorite color is and what your most secret dream is."

Again, she had the feeling he might be trying to distract her from some uneasiness he was feeling. Still, she was happy to do that and so, with his encouragement, she talked. It was amazingly comfortable sitting at the little table, cutting with little scissors, the sun pouring in around them. She marveled at how good it felt to be with him like this, at ease, and yet not at ease the way she had been with Giorgio.

With Connor, something sizzled in the air between them. All that time in the pool together had increased her awareness of him, and that did not change now that they were sitting in her classroom, in chairs too small for them, fully clothed.

She answered all his questions except one.

He didn't miss that, of course.

"And is there a secret dream?"

She thought of the way she had felt when she had learned Marianna was pregnant. Happy for Marianna, of course, and yet...

"No," she croaked.

His scissors stopped moving. He looked across at her. "There is," he said.

"I've given up on the secret dream thing."

"Ah." He obviously did not believe her, but he didn't press. They finished all the costume pieces, and he helped her build a simple set.

How could it be both so easy and so difficult to be with him? He came into her world of paper and glue and paint as easily as she had gone into his world of water. And he did the same thing to it.

An existence that had seemed mundane suddenly sparkled. There was laughter everywhere.

Except as he got ready to leave. He was suddenly very serious. "Can you request a different classroom?" he asked.

"What? Why?"

He shrugged and shoved his hands in his pockets. "You should just ask for one on the first floor, if you can."

"I like this one," she said, feeling stubborn.

"I'm sure you do. Unless there's a fire." His voice, which had been laughter filled only moments ago, was suddenly very grim.

Now, a few days after they had begun, they stood

back from her completed set, costumes and props. The set was lightweight cardboard so that it could be moved easily to the village square the day of the fete.

She sighed with contentment. With his help, it was so much better than anything she could have ever done alone.

He stood beside her. "It's done to your satisfaction?"

"Yes. A whole two days before the fete. I am officially out from under the eight ball."

"That's good," he said. "Because now we can have our date."

She slid him a look. He was covered with splotches of blue paint from painting the sky. He had a relaxed smile on his face.

She was so aware of him. It was dangerous. But she had no fight left in her. She did not want to fight anymore. She wanted to see what would happen between them.

Even if it was the most dangerous thing of all.

"Did you have something in mind?" she asked. Her voice sounded like a mouse squeaking.

"Oh, yeah," he said.

"What?" She hoped he would say something safe, something not that different than watching television at her house. A movie, maybe.

"I want to surprise you with it."

"How do I know what to wear for a surprise?" she asked.

"Anything you wear will be fine."

Did he not understand women at all? "If you could give me a hint," she suggested.

"It will have something to do with the chapel."

"The chapel?" Isabella could not imagine what he

had in mind. The last time she had seen it, the chapel had looked like a construction site, surrounded by scaffolding.

"Trust me."

"All right."

"I'll pick you up just before eight."

"All right."

It was complete surrender, and she knew it. And looking at his face, so familiar to her now, she realized it was a surrender for him, too. It was a surrender to what had been building between them like a thunderstorm on the horizon.

Looking at his face, Isabella wondered when exactly this had happened. When had he come to feel beloved to her?

Had it been as he painted the sky on cardboard or cut the head hole from yet another sunshine? Or had it been before that, when he had drawn her into the swimming pool and taught her to embrace what frightened her most?

Maybe it was before even that. Maybe it had begun that morning they had walked through the dawn to the river and she had felt the mud ooze up between her toes.

Or maybe it had been from the very first moment, when she had put his breakfast outside his door and been assaulted by him in her own home, the beginning of the waking up that had led to this: how she loved her life with Connor Benson in it.

It was a warm evening, so Isabella wore a simple white sundress of eyelet cotton, with narrow straps and a ribbon at the waist and a wide skirt. It did not sing the siren song that her red dress had, but it showed off her coloring and her figure, and it was more her, somehow.

It was as if, with Connor, she was exploring herself and slowly arriving at what that really was.

She saw she had chosen exactly the right ensemble when he arrived at her door. She could see it in his eyes even before he told her that she looked beautiful. Connor looked extraordinary. She had always seen him looking quite casual. Tonight he was in pressed dark slacks and a cream-colored linen dress shirt.

He went down her narrow walk before her and held open a car door. It was a very sleek, sporty car.

"Did you have a car before?" He hadn't ever parked one when he lived with her.

"I had one at my disposal, if I needed it. I prefer to walk. It gives me a better sense of a place. You notice more."

"Is this the car you had?" she asked.

He shook his head. "I traded up."

"Why?" she whispered, looking at the sleek gray convertible with awe.

"It seems to me, my lady, you have missed a few things on the road to romance. Your man wants to show you new worlds and impress you."

Her man? On the road to romance? Was she really ready for this? Isabella could barely breathe as he held open the door for her. It seemed like a long step down into the low-slung sports car, and he took her hand and helped her. She settled back in a deep leather seat.

The car was a dream to ride in, and she loved the way Connor handled it in the narrow streets. There was nothing about him, she realized, that was inclined to show off. And yet he was obviously extremely confident and capable handling the very powerful car. She loved the way one hand rested lightly on the wheel, his other on the knob of the gearshift. The ride seemed over way too soon. When she reached for the door handle, he gave her a meaningful look and she let her hand fall away.

He opened the door for her and then went around to the trunk and opened it as well. He looped the handle of a large wicker basket over his left arm and offered her his right. She threaded her arm through the crook of his elbow and they went up the well-worn path to the palazzo's chapel.

It was as she had remembered, almost completely engulfed in scaffolding.

"It must be American," she said out loud.

"What?"

"A date at a construction site."

"What? Italians don't date at construction sites?" He shook his head, teasing her. "I thought you people had perfected the romantic gesture."

"Why would you think that?"

"My mother calls Italy the land of *amore*."

The land of *amore*. She lived here, and she had missed it! Not that she was going to admit that to Connor.

And then he led her around the back of the chapel.

Isabella gasped. There was a table set up there with a white tablecloth on it. It faced out over a view that seemed to show the rolling, vineyard-covered hills of the entire valley.

Connor placed his picnic basket on the table and pulled back a chair for her. "The sun will be setting—" he glanced at his watch "—in seven minutes. Do you want a glass of wine?"

How could she refuse? He took a bottle out of his basket, dewdrops of condensation running down it. He popped the cork with complete ease. While the wine breathed, he took long-stemmed glasses, plates and cutlery from the bag.

He glanced at his watch. She could see the sun beginning to lower to the edges of the hills. The light was changing, softening all around them.

"What I want to share with you is this way," he said. "I'll let the wine breathe for a moment before I pour it."

What did he mean? The sun would go down over there, in front of them. Was that not what he had brought her here to see, a most wildly romantic gesture? She turned and looked at him. He held out his hand to her, and she took it. Could she ever get used to the feeling of a hand like his closing around hers?

He led her around the chapel and in a side door.

The light inside was suddenly drenched in color, golds and pinks. It was almost as though the chapel had been designed for this moment in time: the setting of the sun. Despite much evidence of work and restoration, when it was suffused with light like this the space seemed sacred.

"I wanted you to see this," he said, and with a sweep of his arm directed her gaze to the side wall of the chapel, by the family pews.

She saw a fresco on the wall of the chapel. Even without the amazing addition of the light from the setting sun, the fresco took her breath away. She moved toward it as if in a dream, staring at the scene before her with utter awe.

The detail of the Madonna and child was stunning: as if each hair on their heads, each eyelash, had been painted individually.

"The color is astounding," she breathed. Connor was

standing right beside her, gazing at the fresco. "Their skin, the color of her robe, the child's lips."

Both Madonna and child had enormous, expressive eyes turned to the heavens, where the clouds parted and a beam of light illuminated them.

"Do you think I can touch it?" she whispered.

"I think so."

She placed her hand on the wall. The sun was touching the wall, and its warmth had seeped into it, making the fresco seem even more like a living thing. "I don't think I've ever seen anything as beautiful as this."

His hand covered hers. "I know. I felt the same way when I saw it. It's been covered all these years. I can't imagine why, and yet it probably preserved the magnificence of the colors. You know, Isabella, I have seen the world at its ugly worst, and I'm not sure why but this restored something in me."

"I understand."

"Do you?"

"Yes, it's like it holds a message. That beauty survives, or wins. It's like it is saying, when all else falls away, the best, the good, will remain."

"That's exactly what I felt when I saw it, not that I could articulate it like that."

"The best," she said quietly, "a mother's love for her child. The Madonna radiates love. Maybe not just for the child. Something bigger. For the world." She could feel the tears clogging her throat, and she bit them back. Even so, he seemed to know what an emotional moment this was for her, because his hand came to rest on the small of her back.

Time slipped away as they explored the fresco together, pointing out incredible details they thought the other might have missed.

Finally, when darkness had fallen so completely that the church was pitched in blackness, Connor ushered her back outside.

He poured the wine and took some candles out of the basket, placed them carefully on the table and lit them. And then he took a dish of still-hot pasta out, wrapped in a tea towel. When he took the towel off, the spicy fragrance of the lasagna made her mouth water. She was not sure if it was because of the painting or because of him that the food tasted as if the angels themselves had prepared it.

"Tell me now about your secret dream," he said softly.

The night was so perfect. Seeing the fresco had brought her secret dreams to the forefront of her mind. It felt right to give him all of her, to hold nothing back.

"Once, I dreamed I would have babies," she confessed.

"Not now? I can picture you with babies. I can picture that look on your face, exactly like the one on the face of the Madonna in the chapel."

"I'm getting very old for this dream," she said, her voice small.

"You think thirty-three is old for having babies?"

"Isn't it?"

He actually laughed. "My mother had my half brother Sammy when she was thirty-six, and my sister, Amelia, a year later. The baby of the family, Henry, arrived when she was forty."

"Thank you for telling me that. It just feels as if everyone having babies is so much younger than me.

Marianna's shower is tomorrow night, and I was trying to think of reasons not to go. Of course, I could not think of a reason not to go that would not raise eyebrows. In Monte Calanetti, celebrating the coming of a baby is mandatory, like giving kisses to strangers on New Year's Eve. But it is very painful watching others have what I wanted."

"You are not kissing any strangers on New Year's Eve," he teased.

Isabella shivered. Would it be reading too much into the teasingly possessive statement to think she could count on Connor to still be part of her life as the village welcomed the new year?

His teasing tone was gone when he spoke again. "Isabella, you and your husband could not have children?"

She shook her head. "He was already too sick by the time we married."

"Aw, Isabella."

"Please don't say that as if I'm to be pitied."

"I'm sorry, that wasn't my intention."

"I wanted to try, even though I knew I would be raising a child alone. Is that selfish?"

"It makes me wonder why you wanted one so badly that you would be willing to raise it alone. That is the hardest thing. I know, because I watched my mom do it. Even if there had been financial security, which I am sure you would have, the emotional burden is huge. The responsibility is a lot to carry alone."

"I see that every day in Luigi," she said.

"And yet?" Connor heard the unspoken as clearly as if she had said it.

She drew in a deep breath. The stars and the wine

and the gaze of Connor, steady and strong, drew her every secret out of her soul.

"And yet, I have always craved a family. A real family."

"Yours wasn't?"

"Oh, my mother and my father stayed together, but only because they both considered it a sin to split up. Our family was a sham. My father always had girlfriends, mistresses. My mother lived in a state of wounded pride and furious anger."

"I'm sorry."

"It's no matter," she said. "Not now. I have my students. They are all my children now. I am lucky in so many ways. And you, Connor? What are your thoughts on children?"

"My own?" he asked. His voice broke in pretended terror, and she laughed, but she was unwilling to let him off the hook so easily.

"I think you would make a wonderful father," she said.

"How, when I have never had that modeled for me?"

"Yes, you have, by men you admired, if not by your own father. I can tell by how you taught me to swim how good you would be at it."

"That's what my mom says, too, when she sees me tussling with my new brothers and sister, that I'd make a great daddy."

"You enjoy being with them?"

"Don't tell anyone, but it's one of my favorite things."

"And why would you not want to tell anyone this?"

"Kind of spoils the whole warrior image. But seriously? I don't think my lifestyle is very conducive to children."

"I think you're wrong. Your lifestyle is about honor, and about standing strong for what you believe. I am not sure you could give a child any greater gift than that."

"Until you come home in a box."

"What is this? Come home in a box?"

"It means to not come home at all."

Isabella wanted to shudder at the harshness of the expression, but she reminded herself there was no room in this man's life for a woman who shuddered at harsh realities.

"And just like that," he continued quietly, "you've made a lot of pain in the world. You've made a Luigi."

"Or maybe, if the love was strong enough, you've left a legacy that is not like the legacy poor Luigi has inherited."

"Maybe," he said, but he did not sound convinced.

The wind came up suddenly and lifted the tablecloth and blew out the candle. By the time they had rearranged the cloth and relit the candle, the serious mood was gone. They joked back and forth while they ate, and when silence fell it was comfortable, soaking up the beauty of the night skyline and the immense sky overhead and the stars that studded it.

Then he slipped his phone from his pocket. She was almost relieved he had made such a wildly inappropriate gaffe in the evening, because she thought to believe in perfection was probably an invitation to fate to prove you wrong. But then Connor searched through the phone and found some music. He put it on, then pushed another button. The phone glowed softly.

"How did you do that?" she asked.

"It's an app—it turns your phone into a light."

"Americans," she teased.

"Yes, we have to have all the state-of-the-art toys."

"If it brings you happiness."

"Isabella, stuff does not bring happiness. This brings happiness." He rose from the table, and he set his phone on the table and held out his hand to her.

"Dance with me?"

She rose from the table and went into his arms with a sigh.

"No words," he said of the music choice. "Not English, and not Italian. I think music and art can speak the language of the heart."

With the stars watching them and tears spilling down her cheeks at the absolute and complete wonder of this moment, Isabella Rossi luxuriated in the feeling of Connor Benson's arms closing around her. Her cheek was pressed into his chest, and she could feel the steady beat of his heart in her skin.

It was homecoming.

It was as if every event of her entire life had served only one purpose and that was to lead her to this moment, dancing under the stars of a Tuscan sky with Connor swaying against her, his hand on the small of her back, his breath fanning the hair on the top of her head.

One song became another. She kicked off her shoes. So did he. The grass was sweet and cool under their feet.

And then, in one smooth movement, he released one of her hands and bent down and retrieved his phone. He shut off the music and the light, plunging them into darkness and silence.

Only it wasn't really silent. She could hear the sounds of the night insects chirping and rubbing their wings, the call of a night bird. She could hear her own breath.

And his. She was certain she could hear the beating of her own heart.

It was no more completely dark than it was completely silent. The houses in the vineyards on the hillsides were matched by the pinpricks of light that shined brilliantly in the black velvet sky above them. His face was illuminated in a sliver of moonlight. She reached up and touched his features, running her fingertips along his forehead and his temples, the bridge of his nose, the faint scrape of whiskers on his cheek.

And then her fingers found the silky plumpness of his lower lip, and he reached out and held her hand there, kissed her fingertips and moaned with a sound of such yearning and longing it sent a wave of tingles up her spine.

His eyes on hers, he turned her hand over and kissed the palm, and the inside of her wrist, and up the length of her arm, feathery little kisses that the stars that watched over them would have approved of. He put that hand away from him and took up her other one and kissed it, just as thoroughly.

And then he tugged, urging her against the length of him.

She went willingly. She'd had hints of what this would feel like—accidental brushings at the pool, going by him in a narrow hallway—but she could not stop herself from sighing at how they fit together so perfectly, how the hard wall of him felt with her body pressed against it. She wrapped her arms around him, melding herself into his contours.

His hands moved her hair away from her face, and then his right index finger went to her chin and tilted it up.

He scanned her face, drank it in. She saw the same look of reverence that she had seen when he looked at the fresco.

"Would it be all right if I kissed you?" he asked huskily.

CHAPTER NINE

OF COURSE IT would not be all right if Connor Benson kissed her, Isabella thought dreamily. Her world would never be the same. It would open places in her that could not be forced shut again. But already her body was trembling in anticipation of welcoming him, and so instead of answering with words, she rose up on the tiptoes of her bare feet and took his lips.

They tasted of wine and starlight and pure masculine perfection. Connor's lips tasted of everything that was beautiful about the world. Everything.

He tangled his hands ever so gently in her hair and tilted his head over hers. The plundering was sweet, his lips claiming her lips, his tongue probing the curves and hollows of her lips and then of her mouth. She could feel the gentle scrape of his whiskers against the tender skin of her face.

She was rocketed into a different world. She was not so much Isabella, and he was not so much Connor. It was more as if they were part of some enormous energy that fused. That energy had been fusing since the dawn of time, drawing men and women together in a way that guaranteed the future of the human race.

That's how big what was between them was: the

whole human race relied on this fusion that was searing, delightful and painful by turns.

It opened up a cavernous hunger in her, to know more, to be more, to be filled to the top. It left her with an aching awareness that until this moment, she had been empty.

She released him and staggered back a step, touching her lips, her eyes wide and searching on his face.

"What?" he whispered.

"I didn't know." And then she was crying again, the night pregnant with overwhelming emotion. "I didn't know that it could be this beautiful."

He reached out over the distance she had created between them, pulled her back gently against his chest, stroked her hair as her tears soaked his shirt. "Shh," he said. "Shh, it's going to be okay."

A star a million years away fell through the night sky, leaving a stunning trail of light behind it.

And she thought that was what she had never really believed. Not in her whole life. She had never really believed it could be okay.

She went to take his lips again, but he shook his head, tucked her head to his chest and continued to stroke her hair.

"I don't think we should start again," he said huskily. He released her, turned to the table and began to pack their things back in the basket.

She hugged herself. A whisper of a breeze touched her, and she felt chilly without the protection of his embrace.

"Why?" Her voice, in her own ears, sounded like a mew of pure need.

"I don't want you to look back and regret an impulse."

"I won't."

"If it's not an impulse, you will still feel the same way tomorrow night," he said.

"I resent that you are choosing now to show off how disciplined you are." She went up behind him and pressed herself into his back, reached around and ran her hand over the marvelous strength of his forearms.

He went very still, and then he turned from the table and caught her up. He kissed her again, but lightly this time, before putting her away from him.

"Tomorrow," he promised her huskily. "Tomorrow night. We could have a second date."

"There is no tomorrow night," she said, aware her tone was sulky. "I have to go to Marianna's shower. As much as I would like to get out of it, I cannot."

"Well, then Sunday. Your day off, correct? We could spend the day together."

"It's the fete."

"Ah."

"Will you come watch?"

"I wouldn't miss it for anything. And after the fete? Are you free?"

"Yes." She felt shy and pleased. She actually felt grateful to him that he had stopped the runaway train of their passion, slowed it down. She thought it showed enormous respect for her.

"Would you let me plan something for after? That will be our second date."

"Yes," she said, and her sigh of happiness felt like that star she had watched fall from the sky.

* * *

When Connor woke the next morning, it seemed to him his whole body was smiling. And that was even though he did not really like his accommodations.

There had not been much available when he had taken his hurried leave from Isabella's house, a small, dark room at the back of someone's house. But it had its own bathroom and a separate entrance and compared to some of the places he had laid his head in his life, it was a palace.

And last night he had been more than grateful that he was not staying under Isabella's roof. Where would that have gone?

Where was it going, anyway? Apparently, at his instigation, it was going to a second official date.

How was he going to live up to the first date? Because really, in the date department, he was pretty sure he had scored a perfect ten, following Justin's instructions to be original.

He wondered what he should do next. But then that question pestered him again. Where was it going, anyway?

He realized, stunned, that he knew where it was going. He knew exactly. It was why he had refused to follow that kiss everywhere it had wanted to go.

He wanted to marry her.

Connor knew he would never feel right about having her in the way he wanted her without doing everything right. She was that kind of woman. Without saying a word she demanded a certain standard. Yes, she had a passionate side, and yes, that was easy to coax to the surface.

She would never be a quick roll in the hay. Underneath that passion, she was old-fashioned and traditional. She was the kind of woman who demanded a man's respect without ever saying a word out loud. With Isabella Rossi, you would either be committed for life or you shouldn't even be playing ball.

Committed for life. He mulled that over. The very thought a month ago would have put him on a plane for anywhere.

But now he was thinking how easy it would be for him to adapt to life in Monte Calanetti. With phones and computers being so high-tech, with global travel being so easy, there was no reason he could not work with Justin and Itus from here.

He even thought that children, whom, with the exception of his half siblings, he'd always found mildly repulsive, would be something he could manage with Isabella guiding him through the pitfalls. Maybe they could have a little girl who looked like her. What if the little girl looked like him, though? Maybe they would be better off to have a little boy.

He got up out of bed, filled with restless energy. He knew how to deal with restless energy, or thought he did. Connor gathered his swim things.

But somehow he never made it to the river. He was stopped by wildflowers that grew by the road. He wasn't going to see her tonight. She was going to a shower. He wouldn't repeat his performance from last time she had gone to a function—he wouldn't be chasing through the streets looking for her.

He would leave the flowers for her to find after school. He wanted her to know he was thinking about her. Bonus: they would make her think of him, too.

Though, when he thought of the reluctance with which she had broken away from their first real kiss, he was happily aware she might not be thinking of much else except him! Being romantic—the thing he'd run in terror from his whole life—had the potential to be all kinds of fun.

He began to plan their second date in earnest. Connor wanted to do even better than he had done on the first one. She would want to relax after all her hard work on the fete. And so he spent the next few hours figuring out where to get a canoe. They would explore the river and find the perfect place, a secluded meadow of wildflowers that could only be reached by the boat.

They would have a picnic supper there. He planned an exquisite menu. He thought of introducing her to the mystical experience of swimming in the dark. And then he would paddle them home, the water so inky dark it would reflect the stars. He hoped he could create the illusion they were paddling through the heavenly night sky.

He left a second vase of flowers on her doorstep, where she would find it immediately after the shower. It contained a note telling her to bring her swimsuit for their second date after the fete. He underlined *swim* so that she wouldn't get any ideas about tormenting him with one of those bikinis.

But then, on thinking about it, he did not want to be in a secluded meadow with her in a bikini. So he tore up that note, and made a new one that simply said what time he would pick her up. He hesitated a long time. Should he conclude with *I love you*? He tried it. And then felt foolish. He tore up that note, too.

On the other hand, he wanted her to know he was

serious. He wanted her to know the whole course of his life felt as if it was changing. He tried a third time.

Dear Isabella,
Life is a river, with calm places and turbulent places. I wonder if you would like to join me on this wild and unpredictable ride? If you are willing, I will pick you up tomorrow evening, after the fete, and we will explore the river.

Instead of signing it with "love," he drew a clumsy heart and signed his name.

He stuffed the note in the vase of flowers before he could change his mind.

And then he went shopping for a swimsuit for Isabella, uncaring of the raised eyebrows and giggles as he went through the selection of women's bathing suits, noting the selection in Monte Calanetti at this time of year was quite a bit better than Isabella had claimed it was.

He purchased a particularly dowdy suit, put the wrapped package under his arm and went back to his humble quarters. He could not wait for tomorrow to come.

As Connor arrived at the town square the next night, it was already filling up with people. A makeshift stage had been set up at the far end of the square, and someone was testing a sound system.

For the first time since he had started planning the second date, he came down to earth. Connor could feel some nervousness tickle along his spine at the number of people in the square. As far as he could see, there was absolutely no security for the event. Didn't the good people of Monte Calanetti know that there were no safe places anymore? Not in the whole world?

He scanned the crowd and relaxed marginally. Really, it was just a family event. The chairs set up in neat rows in front of the stage were nearly full already, but no one seemed to mind. Farther back from the stage area, families were setting up picnic blankets. There were grandmothers and grandfathers, women holding babies, and children threading through the crowd screaming their delight. Young men stood in defensive huddles trying to pretend they did not notice the young women who sashayed by them in their spring clothes.

For all that it seemed benign and happy, Connor could not make himself go into the square and that crush of people to look for one of the remaining seats. He found a tree just on the very edge of the square, leaned his shoulder up against it and watched from a distance.

He could see the kids from Isabella's school, already seated cross-legged on the ground up front, in front of the rows of chairs. He spotted her class easily, their sunshine and flower headdresses making them stand out from the others.

There was Isabella, pacing up front, bending over to adjust a headpiece here, to tap a shoulder there, to smile encouragement or to listen to what one of the children was saying.

She looked extraordinary in a simple shift.

He realized there was no hope at all that the bathing suit he had chosen for her was going to dim her light. She could have been wearing a burlap sack today and she would have looked beautiful.

She was absolutely glowing.

Was that because she had feelings for him that matched his growing feelings for her? Did that light that shined forth from her like a beacon of hope have something to do with him? Did it have something to do with that kiss at the chapel? It felt like quite something to be responsible for a light like that one.

She turned suddenly, as if she could feel the intensity of his gaze on her. Her eyes scanned the crowd and then she saw him.

Despite all the noise and motion that separated them, it was as if the world went still. Her eyes locked on his. She lifted a hand in shy acknowledgment. He lifted his back. She smiled, and the glow about her deepened. She turned back to her responsibilities.

And he turned back to his. He tried to relax, but it was not in his nature. He simply could not be in a situation like this and not be scanning, watching for trouble. It had been a part of his life for too long.

A band took the stage and began to play boisterously, if without great talent. They received wild applause and launched into their second number.

Connor noticed something. His eyes rested on a man who, like Connor, was on the fringes of the crowd. The man was by himself in a sea of families.

The band finished their second number to wild applause, took bows and began to pack up their things. Two of Isabella's children, little girls in matching pink dresses, carried the cardboard backdrop for their performance onto the stage. Isabella's class rose in preparation.

Connor watched, and then his gaze went back to the man. He frowned. It was a very warm day. Why was that man wearing an overcoat? Why was he looking around like that, furtively?

The band had vacated the stage and Isabella's class marched into their places. The boys with their sunshine heads were in the back, the girls in the front. They were so excited, joyous in their moment of being at the center.

Isabella stood off to one side. She darted forward and made a last adjustment and said a stern word to a boy whose sun was looking decidedly crumpled. Connor recognized Luigi, the boy who had run into him and then told him to watch where he was going.

And then she went back to the side again and nodded. She beamed with pride as those innocent young voices filled the air.

Connor did not have to speak Italian to know the song welcomed spring. The suns rose, and the flowers waved happily.

But he was not transported to that place of innocence and hope. In fact, he felt as if the music and the rising suns and the waving flowers were all fading. Because the man was moving through the crowd, snaking his way in and out of the crush of people.

Connor pushed himself away from the tree he had been leaning on. With a sense of urgency, he closed the distance between them, following the man through the crowd. Connor ignored the outrage when he blocked people's views.

The man was nearly in front of the stage now, where the children had been sitting moments ago. He was reaching inside his coat pocket.

Without hesitation, Connor became that huge mountain lion he had been nicknamed for. He went from stalking to pouncing. He launched himself at the man in the coat. They went down in the front of the crowd of people. Everyone was screaming in Italian. The commotion moved like a wave through the crowd until it reached the stage. Isabella, who had been focused on the children, turned, as if in slow motion. Her mouth formed a surprised O. The singing faltered and then ground to a halt.

Connor rolled back to his feet, taking the other man with him. He lifted him up by the collar of the too-warm coat and reached his hand into the pocket. His hand closed around something cold and square.

Wrong shape.

Connor tugged it out and glared at his hand. There was a camera in it.

Connor stared at it. And then, convinced there was danger, he ripped open the buttons of the too-warm jacket. A wrapped birthday gift was hidden in the folds and fell to the ground.

"What's this?" he asked. It looked innocuous, but his training told him it could be anything. The whole point was to make dangerous things appear innocuous.

The man was staring at him with incomprehension. Connor picked up the package, and held it in front of him. "What is this?" he demanded again.

He was hit in the knees from behind and staggered forward a step before whirling to face this new opponent.

Luigi, was there, his face as crumpled as his sunshine headdress. He was screaming in Italian. The man was talking rapidly, both hands raised at his sides, open palmed.

Connor recognized *ma sei pazzo*.

And then Isabella was there, her hands resting gently

on Luigi's shoulders. The little boy turned to her skirt and wept.

She said something to the man in Italian, and seeing her embracing the boy, he thrust the wrapped parcel into Connor's arms and turned and pushed his way through the crowd.

Isabella's eyes, distressed, went to Connor's face. "Luigi's dad," she said quietly. "He wanted a picture of his son in the fete. He wanted to give him a birthday present."

Luigi sobbed something against her skirt, and she stroked his head.

"His dad wasn't allowed to go to his birthday party," she said sadly.

And then a woman pushed her way through the milling, jabbering crowd and grabbed Luigi away from Isabella. The woman turned and marched through the crowd, her chin tilted proudly, half holding Luigi's hand, half dragging him.

"How does this happen?" Isabella whispered. "Presumably they loved each other once. How does it turn to this?"

And then she brushed at her skirt and smiled weakly at Connor. He shoved his hands in his pockets and rocked back on his heels, weathering the dirty looks of the crowd returning to their seats.

"I will see if the children will go on," Isabella said. "I think that would be best, don't you?"

He nodded and watched her weave her way back through the crowd, get onstage and shepherd those distressed children. In minutes, she had comforted them enough that they were able to resume their song.

She had not, Connor noted, said one word of re-

crimination toward him over his overreaction to what
had happened.

But then, she didn't have to. He had enough recrimi-
nation for both of them. He made his way through the
crowds, holding the birthday present along with the
parcel containing the bathing suit for Isabella, which
he had retrieved. No one even seemed to notice him.

This was Italy. He supposed there were passionate
disruptions all the time. But that did not make him feel
one bit better.

What he felt was that he had been living in a fool's
paradise. Was he really tangling their lives together
when she had no idea what she was letting herself in
for?

He went to her house, not knowing what to do with
the gift for Luigi except drop it off there. He saw his
vase of flowers waiting there for her, and in a moment
of pure frustration, he swept them off her stoop with
his shoe.

The glass shattered and flowers were strewn everywhere. His note was soaked in water. Annoyed with
himself, he set Luigi's gift inside her door. Her door
was unlocked, of course—this was Monte Calanetti,
and the only person in the whole town who was out
of step was him. He found her broom and dustpan and
swept up the mess he had made and put it in the bin
under her sink.

He told himself to leave. He could do what needed
to be done over the phone. It would be better that way.

But he did not leave. He went through her house,
stood in the doorway of the bedroom he had used and
thought of the journey they had been on since that first
morning when he had thought she was an assailant.

Normal people did not think like that. Normal people did not go into schools and look for escape routes and try to figure out how you would get out of the building if it burned. Normal people did not drag men in overcoats to the ground in town squares.

From that first day, he should have backed off. What had he done, pressing forward instead?

He stood for a moment in the doorway leading to the bathroom. The showerhead had been fixed, and a new curtain and rod had been installed. The curtain was no longer transparent, and under different circumstances that might have made him smile. But now, standing here, he could remember her wrapped in her shower curtain, and all he felt was an abject sense of loss.

He went back downstairs and stood in her kitchen, memorizing it and saying goodbye.

And then the door squeaked open behind him.

"Hello, Connor."

He turned and looked at her. He had hoped to avoid her. And at the same time, he had hoped for one last chance to look at her.

Just like looking at her house, he realized he was trying to memorize every single thing about her: the upward tilt of her eyes, the puffiness of her bottom lip, the shine of her hair. He was trying to both burn it into his memory and say—

"Goodbye, Isabella."

She looked as if he had struck her. "Goodbye? But—"

"I have to go," he said.

"Go?"

"I'm leaving Monte Calanetti."

"Leaving Monte Calanetti?" she asked, distressed. "But why?"

She had to ask that? After the mistake he had just made at the fete? After he had overreacted so hugely to Luigi's father? After he had destroyed the performance she had worked so hard on? After he had embarrassed himself and her in front of the whole town?

"I've finished the reconnaissance for the wedding." He could hear the chill in his voice. He put up the shield in his eyes. "I'll be back a week before to put everything in place, and then the day it's over, I'll be gone again."

"But isn't this a bit sudden? I thought..." Her voice drifted away. He hated himself for what he had led her to believe.

But wasn't the truth that he hated himself anyway?

"I'm not who you think I am," he said gruffly.

"I have never met anyone less capable of subterfuge than you!" she snapped. "I know exactly who you are, Connor Benson."

For a moment, everything in him went weak. To have this, to have someone know everything about you, and care anyway? Wasn't that what every man really desired?

Beyond anything else, beyond wealth, beyond accomplishment, beyond success, did not the most humble of dreams live in every man? To be cared about for exactly who he was?

But Connor knew, in his case, that was not possible. When Isabella knew the truth, she would not feel the same about him anymore. How could she? He had never felt the same about himself again.

"Isabella, I need to tell you something."

CHAPTER TEN

I NEED TO tell you something. Isabella felt as if her world was going dark and swinging crazily around her. Hadn't every horrible event of her life begun with those words?

Her father, looking up in that café and seeing her standing there, tears rolling down her face, running across the street to her.

I need to tell you something. This is how it is for a man. It doesn't mean I don't love your mother. And you.

Giorgio, just turned sixteen, *I need to tell you something. I have an illness. I have always known I was not well. I might have ten years. And I might not.*

And now this. Isabella pulled one of her chairs out from the table and sank into it. She was so filled with dread she felt as if she could not breathe.

"What? What do you need to tell me?"

He pulled out the chair across from her. Was she ever going to be able to come into this kitchen, this house, again without seeing him here, remembering him? Because he was saying goodbye.

Connor had a dark secret, just as all the men in her life had had dark secrets. She should have known, should never have left herself open to it. Never.

"It's another woman, isn't it?" she asked, her voice shaking. "Of course! How could I have been so naive to think a man like you could love only me?"

He swore under his breath. "It's not another woman."

"You're dying, then," she decided.

"No. I need to tell you why I left the SEALs," he said.

She perked up. Why he'd left his previous job? That didn't sound as if it could be too bad.

"You need to know what kind of man I really am."

"I already know what kind of man you are," she said.

"No, you don't," he said harshly.

The harshness in Connor's voice made her want to cover up her ears so she didn't have to listen to him. It didn't really matter how bad she thought it was. It mattered how bad he thought it was.

"My team had a tough assignment on the Pakistan-Afghan border." He wouldn't look at her. He was looking at his hands. His fingers kept threading and then unthreading. "It was a hotbed of all kinds of activity. We'd gotten some intel about an event that was supposed to go down. But our intel was wrong, or delayed.

"We got there too late. We arrived just as a bomb went off in a school. Within seconds, the whole place was in flames. There were terrified kids everywhere, running. We helped get as many kids out as we could. I thought maybe everyone had gotten out. And then I saw all these little faces pressed against a second-story window."

She remembered his uneasiness in her classroom. She remembered him telling her to try and get on the first floor. She remembered him saying, "I'm sure you do. Unless there's a fire."

Her heart broke for the look on his face as he remembered this, the helpless agony there. He still wouldn't meet her eyes, as if he carried some unspeakable shame within him, as if somehow this was all his fault. She put her hand across the table and laid it on his wrist.

He looked at it for a moment, as if he understood perfectly what she was offering. Her strength and her compassion.

He shook her hand away.

"We had been ordered to stand down." He was looking at her now. His gaze was aloof. She had liked it better when he was not looking at her, not with this look in his eyes.

"The building was deemed too dangerous for us to go into. Do you understand what an order means when you are in the military?"

She nodded mutely.

"It's not open for discussion. At all. But I couldn't do it. I couldn't stand there and look at those kids and hear their terrified voices coming out the window they had smashed. My mom had just had Henry. I had a little brother and a little sister the same age as those kids."

Isabella had never felt the heartbreak she felt looking into his face. She understood that he was trying to close himself off from her. Connor was a man held in the hell of his own memories. And he was not going to allow anyone to shoulder that burden with him.

"In retrospect, there were other things I could have done. We could have organized something for them to jump into. We could have stood under the windows and tried to catch them.

"But no," he said softly. "I had to be the cowboy,

even though I'm from Corpus Christi. You know, I was a wild kid in my youth. The military managed to tame most of that out of me, but not all of it.

"So, they told us to stand down, and I said those words to my superior that Luigi said to me that day in the hallway, and I think I said them with as much pleasure.

"And I went into that building. If you've never been in a burning building, you have no idea. It's darker than night in there, even though it's the middle of the day. The noise is something that you awake in the night thinking you hear—like the wail of a banshee. It's so hot you can feel your clothes melting.

"But none of that mattered. I was in those doors and up those stairs before I could think it through. What I didn't think through? Once I broke the ranks, they all did. My whole squad, eight men, followed me into that fire."

He was silent for a long, long time.

"Only seven came out," he said. "My best friend was unaccounted for. I went back in one more time. He was trapped under a beam that had fallen. His back was broken. He's in a wheelchair to this day. Because of me. He has burn scars over fifty percent of his body because of me."

"What about the children?" she whispered.

"They made it. Every single one them. To this day, Justin will tell you it was worth it."

"Then maybe you should believe him," she said.

The look Connor gave her was furious. "No. Maybe *you* should believe *me*. I made a decision based totally on emotion. It was unacceptable. When I start coming from that place of emotion, my judgment is clouded."

She saw, instantly, where he was going with this.

"You're saying your judgment is clouded about me," she said.

"Look what happened today. I read that situation all wrong. It's an embarrassment."

"I wasn't embarrassed," she said. "I don't think anything you did could ever embarrass me."

For a moment, it looked as if something in him softened, as if he might lean toward her. But no, he leaned away. He heaved himself up from the table.

She got up and stood in front of him. "Please don't go. Please don't carry this one second longer by yourself."

He stared at her. For a second, once again, he hesitated. She saw so much pain and so much longing in his face. She thought she had him.

But then his face hardened, and he put her out of his way. "Like I need a little chit like you to help me carry my burdens," he snapped. "You'd be squished like a bug underneath them. Like a bug."

And then, casting her one more proud look, he was out the door. She followed him. She could not believe the impotent frustration she felt.

"Connor Benson!"

He swung around and looked at her.

"You are the worst kind of coward," she yelled. "You act as if you are the bravest man alive, but when it comes to matters of your heart? You are a complete coward."

His mouth fell open. Then he folded his arms over his chest and spread his legs apart. A warrior's stance if she had ever seen one. It just made her madder. There was a pot of flowers by her door and, propelled by anger, she picked it up. She hurled it at him. He had to step to one side to avoid being hit. The pot smashed harmlessly beside him. He glared at her, and she glared back, and then he turned and walked away, not once glancing back at her.

She watched him walk down the street, his stride long and confident and powerful, the walk of a warrior, until she could see him no more. And then she closed her kitchen door and leaned against it and wept.

What on earth had gotten into her? She was a demure schoolteacher! She did not scream at people in the streets. Or throw pots at them.

Or slap people. Or wear red dresses. Or green bikinis.

Let's face it. Connor Benson had brought out the worst in her.

Or maybe what he had done was make her lose her hold on control, to find at her center she was not demure at all, but passionate and fiery and alive.

Because despite vibrating with anger at him right now, Isabella had to admit she felt as alive as she had ever felt. Despite the fact he had left her, and she knew he was going to use all his considerable strength never to look back, she still felt on fire with life.

She gathered herself and gathered her broom and dustpan and went out into the street and cleaned up the mess she had made. And then she brought it into her kitchen and opened the dustbin. But before she dumped the broken pot and flowers and dirt in, she noticed there was something in there that had not been in there before.

She set her filled dustpan on the floor and hauled the trash out from under the sink. She found the pieces of a smashed vase, and the broken stems of wildflowers, and a water-stained note. She carefully pressed open its folds with her fist. She would know that bold handwriting anywhere. She read the note.

Dear Isabella,
Life is a river, with calm places and turbulent places. I wonder if you would like to join me on this wild and unpredictable ride? If you are willing, I will pick you up tomorrow evening, after the fete, and we will explore the river.

Instead of signing it with "love," he had drawn a quite adorable heart and then signed his name.

But between the time he had written this note and now, everything had changed. Because of Luigi's father, but not really. That incident had just triggered all of Connor's deepest insecurities.

What a terrible burden to carry through life: to think you were in charge of everything, to want to protect everyone, to not allow yourself any mistakes.

It was a hopeless task, of course, protecting everyone. It was impossible. Connor Benson had set for himself an impossible task, and then he was hard on himself when he failed. What he needed most was not, as she had said, someone to help him carry the burden, though he needed that, too. But what he needed most was someone who could gently tell him when he was being unreasonable, when the goal he had set for himself was too much for one man alone.

What he needed was that safe place, where it was okay to make mistakes, where nobody died or was in danger because you had been wrong.

She knew exactly what Connor Benson needed. He needed her. But how on earth was she going to let him know that?

Over the next few days she tried to find clues to where he had gone, but he had disappeared as if he had never been. He was gone completely, without a trace and without a trail. Her initial fire sputtered out. Isabella sank into the deepest despair of her life.

Where there is deep grief, there was deep love.

It complicated her sense of losing Connor that what she felt now was worse than the loss of her husband. It made the wild tumult inside her worse now that she wondered if she had ever truly loved Giorgio. What had it been, if not love?

She could not eat and she could not sleep. Her whole house was a reminder of Connor—the bed he had slept in, the shower he had saved her from, the kitchen table where they had sat together. She was ashamed with how impatient she was with the children at school. But it seemed she spared Luigi, even though his behavior was worse than ever since his father had come to the fete.

Still, she recognized in the child a great mourning, a great sense of loss. She recognized he was acting out in frustration against helplessness.

And then she was shaken out of her own pity when Luigi disappeared. He didn't arrive at school one morning, and she had received no note from his mother saying he would be absent. The whole town was in an uproar. Had he been kidnapped by his father?

The police were called, and a tense day and night later, Luigi was found asleep under a shrub, a backpack beside him, his face tearstained but his spirit as fierce as ever.

"I am not going to have a life without my papa," he screamed, unrepentant, at his mother in front of the police station.

And this time, she heard him. She wrapped her little boy in her arms and said she understood. That she had been wrong to make him suffer because of her pride. That she would change her stance toward Luigi's father, that she would not stand in the way of them loving one another anymore.

Within days, Isabella could see the changes in Luigi. His father was reintroduced into his life. Luigi was calmer. He was happier. He brought her flowers one day, as if to apologize for all he had put her through.

It was a victory of love, and it made Isabella think.

Was she going to mourn for another six years, then? What if she had been wrong? What if deep love didn't cripple you with grief?

What if deep love made you stronger? What if it made you fight to the death for what you wanted? It was the force that had sent a little boy out looking for his father, knowing what all the adults around him had not known—he *needed* that love.

She needed Connor's love. She wanted to be fully alive. She wanted to feel the way she had felt when she was with him.

She realized there were different kinds of love. There was the kind of love Luigi had for his father. And the kind of love Luigi's mother had for her little boy that had helped her overcome her own bitterness and put what was best for him first.

Yes, there was the kind of love that Isabella had had

for Giorgio. Because she had loved Giorgio with gentle compassion did not mean she had loved him less. It meant that she had loved him differently.

And it was all part of her journey to know love completely.

She had to find Connor. She had to convince him not that she was worthy of his love, because she suspected they both knew that. She had to convince him that he was worthy of hers.

She went back to the chapel, sure she could find there some clue to where he would go. What she found was workmen gone for the day and the fresco, reminding her that beauty was true greatness, and that beauty survived when all else fell away.

She went to the river where she had waded with him. It was warmer now, and there were signs the little boys who had a hung a rope and tire from the tree so they could swing out over the water came more often.

There was no one here now, though, and she took off the cover she had put over the plainest of her bathing suits. She hesitated and then climbed the slippery bank, grabbed the rope with both hands and planted her feet on the tire. She swung way out into the river, where the water was definitely over her head, and even though there was a possibility she could lose everything if she let go of that rope, she let go anyway.

It was exhilarating. It felt wonderful to live life without a safety net. It felt wonderful to take chances. It felt wonderful to be brave.

Life was, indeed, a river, with calm places and turbulent places. It was indeed a wild and unpredictable ride. She had never seen it like that before Connor. She wanted to explore completely the wild and unpredictable ride. She wanted to explore it with him.

It came to her—that incident at the fete. It wasn't just that he felt he had made a mistake. It was the whole thing.

It was the realization he could not stop bad things from happening. He could not stop the tragedy of a marriage not working, children being the victims. He said he had seen that before with his SEAL buddies.

If Luigi's father had had a weapon concealed under his coat, Connor could have stopped that particular tragedy from unfolding, but his work had made him so aware of the next one, waiting. His inability to save his friend had made him way too aware how powerless even the most powerful of men could be.

Isabella suddenly felt drenched in light. She felt as if she was the soldier, not him. She had to go get him. She had to rescue Connor from the lonely world of perfection and protection he had made for himself.

And suddenly, there in that deep pool, enjoying the gift he had given her—a freedom from fear—she knew exactly how to find him.

A day later, her confidence felt more shaky as she dialed the number.

"Itus, Arnold speaking."

The voice was curt and no-nonsense. It shook her that it was not a name she was expecting.

"I'm looking for someone named Justin."

There was a moment's silence and then wariness. "You've got him."

"My name is Isabella Rossi. I am looking for Connor Benson."

"You and half the civilized world."

"What does that mean?"

Silence. "What did you say your name was?"

"Isabella Rossi."

"I'm going to guess you're from Monte Calanetti, aren't you?"

"That is correct."

"Ah. I should have guessed."

"Guessed?"

"That there was a reason he came back from there grumpier than a bear with a sore bottom."

"I'm that reason?" Grumpier than a bear with a sore bottom?

"I'm asking you. Are you that reason?"

"I think I might be," she said with a sigh. "I need to talk to him. You don't know where he is?"

"He came back, checked in, made my life miserable for a few days, then cleared his schedule and disappeared."

It confirmed exactly what Isabella had suspected. He had not gone back home and dismissed all that had happened to him. He was somewhere nursing his wounds. Alone. Her heart felt as if it was breaking.

Not for herself. For him. For Connor.

"So, you don't know where he is?" Her disappointment felt as sharp as shards of glass.

"I don't right this minute. But if there's one thing I am very, very good at? It's finding people."

"Who don't want to be found?"

"Especially people who don't want to be found. Up until this point, I thought I'd leave him alone. And I will. But if you want to go find him, I'm okay with that. More than okay with that."

In two hours he called her back. Two hours after that,

she was on a bus to the city to catch a plane, a ticket for the first flight to Switzerland clutched in her hand.

Connor stared out the window of the mountain cabin. There was really nothing as glorious as the Alps in springtime. He wasn't sure why he had picked a place to hide where he couldn't swim, though.

No, that choice had not been an accident.

His whole life he had chased away strong feelings. It was what his military training had taught him to do. Emotion always got him in trouble. He could swim it off, shake off nearly anything with enough punishing physical activity.

So he couldn't swim, but the mountains all around beckoned. He could hike or climb mountains, or go down to that little public house in the village at the bottom of the mountain and drink himself into oblivion.

But it was the oddest thing that had ever happened to him.

Connor *wanted* to feel this. He wanted to feel the devastating loss of Isabella. He wanted to feel the consequences of his actions. He wanted to wake up in the morning and wonder what the point of life was, to feel his all-encompassing emptiness.

He wanted to remember, in excruciating detail, every second they had spent together. He wanted to remember her joy in the pool, and the way her face had looked when she saw the fresco of the Madonna and child.

He wanted to miss her.

He wanted to feel it all intensely. That was his mission. Miss Isabella. And then be over it, completely, and get back to his life.

Except he had expected the getting-over-it part to

be much faster. He was beginning to think the completely part was out of the question. He might have to settle for getting over her a little bit. Enough to function. After all, he'd been in his little cottage in the Alps for a week and if anything, he felt more morose than when he'd begun.

And that did not bode well for whoever knocked on his door. He'd specifically told his landlady he was not to be disturbed under any circumstances.

But of course, she could not control a lost hiker at the door. Or the Swiss equivalent of a Girl Scout selling cookies.

So he swung open the door in a bad temper, ready to be equally unwelcoming to Heidi selling cookies or the lost hiker seeking refuge.

The shock reverberated up his spine when he saw who was there. For a moment, his heart was so filled with gratitude to see the face he had told himself he would never see again that it felt as though he might fall on his knees.

But then he straightened his spine and drew in a deep breath.

He needed to protect her. From himself. From the damaged person he was. From the incomplete person he was. She deserved so much better.

"Isabella." He heard the coolness in his voice and saw the purpose in her posture falter just a bit.

"Connor."

Again, his knees felt weak at the way she said his name. It came off her lips like a blessing, as if she saw all of him and accepted that completely.

"Why are you here?" he asked harshly.

"I'm here to rescue you. I tried to send a Saint Bernard with a cask of whiskey around his neck, but apparently they don't do that anymore."

He did not want to be charmed by her!

"You look horrible," she said softly.

He already knew that! He had looked at his own reflection this morning in the mirror, made the decision not to shave, again. His hair was uncombed, his clothes were rumpled—he looked like a wild man, as if he was holed up in a cave, not in a perfectly civilized cabin.

"Can I come in?"

"There's no point."

She ignored him and slipped under his arm into the cottage.

"Hey!"

"Wow," she said, looking around.

He turned and saw the place through her eyes. It was an absolute shambles. Clothes on the floor, dirty dishes on every surface. There was a bag of groceries by the small kitchen that he had not even bothered to unpack. A trail of cookie crumbs went across the floor and disappeared under a pair of socks.

It was as if it was the first time he'd really noticed it in days. Who had he become? He was a fastidiously neat person.

Undeterred by how the mess spoke to his character, Isabella went over, frowned at the couch and then delicately moved two newspapers and an empty container of chocolate fudge ice cream out of her way. She sat down as if she planned to stay.

"What do you want?" he asked, folding his arms over his chest. He tapped his foot and glanced at his watch. She looked so unperturbed by his show of impatience that he felt almost panicky. He was going to have to be mean to her.

To Isabella? That was impossible.

But it was for her own good. He took a deep breath, soldiered himself. This was what he did. He did hard things. He did impossible things.

"Look, you've traveled a long way for nothing," he said. "If you're going to tell me you can't live without me, forget it. I'm not moved by emotion."

"Hmm," she said, again unperturbed.

He frowned at her.

"I think I came to tell you that you can't live without me," she decided. He contemplated the awful truth of that, and he contemplated the fact she had seen it so clearly. This was not about her. Not in any way. It was about him.

"Well, I can. Live without you. And I will."

"Quit being so damned strong," she said softly. "You've had to be so strong your whole life, Connor. You started working when you were eleven years old to help look after your mom."

"That's hitting below the belt," he said, "bringing my mom into it."

"What is this, below the belt?"

"You're an adult woman—I think you can figure out where men don't like to get hit."

She nodded, mulling that over, but then kept on talking as if he hadn't warned her. "So you've always felt protective of your poor mother, who had you very young and was abandoned by the people who should have supported her. Is it any surprise you were drawn to a profession where you protect people, where you try and fix things? Everything?"

"Look, Little Red Riding Hood, just skip on home. You're playing with the Big Bad Wolf here, and that story does not end well, if you recall."

She cocked her head at him. She didn't look even slightly intimidated. He considered the possibility he was losing his touch.

"You have carried the weight of the whole world for way, way too long," she decided softly.

"Says you."

She sighed as if he was no more irritating to her than Luigi Caravetti yelling swearwords. "I thought we should have a discussion. About the river of life."

He groaned. "Have you no pride? Picking through the garbage?"

"None at all," she said. "Not when it comes to you. It's your turn, Connor."

"My turn?" he said warily.

"Your turn to be rescued."

"You've already said that. Saint Bernards on strike, you have come in their place, without the cask."

"I brought something better than the cask."

He went very still. He knew what she had brought. He could see what she had brought shining from her eyes. He could see it shining from the very fiber of her being.

He could fight anything. That was what he had been trained to do. To fight. And he was so good at it.

But he was not sure that he could fight this. *Don't ask her*, he begged himself, *don't ask her what she brought. You aren't strong enough, Connor, you aren't.*

"What did you bring?" His voice was a rasp.

"You know," she said softly. "You already know what I brought."

Even before she said the words, he could feel his every defense beginning to crumble, like a dam made out of mud and sticks giving way after holding everything in for way too long, so long that its strength had already been compromised.

"I brought love," she said. "I brought my love to rescue you."

"No, please. Isabella, don't do this."

She was up off that sofa in a heartbeat. She navigated the mess on his floor and stood in front of him. She shined with a fierce light.

So, love could be this, too. Not just gentle and sweet and quiet and compliant. But this: as strong as steel forged in a fire.

She put her hands on both sides of his face and forced him to look her in the eyes, look into those great green-and-gold pools of strength and compassion.

"You be whoever you need to be," she said softly. "You be a warrior going to do battle. You be the man who rushes into burning buildings. You be that man who seeks out danger like a heat-seeking missile seeks warmth. You be the man who sees the potential for bad things on a beautiful spring afternoon in the village square. You be the man who would lay down his life to protect a bride on her wedding day. You be those things."

Her words were like the final drops of water adding pressure to the already compromised structure of the dam. Her words broke Connor wide-open. He felt as if he had waited all his life for this one moment, for these words of acceptance, these words of someone seeing him exactly as he was and moving toward him anyway.

She continued to drop words, like healing raindrops, into the brokenness inside him.

"And then you come back to me," she said, and her voice was a promise that he could feel himself moving toward, that every ounce of his strength could not have stopped him from moving toward.

"And you show me all the bruised places," Isabella said, her voice fierce and true, "and the brokenness of your heart. You show me, and me alone, what it has cost you to be these things. And you let me place poultices on your bruises, and you let me knit my love around your wounds.

"Connor, I will be the place where you lay down your sword. I will be the place where you see that beauty wins. I will be the home that shows you that love survives all things, and makes all things possible."

He was staring at her. His heart was pounding as if he had run a race, and he could see the finish line. She, Isabella Rossi, was the finish line, and he reached out for her.

He reached out and scraped his hand down her cheek. He realized she was crying, and he was pretty sure she did not know that herself.

"You look just like her right now," he said, his voice soft.

"Who? Who do I look like?"

He gazed at her, feeling as if he could never get enough. When he spoke, his voice was hoarse with emotion. "The Madonna in the fresco. You look just like her."

He stared at her, not able to look away, held by the light that had infused her face, aware that he was in the presence of the purest and most powerful thing in the world.

Rarely, like in the fresco, someone captured the essence of this power, the heart of it, the spirit of it. An unknown Renaissance artist had followed inspiration, obeyed it and been allowed to capture it.

It was love.

It was all that it was to be human at its highest and its best. It was what Connor had fought his whole life for, without ever being able to give it a name.

He realized he was like the man in Greek mythology, just as Isabella had said, a long time ago. He *was* like Itus. He was being offered the opportunity to walk among gods. For that was what it was for a man to know love. It was to walk in glory. It was to experience things beyond what a mortal man had a right to expect.

He did not deserve this. He knew that. And he also knew that it didn't matter. That he was not strong enough to refuse what was being offered to him.

Connor Benson did what he had never done, not in his whole life. Even when he was a child, he had stood strong, he had been ready to fight for what he felt was right. But now, standing here before Isabella, drenched in the light, he bowed before her, and before the presence of a force greater than himself.

He laid down his weapons. He laid his head on her shoulder. He surrendered. He ate the food that was offered to him.

He felt Isabella's hand, cool and strong, on the back of his neck. He felt her tears anoint him. And he drew her into the warmth of himself and held her in a way that reflected the truths he had just learned.

He held Isabella as if he would never let her go.

He was a man who had crossed deserts, navigated jungles, climbed mountains. He was a man who had fought to give others something that he had not named. But now that he was there, in the circle of its light, he recognized the name of it.

Home.

Connor Benson was home.

* * * * *

HIS
LOST-AND-FOUND
BRIDE

SCARLET WILSON

This book is dedicated to my fellow authors
Susan Meier, Jennifer Faye,
Michelle Douglas, Cara Colter, Teresa Carpenter,
Rebecca Winters and Barbara Wallace.
It has been so much fun creating this series with you!

PROLOGUE

'*SIGNOR! SIGNOR, VENGA ORA!*'

Logan Cascini was on his feet in an instant. As an architect who specialised in restoring old Italian buildings, to get the call to help transform the Palazzo di Comparino's chapel for a royal wedding was a dream come true.

The property at the vineyard was sprawling and over the years areas had fallen into disrepair. His work was painstaking, but he only employed the most specialised of builders, those who could truly re-create the past beauty of the historic chapel in the grounds and the main *palazzo*. Most of the buildings he worked on were listed and only traditional building methods could be used to restore them to their former glory.

Timescales were tight in order to try and get the chapel restored for the royal wedding of Prince Antonio of Halencia and his bride-to-be, Christina Rose. No expense was being spared—which was just as well considering he had twenty different master builders on-site.

'*Signor! Signor, venga ora!*'

He left his desk in the main *palazzo* and rushed outside to the site of the chapel. His stomach was twisting. *Please don't let them have found anything that would hold up the build.* The last thing he needed was some unexpected hundred-year-old bones or a hoard of Roman crockery or coins.

This was Italy. It wouldn't be the first time something unexpected had turned up on a restoration project.

He reached the entrance to the ancient chapel and the first thing that struck him was the fact there was no noise. For the last few weeks the sound of hammers on stone and the chatter of Italian voices had been constant. Now every builder stood silently, all looking towards one of the walls.

The interior of the chapel had been redecorated over the years. Much of the original details and façade had been hidden. The walls had been covered first in dark, inlaid wood and then—strangely—painted over with a variety of paints. Every time Logan came across such 'improvements' he cringed. Some were just trends of the time—others were individual owners' ideas of what made the building better. In restoration terms that usually meant that original wood and stone had been ripped away and replaced with poorer, less durable materials. Sometimes the damage done was irreparable.

His eyes widened as he strode forward into the chapel. Light was streaming through the side windows and main door behind him. The small stained-glass windows behind the altar were muted and in shadow. But that didn't stop the explosion of riotous colour on the far wall.

A few of the builders had been tasked with pulling down the painted wooden panelling to expose the original walls underneath.

There had been no indication at all that this was what would be found.

Now he understood the shouts. Now he understood the silence.

Beneath the roughly pulled-back wood emerged a beautiful fresco. So vibrant, the colours so fresh it looked as if it had just been painted.

Logan's heart rate quickened as he reached the fresco. He started shaking his head as a smile became fixed on his face.

This was amazing. It was one of the most traditional of frescoes, depicting the Madonna and Child. Through his historical work Logan had seen hundreds of frescoes, even attending a private viewing of the most famous of all at the Sistine Chapel.

But the detail in this fresco was stunning and being able to see it so close was a gift. He could see every line, every brushstroke. The single hairs on Mary's head, baby Jesus's eyelashes, the downy hair on his skin, the tiny lines around Mary's eyes.

Both heads in the fresco were turned upwards to the heavens, where the clouds were parted, a beam of light illuminating their faces.

Part of the fresco was still obscured. Logan grabbed the nearest tool and pulled back the final pieces of broken wood, being careful not to touch the wall. Finally the whole fresco was revealed to the viewers in the chapel.

It was the colour that was most spectacular. It seemed that the years behind the wood had been kind to the fresco. Most that he'd seen before had been dulled with age, eroded by touch and a variety of other elements. There had even been scientific studies about the effects of carbon dioxide on frescoes. 'Breathing out' could cause harm.

But this fresco hadn't had any of that kind of exposure. It looked as fresh as the day it had been painted.

His hand reached out to touch the wall and he immediately pulled it back. It was almost magnetic—the pull of the fresco, the desire to touch it. He'd never seen one so vibrant, from the colour of Mary's dark blue robe to the white and yellow of the brilliant beam of light. The greens of the surrounding countryside, the pink tones of Jesus's skin, the ochre of the small stool on which Mary sat and the bright orange and red flowers depicted around them. It took his breath away.

He'd hoped to restore this chapel to its former glory—but he'd never expected to find something that would surpass all his expectations.

'*Signor? Signor?* What will we do?' Vito, one of the builders, appeared at his elbow. His eyes were wide, his face smeared with dirt.

'Take the rest of the day off,' Logan said quickly. 'All of you.' He turned to face the rest of the staff. 'Let me decide how to proceed. Come back tomorrow.'

There were a few nods. Most eyes were still transfixed on the wall.

There was a flurry at the entranceway and Louisa, the new owner of the *palazzo*, appeared. 'Logan? What's going on? I heard shouts. Is something…?' Her voice tailed off and her legs automatically propelled her forward.

Louisa Harrison was the American who'd inherited Palazzo di Comparino and hired him to renovate both it and the chapel back to their former beauty. She was hard to gauge. Tall and slim, her long blond hair was tied up in a ponytail and she was wearing yoga pants and a loose-fitting top. Her brow was furrowed as she looked at the fresco and shook her head. 'This was here?' She looked around at the debris on the floor. 'Behind the panelling?'

He nodded while his brain tried to process his thoughts. Louisa would have no idea what the implications of this could be.

She turned back to face him, her face beaming 'This is wonderful. It's amazing. The colours are so fresh it's as if the painter just put down his paintbrush today. I've never seen anything like this. Have you?'

He took a deep breath and chose his words carefully. 'I've seen a few.' He gave a nod to the wall. 'But none as spectacular as this.'

She was still smiling. It was the most animated he'd seen her since he'd got here. Louisa rarely talked to the tradesmen or contractors and when she did it was all business. No personal stuff. He'd learned quickly that she was a woman with secrets and he still had no idea how she'd managed to inherit such a wonderful part of Italian history.

But her intentions seemed honourable. She'd hired him after going along with the request for a wedding venue from Prince Antonio. And with his growing reputation, thriving architecture business and natural curiosity there had been no way he'd turn down the opportunity to do these renovations.

'It will be the perfect backdrop for the wedding,' Louisa said quietly, her eyes still fixed on the fresco. 'Won't it?'

He swallowed. Exactly how could he put this?

'It could be. I'll need to make some calls.'

'To whom?'

'Any new piece of art has to be reported and examined.'

She wrinkled her nose. 'And a fresco falls under that category?'

He nodded. 'A fresco, any uncovered relics, a mosaic, a tiled floor...' He waved his hand and gave a little smile. 'We Italians like to keep our heritage safe. So much of it has already been lost.'

'And you know who to call? You can sort this all out?' He could almost hear her brain ticking over.

He gave a quick nod.

'Then I'll leave it to you. Let me know if there are any problems.' She spun away and walked to the door.

Logan turned back to the wall and stood very still as he heard the quiet, retreating footsteps. The enormity of the discovery was beginning to unfurl within his brain.

He could almost see the millions of euros' worth of plans for the prince to marry here floating off down the nearby Chiana River.

In his wildest dreams the prince might get to marry his bride with this in the background. But Italian bureaucracy could be difficult. And when it came to listed buildings and historic discoveries, things were usually painstakingly slow.

He sucked in a deep breath. The air in the chapel was still but every little hair stood up on his arms as if a cool breeze had just fluttered over his skin. He knew exactly what this fresco would mean.

He knew exactly who he would have to contact. Who would have the expertise and credentials to say what should happen next. Italy's Arts Heritage Board had a fresco expert who would be able to deal with this.

Lucia Moretti. His ex.

CHAPTER ONE

LUCIA STARED OUT of the window, sipped her coffee and licked the chocolate from her fingers.

If her desk hadn't been on some priceless antiques list somewhere she would lift her aching legs and put them on it. She'd just completed a major piece of work for Italy's Art Heritage Board. Months of negotiations with frazzled artefact owners, restorers and suppliers. Her patience had been stretched to breaking point, but the final agreement over who was going to fund the project had taken longest. Finally, with grants secured and papers signed, she could take a deep breath and relax.

She pushed her window open a little wider. Venice was hot, even for a woman who'd stayed there for the last twelve years, and the small-paned leaded-glass window obstructed her view out over the Grand Canal. A cruise ship was floating past her window right now—in a few months these larger ships wouldn't be allowed along here any more. The huge currents they unleashed threatened the delicate foundations of the world-famous city. So much of Venice had been lost already—it was up to the present generation to protect the beauty that remained.

Her boss, Alessio Orsini, put his head around the

door. His eyes were gleaming and she straightened immediately in her chair. Alessio had seen just about every wonder of the world. There wasn't much left that could make his eyes twinkle like that.

'I've just had the most interesting call.' She waved her hand to gesture him into her room, but even though he was in his late seventies he would rarely sit down.

'What is it?'

He gave a little nod. 'There's been a discovery. A new fresco—or rather an old one. Just been discovered in Tuscany during a chapel restoration. I've given him your number.' He glanced at her desk. 'Seems like perfect timing for you.'

She smiled. Alessio expected everyone around him to have the boundless energy he had. But her interest was piqued already. An undiscovered fresco could be a huge coup for the heritage board—particularly if they could identify the artist. So many frescoes had been lost already.

It seemed as though the whole of Italy was rich with frescoes. From the famous Sistine Chapel to the ancient Roman frescoes in Pompeii.

The phone on her desk rang and she picked it up straight away. This could be the most exciting thing she'd worked on in a while.

'*Ciao*, Lucia.'

It was the voice. Instantly recognisable. Italian words with a Scottish burr. Unmistakable.

Her legs gave a wobble and she thumped down into her chair.

'Logan.' It was all she could say. She could barely get a breath. His was the last voice in the world she'd expected to hear.

Logan Cascini. The one true love of her life. Meeting him in Florence had been like a dream come true. Normally conservative, studying art history at Florence University had brought Lucia out of her shell. Meeting Logan Cascini had made it seem as though she'd never had a shell in the first place.

He'd shared her passion—hers for art, his for architecture. From the moment they'd met when he'd spilled an espresso all down her pale pink dress and she'd heard his soft burr of Scottish Italian she'd been hooked.

She'd never had a serious relationship. Three days after meeting they'd moved in together. Life had been perfect. *He* had been perfect.

They'd complemented each other beautifully. He'd made her blossom and she'd taught him some reserve. He'd been brought up in a bohemian Italian/Scots family and had often spoken first and thought later.

She'd had dreams about them growing old together until it had all come to a tragic end. Getting the job in Venice had been her lifeline—her way out. And although she'd always expected to come across him at some point in her professional life she hadn't realised the effect it would have.

Twelve years. Twelve years since she'd walked away from Logan Cascini. Why did she suddenly feel twenty years old again?

Why on earth was he calling her after all this time?

He spoke slowly. 'I hope you are well. Alessio Orsini suggested you were the most appropriate person to deal with. I'm working in Tuscany at the Palazzo di Comparino in Monte Calanetti. I'm renovating the chapel for the upcoming wedding of Prince Antonio of Halencia and Christina Rose, and yesterday we made the most amazing discovery. A fresco of the Madonna and Child. It's exquisite, Lucia. It must have been covered up for years because the colours of the paint are so fresh.'

His voice washed over her like treacle as her heart sank to the bottom of her stomach. How stupid. Of course. Alessio had just told her he'd given someone her number. He just hadn't told her *who*.

Logan Cascini was calling for purely professional reasons—nothing else. So why was she so disappointed?

It wasn't as if she'd spent the last twelve years pining for him. There was a connection between them that would last for ever. But she'd chosen to leave before they'd just disintegrated around each other. Some relationships weren't built to withstand tragedy.

She tried to concentrate on his words. Once she'd got over the initial shock of who was calling, her professionalism slipped back into place.

This was work. This was only about work. Nothing else.

Being involved in the discovery and identification of a new fresco would be amazing. She couldn't believe the timing. If she'd still been caught up in negotiations, Alessio could have directed this call to someone else on the team. Even though frescoes were her speciality, the Italian Heritage Board expected all their staff to be able to cover a whole range of specialities.

She drew in a deep breath. Her brain was still spinning, still processing. This was the man she'd lived with, breathed with. What had he been doing these last few years?

Her heart twisted in her chest. Was he married? Did he have children?

'Lucia?'

His voice had been brisk before, but now it was soft. The way it had been when he'd tried to cajole or placate her. Just the tone sent a little tremor down her spine.

She cleared her throat, getting her mind back on the job. She had to take Logan out of this equation. This discovery could be career-changing. It was time to put her business head on her shoulders.

'What can you tell me about the fresco?'

He hesitated. 'I almost don't know where to start.' His voice was echoing. He must be standing in the chapel now. She squeezed her eyes shut. She didn't need to imagine Logan—his broad shoulders, thick dark hair and oh-so-sexy green eyes. He was already there. Permanently imprinted from the last time she'd seen him.

After all the emotion, all the pent-up frustration and anger, all the tears, she'd been left with his face on her mind. A picture of resolve. One that knew there was no point continuing. One that knew walking away was the only way they would both heal.

She'd known he wouldn't come after her. They had been past that point. He might not have agreed but he'd realised how much they'd both been damaging each other.

The vision of him standing in the stairwell of their apartment, running his hand through his just-too-long hair, his impeccable suit rumpled beyond all repair and his eyelids heavy with regret had burned a hole in her mind.

'Just tell me what you see.' She spoke quickly, giving her head a shake and trying to push him from her mind.

He sighed. 'I can't, Lucia. I just can't. It's just too... too...magnificent. You have to see it for yourself. You have to see it in the flesh.'

Flesh. Every tiny hair on her arms stood on end. Seeing it in the flesh would mean seeing *him* in the flesh. Could she really go there again?

'Wait,' he said. She could hear him fumbling and for a second it made her smile. Logan wasn't prone to fumbling. 'What's your email address?'

'What?'

'Your email. Give me your email address. I've just taken a photo.'

She recited off her email address. It was odd. She didn't even want to give that little part of herself away to him again. She wanted to keep herself, and everything about her, sealed away. Almost in an invisible bubble.

That would keep her safe.

Being around Logan again—just hearing his voice—made her feel vulnerable. Emotionally vulnerable. No one else had ever evoked the same passion in her that Logan had. Maybe it was what they'd gone through together, what they'd shared that made the connection run so deep. But whatever it was she didn't ever want to recreate it. She'd come out the other side once before. She didn't think she'd ever have the strength to do it again.

Ping. The email landed in her inbox and she clicked to open it.

As soon as the photo opened she jerked back in her seat. Wow.

'Have you got it?'

'Oh, I've got it,' she breathed. She'd spent her life studying frescoes. Most of the ones she'd encountered were remnants of their former selves. Time, age, environment had all caused damage. Few were in the condition of the one she was looking at now. It was an explosion of radiant colour. So vivid, so detailed that her breath caught in her throat. She expanded the photo. It was so clear she could almost see the brushstrokes. What she could definitely see was every hair on the baby Jesus's head and every tiny line around Mary's eyes.

'Now you get it,' said the voice, so soft it almost stroked her skin.

'Now I get it,' she repeated without hesitation.

There was silence for a few seconds as her eyes swept from one part of the fresco to another. There was so much to see. So much to relish. The palm of her hand itched to actually reach out and touch it.

'So, what now?'

The million-dollar question. What now indeed? 'Who owns the property?' she asked quickly.

'Louisa Harrison—she's an American and inherited the property from a distant Italian relative. She hired me to renovate the *palazzo* and chapel for the upcoming royal wedding.'

Lucia frowned. 'What royal wedding?'

Logan let out a laugh. 'Oh, Lucia, I forget that you don't keep up with the news. Prince Antonio of Halencia and Christina Rose. It's only a few short weeks away.'

'And you're still renovating?' She couldn't keep the surprise from her voice. All the Italian renovation projects that Logan had been involved with before had taken months to complete. Months of negotiation for the correct materials sourced from original suppliers and then the inevitable wait for available master craftsmen.

This time he didn't laugh. This time there was an edge to his voice. 'Yes. I have around forty men working for me right now. This fresco—it was more than a little surprise. There was wood panelling covering all the walls. Every other wall we've uncovered has been bare. We expected this one to be the same.' He sighed. 'I expected just to use original plaster on the walls. It should only have taken a few days.'

Now she understood. This discovery was amazing—but it could also cause huge hold-ups in Logan's work. She'd known him long enough to know that would be worrying him sick.

Logan never missed a deadline. Never reneged on a deal. And although she hadn't heard about this wedding she was sure it must be all over the media. If Logan couldn't finish the renovations of the church in time the whole wedding would be up in the air and his reputation would be ruined.

Not to mention his bank balance. She'd no idea who the owner was, but there was every chance she'd put a clause in the contract about delayed completion—particularly when it was so vital.

'I'll come.' The words were out before she really thought about it. She grabbed a notebook and pen. 'Give me the address and I'll make travel arrangements today.' As her pen was poised above the paper her brain was screaming at her. *No. What are you doing?*

She waited. And waited.

'You'll come here?' He sounded stunned—almost disbelieving.

Her stomach recoiled. Logan obviously had the same reservations about seeing her as she had about him. But why—after twelve years—did that hurt?

But he recovered quickly, reciting the address, the nearest airport and recommending an airline. 'If you let me know your flight details I'll have someone pick you up.'

His voice was still as smooth as silk but she didn't miss the implication—Logan hadn't offered to pick her up himself.

It didn't matter that she was alone in her office, she could almost feel her mask slipping into place. The one that she'd used on several occasions over the years when people had started to get too close and ask personal questions. When past boyfriends had started to make little noises about moving to the next stage of their relationship.

Self-preservation. That was the only way to get through this.

'I'll email you,' she said briskly, and replaced the receiver. She ignored the fact her hands were trembling slightly and quickly made arrangements on her computer. Alessio would be delighted at the prospect of a new fresco. As long as it wasn't a complete fake and a wasted journey.

But it didn't sound like a fake—hidden for years behind wood panelling in a now-abandoned private chapel. It sounded like a hidden treasure. And even though she didn't want to admit it, Logan was so experienced in Italian architecture and art he would have enough background knowledge to spot an obvious fake.

She sent a few final emails and went through to give the secretary she shared with five other members of staff her itinerary for the next few days. It was five o'clock and her flight was early next morning. She needed to pick up a few things and get packed.

She turned and closed her window. Venice. She'd felt secure here these last few years. She'd built a life here on her own. She had a good job and her own fashionable apartment. There was security in looking out her window every day and watching the traffic and tourists on the Grand Canal. The thought of heading to Tuscany to see Logan again was unsettling her. She felt like a teenager.

She picked up her jacket and briefcase, opening her filing cabinets to grab a few books. She had detailed illustrations of just about every fresco ever found. There were a few artists who'd lived in Tuscany who could have painted the fresco. It made sense to take examples of their work for comparison.

She switched on her answering-machine and headed for the door. She needed to be confident. She needed to be professional. Logan would find this situation every bit as awkward as she would.

She was an expert in her field—that's why she'd been called. And if she could just hold on to the *career-defining* thought and keep it close, it could get her through the next few days.

Because if that didn't, she wasn't sure what would.

CHAPTER TWO

LUCIA STEPPED DOWN from the chartered flight with her compact red suitcase in her hand. She'd spent most of the flight going over notes, trying to determine who the likely artist of the fresco would be.

The style was vaguely familiar. But there were a huge number of fresco artists spanning hundreds of years. Often the date of the building helped with the determination of the artist, but it seemed that Palazzo di Comparino had existed, in some state, for hundreds of years. The chapel even longer. There were a number of possibilities.

The airport in Tuscany was private—owned by some local multi-millionaire—so she was practically able to walk down the steps into the waiting car.

She gave a nod to the driver. '*Grazie*, I will be staying at Hotel di Stelle.'

He lifted her case in the trunk of the black car. 'No, *signorina*. A room has been prepared for you at Palazzo di Comparino.'

Her stomach clenched. She'd been definite about booking her own accommodation. Working with Logan was one thing, living under the same roof—even for a few days—was too much.

'No, I insist. I must stay at the hotel. Can you drop my bag there, please?'

He gave a little smile and climbed into the driver's seat. The Tuscan countryside flew past. The roads in the area were winding, climbing lush green hills, passing hectares of olive groves and vineyards, filling the air with the aroma of Mediterranean vegetation. Tuscany was known for its rolling hills, vineyards and fine wines and olive oil.

It was also unique in its representation of class. Every kind of person stayed in these hills. They passed a huge array of houses and tiny cottages dotted over the countryside. Medieval villages, castles—some ruins, some renovated—and old farmhouses crowning hilltops.

After thirty minutes the car passed an old crumbling wall and turned onto a narrow road lined with cypress trees, then rolled into the picturesque village of Monte Calanetti. Lucia put down her window for a better view. The village had two bell towers that were ringing out the hour as they arrived. There was also a piazza surrounded by small shops and businesses, cobblestoned walkways going up and down the narrow streets and a fountain where a few children were walking around the small wall surrounding it and splashing water at each other.

There was an old well on one side next to red-brick houses with gorgeous flower boxes and laundry strung overhead.

A few blue and red scooters whizzed past, ridden by young men with their trousers rolled up at their ankles and their hair flapping in the wind. Helmets didn't seem to be a priority.

She smiled. It was gorgeous. It was quaint. It could

be a setting for a film. Every character that was needed
was there—the small wizened woman hanging her
washing from a window, the young mother hurrying
past with her child, a shopkeeper standing in a doorway
and a couple of young girls whispering and watching
the guys zipping past on their scooters.

The car turned onto another winding road, again
lined with cypress trees. It only took a few moments
for the *palazzo* to come into sight.

It was a sprawling, grand building with lots of little
scattered buildings around. Lucia twisted in her seat,
but it wasn't until the car pulled up outside the sweeping
entrance of the *palazzo* that she finally saw the building she was after on the other side of the courtyard.

An old traditional chapel. Dark stonework, arched
windows and door. It had two stained-glass windows,
which had obviously been added at a later date than
the original build.

But before she had a chance to focus on the beauty
of the building something else took her breath away.

Logan, emerging from the entrance of the chapel.
It had been twelve years since she'd seen him and she
hadn't quite expected the jolt that was running through
her body.

He ran his fingers through his dark hair, which was
still a little too long. Logan had always been stylish,
had always dressed as if the clothes had been made personally for him. Today he had on cream suit trousers
and a pale blue shirt, open at the throat with the sleeves
pushed up. Only Italian men could get away with cream
suits. She imagined his cream jacket would have been
discarded somewhere inside the chapel.

It wasn't just that he'd aged well. He'd aged *movie*

star well. He was still lean, but there was a little more muscle to his frame. His shoulders a bit wider, his shape more sculpted. He lifted his head and his footsteps faltered. He'd noticed her at the same time she'd noticed him, but she could bet his body wasn't doing the same things that hers was.

The car halted and the driver opened her door. There was no retreat. There was nowhere to hide.

She stared down at her Italian pumps for the briefest of seconds, sucking in a breath and trying to still the erratic pitter-patter of her heart. Thank goodness she'd taken off the stilettos. She'd never have survived the cobbled streets of Monte Calanetti.

She accepted the extended hand of the driver and stepped out of the car, pulling down her dress a little and adjusting her suit jacket. The cool interior of the car had kept the heat of Tuscany out well. It was like stepping into a piping-hot bath. This situation was hot enough without the sun's intense rays to contend with.

Logan walked over. His faltering footsteps had recovered quickly. He reached out his hand towards her. 'Lucia, welcome.'

For the briefest of seconds she hesitated. This was business. *This was business.* She tried to appear calm and composed, even though the first little rivulet of sweat was snaking down her back.

She grasped his hand confidently. 'Logan, I hope you've been well. I take it that is the chapel?' She gestured to the building from which he'd emerged.

Straight to the point. It was the only way to be. She had to ignore the way his warm hand enveloped hers. She definitely had to ignore the tiny sparks in her palm and the tingling shooting up her arm. She pulled her hand back sharply.

If he was surprised at her direct response he didn't show it. His voice was as smooth as silk. 'Why don't we go into the main house? I'll show you to your room and introduce you to Louisa, the owner.'

He waved his hand, gesturing her towards the *palazzo*, and she could instantly feel the hackles rise at the back of her neck.

'That won't be necessary. I'm not staying. I've booked a hotel nearby.'

Logan exchanged a glance with the driver, who was already disappearing into the *palazzo* with her red case. 'Why don't you have some refreshments in the meantime? I'd still like to introduce you to Louisa and I'm sure you'd like to see around the *palazzo*—we've already renovated some parts of it, including the room Louisa has set aside for you.'

He was so confident, so assured. It grated because she wished she felt that way too. She was trying her best to mimic the effect, but it was all just a charade. Her stomach was churning so wildly she could have thrown up on the spot. It wasn't just the intense heat that was causing little rivulets of sweat to run down her back, it was Logan. Being in his presence again after all these years and the two of them standing here, exchanging pleasantries, as if what had happened between them hadn't changed their lives for ever, just couldn't compute in her brain.

Business. She kept repeating the word in her head. She was probably going to have to keep doing this for the next few days. Whatever it took to get through them. She had to be professional. She had to be polite. The

Italian Heritage Board would expect her to discuss her findings and proposals with the owner directly—not through a third party. Maybe this way she could take Logan out the equation?

She gave a nod and walked over the courtyard towards the *palazzo*. The first thing she noticed as she walked into the wide entrance hall was the instantly cool air. The *palazzo* may be hundreds of years old but it seemed as though the amenities had been updated. She gently pulled her jacket from her back to let some air circulate.

Logan showed her through to a wide open-plan sitting area. Glass doors gave a wide, spectacular view over the vineyards. She was instantly drawn to the greenery outside.

'Wow. I've never really seen a working vineyard before. This is amazing.'

A beautiful slim blonde emerged from another doorway, her hair tied in a high ponytail, wearing capri pants and a white top. She smiled broadly and held out her hand. 'Welcome. You must be Lucia. Logan told me to expect you. I'm Louisa.' She nodded to the view outside. 'And I knew nothing about vineyards either before I arrived here.'

Lucia shook her hand easily. Should she be cautious? What exactly had Logan told her?

Her eyes flitted from one to the other. Was there a relationship between Logan and Louisa? She watched for a few seconds. Logan had his hands in his pockets and was waiting in the background. He wouldn't do that if he were in a relationship with Louisa and this was their home.

Louisa nodded towards the doorway that must lead

towards the kitchen. 'Can I get you coffee, tea, water or...' she gave a smile '...some wine?'

Of course. She was in a vineyard. Would it be rude to say no? She was Italian, she loved wine. But she was here for business, not pleasure. 'Just some water would be lovely, thank you.'

There was a few seconds of uncomfortable silence as she was left alone with Logan again. He moved over next to her, keeping his hands firmly in his pockets.

'How is your job at the heritage board? Do you like it?'

She gave a brief nod but kept her eyes firmly on the vineyard outside. 'It was always the kind of job that I wanted to do.' She left everything else unsaid. If things had turned out differently there was a good chance that she would never have taken the job in Venice. It would have been too far away from the life they had planned together in Florence.

Something inside her cringed. It was almost as if she'd wanted things to turn out this way and that just wasn't what she'd meant at all.

But Logan didn't seem to notice. He just seemed more concerned with filling the silent space between them. 'And how do you like living in Venice, compared to Florence?' It was his first acknowledgement of anything between them. They'd lived together in Florence for just over a year.

Louisa came back out of the kitchen holding a glass of water. 'You've lived in Florence and now Venice? How wonderful. What's it like?'

Lucia took the water gratefully. Her throat was achingly dry. For the first time since she'd got here she felt on comfortable ground—questions about Venice were always easy to answer. 'Venice is amazing. It's such a welcoming city and it absolutely feels like home to me now. It is, of course, permanently full of tourists, but I don't really mind that. My apartment is on the Grand Canal so at night I can just open my doors and enjoy the world passing by on the water. Some nights it's calming and peaceful—other nights it's complete chaos. But I wouldn't have it any other way.'

Louisa gave a visible shudder. 'Too many people for me. Too much of everything.' She looked out over the vineyards. 'I can't imagine what this place will be like when the royal wedding takes place. There will be people everywhere.' She gave a shake of her head. 'All the farmhouses and outbuildings are being renovated too. Logan's the only person staying in one right now while we still have some quiet about the place.'

Lucia didn't smile. Didn't react. But her body was practically trembling with relief to know she wouldn't be under the same roof as Logan.

Now she might consider staying in the *palazzo* for the next couple of days.

Louisa gave her a smile. 'I intend to stay out of the way as much possible. Now, about the fresco. What happens next? You do understand that we are under an obligation to get the rest of the restoration work finished as soon as possible?'

Lucia could hear the edge in her voice. The same strong hint that had come from Logan. She chose her words carefully. 'It all depends on the fresco itself. Or, more importantly, the artist who created it.'

'Will you know as soon as you look at it?'

She held out her hands. 'It would be wonderful if we could just look at something and say, "Oh, that's by this artist…" But the heritage board requires authentication of any piece of work. Sometimes it's by detailed comparison of brushstrokes, which can be as good an identifier as a signature—we have a specialised computer program for that. Sometimes it's age-related by carbon dating. Sometimes we have to rely on the actual date of the construction of the building to allow us to agree a starting point for the fresco.'

Louisa smiled and glanced over at Logan, who looked lost in his own thoughts. 'Well, that's easy, then. Logan has already been able to date the construction of the *palazzo* and chapel from the stone used and the building methods used. Isn't that right, Logan?'

He turned his head at the sound of his name, obviously only catching the tail end of the conversation. He took a few steps towards Lucia. 'The buildings were constructed around 1500, towards the end of the Italian Renaissance period. The fresco could have appeared at any point from then onwards.'

It didn't matter how tired she was, how uncomfortable she felt around Logan—it was all she could do not to throw off her shoes and dash across the entrance courtyard right now to get in and start examining it.

She gave a polite, cautious nod. 'I'm keen to start work with you as soon as possible, Louisa.'

Louisa's eyes widened and she let out a laugh. 'Oh, you won't be working with me.' She gestured towards Logan. 'You'll be working with Logan. I have absolutely no expertise on any of these things. I've started to call him Mr Restoration. Anything to do with the work has to be agreed with him.'

Lucia eyes fell to the empty glass on the table. Where

was more water when she needed it? This was the last thing she wanted to hear.

She smiled politely once again. 'But, as the owner, I need to agree access with you and have you sign any paperwork the heritage board may require. I also need to be able to come to and from the *palazzo* at my leisure. I will be staying at a nearby hotel.'

'What? Oh, no. You're staying here. Come, and I'll show you to your room.' She was on her feet in an instant. 'We have renovated some parts of the *palazzo*, you know.' She waved her hand. 'And it will all be finished before the wedding.' As she reached the door she turned, waiting for Lucia to follow her.

The corners of Logan's lips were turning upwards.

'Ms Harrison, I really don't want to put you to any trouble. I'm more than happy to stay in a hotel and just travel to and from the *palazzo*. It will only be for a few days. I don't expect my research to take any longer than that.'

Louisa shook her head. 'Nonsense. You'll stay here. I insist. As for the paperwork, Logan will need to read that first and explain it to me. My Italian is still very rusty.'

Louisa had already started up a flight of stairs, obviously expecting Lucia to follow her. 'You're going to have a beautiful view over the vineyard. And you're welcome to use the kitchen if you want.' She paused. 'But there's a really nice restaurant in Monte Calanetti you should try.'

She wanted to object. She wanted to get away from here. But it was important that she have some sort of relationship with the owner. And because of that the words were sticking in the back of her throat. Louisa hadn't stopped talking. She was already halfway up the stairs. It obviously didn't occur to her that Lucia might continue with her objections. 'I'm sure you'll love the room.'

Lucia sucked in a breath. She wasn't even going to look in Logan's direction. If she saw him smile smugly she might just take off one of her shoes and throw it at him in frustration. At least she had the assurance that he wouldn't actually be under the same roof as her.

Just achingly close.

'I'll be back in five minutes. I want to see the fresco,' she shot at him as she left the room.

She walked up the stairs after Louisa and along a corridor. This *palazzo* had three floors—it was unusual, and had obviously survived throughout the ages. The person who'd built this had obviously had plenty of money to build such a large home in the Tuscan hills. Even transporting the stones here must have been difficult. What with the land, and the vineyard, along with all the outbuildings she'd spotted and the chapel, at one time this must have been a thriving little community.

Louisa took her into a medium-sized room with a double bed and wooden-framed glass windows overlooking the vineyard. Everything about the room was fresh and clean. There was white linen on the bed and a small table and chair next to the window, with a classic baroque chair in the corner. A wooden wardrobe, bedside table and mirror on the wall completed the furnishings.

A gentle breeze made the white drapes at the window flap, bringing the scents of the rich greenery, grapes and lavender inside. Her red case was presumptuously sitting next to the doorway.

'I'll bring you up a jug of water, a glass and some wine for later,' said Louisa as she headed out the door. 'Oh, and we don't quite have an en suite, but the bathroom is right next door. You'll be the only person that's using it.'

She disappeared quickly down the hall, leaving Lucia looking around the room. She sank down onto the bed. It felt instantly comfortable. Instantly inviting. The temperature of the room was cool, even though the breeze drifting in was warm, and she could hear the sounds of the workers in the vineyard.

She closed her eyes for a few seconds. She could do this. Two days tops then she could be out of here again.

Logan. Seeing him again was hard. So hard. The familiar sight of Logan, the scent of Logan was tough. She couldn't let him invade her senses. She couldn't let him into her brain, because if she did a whole host of other memories would come flooding back—ones that she couldn't face again.

This is business. She repeated her mantra once more.

The smell of the Tuscan hills was wrapping itself around her. Welcoming her to the area. Her stomach grumbled. She was hungry, but food would have to wait. She wanted to see the fresco.

She walked over and grabbed her case, putting it on the bed and throwing it open.

It was time to get to work.

Logan had finished pacing and was waiting for Lucia to appear. He'd walked back out to the courtyard and was leaning against the side of the doorway to the chapel with his arms folded across his chest.

It was much warmer out here, but he thrived in the Italian sun.

Seeing Lucia had been a shock to the system. His first glance had been at her left hand but there had been no wedding ring, no glittering diamond of promise. He was surprised. He'd always imagined that after twelve years Lucia would have been married with children. The fact she wasn't bothered him—in more ways than one.

She'd been hurt, she'd been wounded when they'd split. Even though it had been by mutual agreement. But he'd always hoped she'd healed and moved on. When he'd heard she was working for the Italian Heritage Board he'd assumed she'd pulled things together and was focusing on her career. Now he was suspicious she'd *only* focused on her career.

Lucia had aged beautifully. She was still petite and elegant. Her pale pink suit jacket and matching dress hugged her curves, leaving a view of her shapely calves.

And she'd kept her long hair. It was maybe only a few inches shorter than it had been the last time he'd seen her. He liked it that way. Had liked it when her hair had brushed against his face—liked it even more when her long eyelashes had tickled his cheek as she'd moved closer.

It was odd. Even though there were lots of parts of his body that could have responded to the first sight of her, it had been his lips that had reacted first. One sight of her had been enough to remember the feel of her soft lips against his, remember the *taste* of her. And as she'd stepped closer he'd been swamped by her smell. Distinctive. Delicious. In any other set of circumstances…hot.

But not in these circumstances. Not when delays on this project could result in a late completion penalty that could bankrupt his company. Louisa was serious about this place being ready for the royal wedding. She was depending on it.

He straightened as Lucia appeared, walking briskly across the courtyard. She'd changed and was now wearing flat shoes, slim-fitting navy trousers, a pale cream top with lace inserts on the shoulders and a dark silk scarf knotted at her neck. She had a digital camera in her hand.

He was disappointed that her legs were no longer on display.

She stopped in front of him, meeting his gaze straight on. She'd changed a little over the years. There were a few tiny lines around her eyes, but the rest of her skin was smooth. She, like him, had naturally olive Italian skin. Her dark brown gaze was uncompromising. 'Show me your fresco, Logan.'

It was the most direct he'd ever heard her. He tried not to smile. Twelve years had instilled a new-found courage in her. He liked it.

But something else swamped him for a few seconds. There had been a time in his life that Lucia had encompassed everything for him. She'd been the centre of his universe. He shifted self-consciously on his feet. He'd never felt that way again—he'd never *allowed* himself to feel that way again.

It was too much. Too much to have so much invested in one person when your life could change in an instant and everything come tumbling down around you both.

It didn't matter that seeing Lucia again after all these years was swamping him with a host of memories. It was time to put all those feelings back in a box. A place where they were best left.

He gestured towards the entranceway. 'It's all yours. Let's go.'

She walked ahead of him, her tight bottom right in his line of vision. He lifted his eyes to look straight in front of him and smiled as her footsteps faltered as she saw the fresco.

'Oh...whoa.'

He smiled as he stepped alongside her. 'Pretty much what I said too.'

She lifted her camera then put it back down and walked right up to the wall. She lifted her hand but didn't actually touch it. 'It's been covered for...how long?'

Logan shook his head, his hands on his hips. 'I couldn't say for sure.' He pointed to the corner of the room where debris was stacked. 'The wood panelling could be between three and four hundred years old.'

She glanced at the wood and turned back to the fresco. This time she did lift her camera and started snapping, first capturing the full work then systematically snapping detailed sections. Images that she could take time to pore over later.

When she finished she placed the camera on the floor then picked up some tiny fragments of clay that were on the floor—obvious remnants from the uncovering of the fresco. She gathered them in little plastic bags, labelled them, then put them in her bag. Once she'd finished she moved so close to the fresco that her nose was only inches away.

She lifted her fingers. It was obvious she was itching to touch it, but, she was resisting the temptation. 'I can see the movement,' she said quietly. 'I can see the brushstrokes. What kind of brush do you use to paint individual hairs? This is amazing.'

Logan waited, watching her relish her first viewing of the fresco. It was strangely exhilarating. He could see the wonder on her face, see the excitement in her eyes. Just watching her sent a little buzz through his body. Memories were sparking. This was part of the Lucia he'd loved. The wonderful, passionate girl who'd embraced life to the full. When they'd first met she'd been quiet, reserved as a result of her upbringing. But studying in Florence had made her blossom into the beautiful woman he'd quickly grown to love. The buzz, culture and bright lights had been a nurturing environment for the young artistic woman. And the two of them meeting had seemed to spark her even further. All his first memories of Lucia had been about their drive, their passion and their instant connection.

He could feel it even now—twelve years on. The palms of his hands were actually itching to reach out and touch her—just the way hers were obviously itching to touch the fresco. Parts of Lucia had been so easy to read.

Other parts she'd kept tightly locked up and tucked away. Those had been the parts that had sealed the end of their relationship. Every person grieved differently. But Logan just couldn't understand why she'd been unable to talk to *him*, why she'd been unable to share with *him*. After all, he'd been going through exactly the same thing.

He took a deep breath. 'What do you think?'

'The fresco was prepared in sections. *Giornate*—done on a daily basis with small sections of plaster laid at a time to be painted—much in the same way that Michelangelo carried out the work at the Sistine Chapel.'

Logan was incredulous. 'You think this was done by Michelangelo?'

She laughed. 'Oh, no. Of course not. The artist of the time just used the same techniques. Michelangelo used different skin tones from those used here.' She leaned back critically. 'Different draping of the clothes. This definitely isn't his work.'

She finished snapping a few more shots with the camera and turned to face him again. 'I have a program on my computer that I can upload these pictures to. It finds similarities between frescoes and gives the most likely artists.'

He shook his head. 'Why do I feel as if you don't really need it? What's your gut instinct?'

She shook her head. 'I'm not sure. It could be one of a few possibilities.'

He pressed her again. 'But you think...' He let his answer tail off.

She brushed her hair off her shoulder. 'I think there's a chance it's a lesser-known Renaissance painter. His name was Burano.' She gave a wry smile. 'The same as one of the islands in the Venetian lagoon.'

Logan's brow creased. 'He was from Venice, then?'

She nodded.

'So what was he doing in Tuscany?'

She turned back to face the fresco. 'That's my question too. That's why I'm hesitant. I could be wrong. Journeying between Venice and Tuscany in Renaissance times wasn't easy, but we both know the European Renaissance started in Tuscany and centred in Florence and Siena.' She raised her eyebrows. 'Venice was the late starter.'

She walked back to the entranceway. 'Give me some time to run the program and see what it comes up with.'

Logan held out his hand as she made to leave. 'And in the meantime?' He spun around. 'Time is marching on, we've still got work to do in the chapel—even if we aren't anywhere near the fresco.'

She looked around and gave a little nod. 'Let me give you some recommendations on the best way to protect it in the meantime from dust, plaster and paint.' Her gaze connected with his. 'This could be a really amazing discovery, Logan.'

It was the way she'd said his name. Her accent, her lilt. He'd heard it on so many occasions. Last thing at night, first thing in the morning. In the heat of passion and in the depths of despair.

He just hadn't admitted how much he actually missed it.

His feet were rooted to the spot. But Lucia's weren't. She was headed out the door. She was leaving. Who knew how long she would actually stay here. He could get up tomorrow morning and discover her gone.

'Have dinner with me?'

'What?' She stopped. She looked shocked.

'Have dinner with me,' he repeated, stepping closer to her. The words had come out of nowhere. He couldn't take them back. He didn't *want* to take them back.

'We have things we need to discuss.' He saw a wave of panic flit across her eyes. '*Business* we need to discuss.'

'Oh, of course.' She glanced down at her digital camera. 'My program will take a few hours to run.' She was stalling. Of course she was. The last thing she'd want to do was have dinner with him.

'Then you'll have a few hours to kill,' he said quickly. This was embarrassing. Logan Cascini wasn't used to women saying no to him. But Lucia wasn't just any woman. Lucia was the woman he'd once loved. Sure, it felt awkward. Sure, this wasn't an ideal situation.

But this was the first time he'd seen her in twelve years. If this fresco turned out to be important, it could have significant repercussions for his business. He had to keep on top of this.

He almost laughed out loud. His mind was giving him all the rational, professional reasons for having dinner with Lucia. But his heart was giving him a whole host of completely irrational, emotional reasons for having dinner with Lucia.

None of them professional. All of them personal.

His mouth kept talking. 'We can discuss any paperwork that will need to be completed. I'll need to translate everything for Louisa, and if there's going to be any extra expenses we'll need to discuss those too. There's a nice restaurant in Monte Calanetti. It will give you a chance to see the village.'

She was hesitating, looking for a reason to say no, and he wasn't prepared to accept that.

He walked around her in long strides. 'Leave the arrangements to me.'

'Well, I... I...' She was still murmuring while he left.

CHAPTER THREE

FOUR DIFFERENT OUTFITS. That's how many she'd tried on. She hadn't brought that many clothes as she'd only expected to be here a few days and hadn't expected to be socialising at all, let alone socialising with the man she used to live with. Two suits, one pair of trousers, one extra skirt and a variety of tops were all that her trusty red case held.

A white shirt, a pale pink shirt and a bright blue one were currently lying on her bed. She was wearing a flared white skirt and red shirt. And against all her better judgement a bright red pair of stilettos.

The shoes gave some height to her diminutive stature. Right now she was praying that the restaurant wasn't in the middle of the cobbled streets of Monte Calanetti.

Logan was waiting outside for her in an idling car. She'd expected him to drive something black and sleek but instead he was in a four-wheel drive.

He gave her a nod as she opened the door and climbed in. Catching sight of her shoes, a glimmer of a smile appeared on his face. 'We're going to the local restaurant—Mancini's. I hope you like traditional food.' His eyes were gleaming.

She was nervous. And she couldn't quite work out why. Logan had changed into a white open-necked shirt and dark fitted trousers. His dark hair still had that rumpled look that she'd always loved. It was like a magnet—all she wanted to do was lift her hand and run her fingers through it.

She shifted her legs nervously in the car, crossing them one way then the other. If he noticed he didn't say anything. She eyed her shoes warily. 'Where is the restaurant?'

Logan was completely cool. He didn't seem at all unsettled at being around her. 'It's a converted farmhouse on the edge of the village. The chef's family have owned the restaurant for years, his wife-to-be is the maître d'—she's from the US.' He gave a little smile. 'It's an explosive combination.'

With Logan this was all about business. She would clearly have to adopt the same attitude.

He pulled up outside the restaurant, switched off the engine, and before she even had a chance to think he had come around the car and was opening her door and holding out his hand towards her.

She stared at his tanned hand and fingers. *Touch him.* She'd done it once. Her palm had burned for around an hour afterwards. Did she really want to touch Logan Cascini again?

How on earth could she say no?

She placed her hand in his. The sparks didn't fly this time. Probably because she was a little more prepared. This time it was a warm buzz, a little hum running up her arm and straight across to her heart.

Twelve years on, and he could still do it to her.

It was unnerving. She could hardly keep her thoughts straight.

The first glimpse of Logan had sent tingles around her body. But that had been quickly followed by a rush of emotions associated with bad memories. Memories that were locked away deep inside her.

There was a reason she wasn't happily married with a family. There was a reason she always backed off when a few dates started to turn into something else.

Professionally, her life was good. She had a gorgeous apartment, a motivating and challenging job, along with a whole host of good friends and colleagues.

That would be enough for most people. That *should* be enough. And right up until she'd glimpsed Logan again it had been.

Now she felt…unbalanced.

She walked into the farmhouse converted into a restaurant. Thankfully there were no cobbles outside and the added height from her stilettos seemed to buffer her confidence a little.

It was cute. There were shutters on the windows and exposed brickwork on the walls. Wooden tables filled the dining room, but they weren't all uniform, like in most restaurants. They were all different shapes and sizes, perfect for all numbers of guests, and it gave an old-world charm to the place.

They were shown to their table and the waiter lit the candle, then handed over the wine list. He nodded at Logan and pointed to the back wall. 'As you can see, we have a wide variety of wines from all the local vineyards. If you need a recommendation just let me know.'

Lucia ran her eyes down the list and sighed. Italians

were passionate about their wine and the wine list was thicker than the actual menu.

'What's your preference?'

Couldn't he remember? Had he forgotten everything about their time together?

Before she had a chance to speak he waved to the waiter. 'Can we have some bread, olives and some oil while we decide?'

The waiter gave a nod and disappeared. It seemed he hadn't quite forgotten everything after all. Lucia had always enjoyed taking her time to peruse a menu, and Logan had always been starving.

She swallowed, her fingers drifting back to the file she'd brought with her. This made it seem more real. This was work. The reason she'd agreed to dinner tonight.

She licked her lips. Nerves were doing strange things to her. 'I think I'd like to keep things simple. I'd like to have some white wine, I think, something light. A *frascati*.'

She knew he'd be surprised. During their time together they'd both favoured red wines, Merlots and Chiantis.

'And I like the look of the set menu. Sometimes it's nice to have someone else pick for you.'

She'd only glanced at the set menu and nothing had jumped out at her. Most restaurants offered a set menu of some of their best dishes. She only hoped Mancini's was the same.

In years gone by she'd been picky about her food, sometimes refusing to go to some restaurants if they didn't serve a particular dish that she liked. But she wanted to start this meeting by letting Logan realise that he didn't really know her any more. Just because he was working on this project it didn't mean that he'd get any special treatment. And she wasn't swayed by a royal wedding either.

She took her job seriously. If the fresco had been by Michelangelo everything would have ground to a complete halt. She was fairly certain it was by a lesser-known artist—one who was still recognised and his work would be protected. But the chapel was fairly well maintained. There was no damp, no immediate threat to the fresco—just the new work that was going on to make it ready for the wedding.

Once the identification part was done, things should be fairly straightforward.

Logan set his menu on the table. 'Both are fine with me.' He had a hint of a smile on his face. As if he knew she was trying to be different but it was all really just a pretence. 'How have you been, Lucia?' he asked huskily. That voice. That accent. Little waves were rolling down her spine. It was the memories. It was anticipation of what had used to come next when Logan had spoken to her like that.

Those days were long gone. Vanished for ever. It didn't matter that the words were bland and perfectly normal. It was the *way* he said them that counted.

'Twelve years is a long time, Logan.' Her voice was sharp.

He waited a few seconds before answering. His voice was low. 'You're right. It's been a very long time. Almost a lifetime ago.'

What did that mean? That for him it was gone, forgotten about? How could anyone forget losing a child? She could feel herself bristle.

'How have you been?' She bounced the question back to him. Her insides were curling up in case he told her—even though he didn't wear a ring—that he was indeed married with a houseful of children.

He nodded slowly. 'I've been busy. Building your own business takes time.' He shrugged. 'Nearly all of my time. I like to be on-site for the restoration projects. I like to make sure that everything is going to plan.'

She felt her shoulders relax a little. 'You don't like to sit in your office and drink coffee?' It was something they used to joke about years ago. Creative people ending up in jobs behind desks, drinking endless cups of coffee.

He gave a smile and shook his head as the waiter approached again, taking their order and returning a few moments later to pour the wine and leave the bread, olives and oil on the table.

Lucia took a sip. The first taste was always sharp. The second much more pleasing as her taste buds adjusted.

'Where are your offices?'

He tasted his wine too and nodded in approval. 'Florence. But I don't spend much time there.'

She tried not to raise her eyebrows. Office space in Florence was expensive. His business had obviously done well. 'Do you still live in Florence?'

He hesitated a second. And she wondered if she'd just stepped over some invisible barrier. They'd lived in Florence together. But she didn't expect him still to be in the small one-bedroomed flat a few minutes from the university.

He nodded and dipped a piece of bread in the oil. 'I have an apartment overlooking Piazza Santa Croce.'

'Wow.' She couldn't help it. It was one of the main areas of Florence. Apartments there weren't cheap and although the existing buildings were old, they'd usually been refurbished to a high standard, hence the expensive price tags.

She gave a little nod of her head. 'I can see you staying there. Did you get to renovate the place yourself?'

He shook his head. 'If only. The apartment was renovated before I got there. But all the original architecture is still there. That's what's important.'

'Do you like staying there?' She was dancing around the subject that was really in her mind. *Did anyone stay there with him?* It shouldn't matter to her. Of course it shouldn't. But she couldn't help but feel a natural curiosity. And there was no way she would come right out and ask the question.

'It's fine. It's Florence.' He looked at her carefully. 'I've always loved living in Florence. I just don't get to stay there as much as I would like.'

'Really? Why not?' *Because your wife and child stay somewhere else?*

He shrugged. 'I've spent the last ten years building up my business. I go wherever the work is. It takes time, energy and commitment. When I'm doing a restoration—like now—I like to be on-site. I've stayed in my apartment probably only three months of the last year.'

'I see,' she said quietly, as the waiter appeared and placed their starters in front of them—wild mushroom ravioli with butter and Parmesan sauce. She was glad of the distraction. Glad to stop being watched by those too-intense green eyes.

It made sense. Logan had always been passionate about everything he'd been involved in. From his work, to his family, to his relationships. But it sounded very much like he didn't have anyone back in Florence to worry about.

'How are your family in Scotland?' she asked.

He smiled. 'They're good. They have three restaurants in Glasgow now. The one in George Square is still the main one and my *nonna* refuses to get out from behind the bar. She still sits there every day and criticises what everyone else does.'

Lucia laughed. She'd met his *nonna* on a few occasions. She was fiery little woman who was both fiercely protective and critical of her family.

'They still ask after you,' he said quietly.

Her laughter died and she swallowed quickly. There was a little tug at her heartstrings. Although both families had roots in Italy, Logan's family were much more welcoming and outgoing than her own. She'd felt more at home in their house in Glasgow than in her own mother and father's house in the small town of Osimo.

She didn't reply. She couldn't reply. Too many memories were starting to flood back. This was the problem with seeing Logan after all this time. All the things she'd literally pushed to the back corners of her mind were starting to poke their way through again.

But it wasn't just unhappy memories that were crowding her thoughts. Logan had other little places in her mind. Just sitting here with him now made a little warm glow spread throughout her body. His eyes, his accent, the way he ran his fingers through his hair when he was searching for the right words. Beautiful, sunny days in Florence, long afternoons drinking endless cups of coffee and dusky evenings with wine leading to long nights together.

Passionate. Intense. The two words that sprang to mind to describe their relationship. The third word was tragic. But she didn't even want to go there.

She was still toying with her food, wondering if either one of them would bring up the elephant in the room.

But Logan wasn't ready to go there yet. 'What do you think of Louisa?'

She put down her knife and fork. It was a curious question. The Logan she used to know would size someone up in a matter of minutes. The fact he was asking about Louisa meant he obviously wasn't quite sure.

She frowned. 'I'm not sure. I haven't really had a chance to talk to her yet. She's American, isn't she? How did she manage to own a vineyard in Tuscany?'

'From what I know, she inherited it. She's the last living relative of Signor Bartolini. It seems she might have inherited some time ago but has never visited before. As far as I can make out, Nico—who owns the neighbouring vineyard and who was a friend of Signor Bartolini—has kept it semi-functioning for the last few months. But I'm not entirely sure that Nico and Louisa have hit it off.'

She nodded thoughtfully. She hadn't met Nico yet but had heard him yelling instructions to some of the vineyard workers. He was obviously intent on keeping the vineyard working.

Logan took a sip of his wine. 'How do you find Venice?'

'It took a little getting used to. Florence was always busy, but Venice is off the scale. Cruise liners come in every day and the Piazza San Marco is so busy you can barely move.'

He gave a little nod. 'Where are you staying?'

'I was lucky. I managed to get an older apartment—much like you—on the Grand Canal. My building and street are off the main thoroughfare, but any time of the day or night I can open my doors and look out over the canal. There's never a quiet moment out there.'

'Do you live alone?' She sucked in a breath but couldn't help the amused smile that appeared on her face. It seemed that Logan didn't mind being direct. She'd skirted around the issue but he had no intention of doing that.

A tiny little part of her wanted to lie. Wanted to tell him she had a billionaire husband and three perfect children at home. But she had never been a person to tell lies. Her secret hopes and desires for her own life were just that—secret.

'Yes. It's just me. I lived with someone for a while but things didn't work out. I was consumed with work and didn't really have time for a relationship. It turned out he really didn't want a career woman for a wife anyway.'

She said the words flippantly, not giving away how much it had hurt at the time. But time, in some cases, gave a chance for reflection. That relationship would have always come to an end.

Logan's eyebrows had risen as she'd been speaking. Wasn't she supposed to move on?

But it seemed he'd opened the door now and given her a right to ask whatever she wanted. 'Why haven't you got married and settled down?' she asked.

The waiter appeared, clearing one set of plates and setting down their main course—Tuscan veal chops with Parmesan *tuilles*. The smell drifted up around her.

She picked up her fork and sighed. 'This is the kind of thing I wish I had the time and talent to make.'

'Your cooking talents haven't improved with age?' He laughed. Lucia's cooking attempts had been a constant source of amusement for them. She'd once declared she could burn water—and she probably could.

The initial preparation and cooking attempts hadn't been a problem. Distraction had been the problem. Something else had always managed to crop up while she was supposed to be watching a timer or stirring a pot.

'How have you survived without someone to feed you?'

She gave a resigned nod of her head as she tasted some of the succulent veal. 'I eat out. A lot. The kitchen and I will never be friends.'

He laughed. 'I should get Nonna to package up some food for you.'

She waved her fork at him. 'Nonna should package up food for the world. She could make a fortune if she released a recipe book, or sold them to a food manufacturer.'

Logan's eyes connected with hers. 'You really expect Nonna to reveal her secret family recipes to an unsuspecting world?' He was teasing. She could tell. This was the way it used to be with them. Constant joking back and forth.

She shrugged. 'I'm just saying you have an untapped family fortune out there. That could be your nest egg, you know.'

He shook his head. 'I don't think I'd live to tell the tale.'

'Probably not.' She took a sip of her wine. This wasn't

quite as bad as she'd feared. Logan wasn't being difficult, he was his usual charming self. She'd just forgotten how hypnotic those green eyes could be. Every time
his gaze connected with hers she had to blink to remind
herself to breathe.

Logan had always been charming. His family had
joked he could charm the birds from the trees and the
gods out of Olympus. And she'd loved it. She'd loved
the way he could make her feel like the most important woman on the planet. Because even though Logan
had been a charmer, he'd also been a one-woman man.
He'd never shown a glimmer of interest in anyone else
when he'd been with her. She'd felt assured in his love.

It had been a long time since she'd felt so cherished.

A little warm wave rushed over her skin as she
smiled at him and took another sip of her wine. She
was relaxing more as the night went on, remembering
the good times instead of the bad.

Logan didn't deserve the negative associations that
she'd built up in her brain. He deserved much more
than that.

But if that was how she remembered him, how did
he remember her?

This was more like the Lucia he'd once known. It was
the first time he'd seen a genuine smile since she'd got
here. When she'd walked outside to meet him earlier
his heart rate had rocketed. With her perfect hourglass
figure, the white flared skirt, fitted red shirt and silk
scarf knotted around her neck she'd looked like a nine-
teen-fifties movie star. As for those killer red stilettos...

With her tumbling locks and red lips her picture
could have adorned a thousand walls. His fingers

couldn't decide whether they wanted to unknot the scarf around her neck and pull it free, or run down the smooth skin on her tanned legs towards those heels.

Lucia. It was odd. She tried to act so independent, so aloof, but there was an inherent vulnerability about her that made him lose focus on everything else. He felt strangely protective and proud of her. The last time he'd seen her she'd been a shell of her former self. Losing their child had devastated them both.

Although the pregnancy hadn't been planned they'd both been delighted when they'd found out a baby was on the way. They'd spent hours talking about their future together and making preparations for their baby. At one point it had seemed that the whole apartment had been full of brochures for cribs, cabinets, prams and high chairs.

The twenty-week scan had revealed a perfect daughter waiting to be introduced to the world.

No one could explain the unexpected premature labour.

No one could explain why Ariella Rose hadn't managed to take those first few vital breaths.

Of course, the doctor had tried to say that her lungs hadn't been developed enough and there had been no time to give Lucia steroids to help Ariella's lungs mature.

It had been that terrible time when doctors tried to decide if a baby's life was viable or not.

Some babies did breathe at twenty-three weeks.

Ariella Rose hadn't.

The beautiful, vivacious woman he'd known had disintegrated before his eyes, their relationship crumbling around him. He'd spent months desperate to get her to talk to him. But Lucia had put up walls so thick nothing had penetrated.

Every time he'd tried to draw her out of her shell she'd become more and more silent and withdrawn. He'd pulled back too, focusing on his work, because right then that had been all he'd had. But Lucia had slipped through his fingers like grains of sand from the beach.

He'd been grieving too, watching the days tick by on the calendar, waiting for the day they would have welcomed their daughter into the world.

That had been the day Lucia had packed her cases and left.

No amount of pleading had dissuaded her. Florence had had too many bad memories for her—too many painful associations. She'd accepted a job in Venice. She'd wanted to leave, and she hadn't wanted him to follow.

Now his insides twisted. He'd always regretted that he hadn't fought harder. Hadn't found the words to persuade her to stay.

It was almost a relief to see her now. There was a stillness about her—something reserved that hadn't been there before they'd lost their daughter. He could still see a remnant of sadness in her eyes.

But this Lucia was different. She had a different kind of confidence around her. She was a little more self-assured. She'd been through the worst and come out the other side. There was a real resilience there that bubbled underneath the surface.

Her clothes and demeanour were back to the woman he remembered. She'd always worn her stilettos with pride, as if to take someone to task for her diminutive height. And her hair was every bit as tempting as it had always been. It had always felt like silk and smelled of roses. Even now, there was a faint floral aroma drifting across the table towards him, curling its way around him and kicking his senses into gear.

The waiter appeared to clear their plates. 'Dessert?'

'No, thank you.' They both answered in unison and Lucia threw her head back and laughed.

Now his fingers were definitely itching to reach across and tug that scarf from her neck and reveal the paler sensitive skin around her décolletage.

It was her tender spot. The area that when kissed sent her into a spin. It had always been guaranteed to make her go weak at the knees.

He shifted uncomfortably in his chair. Parts of his body were awakening that shouldn't—not in a public restaurant. 'Do you want to have coffee?'

She shook her head. 'I'm tired. I still need to do some work online.'

Work. Of course. The reason they were here. He'd barely even discussed the project with her. He was normally so pedantic about every detail of his build. It seemed that even being around Lucia for a few hours was making him lose focus.

He should be worrying about delays. He should be panicking that his business could be affected by the non-completion clause in his contract.

If things weren't ready on time for the royal wedding he might have to face the wrath of the wedding planner, Lindsay Reeves. She was already phoning him twice a day for updates and photos of the chapel.

He took a deep breath and tried to collect his thoughts. 'Can we continue our work in the chapel?'

This was useless. Now he was looking at those deep brown eyes. Lucia's eyes had always been able to draw him in completely. In twelve years they hadn't lost their magic.

People said that eyes were the window to the soul. Lucia's brown eyes were very dark, very deep and flecked with gold. He could get lost in them completely. Always had.

She blinked. 'In truth, probably not. Give me another day. I have a few ideas. If I needed to go elsewhere to verify who painted it, would you have someone who could ensure the safety of the fresco?'

He straightened in his chair. 'Why would that be needed? It's been safe for the last five hundred years beneath the panels in the chapel?'

She gave an apologetic smile. 'But now it's been discovered. Now it's open to the elements. And now we have a whole host of tradesmen who know that it exists.' She shrugged. 'What if people have thoughts like you first did? What if they think that there is a tiny possibility this could be a Michelangelo work? What if someone tells the press?'

She held out her hands. 'In the space of a few hours this whole village could be swamped by a whole host of people—not all of them with good intentions.' She spoke with complete sincerity. He'd always respected Lucia's ambition, but he was now seeing a true glimpse of her professional expertise.

He nodded slowly. 'Of course. Louisa has already expressed some concerns about publicity. She's worried enough about the royal wedding without having to deal with something else.' It was easy to know who to discuss this with. 'Connor Benson is the head of security for the royal party. He'll know exactly how to keep things safe and protect the fresco in the meantime.'

She gave him an amused smile. 'Isn't he more at home looking after real-life people than artefacts?'

Logan lifted his hands. 'He has the skill and expertise we need. What's more important is that I trust him. If he says he can keep the fresco safe, then I believe him.'

He signalled to the waiter for the bill. Lucia had told him she still had work to do. It didn't matter that he wasn't in a hurry for this evening to end. He had to respect the job she was here to do.

It only took a few minutes to pay the bill and head back out to the car. The sun was setting behind the deep green Tuscan hills, sending shards of orange and red across the sky.

Lucia took a deep breath as they stepped outside. 'How beautiful.' She spun around in her heels, her skirt swishing around her, a relaxed smile on her face.

He caught her arm as she spun, feeling her smooth skin against his palm. 'You've never experienced a Tuscan sunset. It really is something, isn't it?'

The evening was still warm and pleasant. 'Why don't we go for a walk before we head back to the *palazzo*?' The words were out before he thought about it and he could sense her immediate reluctance.

But what struck him straight away was the way his stomach curled. He hated seeing Lucia like this, prickly and difficult around him. Towards the end of their relationship she'd been so flat. Almost emotionless, as if everything had just been drained from her. It had just been another stage of grieving—he appreciated that now.

But at the beginning she'd been bright, bubbly and vivacious. He didn't know this prickly and difficult version. More importantly, he didn't know how to *act* around her.

He waved his hand. 'Of course, if you want to head straight back, that's fine. I just thought you might want to have a chance to see around Monte Calanetti a little.'

It was official.

She was caught between a rock and a hard place.

Strange as it seemed, getting a sense of the village might actually help her identify who the artist of the fresco might be. Often, if someone had stayed in an area there might be historical stories or some folklore about them. Sometimes getting a sense of a place, seeing other work done in the area could actually help. And, in some respects, Logan's brain worked exactly the same way that hers did.

She sucked in a breath, holding it for a few seconds, her eyes fixing on her red stilettos. They'd seemed like a good idea at the time. But she'd seen the streets of Monte Calanetti. Cobbles. Everywhere. She'd probably land on her back.

She bit her lip. Logan's gaze was fixed on the sunset, his face basking in the orange glow. Her reserve softened. With his dark hair, tanned skin and dark suit jacket he was definite movie-star material. Age suited him. The little lines around his eyes gave him even more charisma, and Logan had oozed it already.

'Okay, then.' *Where had that come from?*

She was almost as amazed at her words as Logan was, judging by the expression on his face. He recovered quickly. 'Great, let's go.'

He drove the car into the town centre and parked outside a bar. He walked swiftly around and opened the door, holding his hand out to her as he had before.

She didn't hesitate. Didn't think about the contact. She was making too much of this. It was probably just all in her head anyway.

Wrong move. She could almost see the spike of electricity.

One of her heels automatically slipped in a gap in the cobbles and he caught her elbow, sliding one arm behind her waist. She pretended it was nothing. Nothing—to feel his body right next to hers.

Her throat was so dry she couldn't even swallow. This wasn't supposed to happen. She was in self-protect mode.

She could smell him. Smell his woodsy aftershave, his masculine scent winding its way around her body. So familiar. So scintillating.

He slammed the car door, keeping one hand around her waist. 'Don't want you to stumble,' he said throatily.

It was an excuse. She knew it was an excuse to keep her close. But she didn't feel in a position to protest. The likelihood of her landing on her backside had just increased tenfold. The cobbles weren't the only thing affecting her balance around here.

He steered her towards the centre of the square, near a fountain and old brick well.

Now Lucia really had a chance to see the beauty of the square, the most quirky thing being that it wasn't exactly a square. The fountain was similar to lots found in small Italian villages. Built with travertine stone, it was circular with a sleeping nymph at its centre. The old well was solid with mismatched stones. Like most of Italy's traditional village wells some modernisation had taken place and water from the well could be accessed via a pipe at the side. Logan pressed the button and reached over for her hand. She didn't have time to pull it back before cool, clear water poured over their fingers.

He lifted his hand, letting the drops fall into his mouth. Her legs quivered. She put her fingers to her lips and tasted the cold water. It was surprisingly fresh. She smiled as a drop trickled down her chin.

Logan moved instantly and caught the drop with his finger. She froze. Before it had just been touching hands, arms. Even holding her close, she was still completely clothed.

But touching her face was different. Touching her face was a complete and utter blast from the past. Logan had always touched her face—just before he kissed her.

It had been their *thing*. She'd used to close her eyes and he'd trace his finger over her skin like butterfly kisses. It had always driven her crazy.

And even though she willed it not to happen, as soon as he touched her chin her body reacted. She closed her eyes.

This was something she wasn't prepared for. This was something she'd *never* be prepared for. She sucked in a sharp breath and forced her eyes back open.

Their gazes meshed. So focused, so intense it made her want to cry.

Logan's deep green eyes were so clear, so solid. He was everything she'd ever wanted. Everything she'd ever needed. The person she'd love for ever. The person she'd never forget.

Something flashed across his vision. Panic. Something she'd never seen before in Logan's eyes. He was the calmest, most controlled man she'd ever known.

He pulled his finger back and stared at it for a second, as if he were being hit with the same overload of memories she was.

She wobbled, adjusting her weight in her stilettos. Logan blinked and lifted his hands onto her shoulders, walking her back a few steps to the edge of the fountain. She sagged down, breathing heavily, trying to ignore the pitter-patter in her chest.

She adjusted her position at the edge of the fountain and her eyes fixed on the nymph in the centre of the cascading water. It was exquisite. Serene and beautiful, holding a large clamshell above her head.

Logan stepped in front of her. She was so conscious of him, of his strong muscular thighs barely hidden inside the dark suit trousers. He didn't speak. He didn't try to touch her again.

Her brain tried to clear a little. This was ridiculous. She wasn't the young woman she'd been the last time she'd been around Logan. She'd lived and aged twelve years. Sometimes inside it felt like she'd aged another forty.

She tried to focus her attention on something else. Something safe. The sculpture of the nymph.

Most nymphs were naked. This nymph wasn't. It was clothed. In a cloak. A cloak with characteristic folds.

She straightened up.

'What is it?' Logan crouched down next to her.

She pointed to the nymph. 'Do you know anything about this?'

He touched the wall of the fountain where she was sitting. 'About the fountain?'

She shook her head. 'No. About the nymph. Do you know who sculpted it? Is there any village history that would tell us?'

His eyes were fixed on hers. 'I know the legend attached to the fountain.'

Her heart started to beat faster. 'What's the legend?' She was watching the fine billowing mist that seemed to glow in the lowering sun. Of course. Every village fountain in Italy would have a legend.

He gave her a wistful kind of smile. 'They say that if you toss a coin and it lands in the clamshell you get your wish.'

Her stomach clenched. It wasn't exactly what she'd wanted to hear. But it reached into her and grabbed a tiny part of her soul. Oh, she had a whole host of things she could wish for. But most of them were in the past. And nothing would change that now.

Wishful thinking. That's all that could happen around this fountain. And a fanciful legend didn't help her identify the sculptor. 'Do you know anything else? Anything more realistic?'

He looked as if he'd been stung. He frowned. 'I have no idea. Is it important?'

She stood up and spun around to face it. 'It could be. See the folds of the cloak?'

He leaned forward. 'Yes…' His voice was hesitant.

She touched his arm. 'Does it look familiar to you?'

His face broke into a smile, there was a mischievous twinkle in his eyes and he held up his hands. 'Is yes the right answer?' It was clear he had no idea.

But something had sparked a fire within her. 'I think it might. Most Renaissance artists didn't just paint— they also sculpted. It could be the nymph was sculpted by the same person who painted the fresco. The folds of the cloak are quite characteristic. If I can compare the fresco and the nymph to the works of art that are held in Venice, it could help identify the artist.'

He started to nod his head in recognition. 'You still think its Alberto Burano?'

She smiled. 'It could be.'

This was work. Work she could do. Talking about work made her feel confident again. Made her feel safe.

'So what happens now? How long will it take you to find out?'

She paused. Of course. 'These things can take weeks—sometimes months. The Italian Heritage Board is cautious. We have to be careful before we make any kind of declaration about the potential artist of any fresco. It can always be challenged by others.'

Logan shook his head. 'But what happens in the meantime? Can the wedding still go ahead in the chapel? Louisa is absolutely adamant that things must go to plan. I suspect she's counting on the money from the royal wedding to help her complete the renovations on the *palazzo*. If we can't progress...' His voice tailed off.

There were deep furrows in his brow. He put his hands on his hips and stared out across the village. It was obvious that something else was bothering him.

'If we can't progress—what?'

He let out a deep breath and turned to face her. 'We have a non-completion clause in the contract. It's standard practice in the renovation business.'

'What happens if you don't complete on time?' Now she understood why he looked so worried.

He couldn't meet her gaze. Her brain whirred. She

knew exactly what would happen. Logan's company would have to bear the brunt of any costs.

Something twisted inside her. It had been a long time but Logan had been the father of her child. She knew exactly how much something like this would matter. If he failed to complete this job his reputation would be ruined—he could kiss his company and all his hard work goodbye.

'Is there anything I can do to help prevent the delays?' There was an edge to his voice. Determination.

From the second she'd got here all she'd wanted to do was get away. Being around Logan was claustrophobic, too cluttered—stifling, too many memories.

But she couldn't let his business fall apart because of things he had no control over. This wasn't his fault.

She hesitated. 'There will be a whole lot of paperwork that will need to be completed in Venice. That's always the thing that causes the most delays. If Louisa will allow you to be a signatory for her it could make things much easier. As you know, Italian paperwork can be complicated.'

'You want me to come to Venice?' He sounded a little stunned.

But so was she. Had she really just suggested that?

'Well…it might move things along more quickly. I will be working on the comparisons with other frescoes. If you could find any history of the village that might link Alberto Burano to being here it could also be a huge benefit.'

He nodded slowly. She could almost see him thinking everything over, weighing up the best way forward.

He stepped forward. A little closer than she expected and as she breathed in all she could smell was his woodsy aftershave.

'What day do you want me in Venice?' His voice was determined.

'Friday,' she said quickly, trying not to think about it too much.

Friday was only a few days away. She would have done some of the groundwork before he got there.

He seemed to wait a few seconds before he replied. His voice was low and husky, sending shivers down her spine. 'Friday it is.'

What had she just done?

CHAPTER FOUR

THE HEAT IN Venice was stifling. It seemed the whole world had descended on it to hear one of the world's biggest rock bands play in a concert. Piazza San Marco was positively heaving, the streets crowded beyond measure and tourists juggling to pay the inflated prices in the surrounding cafés and bars.

Venice was always hot in the summer and Lucia was used to it. Living in the middle of permanent tourist attractions meant it was rarely quiet but today was the busiest she'd ever seen it. The queue of people to get inside St Mark's Basilica snaked around the centre of the piazza twice.

Lucia glanced at her clock again. She'd expected Logan to call her over an hour ago. When they'd made the arrangement for him to come and help complete the paperwork she'd had no idea about the rock concert. It hadn't even been on her radar. She didn't want to think about what Venice Marco Polo Airport was like right now. She knew that the wait for the water buses was over an hour and that everything was going much slower than expected.

But the heat in her office was becoming claustrophobic. Even with her windows opened wide over the

Grand Canal there was no breeze. She glanced at the clock again and pulled her fitted blouse away from her back. The air conditioning rarely worked at the Italian Heritage Board. Today was no exception.

She gathered up the papers she might need, closed her windows and headed for the door. Her mobile sounded just as she walked down the stairs. Logan. She answered quickly, but could barely make out his voice for the background noise. 'Logan, where are you?'

She walked out into the bustling crowds, her feet turning automatically in the direction of San Marco, the waterbus drop-off on the Grand Canal. His voice was lost as she struggled to hear, so she continued through the thronging crowds towards the drop-off point. There, in the distance, she could see Logan and a smile flickered to her face.

His bag was clutched in one hand, alongside a pale beige jacket and his mobile phone. His white shirt was wrinkled, his hair rumpled and his face red. It was the first time in her life she'd ever seen Logan looking hot and bothered. It was kind of nice to know that could actually happen to him too.

He ran his fingers through his hair and looked around him, scanning the crowds. The rock concert had obviously caught him equally unawares.

She lifted her hand and waved at him, snaking her way through the people. A flash of relief was all over his face and gave her an unexpected glow. He moved towards her. 'Lucia, thank goodness.' He held up his hands. 'This place is even madder than usual. It wasn't until I hit the airport that I heard about the concert. I guess I should have got an earlier flight. The queue for the water taxis and buses was a mile long.'

She gave a nod and glanced at his bag. 'You look hot. How about we find somewhere to sit down and get something cool to drink?'

Logan let out a long breath, his brow furrowed. 'Do you think you'll be able to find anywhere?'

Lucia gave a little nod of her head. 'You forget, Logan. I've been here more than ten years. I know all Venice's best kept secrets.' She nodded her head for him to follow and weaved through the crowds. She was glad she'd opted out of wearing her normal business attire today. In these conditions she would have sweltered in her fitted suit dress. Instead, the lighter short-sleeved white blouse and knee-length navy skirt helped to keep her cooler. She pulled her sunglasses down from her head and snaked her way through the cobbled side streets of Venice. These were instantly cooler out of the sun's blistering rays and after a few minutes' walk they were away from the madding crowds.

She pointed towards a café with tables and parasols set on the street. Logan gave a sigh of relief and sank down into a chair. 'Perfect,' he said.

The waitress appeared instantly and they both ordered two drinks, one cool and one coffee for later.

She was still amused by how flustered he looked. 'I'm sorry about being so late, Lucia. I hope I haven't ruined your schedule for the day.'

She shook her head. 'No problem. I'd just decided to leave a little earlier because it was so hot. I'm happy to meet you outside rather than in the office.' She pulled out her files. 'I brought the paperwork with me. We can do it now, if you like.'

The waiter appeared and put their drinks on the table. Logan finished his cool drink within a few seconds, then sat back in his chair and sighed. He gave her a quirky smile and held up his hands. 'I don't remember Venice ever being this hot. What on earth is happening?'

She shrugged her shoulders. 'A cross between a heat wave and an extra twenty thousand people descending on the city at once?' She pushed the papers over towards him. 'These are the ones I need you to complete. Then we can file the fresco as a "new find" with the Heritage Board. They are the ones that can authorise any restoration that might need to take place.'

Logan was scouring the papers. He lifted his eyes towards her. 'And who would do that?'

She paused for a second, wondering if it was an answer he really wanted to hear. 'It would probably be me. I've done most of the work on all of the last frescoes that needed to be restored. It used to be my boss, Alessio Orsini, who handled fresco restoration, but once he'd trained me and overseen my work a few times he was happy to hand over the reins. I think he's looking to retire soon.'

Logan nodded slowly. He sat down his pen. 'How would you feel about working in Tuscany? There is a good chance that I'll still be there for the next few months.'

Logan was being cautious, but for some reason she felt as if a little man with icy feet was marching down her spine. It was almost as if he didn't want her there. She felt insulted.

She looked at him steadily. 'I'll go wherever I'm needed. My job is very important to me. The other personalities involved aren't important.' She picked up her cappuccino and took a sip, breaking the little caramelised biscuit at the side into pieces.

'That's not what I meant.' He reached over and grabbed her hand.

It was unexpected. A little part of the biscuit dropped from her hand onto the cobbled street.

Her eyes fixed on it lying amongst the cobbles, rather than looking at his hands or his face. She didn't pull her hand back. 'I get it, Logan. You'd rather not have to work with me. But I won't compromise on my job. We're just going to have to both be professional about it.' She lifted her gaze to meet his.

His eyes widened. 'No, Lucia. You're reading this all wrong.' He squeezed her hand. 'I know we had a difficult past. And seeing you after all these years…it's been…' He seemed to struggle to find the right word. 'It's been hard.'

She felt her heart squeeze.

He moved the position of his hand. This time his thumb was inside her palm, moving in tiny circular motions, while the rest of his hand rested over hers.

He lowered his voice. 'But it's been good to see you, Lucia. Really good. It's left me wondering why we didn't do this earlier.'

She didn't hesitate. 'Because it would have been too hard.' Her gaze was steady on his. 'And you're right, it is still hard.'

'But it doesn't have to be?' There was an edge of optimism in his voice. A little glimmer of hopefulness.

Tears prickled in her eyes. A lump rose instantly in her throat. This was dangerous territory. Business was business, but this was something else entirely. She swallowed. 'I think it always will be. There's too many memories. Too many associations.'

He didn't move. Didn't flinch. Logan had always

been like this. His thumb kept moving in little circles, the way it always had when he was trying to soothe her. And for the most part it worked. Logan had always been cool, almost like the eye of a storm. Few things made him ever raise his voice. Few things made him rattled.

She looked at him again. He was still her Logan. Still so handsome. Still so protective. Grief had made his love feel suffocating. But the truth was Logan had never been suffocating. He'd encouraged her to blossom and grow while they'd been in Florence together. He'd be the very person to tell her never to hide her light under a bushel.

Why on earth hadn't he met someone over the last twelve years? Why wasn't he married with children? It had always been what he wanted. And he'd seemed to cope so much better with the death of Ariella Rose than she had.

He'd been grief-stricken for sure. The plans they'd made for baby furniture and paraphernalia had silently disappeared. He'd spoken to the doctors regarding a proper burial. Things were difficult when a baby was so young. But Logan's calm and assuring manner had persuaded them to go along with his wishes and they'd got to lay Ariella Rose to rest in a cemetery just outside the city walls.

The short ceremony by the priest had been beautiful, the flowers and funeral arrangements all carried out by Logan—she'd been too numb to help with any of it.

It was only now, in hindsight, that she could appreciate just how hard that must have been for him. She hadn't been the only one to cry over the death of their daughter. And after he'd spent days trying to get her talk and she hadn't responded he'd finally stopped and mirrored her behaviour. Closing in on himself and shutting out the world around him.

He finally replied. 'Let's just see how things are. I'm glad we've met again, Lucia. I'm glad that you're settled in an amazing city and doing a job that you love.'

There it was. The unspoken words.

I'm glad you've finally moved on.

But had she?

All he wanted to do was reach across the table and hold her. Lucia was at her most fragile right now. He could see the hidden pain in her eyes and he hated it that he was the person who had done that to her. Hated that her association with him was her most painful memory.

He had painful memories too. But he was still able to remember the good times in Florence—running through one of the fountains during a rainstorm, watching her face when he'd come home with every flower that the street vendor had been selling, sneaking out in the morning to buy her favourite pastry and watching her nose twitch as she'd woken up to the smell. For a long time Lucia had been his joy—and the feeling had been mutual. He only wished he was still hers.

She'd haunted his dreams on and off for years. Dreams about them meeting again in some random place, having dinner together, or catching each other's eye across a crowded room.

He'd always dreaded hearing the news that she was happily married or settled with a family of her own, but somehow seeing her like this was equally hard. More than anything he wanted Lucia to be happy.

Seeing her again was sparking a whole host of emotions that he'd long forgotten. He'd never imagined that the spark between them would still feel so electric. He'd never imagined that once he'd stared into those brown eyes again he'd feel rooted to the spot and never want to break away.

Lucia brushed her chocolate hair from her shoulder. It was a little shorter than he remembered and it suited her. She pulled her hand back steadily, keeping her gaze on his. He could almost see her retreating back into herself and putting a carefully drawn line between them.

She picked up her coffee cup. 'How soon do you think you'll get the paperwork completed?'

Business. That was all she wanted to discuss with him. Even after all this time.

He nodded, picking up the biscuit from the side of his cappuccino and placing it on her saucer. He didn't miss the little hint of a smile from her.

'How soon can you tell me I can finish my renovations?'

She blinked. 'Well…' She paused. 'Actually, I'm not sure. We have to file your paperwork, then I need to do some investigating. I've made a private appointment tomorrow to view another fresco by the artist we think is involved.'

He sat back in his chair. 'Well, that's fine. I'll come with you.'

She looked surprised. 'Why would you want to come with me?'

He shrugged. 'There's not much point in me going back if I can't give Louisa good news. She needs to know that the renovations and wedding plans can continue. At the moment most of the work in the chapel has ground to a halt. There's still work ongoing in the *palazzo* but it doesn't require my supervision every day.

The chapel will be the difference between this wedding going ahead or not.'

Lucia looked thoughtful. Her fingers started twiddling with a strand of her hair and she crossed her legs, giving him a flash of her tanned skin. 'What do you know about the royal couple?'

He shook his head. 'Virtually nothing. I've mostly dealt with Lindsay, the wedding planner.' He laughed. 'Now, there's a woman I don't want to call to say there's an issue with the chapel.'

Lucia smiled. 'Will she chew you up and spit you out?' There was a little spark of amusement in her eyes. It suited her. It made her more like the Lucia he remembered. The Lucia he *wanted* to remember.

'In a heartbeat,' he said quickly. 'There's no point in going back until I know I'm safe.'

Lucia frowned. 'Where have you made arrangements to stay?'

This time he frowned too. Oh, no. 'Well, I haven't. Not yet anyway.' His brain started spinning. 'There's a small boutique hotel I stay in if I ever come to Venice. I can give them a call.' He pulled his mobile from his pocket and started dialling.

Lucia shook her head and held out her hands. 'Have you seen this place? I've never seen Venice this busy. I think everywhere will be packed out.'

So do I. He was cringing inside. He'd known as soon as he'd arrived that he would never make his flight back. It was leaving right around now. And he hadn't even made any attempt to book another. With this number of tourists he imagined that every flight and train journey, in and out of Venice, was booked for the next few days.

He pressed the phone to his ear. 'Hi, there, it's Logan Cascini. I wondered if there was any chance of reserving a room for the night.'

He listened to the reply and tried to stop the sinking feeling settling over him. 'No problem. Can you recommend anywhere else?'

The crease across Lucia's brow was deepening.

He listened to the receptionist telling him what he already knew. Venice was packed. Every hotel was fully booked for the next two days. He cut the call and gave his best attempt at a shrug. 'I'll try somewhere else.'

Lucia sucked in a breath. 'Why do you want to stay, Logan? There isn't anything that you can actually do. Did you book a flight back to Tuscany?'

Her tone was almost accusatory. He pressed a button on his phone and spun it around, showing her his online boarding card for the flight that was due to take off any minute.

Her eyes widened. 'Oh.'

She bit her lip again. 'Why do you even *want* to stay?'

The same question again. This time with a different emphasis on the words. It was obviously preying on her mind, just like it was preying on his. When he'd booked his flight he'd planned to be in Venice for four hours and leave again later today and go straight back to Tuscany. It had all seemed straightforward. Except in his mind, where a little voice kept niggling at him.

This was the contact he'd always imagined making. The renovations were a perfect excuse to be around Lucia. He hadn't planned it. It had surprised him just as much as it had surprised her. But sometimes fate had a mysterious hand in things.

After the first few awkward moments curiosity had been killing him about Lucia. He wanted to know everything about the last twelve years. He wanted to know her plans for the future. If she was happy. If she was settled.

And absolutely none of it was his business. But that didn't stop the little craving that had always been there growing into something a whole lot bigger.

There would always be something between them. Right now, it still felt as if there was a big black cloud hanging over them. But for him, he could see little remnants of sunlight struggling to get through. And he wanted them to get through. So badly.

But still something was holding him back. Holding him back from saying their daughter's name and asking Lucia if she was ready to talk about her.

So he took the easy way out. The safest way out, if he wanted to still have contact with Lucia.

'I want to stay because I want to help move this project along. I would love to see Burano's fresco. I would love to see how it compares to the Madonna and Child and to the nymph sculpture. You know I love this stuff just as much as you do.'

Part of him felt guilty. These were careful words, designed to push the little buttons inside her and help things spark along.

There was a glimmer in her eyes. He was talking her language. A language she related to and understood.

He pulled something from his bag. 'Look at this. You told me to try and find any evidence that Burano had been around the village. I've photocopied something from the local museum. One of the guest houses had an ancient register. People used to stay for months at a time.' He pointed to a blurred entry from 1530. 'I thought that might be Alberto Burano.'

She screwed up her nose and squinted at the blurred entry. It was difficult to judge but he could see the glimmer of excitement behind her eyes.

'I'm sure we'll have a sample of his writing somewhere at the heritage board.' She met his gaze. 'This could be really important, Logan. You did well to find this.'

It was the first note of approval he'd had from her and it made his heart swell in his chest. He wasn't going to tell how he'd had to bribe the local museum curator to let him riffle through all the old paperwork. He wasn't going to let her know he'd spent all of last night checking through mountains of ancient chests in order to find anything that might help.

'Can I take this?' she asked, holding up the photocopy.

He nodded as he zipped up his bag again.

'This can definitely help.' She looked around them. The number of people in the quiet street was starting to pick up. 'But where will you stay?'

The million-dollar question. He shrugged as he desperately tried to think of someone, *anyone* he still knew in Venice.

His fingers flicked through the numbers on his phone. He had a multitude of contacts in Florence, Rome and Pisa. Venice? Not so much.

'You can stay with me.'

The words came out of the blue. It was absolutely the last thing he was expecting to hear.

'What? No, I couldn't possibly put you to any trouble.' His stomach clenched.

He couldn't miss the expression on her face. She was saying the words, but it was reluctantly—this wasn't a warm invitation.

And he hated that. He hated that she felt obliged to offer him somewhere to stay—when it was obvious she didn't really want to.

That hurt.

But the reality was that he really didn't have anywhere else to go. Chances were he could spend the next two hours phoning every hotel and just get the same answer—fully booked. There was a strong likelihood he wouldn't find a bed for the night.

Part of him wanted to refuse graciously and just walk away.

But something else was burning inside…a persistence.

Lucia used to be his. She used to fill his whole world. And he knew that the feelings had been mutual.

They were both adults. They were twelve years away from their shared past. Determination was overcoming him.

He didn't want to walk away from Lucia—no matter how awkward she felt.

In another world she would love him just as much as she always had, and would be delighted to offer him somewhere to stay and he would be delighted to accept.

But in another world they wouldn't have lost Ariella Rose.

His fingers itched to reach over and touch her soft hand.

Her own hands were knotted together, turning over and over in her lap.

The rational part of his brain kicked in. He needed

to get this job back on track. He needed to finish the renovations at the *palazzo* and the chapel.

And the history-loving part of him would love to see the other fresco. This wasn't such an unreasonable offer to accept. Another night in Venice might give him a little time to get to know Lucia again.

And it seemed as though the rest of Venice might be attending a concert somewhere, leaving the beauties of Venice still to be explored...

He lifted his gaze to meet hers. 'Thank you, Lucia. You're right. I probably won't be able to find anywhere else to stay. As long as you're sure it's not too much trouble, I'd be delighted to stay.'

CHAPTER FIVE

WHAT HAD SHE just done?

Was her apartment even reasonably tidy? She didn't have any food. Well, not the kind of food to entertain with and make dinner for a guest. Chilli-flavoured crisps and orange-flavoured chocolate might be her favourite dinner but she couldn't offer it to a guest. What on earth had she been thinking?

She was desperately hoping that she appeared outwardly calm. But her heartbeat was thudding against her chest at a rate of knots. Logan gestured to the waiter and settled their bill, picking up his bag and giving her a casual smile. 'Shall we finish this paperwork back at your place?'

It was a reasonable, rational question. He couldn't possibly imagine the way the blood was racing around her system and the breath was sticking in her lungs.

'Of course,' she said as coolly as possible, with a nod of her head as she stood up.

'How far away do you live?' he asked.

She tried to smile. 'Well, that depends entirely on traffic and the time of day.'

She weaved her way through the cobbled streets towards the water-taxi stop. 'I'm only two stops along. It only takes a few minutes.'

They were lucky. The water taxis on this side of the canal weren't quite so busy. They jumped on and back off within five minutes.

Her skin was prickling. Every little hair on her arms was standing on end even though the sun was splitting the sky. Now that Logan had had a chance to cool down he was back to his normal, unruffled self. She kind of wished he was still as flustered as he had been for a few moments earlier. It made him seem less infallible. A little more vulnerable—just like she felt.

But Logan had never been vulnerable. He'd always been rock solid. Even in grief.

He jumped out of the taxi before her and held out his hand for her as she stepped from the bobbing boat. She lifted her head and tried to walk with confidence. Although her apartment overlooked the Grand Canal the entrance of the traditional building was around the back. It had been hundreds of years since people had entered directly from the canal, and the original entrance had long since been plastered over.

She couldn't hide her smile. The architect in Logan could never be hidden. His eyes were roaming over the traditional building, his smile growing wider by the second. 'You stay in an old Venetian palace?'

The admiration and wonder in his voice was obvious. She'd always known Logan would approve of her choice. The fifteenth-century building facing the Grand Canal was one of the most photographed in the district. It had distinctive Venetian floral Gothic-style architecture. The façade was pink plaster facing with intricate white detailing around all the windows and balconies that overlooked the canal. The arches on the balconies were topped with delicate quatrefoil windows, resembling flowers with four petals.

She gave him a smile as she opened the entranceway. 'Just wait until you see the inside. We have our own high ceilings, beams, alcoves and frescoes. The whole place is full of original features.'

Logan was nodding, his eyes wide as they stepped inside. She'd always loved this about him. The way a glimpse of architectural details of a building could capture his attention instantly. He would become instantly enthralled, desperate to know more about the building and its history. Architecture had always been Logan's dream. But renovating ancient buildings? That was his calling. Always had been.

A bit like hers had been painting.

The memory swept through her like a gust of stormy weather.

Another part of life put into a box. When she'd first got together with Logan, their apartment had been littered with brushes, easels and oils. She had painted all the time, usually wearing nothing more than one of his shirts. She'd loved the feel of having him right next to her as she'd created, and if he hadn't been there, the scent of him—his aroma and aftershave—would usually linger on one of his shirts waiting to be washed. Thoughts of Logan had always fired her creative juices.

A warm feeling crept across her stomach. Logan had always loved finding her like that, his shirt loose around her body and her hair twisted on top of her head with an errant paintbrush holding it in place. He'd usually pulled it free, followed by the shirt, and the following hours had been lost in a rush of love.

But that light had flickered out and died along with the death of their daughter. For a long time she couldn't even bear to look at a paintbrush, let alone hold one.

Working for the heritage board had helped her heal. She didn't paint her own creations any more. But she did paint. Restoration work was painstaking. In every fresco she restored she tried to re-create the passion and drama that the original artist had felt when he'd envisaged the work.

There was still a little part of her that longed to feel like that again too.

There was a lift inside her building but Logan was captivated by the grandiose staircase inside the entranceway. As it curved upwards there were archways hollowed out in the plaster in the walls. A long time ago each had been painted individually and had held sculptures. In between each hollowed archway was a large circular fresco embedded into the plaster on the walls.

Logan moved quickly up the stairs, stopping to admire each individual one. 'These are amazing,' he said, his hand hovering about them. Logan's professional expertise knew far better than to actually touch.

She followed him upwards. A warmth was spreading through her. She was proud of her home—and secretly pleased that the man she'd shared part of her life with loved it just as much as she did.

As they walked upwards she leaned a little closer and whispered, 'I might have restored some of these.'

His head shot around towards her. 'You did?'

She nodded as his eyes fixed on the walls again. His fingers were still hovering just above a fresco of Moses. 'You've made an amazing job of these.'

'Thank you,' she said simply, as they reached her

floor and she pulled out her key and opened the apartment door.

He walked inside and looked around. Her living area was spacious and held a dining table and chairs and two wooden-footed red sofas. As with most Italian traditional apartments the floor was marble. A dark wooden bookcase adorned one wall, jam-packed with books.

But the most spectacular aspect of the apartment was the view. Lucia strode across the room and pulled open the black-and-gilt-edged glass doors. The warm air and noise from the Grand Canal below flooded in. It was like flicking a button and bringing the place to life. Next to the doors was a small wooden table, a chaise longue and an armchair. It was like having a real-live television. You could sit here all day and night and watch the world go by.

She knew his head must be spinning. This apartment was sumptuous. Well out of her price range. She stood shoulder to shoulder with him, watching the *vaporetti* and private boats motor past. On the other side of the canal stood another magnificent long-abandoned palace. Renaissance in style again, with Gothic-styled windows and ornate frescoes on the outside of the building.

He turned towards her and smiled. 'It's almost like your perfect view, isn't it?' There was an edge of curiosity in his voice. But he wasn't going to ask the question out loud. Logan was far too polite for that.

'Coffee?' she asked, as she walked towards the kitchen. It was right next door to the open living area and again had windows looking out on the canal. He nodded and walked in next to her, sitting down on one of the high stools looking over the canal. She switched on her coffee-machine and put in her favourite blend.

She leaned back against the countertop. 'I haven't always stayed here,' she said quietly. 'After I'd been in Venice for two years one of my colleagues retired from the heritage board. They subsidise our living arrangements because—as you know—Venice can be very expensive.' She held out her hands. 'I sort of inherited this place. I pay roughly the same as we did for our apartment in Florence.' She watched his eyebrows rise and couldn't stop the smile. 'It was like all my Saturdays at once.' She laughed as she watched the coffee brew and pointed across the waterway. 'Do you know, they actually asked me how I'd feel about staying here? It was all I could do not to snatch the key and just run.'

The warm feeling was spreading further. She rarely brought friends back to her apartment. This place was her sanctuary. From the moment she'd stepped inside it had always felt like that.

She'd thought having Logan here would be unbearable. She'd been so busy focusing on all the negatives she hadn't even considered the positives.

He was fascinated by the building's history and traditional architecture. He respected the heritage just as much as she did.

She poured the coffee into two mugs and set them on the table, watching the steam rising while she frothed some milk and added it to the mugs.

She gestured with her hand. 'Come and I'll show you where your room is.'

She hadn't even had time to prepare anything and she had to hope that nothing was out of place in her barely used guest suite. She led him down the corridor off the kitchen. It was the only place in her apartment that didn't have natural light.

He grabbed her elbow as they walked down the corridor. 'Are you sure this is okay?'

She turned to face him. He was much closer than she'd expected, his warm breath hitting her cheek. For a second she was frozen. This was as up close and personal as she'd been to Logan in years. The closeness took her breath away.

Even in the dim light of the corridor his green eyes made her struggle to think clearly. He was worried. He was worried about her. And glances like that brought back painful memories.

A tiny little part of her wished that Logan was looking at her in a different way. The way he used to, with passion and laughter in his eyes. She wanted to reach up and touch him. Touch the skin on his cheek, the shadowed outline of his jaw, and run her fingers through his dark hair. She wanted him to step forward just a few inches to see if their bodies still fitted together after all this time.

Her heart was racing and Logan blinked. He was staring at a spot on her neck where she was sure he could see the rapid beating of her pulse.

She took a deep breath and turned away, trying to blink back threatening tears. This was why everything about this was a bad idea.

She swung open a dark wooden door, flooding the corridor with light and stepping into a white and blue room. It was still traditional. A double bedroom with a window overlooking the canal, pale blue walls and fresh white bed linen. It wasn't quite as sumptuous as the other rooms in the house as it was rarely used.

She nodded her head. 'The bathroom is next door. Don't worry, we won't have to share. The box room was converted to an en suite. Would you like some time to settle in?'

He shook his head. 'Your coffee smells too good to let it go to waste. Let's finish the paperwork then we can decide where I'm taking you to dinner.' There was a glimmer in his eye. 'I don't expect you to cook for me—not if I want to live to tell the tale.'

He'd caught her unawares and she threw back her head and laughed. 'I offer you a room for the night and this is the thanks I get?'

He gave her a steady smile. 'Let's just wait until dinner.' She could almost hear his brain ticking over and her stomach gave a little leap.

What on earth did he have planned?

Logan washed up and changed his wrinkled shirt. Thank goodness he always had a spare in his bag.

He looked around the room. It was comfortable but sparse—it was clear this room didn't get much use. Didn't Lucia have friends to stay? She'd had a few girl-friends at university but he had no idea if they'd kept in touch.

He sighed and looked out of the window. It was ridiculous but he was having a hard time with this.

Lucia had a job she loved and a fabulous apartment in one of the most cosmopolitan cities in the world. He should be overjoyed for her. In his head, all he'd ever wanted was for her to be happy. In a twisted kind of way this was his ideal situation.

She was happy. She was settled. But there was no husband and kids on the scene to let the tiny leaves of jealousy unfurl. To let him know that she'd taken the final steps.

He couldn't quite work out why he was feeling so unsettled. All he knew was that there was something in her eyes. A guarded part. A hidden part. A little piece of her that didn't look quite…alive.

That was what bothered him. Lucia had a fabulous life. But was she really living?

He glanced around. While this room was sparsely furnished, the rest of the apartment was sumptuous. The reds and golds complemented the grandeur of the ancient palace. There were lots of similar buildings scattered across Venice. It seemed everyone who'd ever been slightly royal had built a palace in Venice. It was no wonder the heritage board wanted to keep someone in here.

He walked through to the main room. Lucia was sitting in a chair next to the open doors, the sights and sounds of the Grand Canal drifting up towards them. She'd changed into a purple jersey wrap-around dress, her dark chocolate-brown hair falling over her shoulders in waves. Her legs were curled up underneath her and she was reading a book.

Sitting on the table next to her was a glass of red wine. He smiled. 'Merlot or Chianti?'

Her head lifted in surprise. 'What do you think?'

He glanced out at the busy traffic on the Grand Canal. 'A warm summer evening? An aperitif before dinner?' He put his finger on his chin. 'I'm trying to think what you've planned for dinner—will it be meat or pasta?'

She used to be so fussy. He could imagine there were only certain local restaurants that she'd visit.

She held up her glass towards him. 'Maybe it will be both?'

She was teasing. He shook his head and pointed to the glass. 'It must be Merlot. It's too warm an evening for steak. You're planning for pasta.'

Something flickered across her face. She didn't like it that after twelve years he could still read her. She gestured towards the dining table where the bottle of wine and another glass sat. 'Find out for yourself.'

Logan walked over and filled his glass, resisting the temptation to smile. 'Where do you think we're eating tonight?'

She raised her eyebrows. 'What makes you think we'll be eating anywhere? Haven't you heard—it's the busiest night of the year in Venice?'

He sat down on the chaise longue next to her chair. 'But I might know an out-of-the-way place that the tourist hordes don't know about—like Erona's in Florence.'

There was a flash of something behind her eyes and she stood up quickly. He'd upset her.

She didn't want direct reminders of their time in Florence. 'You're not from here. How would you know where to eat?'

'Let's just say that your boss, Alessio, gave me a few hints.'

She slid her feet into a pair of red-soled black patent stilettos with impossibly high heels.

'Wherever we're going, I hope they have flat surfaces,' he muttered. Alessio had told him to get to the restaurant—just not what the streets around it were like.

'Let's go, Logan. Our viewing is early tomorrow morning. I want to get an early night.'

The words sent a flurry of sparks across his brain. An early night. With Lucia Moretti. It was enough to send his whole body into overdrive.

His eyes focused on her behind as she crossed the room ahead of him in her impossibly high heels. Her dress clung to every curve.

He swallowed. This was going to be a long, uncomfortable night.

Venice was virtually silent at this time in the morning. The private motor boat glided through the water towards the Venetian island of Giudecca.

Logan was curious. 'I thought all the artefacts of historical value would have been commandeered by the Italian Heritage Board?'

Lucia gave a sigh. 'In theory, they can. But part of this island is private—has been since before Renaissance times. It's owned by the Brunelli family. They built the church here and commissioned the artist, Burano, to paint the fresco. Technically, we're just their guests. We're allowed access to the fresco on request. You'll understand why when you see it—it's a little unusual.'

The boat came to a halt at the dock and they disembarked onto the wooden structure. A white stone path led them directly to the church, where a dark-suited man was waiting for them. Logan recognised him immediately—Dario Brunelli was frequently nicknamed Italian's most eligible bachelor. *He knew Lucia?*

'Lucia,' he said swiftly, bending to kiss her on both cheeks, 'it's good to see you again. How have you been?'

His familiarity with Lucia grated instantly. Her reaction was even worse—she seemed relaxed in his company. 'I'm good, thank you.' She turned towards Logan. 'Dario, this is Logan Cascini, a specialist restoration architect from Florence. He's working with me on the project in Tuscany.'

It was completely true. But it made it sound as if they'd only just met. As if there was no shared history between them at all.

For a second he held his breath, wondering if Dario was having the same thoughts that he'd had this morning when he'd first seen Lucia. Her cream fitted business suit and pale pink shirt hugged her curves. The knee-length skirt exposed her slim legs. And her dark hair and eyes complemented the package perfectly. Lucia looked good enough to eat.

Dario nodded towards Logan but it was clear his focus was on Lucia. 'So, do you think you've found another of Burano's frescoes?'

Lucia's smile was broad. 'I think there is a distinct possibility. With your permission, I'm going to take some high-resolution digital shots to compare the brush-strokes.'

Dario was nodding enthusiastically. 'In Tuscany? I wonder how in the world Burano ended up working there? Wouldn't it be wonderful if it was another of his works?'

A Renaissance art lover. The passion and enthusiasm in his eyes was for the art, not for Lucia. Not for his woman.

Where had that come from?

Cold air prickled his skin and he shifted on his feet. Lucia hadn't been his woman for twelve years—she hadn't wanted to be.

And he'd had to live with that. He'd had to support the fact she wasn't able to continue their relationship and allow her the space she'd needed to heal. No matter how much it had ripped his heart in two.

No one else had ever come close to the love he'd

felt for Lucia. How could they? She'd been the mother of his child. And even though that was something she wanted to forget, her place in his heart had been well and truly cemented there.

But even he hadn't realised how much.

'Forgive me.' Dario nodded. 'I have to go. I have business to attend to. Please, take all the time you need.'

Lucia gave a gracious nod of her head as Dario walked swiftly down the path towards the waiting motorboat.

She turned and pressed her hand against the heavy wooden door of the church and smiled at Logan. There was a gleam of something in her eye. He only hoped it was for the contents of the church and not for the retreating back of Dario. The spike of jealousy had been unexpected—a feeling he hadn't dealt with in years.

'Ready?' she asked.

He nodded and she pushed the door and it groaned and creaked loudly on its hinges as it swung back. The church wasn't lit.

The only light that streamed in came through six muted stained-glass windows above the altar.

It took a few seconds for his eyes to adjust to the dim light. He caught his breath.

The fresco on the wall was magnificent and stretched from one end of the church to the other. His feet moved automatically towards it.

Over his years in Italy he'd seen many frescoes— but none quite like this. It was completely and utterly unique, almost like a timeline through the first book of the bible.

She rested her hand on his arm. 'I've never seen anything like it before, and I'm quite sure I'll never see anything like it again.' He could hear the amusement in her voice at his reaction. 'It's a little different from the Madonna and Child, isn't it?'

He shook his head as he took in more and more of the fresco. He recognised the characters—at least, he thought he did. Adam and Eve, Noah, Moses, Jacob and his sons. But the thing that made these characters unique was the fact they were all completely naked.

He spun to face her. 'What on earth...?'

She laughed. 'I know. It's why the Italian Heritage Board hasn't bothered to make demands on the family. The Catholic Church would be outraged by these scenes.'

Logan moved forward. He just couldn't stop smiling. He was trying to think rationally. 'Adam and Eve—you might expect them to be naked. But the rest...' He kept looking at the scenes. 'It's amazing. I mean, apart from their nakedness the depictions are accurate. Eve with the apple, Moses leading the Israelites through the Red Sea, Noah on the ark, and Jacob with his twelve sons.' He let out a laugh. 'Joseph is even holding his multi-coloured coat instead of wearing it.'

She shrugged her shoulders. 'Naked bodies were pretty much the fashion during Renaissance times.' Her brow creased slightly. 'But usually they had something—anything—draped around about them. These ones are totally original.'

Logan stepped back a little. 'But there's something else, isn't there? I can't quite put my finger on it.' He paused, staring hard at the scenes, looking between one and another.

She nodded, with an amused expression on her face. 'Give it time, Logan. You'll get it.'

She was teasing him. It was almost like throwing down a challenge. So he took a few minutes, concentrating hard until, finally, the penny dropped.

He turned to her in amazement. 'It's the faces, isn't it?' He stepped right up to the fresco, staring first at the face of Adam then at the face of Moses, then Noah. 'It's the same face.' His eyes scanned one way, then the other. 'It's the same man and woman in every scene.'

Lucia was laughing. 'You're right. The family don't have any official records about who commissioned the fresco. The name of Burano has just been passed down through the family. That's why we'll have to do a comparison. And we're not quite sure why it's the same faces in all the scenes. I've spoken to the family about it at length. We think there's something a little narcissistic in it. We think that when the original Brunellis commissioned the artist they asked for the faces to be made in their image.'

Logan let out a burst of laughter. 'You mean, even all those years ago we had fame-hungry people?' He shook his head. 'Wow, just wow.'

He took another few seconds and stopped in front of the young Joseph holding the coat. 'I still can't believe they wouldn't let Joseph wear his multi-coloured coat.'

She bent down in the front of the fresco. In the dim light he could see her dark eyes were still gleaming. 'Yes, but look at the folds in the cloak. What do you see?'

He looked closer. 'Of course. They look exactly like the folds in the Madonna's dress in the fresco in Tuscany. That's what you noticed.'

There wasn't a sound in the dark church. They were entirely alone, crouching on the floor. The lack of artificial light was almost like a safety blanket around them.

His face was only inches from hers. Their gazes meshed. It was a moment. An instant. For just that second she had the same passion and wonder in her eyes that she'd had twelve years ago. Twelve years ago when they'd thought they could conquer the world.

He'd been trying so hard to hold his tongue, trying to keep a handle on how he felt about everything, but the memories of Lucia were just overtaking him. The spark of jealousy, the protectiveness, the connection between them. He was like a pressure cooker just waiting to go off.

Her pupils were dilating in front of him, the blackness overtaking the chocolate brown of her eyes. He was pretty certain his were doing exactly the same.

All of a sudden he couldn't stop himself. He leaned forward, just a few inches, and caught the back of her head in his hand, tangling his fingers through her hair as he pulled her towards him.

And then he stopped thinking entirely...

She was instantly transported back twelve years. The familiarity was astounding.

No one had kissed her like this in twelve years.

No kiss had felt so right.

No kiss had felt so perfect.

Her body moved on automatic pilot, ignoring all the little neurons that were firing in her brain. Ignoring every single rational thought that might be there.

She could only act on instinct. Her hands slid through his thick, dark hair, her fingers tugging and pulling at his head. She could taste him. She could smell him.

Everything about him was familiar. His scent was winding its way around her like a coiling snake. Her hands moved, sliding across his muscled shoulders and arms and down the planes of his chest.

His lips never left hers. Their teeth clashed, his tongue tangling with hers. Crouching on a floor wasn't comfortable for kissing. Logan sensed that and pulled her up against him, his strong legs lifting them both upwards, keeping their bodies in contact the whole time.

She could feel his heart thudding against her chest. Feel her breath catching in her throat.

It was so easy to be swept away. It was so easy to forget about everything else. His fingertips brushed across the front of her breasts as she sucked in a sharp breath, then rounded her hips and stopped firmly on her behind, pulling her even closer to him.

There was no mistaking his reaction to her. There was no mistaking he was every bit as caught up in this as she was.

So when he stopped kissing her she was shocked.

He pulled his lips back from hers and rested his forehead against hers, breathing heavily. His body was still interlocked with hers. It seemed he had no intention of moving.

Her hands, resting against his chest, clenched.

Embarrassment swamped her. She wanted to step back but couldn't.

What on earth was he thinking?

Then, to her surprise, he let out a deep laugh. It wasn't a mocking laugh. It wasn't derogatory. It was more one of astonishment.

In the dark church his voice was husky. 'So that's what I've been missing.' He took a deep breath. 'I sometimes wondered if my mind was playing tricks on me. If I'd imagined how good it was.'

He was echoing her thoughts. She'd felt exactly the same way. Any time she'd allowed memories of Logan to sneak into her brain, she'd always thought it couldn't possibly have been as good as she remembered it. Everything before Ariella Rose, that was.

The portcullis that was always stiffly in place was shaken a little. The thick gate had risen just a tiny bit, leaving the thinnest gap underneath. The black cloud of self-protection that usually cloaked her was thinning in patches.

Their foreheads were still touching. She could feel his warm breath on her cheeks. 'It wasn't all that bad, was it?' she whispered.

His fingers stroked through her soft hair. 'Some parts were really good,' he breathed quietly.

She stayed where she was—for a few more seconds.

This was only a moment of madness. A tiny little step back in time.

It wasn't real. None of this was real.

Real life meant that now she lived and worked in Venice and Logan lived and worked in Florence.

The meeting at Tuscany was merely a blip. The next few weeks of working together would only be a continuation of that blip. She could almost feel the protective coating going around her heart. She had to be careful. She had to be sensible.

She lifted her head back from his, trying to ignore the warm feeling of his beating heart beneath her palm.

It was time to put all the safeguards back in place.

She gave him a rueful smile and stepped back, freeing herself from his grasp.

The movement jolted Logan. He straightened his

back, watching her carefully. It was almost as if he knew what was coming next.

'We don't really have time to reminisce, Logan. I have work to do. You have work to do. The sooner we can verify the artist of the fresco, the sooner we can both move towards our goals.'

What were her goals? She'd always been clear about them in the past, but right now they were looking pretty muddy.

Silence hung in the air between them. It almost shimmered in the slowly brightening daylight.

She could almost hear him processing what she'd said.

He chose his words carefully as he stepped forward and gently touched her cheek. 'You're right, Lucia. It's best we leave things as they are.' He nodded his head. 'We both need to focus on work.'

Something squeezed in her chest. For a few seconds she felt as if she couldn't breathe.

Part of her wished he'd said no. Part of her wished he'd pull her back into his arms and kiss her all over again. Acknowledge this thing that shimmered in the air between them and refuse to walk away from it.

But that was all a fairy tale. This was real life. She could tell from the slight waver in his voice that he was saying what he thought he should. This was just as hard for him as it was for her.

If this was anyone else she might think they were toying with her. But Logan just wasn't capable of that kind of thing. Not after what they'd shared.

This was for the best. It didn't matter that little parts of her brain were screaming at her. Every female hormone she'd ever possessed was currently marching in a charge towards all parts of her body.

She blinked back the tears that were hovering behind her eyes. His fingers felt like butterfly wings on her skin. It was all she could do not to tilt her head towards his hand.

She bent down and picked up her papers, which were strewn on the floor, trying not to acknowledge her trembling hands.

His feet took a step backwards. She could sense him bending over her, probably reaching towards her, then he took a few further steps back. It was almost as if he forcing himself into a position of retreat.

She straightened up and fixed a false smile on her face. 'Let's get to work, Logan. Can you see if we can find some light?' She pulled her camera from her bag. 'The sooner we get these pictures, the sooner we can move forward.'

She tried not to wince at her choice of words.

But Logan's expression was resolute. Guarded. She had no idea what was going on behind those green eyes.

He gave a brief nod. 'Of course.' And walked back towards the door to let in some light.

She turned back to the fresco.

Work. The only thing that was currently keeping her sane.

CHAPTER SIX

WORK WAS THE easy part. It didn't take any time at all for Lucia to take the photos and to take the boat trip back to her office. The rest of Venice had woken up now, with the city becoming loud and colourful as their boat glided back through the water.

The Italian Heritage Board building was every bit as exuberant as Logan had expected it to be. The architecture was a welcome distraction, with some of the really exclusive Renaissance pieces of art housed in the building.

Lucia had uploaded the pictures to her computer and was running a comparison computer program that would take a few hours.

All they could do was wait.

And waiting was something Logan Cascini had never been good at.

After that kiss he was finding it difficult to keep his cool, collected manner in place. One touch of Lucia's lips had been enough to ignite all the sparks in his brain and frustration had been building ever since.

He'd had enough. Not of Lucia. He'd had enough of them being in the same room together and not talking about the big elephant between them. Ariella Rose.

It was twelve years on. It was time. Even if Lucia still felt that it wasn't.

There was no way he was getting on that plane back to Tuscany without tackling the subject. No way at all.

But how?

She had barriers erected so tightly around her she might as well have been wearing a spacesuit. The kiss had been one thing. She'd probably already written it off as a blip.

But Logan couldn't do that. He wanted more. Much more.

No wonder every other relationship he'd had had fizzled out. No wonder he'd never wanted to commit to someone else.

This was nothing to do with losing his daughter. This wasn't about the fear of another pregnancy or another child.

It was much more primal than that. It was about the fear of never finding someone he had the same chemistry with, the same connection with, as he had with Lucia.

Life was hard. Life was tough. But twelve years of drifting had given him new determination.

Seeing Lucia for the first time again had been like a lightning bolt. Kissing her again…well, that had been so much more.

It was time to face things head-on.

He turned from the view of Venice to face her. She was sitting behind her desk, twiddling her long dark hair around one finger.

He reached forward and grabbed her other hand, pulling her to her feet. 'Let's go.'

She looked shocked. 'Let's go where?'

He held out his other hand. 'Out there. Let's see Venice.' He pointed to the screen. 'You already said the computer program would take a few hours. Let's spend them wisely.' He grinned at her. 'Today I am a tourist. Today I want you to show me Venice.'

A hint of a smile appeared on her face. She waved towards the window. 'But it will be crazy out there. There's another concert tonight. We'll have all of last night's gig-goers and all of tonight's too.'

He raised his eyebrows. 'What, we can't handle a few tourists?'

She shook her head and let out a little laugh. 'Now I know you're definitely crazy.' She picked up her handbag and swung it over her shoulder. 'You're right, the program will take another few hours, and as long as we start with ice cream I'm in.'

He held out his hand towards her.

She hesitated. She wavered. He could see it in every inch of her body. She finally let out the breath she'd been holding and put her hand in his.

'Let's go.'

It was hotter than hot. Her jacket was hanging over the top of her shoulder bag to try and deter any pickpockets and her shirt was in danger of sticking to her back.

The queue for ice cream was snaking its way out the door of her favourite gelateria. She tugged Logan towards the end of the queue. His hand was still in hers. It felt odd, but she hadn't quite managed to pull her hand free of his.

The walk through the twisting cobbled streets had been like a step back in time. She'd noticed the women's admiring glances. Logan was every woman's Italian dream—dark-haired, broad shouldered, well dressed and devilishly handsome. His unexpected bright green eyes added a little twist.

And he was free with his natural charm. He nodded and smiled at the numerous pairs of acknowledging eyes. A tiny swell of pride surged in her chest. Memories flickered in her brain. People thought they were a couple. People thought that Logan was hers.

He turned to face her as the queue slowly moved forward. 'What kind of ice cream do you want? I take it you've sampled them all?'

She gave a little smile. 'All in the name of research. Dark chocolate and *limon* are my two favourites from here.'

He nodded at her choices. 'In that case we'll get one of each. Why not try everything you like?' He was smiling as he said the words, and the woman in front turned around with a gleam in her eyes.

Lucia shifted on her feet. She didn't want to allow the tiny seeds in her brain to flower and grow.

Logan reached the front of the queue, ordering their ice creams and only releasing her hand when he reached to pay for them. They walked out into the building heat and he held both hands out towards her. 'What'll it be? The dark, tantalising chocolate or the sweet, zesty lemon?'

He was teasing her. But the surprising thing was, she kind of liked it.

She held her hand out for the chocolate. 'I'll start with dark and delicious.' Her fingers brushed against his. 'But don't count on getting to finish the lemon yourself,' she said smartly as she walked past.

Within seconds he was walking shoulder to shoulder

with her. 'Where do you want to play tourist, then?' she asked. 'I can't imagine that you want to visit Piazza San Marco, St Mark's Basilica or the Clock Tower.'

He shook his head. 'Too busy, and anyway I much prefer Piazza San Marco at night. Much more romantic,' he added.

She ignored the comment.

He pointed over in the distance. 'What I'd really like to do is catch a *vaporetto* to San Giorgio Maggiore and go up the campanile. It's still early. There will hardly be any crowds.'

She gave him a sideways glance as she veered towards the nearest *vaporetto* stop. 'Hmm, so you're still a tourist at heart, then?'

He shrugged. 'It's been a few years since I've been in Venice. But I'm an Italian, I still know where to go to get the best view of the city.' He held out his ice cream towards her. 'Swap?'

She nodded. The dark chocolate was starting to taste a little bitter. She took a nibble of the lemon and sweet, tangy zest nearly made her taste buds explode. But her brain didn't have time to focus on that because Logan had slung his arm around her shoulders and was walking easily next to her as if they did it every day.

And it *did* feel like they did it every day. She fitted under his arm. Always had—always would.

He chatted as they made their way along to the *vaporetto* stop, joining the small number of waiting people and climbing on board as soon as it arrived. Most of the rest of the passengers were heading to Murano—the island famous for its glassware. He glanced at her as the boat stopped. 'Did you want to get off here?'

She shook her head. 'I love Murano glass—I have the

most gorgeous red and gold vase in my apartment—but I don't like the hordes of tourists, or what they make for them. If I see one more orange fish in a clear square cube I'll scream.'

She was standing near the front of the boat and he laughed and pulled her down next to him as the next load of passengers climbed on board. 'You old Venice snob.'

'Oh, come on, you were exactly the same way in Florence. You hated the millions of ornaments of the cathedral and baptistery.'

He lifted his ice cream towards her. 'Guilty as charged.' Then he glanced at the activity on the Grand Canal. 'But sometimes it's nice to play tourist.'

They sat in silence for a few minutes as the boat glided along the canal. It was busy this morning, making the ride a little bumpy, and she inched closer and closer to him. His arm stayed loosely on her shoulders as they reached the stop for San Giorgio. Ice creams finished, they wiped their hands on the napkins provided and climbed out of the boat.

It was getting hotter but most of the tourists hadn't reached the island yet and the queue for the lift to the top of the campanile meant they only had a ten-minute wait.

Logan shook his head as they approached. 'This is one of the architectural glories of Venice. Palladio is one of my favourite architects. Look at it, the gleaming white Istrian marble façade and lithe brick and bell tower—why, it almost seems to float in the middle of the Bacino San Marco, supported on its own tiny island. It's only a few hundred yards off St Mark's Square but most people just take a photo on the way past. They have no idea it's decorated with works by Tintoretto,

Carpaccio and Jacopo Bassano. This is the one place in Venice I just wouldn't want to miss.'

Lucia smiled at him. The passion and enthusiasm in his voice was so good to hear. She could see heads turning at his voice, obviously relieved they'd chosen this venue to visit.

The lift opened to take them up the sixty-metre-high bell tower and a few minutes later they stepped out on to the observation deck. Logan held out his arms and spun around. 'And this is why I love this place. Hardly a queue to get in, only a couple of euros and no crowding up here. The view is perfect.' He pointed across the water towards the campanile San Marco. 'While our brother over there has long lines, a higher price tag, is crowded and doesn't have the same panoramic views.'

Lucia grinned. 'But you can get a full-on postcard shot of the Piazza San Marco just across the water.' She pulled out her phone and held it in front of her, snapping a quick photo.

'Hold it.' Logan pulled out his own phone, but put his hands on her shoulders and turned her, so instead of having a background shot of Piazza San Marco he had a full shot of the Grand Canal. 'Smile,' he said as he held up his phone. 'You know, on a clear day you can see right across the Adriatic Sea and all the way to the Alps.'

The smile was still on her face and she didn't have much time to think about the fact that Logan would now have a picture of her on his phone. As soon as he'd snapped the shot he walked over and leaned his elbows on the balcony, looking out at the panoramic view. 'This is what Venice should be about,' he said quietly.

She spun around and put her elbows next to his. There were a few other people wandering around on the observation deck, but it was nowhere near as busy here as it was on the other side of the water. St Mark's Square was already packed. It seemed most of the people who'd attended the concert hadn't had much sleep.

She could hardly blame them. Anyone who was lucky enough to visit Venice—even for a few hours— usually tried to squeeze in as many of the sights as they possibly could.

Something flickered through her brain. With one concert last night and another tonight there would be a whole host of new people in and out of the city today. 'You won't be able to get a flight home today either, will you?'

A gentle breeze blew across her skin. She wasn't quite sure how she felt about this. Having Logan stay over one night had seemed like an unavoidable hiccup. Having him stay for two nights was something else entirely.

He didn't answer for a few seconds, fixing his eyes instead on the hustle and bustle of the masses of people on the other side of the canal. 'I'm sorry, Lucia.' He ran his fingers through his hair. 'I had no idea about any of this. I didn't mean to put you in a difficult position.'

He looked a little uncomfortable but not entirely unhappy. She'd hardly slept a wink last night. How could she, knowing that the person she used to love with her whole heart had been lying naked next door?

Logan had always slept naked, hating anything on his skin once he was in bed. The only thing he'd ever wanted next to his skin had been her.

She was trying so hard to seem cool, to seem professional. The atmosphere between them today had been lighter, less pressured.

Exactly the opposite from what it should have been after that kiss.

But that kiss had ignited the good memories in her brain. Before that, everything about Logan had been a build-up of frustration and a reminder of grief.

It was almost as if that kiss had brought alive the side of her brain she'd shut off. She just didn't know what to do with it.

'It's fine, Logan,' she said quickly, as she held out her hand towards the busy St Mark's Square. 'The hotels will be every bit as busy again today. Don't worry.'

His head turned towards her and he lifted his hand, running one finger down her arm towards her hand. 'But I do worry, Lucia. I'll always worry about you.' His voice was low, husky and it sent a little tremble up her spine.

She couldn't turn to face him, just kept looking out at the people of Venice as her skin tingled and his hand slid over hers, slowly interlocking their fingers.

Her breath caught in her chest. Just when she'd thought she was safe around Logan. Just when she'd thought she could relax, he did something like this.

Something that made her catch her breath and nibble her bottom lip.

It was the closeness that made her feel vulnerable. Made her feel as if she was on the verge of opening herself up to a whole host of hurt. She'd spent so long protecting herself, hiding herself away.

Logan was a whole part of her life that she'd chosen to close the door on. But having him standing next to her, his breath warming her cheek and his hand interlocked with hers, was like dangling her over a precipice she wasn't ready for.

And it was as if he could sense it. He didn't go any further. Didn't make any other move. Didn't bring up the biggest subject in the world.

Logan was carefully skirting around the edges of her life. But he wouldn't stay there for ever.

'How do you enjoy living and working in Venice?'

She swallowed, trying to push all other thoughts away. 'I love Venice. But it's not the city that captures my soul. I still miss Florence.'

The words took her by surprise. She'd always felt like that. She'd just never said it out loud.

He was facing her again and she could feel his eyes watching her carefully. She wondered if he'd pick her up on what she'd just said. But he didn't. He let it go, keeping things in safe territory. 'How do the restorations work?'

She lifted her other hand and pulled her hair off her neck. It was getting even hotter. 'I've done at least one every year I've worked for the heritage board. Always on frescoes. If they decide the fresco in Tuscany is genuine and is to be restored, then that will be my job.'

She knew why he was asking. He would be in Tuscany for the next few months and he was trying to think ahead. If a few days were difficult, how would they manage to work in the same environment for a few months?

At least, she thought that's what would be on his mind.

It couldn't be the kiss. It *wouldn't* be the kiss. Not when there was so much more to think about.

'How do you feel about coming down to Tuscany?'

It was work. Of course it was work. She didn't know whether to feel disappointment or relief. The touching and handholding was nothing. It was just Logan back to his usual charming self, trying to make everyone around him feel good.

She stared at the packed street across from her and smiled. 'While I love Venice, and I love my apartment, the summer months are extremely busy. Tuscany seems a lot more peaceful than here. It might be nice to have some clean fresh air and some quiet to be able to concentrate on the restoration work.' She turned her body towards him, finally relaxed enough to give him a smile. 'I think I'll like it.'

But Logan wasn't staring at her the way she'd thought. He'd moved his thumb underneath their interlocked fingers and was gently making circles on the underside of her palm, This was what he'd used to do when he was deep in thought...when he was contemplating something carefully. His eyes were lowered and his voice quiet. 'How would you feel...?'

She inched a little closer to hear him.

He tried again. 'How would you feel if I asked you to stay with me when you came back to Tuscany, instead of in the main *palazzo* with Louise?'

Now he did look up. But he didn't have the quiet assuredness that usually always possessed him. Now he looked wary.

The words were very unexpected. She'd just gone back into that 'safe' zone, the one where no one could touch her and no one could threaten her. His words catapulted her straight back out.

The voices in the background blended together into one constant murmur as the rapid beating of her heart thudded in her eardrums. His thumb hadn't stopped moving in those little circles. It was almost as if he'd been trying to prepare her, to soothe her, before he'd asked the question.

Her brain felt jumbled. She didn't quite know what to say. 'I don't think... I don't think that would work,' was all she could fumble out.

His fingers tensed around hers. 'Why? Why wouldn't it work? You're my oldest friend. Twelve years have passed, Lucia, and you and I are still trapped there. Why aren't you married to someone else with a houseful of kids? Why aren't I?'

Now it was too much. That little question had turned into a whole lot more. She was standing overlooking this beautiful city, people all around her, and yet she felt hideously exposed. If she could transport herself, right now, back into her bed and under her covers, that's exactly what she'd do.

'I don't want to be married,' she blurted out, causing a few heads to turn in their direction. Instantly, she understood what she'd done. People were casting their eyes down in sympathy, as if Logan had just proposed and it had gone horribly wrong.

She shook her head. 'I'm happy with my work. I'm happy with my life.'

He put his hand behind her waist and pulled her towards him. His voice was quiet but there was an edge of frustration that only she could hear. Only she could understand.

'Look at me, Lucia. Look at me and tell me that you've tried to have other relationships. Tell me that you've met some suitably nice, handsome men—just like I've met some beautiful and good women—but something just hasn't been right. It hasn't felt the way it used to feel—the way it *should* feel. You could never go on and take the next step because you knew, deep down, that you'd ultimately hurt this good and loving person. You'd never quite love them the way that they loved you.'

It was almost as if he'd stepped inside her brain and was reading her mind and all her past memories. All her hidden regrets. She could see them all reflected on his face. He knew this, because he'd been living this life too.

That kiss had catapulted him into another space. Given him a painful reminder of what he wanted to capture again. Just like it had her.

She put her hand up to her chest, which was hurting, tight.

She was still shaking her head, aware of the anxious glances around them. 'I don't know, Logan. I just don't know.' She looked up and met his gaze. He looked hurt. He looked confused and something twisted inside her. It had been a long time since she and Logan had been like this.

Last time around she'd felt numb. She'd been unable to cope with her own grief so she certainly hadn't coped with his. But now he looked just as exposed as she felt.

His hair was mussed from where he'd run his fingers through it. The wind was rippling his shirt around his shoulders and chest. She almost hated the fact he could relate to how her life had turned out. To how every relationship she'd had since him had turned out.

But she hated even more that he'd mirrored her life with his own. She'd told herself that she'd always hoped Logan would move on, meet a girl, fall in love and have a family of his own.

Seeing him in Tuscany a few days ago and feeling

that flicker of excitement when he'd told her he was unattached had revealed a side to her she didn't like.

He was fixed on her with those green eyes. They were burning a hole into her. To the rest of the world they would be the picture-perfect couple with the backdrop of Venice behind them. No one else would know the way their insides had been ripped out and left for the vultures.

Her heart squeezed. She was bad. She was selfish. Part of her did wish Logan had a happy life but then again part of her always wanted him to belong to her. But at what price?

He hadn't moved. One hand was still wrapped around her waist, pressing her body against his, the other interlocking their fingers. She could break free if she wanted to. But after all these years she just didn't know how.

He blinked. 'I won't pressure you any more. I won't bring it up again. Just promise me you'll give it some thought. You can tell me before I return to Tuscany tomorrow.'

She gave the briefest nod and it coincided with a swell of relief from her chest as he stepped back, breaking their contact. In their exposed position on the observation deck a gust of wind swept between them. It startled her, sweeping away the feeling of warmth from Logan's body next to hers.

The expression in Logan's eyes changed. Gone was the tiny smudge of vulnerability that she'd seen before. It had been replaced by the determined, focused look she knew so well.

'Are we done with photos?' he asked, just a little brusquely.

She nodded as she pushed her phone back in her bag. He took her hand again, firmly this time, no gentle touch, as if he was determined not to let her escape. They walked back to the lift. 'Tonight I'm going to pick the venue for dinner.'

It was clear there was no point arguing. She gave a brief nod as the doors slid closed in front of them.

The stiff atmosphere remained for the next thirty minutes. His hand grasped hers rigidly as they boarded the *vaporetto* and made the short journey back to Piazza San Marco.

It was even more crowded but Logan seemed to have got his bearings in the city and led her through some of the backstreets. Her phone rang just as they were about to cross one of Venice's bridges.

She pulled it from her bag. 'It's work,' she said. 'I need to take it.'

'No problem. I'll have a look in some of the shops around here.'

As her boss spoke rapidly in her ear she lost sight of Logan's broad shoulders in the crowds. It was twenty minutes before the conversation was over and Logan appeared at her side holding a large loop-handled bag with a designer logo on the side. He held it out towards her.

'What is it?'

'Yours. For tonight.'

She was more than a little surprised. She opened the bag and saw a flash of red but he shook his head.

'Leave it. You can try it on when we get back to the apartment.'

In some ways she should feel flattered. Logan had always had exquisite taste. He'd bought her clothes in the past and she'd loved every single item. But they weren't a couple any more—they weren't lovers and she wasn't sure this felt entirely appropriate.

'Why on earth would you buy me something?'

He shrugged his shoulders. 'It's a thank-you gift,' he said casually. 'A thank you for letting me stay at your apartment when I obviously should have planned better.' He made it sound so matter-of-fact, so easy and rational. But the contents of the bag didn't seem impartial.

Red was her favourite colour. And although she hadn't had a chance to examine the dress she was sure it would fit perfectly and be a flattering style. It was all part of Logan's gift.

'What was your call?' He wasn't giving her time to think about this too much. Probably in case she started to object.

She gave a little smile. 'The electronic comparison of brushstrokes indicates the fresco is indeed by Burano. The paint sampling won't be completed until early next week.'

'When?'

'Probably Monday. Technology is a wonderful thing these days. They will be able to give me an exact match of the product and colours that Burano used in his fresco for the restoration work.'

They started to walk across the bridge now, stopping in the middle just as a gondola with some tourists on board passed underneath. 'And how long do you think the restoration work will take?'

She put her elbows on the bridge next to him. The sun was beating down now, rising high in the sky above them. She gave a nervous laugh. 'That's the one thing that doesn't happen quickly. Probably around a few months.'

'And it will be definitely you who does the work?'

Was it possible he didn't want her to be working next to him, no matter what he'd been saying? Maybe Logan was only looking for a quiet life. Maybe he was only trying to keep her onside to make sure his project didn't miss his deadline?

But he didn't look unhappy. He still had that determined gleam in his eye. He pointed to a baker's shop on the other side of the bridge. 'Why don't we grab some food and head back to the apartment? It's going to be too hot for sightseeing this afternoon and we both have work we can probably do before dinner tonight.'

She gave a nod of her head. It made sense—even if the thought of sharing her apartment space with Logan all afternoon made it feel as if the walls would close in around her.

'Where are we going later?' she asked, as they walked over the other side of the bridge.

He tapped the side of his nose. 'Leave that to me.'

CHAPTER SEVEN

IT WAS RIDICULOUS and he knew it. Why did he feel as if so much rested on one night?

He'd planned everything to perfection, pulling strings wherever he could. What he wanted most was for Lucia to be relaxed around him, maybe just enough to let her guard down and let him in.

It sounded cold, it sounded calculating. It was anything but.

He needed her to open up to him, to talk to him. It's what they both needed in order to move on with their lives.

It didn't matter that he had hopes for the direction in which they moved. He had to push those aside right now. He wanted her to talk. He couldn't see any further forward than that.

'Are you ready?'

He'd been pacing in the main room for the last half hour, watching the sun beginning to lower in the sky, bathing Venice in a beautiful orange glow.

'I'm ready.' Her voice sounded a little shaky and he spun around.

She looked a picture. The red dress was exactly as he'd envisaged it, hugging her curves in all the right places. He'd known as soon as he'd seen it that it was perfect for her. A red jersey underlay with red crochet lace on top, it reached her knees and only gave the tiniest hint of skin underneath. Lucia had never liked anything too revealing.

She was wearing her black patent impossibly high heels with red soles and clutching a sequin bag in her hand. But something wasn't quite right.

She flicked her long hair on her shoulders and meshed her fingers together. Lucia was wound tighter than a spring.

He walked over and handed her a glass of red wine. 'Let's sit down for five minutes. We have time.'

He gestured towards the chaise longue.

She waited a few seconds. Her nerves seemed to emanate from her, and even the hand holding the glass had an almost imperceptible shake. After a few moments she sucked in a deep breath and walked across the room.

'Thank you for the dress. It's perfect,' she said simply, as she sat down and crossed her legs.

'I knew it would suit you,' he said calmly. 'You look stunning.' It was true and he was quite sure that every man in Venice who saw her would agree during the course of the evening.

She took a sip of her wine. 'Are you going to tell me where we are going for dinner?'

He smiled. 'We're in Venice. We're going to Rubins overlooking Piazza San Marco. Where else would we go?'

A hint of a smile appeared on her face as she relaxed back and took another sip of wine. 'How on earth did you manage that? You couldn't find a hotel room, but you managed to get into the most exclusive restaurant in Venice?'

He wrinkled his nose. 'Let's just say I might have helped them at some point with an architectural matter. Unfortunately, they don't have beds for the night—so dinner it is.'

He actually couldn't believe his luck. The restaurant overlooking Piazza San Marco and based in the Procuratie Nuove had had issues a few years ago when some of the stonework around the elaborate archways had started to crumble. Logan had been able to help them find the same stone, from the original source, to allow complete restoration. It hadn't been an easy task. And right now he would take any advantage he could get.

They sat for a few minutes longer, watching the world go by on the Grand Canal, as she finished her wine.

He stood up and held out his hand towards her. 'Are we ready?'

She nodded and slid her hand into his. The momentum of pulling her up made them almost bump noses and she laughed and put her hands on his chest. 'Where did this dark suit come from? You surely didn't have this in your bag?'

He shook his head. 'I picked it up an hour ago when you were getting ready. I think you've seen enough of the cream jacket and trousers.'

Her eyes ran up and down his body. It was amazing how that tiny act could make his hairs stand on end and make him feel distinctly hot under the collar.

She gave an approving nod. 'I like it,' she said as she stepped away. 'I like it even more that you didn't bother with a tie.' She spun towards him in her heels. 'I never did like a man in a tie.'

His heart leapt in his chest. Her mood was lifting. She was definitely beginning to relax. He caught her elbow and spun her back towards him, resting his other hand on her hip.

He wanted this to be the start of something new. He wanted a chance to make things work with the only woman he'd ever really loved.

He knew they both had to move on. He knew they might not be able to move on together. And he knew at some point they had to talk about Ariella Rose.

But his heart was squeezing in his chest.

Tonight could be perfect. Tonight could just be about them. And somehow he knew that if he gave her the guarantee of no pressure, it could change everything.

'What do you say that for tonight I promise you that I won't mention Ariella Rose. We won't talk about what happened. And we'll only concentrate on the here and now. We'll only concentrate on the good things.'

He slid his hand through her silky soft hair.

She'd outlined her eyes in black and put on some lipstick that matched her dress. Right now Lucia was every bit the Italian siren.

Tonight wasn't about upsetting her. Tonight wasn't about grieving.

Tonight was about reminding her how good things had been between them. Reminding her what it felt like to truly connect with a person—and hoping she might realise that some things were worth fighting for.

She blinked quickly, trying to lose the obvious sheen on her eyes. Her voice was shaky. 'You promise?'

'I promise.' He didn't hesitate. This was the only way. The only way to try and take the steps to move forward. He wouldn't leave Venice without having that

conversation with her but for tonight—just for tonight—
he wanted to capture just a little of the old Lucia and
Logan again.

She locked up the apartment and they headed downstairs. He gestured her towards the other entrance of the
building, the one that looked out over the Grand Canal
and had a private mooring dock.

She shook her head. 'We never use that any more.'

He smiled as he pulled at the older doors. 'Well, tonight we're going to.'

Her stomach had been doing little flip-flops since early
afternoon and didn't seem to want to stop any time
soon.

The dress he'd bought her was beautiful, elegant
without being revealing and still managing to fit like
a second skin. It might as well have been made especially for her.

When she'd put it on she'd felt a surge of confidence
she hadn't felt in years. And seeing Logan in his dark
suit had almost toppled her off the edge where she was
dangling. It was like recapturing a moment from twelve
years ago, when they'd used to dress up regularly and
go out eating and dancing together. Back when neither
had had a care in the world and she'd had no idea what
could lie ahead.

Logan's green eyes were twinkling as he opened the
door to the Grand Canal. Bobbing on the water was a
sleek black gondola edged in red and gilt with its own
private canopy.

Lucia sucked in a breath. 'What on earth have you
done?' She knew exactly how much these cost to hire.
Every night the Grand Canal was full of wide-eyed

tourists bobbing around in these private hired gondolas. Most of the local Venetians laughed at them being taken advantage of. She'd never guessed Logan would fall into the trap.

'I've decided to start this evening the way it should continue.' He was smiling and his voice was steady. She could swear the orange-bathed canal was almost shimmering behind him. It made the whole evening just seem a little magical.

She glanced down at her towering stilettos as the gondolier held out his hand towards her. Her footsteps were slightly tottery as she stepped over the dark water of the Grand Canal. While it could seem terribly romantic, she didn't want to land in it and re-emerge like a creature of the black lagoon.

Logan jumped over easily, catching hold of her waist and steering her towards the red velvet love seat on the gondola. She laughed as they plonked down onto the seat under a black canopy and the gondola started gliding along the canal.

It was the first time in her life she'd felt like a tourist in Venice. Logan's arm slid easily behind her back. The love seat was unsurprisingly small, making sure they sat snugly together, his leg touching the length of hers.

It had been years and years since she'd done anything like this.

There was something magical about Venice in the early evening. Voices were hushed, music floated through the air, and quiet had fallen over the city.

'This is lovely,' Lucia murmured. Logan gave her shoulder a little squeeze.

As she watched the world go by she started to relax into his hold. He'd promised her there would be no pressure, no tension tonight. A tiny part of her coiled-up stomach didn't exactly believe him. It was hard to be around Logan and not think about Ariella Rose at all—and she was sure he must feel the same way.

But for tonight it might be nice not to focus on the hurts of the past. It hadn't been Logan who had hurt her. She'd never felt let down by him, or felt animosity towards him.

He was just the biggest reminder of Ariella Rose, and until her head could get around that...

The gondolier moved smoothly through the traffic. She had no idea where they were going but it was obvious he was going the picturesque route, winding their way through lesser canals and under bridges. She could see tourists pointing and taking pictures. Thank goodness for the canopy as it gave some ounce of privacy without spoiling their view.

There was something nice about the sound of the water lapping gently at the side of the gondola. Logan took his arm from her shoulder and bent forward, bringing out a bottle of chilled Prosecco and two glasses. He popped the cork and filled them up, handing hers over and holding his towards her. 'Here's to a fabulous night in Venice.'

She clinked her glass against his and sipped, letting the bubbles explode across her tongue and tickle her nose. 'Here's to an unusual night in Venice,' she said.

He raised his eyebrows. 'You mean you don't travel by gondola every night?'

She shook her head. 'I mean I haven't travelled in a gondola *ever* since I got here.'

'Really?' He seemed surprised.

She shrugged her shoulders. 'Think of it this way.

If you lived in Pisa, how many times would you actually climb the tower?'

He wrinkled his brow. 'I get where you're coming from but this is me—remember?' He turned a little more to face her. She could see the faint shadow on his jawline. He'd probably only shaved a few hours ago but that didn't quell the rapid growth of his potential beard. Her fingers itched to reach out and touch.

Logan wasn't finished. 'Remember when we stayed in Florence? How many times did we keep visiting the baptistery at the Duomo or stand underneath the Renaissance dome?'

She shook her head. 'That's because you're an architect junkie and those things were right on our doorstep.' She raised her eyebrows at him. 'I do remember you found a way to charm guards at every attraction and skip the queues.'

He gave a wave of his hand and glanced at her mischievously. 'There's a reason Italian men were born with charm. Anyway, we were natives. The guards knew that.'

'Only because you slipped some money in their hands.'

He gave a deep laugh. 'I don't know what you're taking about.' There were crinkles around his green eyes and her heart gave a little lurch.

Logan Cascini was really every woman's dream guy. She'd forgotten just how much fun they used to have together. It was unusual to meet a guy who shared her passion for the arts as much as he did.

From what most of her girlfriends told her, it was unusual to feel so connected, so in tune with a guy as she had with Logan. Most of her friends went for tempestuous and volatile relationships with plates smashing and clothes being tossed out of windows.

Life with Logan had been passionate but fulfilling. Something she'd never found again.

The gondola slid up next to the service point for disembarkation. It rocked precariously as she tried to stand up and she wobbled as the gondolier leapt ashore and held his hand out towards her.

As her feet landed on steady ground she turned towards Logan again. They were right at the edge of Piazza San Marco—the busiest place in Venice. The crowds might be a little quieter because of the planned concert but it was buzzing with excitement.

'Ready?'

He nodded towards the gondolier, tipped him and slid an arm around her waist, steering her towards the Procuraties. The sun was even lower in the sky now. The Procuraties were lit at night with tiny white lights. It was like a thousand glittering candles flickering in the night. There was no denying the beauty of the setting.

Music drifted down towards them. Some of these restaurants were known as the finest in the world, with Michelin-starred chefs and award-winning menus.

He pointed to a set of stairs heading up towards Rubins. 'After you.'

She felt her stomach flip over. He was being so formal around her. So controlled. The tiny bit of laughter on the boat had been the one true time she'd glimpsed the real Logan. That was who she wanted to spend the evening with.

The restaurant was beautiful. White linen tablecloths, more flickering candles and a harpist playing in the corner. It was full of couples dining in the dimmed lights, capturing a moment in one of the most beautiful cities in the world.

Logan held out her chair as she sat at the table then ordered them some wine. The waiter gave them thick, leather-covered menus. Lucia gave a smile as the wine appeared and was poured. 'It looks like we could have finished the wine by the time we get through this menu.'

Logan smiled at the waiter and closed his menu. 'What do you recommend?'

In the end they ordered a mixture of duck stuffed ravioli, white truffle pasta, fish carpaccio and some veal escalopes with Dobbiaco cheese.

The food was delicious and the wine kept flowing, almost as much as the easy chatter.

'What do you have to work on after the Tuscany project?'

Logan smiled at her. 'I could tell you, but I might have to kill you.' He tapped the side of his nose.

She leaned forward. 'Oh, don't go all James Bond on me. Is it something good?'

He leaned forward too, his voice low. 'It's something great. I'm just waiting for the final word. Let's just say I'll be working on something in Rome. Something I would absolutely love to work on and which could really put my restoration business under the spotlight.'

'Doesn't the chapel and *palazzo* restoration in Tuscany already do that? I'd have thought the royal wedding would mean everyone involved would benefit from the publicity.'

He gave a sigh. 'It does. But this is different, this is real Renaissance architecture. Something special that's needed to be restored for a number of years.'

She shook her head as she kept eating the delicious food. 'You make it sound like my dream job of being asked to restore the Michelangelo frescoes.'

'It's close.'

She almost dropped her fork. 'Really?'

He nodded. 'They are considering a number of different companies. The work definitely needs to be done, it just depends who wins the contract.'

She frowned. She knew just how passionate Logan was about his work, just how particular. 'There can't be many firms that have as good a reputation as you have.'

He met her gaze. 'Thanks for the compliment. Any chance you could be on the selection committee?'

She threw back her head and laughed. The wine was starting to kick in. The venue was exquisite and the food delicious. As for the company...

Logan put down his knife and fork. 'Honestly, what would you do if you got asked to do some restoration work on one of Michelangelo's frescoes?'

His face was completely serious. What on earth had he been asked to do?

'Honestly? I would probably die of shock. And I would be too scared to even contemplate doing something like that.'

He tilted his head. 'But you work for the Italian Heritage Board. Isn't that exactly the place that should be asked to do these things?'

She shook her head. 'We're just one organisation. I would be terrified. The pressure would be overwhelming and the criticism—before I even started—would be even more so.' She sat back in her chair. 'When it comes to things like that, I prefer just to admire along with the rest of the general public.'

'And Burano?'

She shook her head. 'His work isn't as well known. Isn't as criticised. The Madonna and Child hasn't been seen in generations. It isn't even on official records. Restoring it to its former beauty will be an act of joy.'

She could see him suck in a breath at her words. He paused, then looked up between heavy lids, 'And do you think everything can be restored—even people?'

Her skin chilled and her throat closed over. It was almost as if someone had stood behind her and poured icy water over her head.

He'd promised. He'd promised he wouldn't mention this tonight. She stood up swiftly, her chair toppling over behind her.

Logan was on his feet in an instant. It was almost as if he'd realised what had slipped out of his mouth. He walked swiftly over to the waiter, thrusting a bundle of notes at him.

Lucia didn't wait, she turned on her impossibly high heels and took off down the stairs.

But Piazza San Marco wasn't ready to give up on her yet.

As they'd had dinner, a small string quintet had been setting up downstairs outside one of the neighbouring restaurants. With the whole square bathed in flickering lights, the silhouette of the Basilica and Clock Tower at one end and the outlined string players in the middle her feet came to an abrupt halt.

Even she knew that running through the middle of a quintet in the piazza wasn't her best idea.

As she sucked in some air to try and still her thudding heart, she felt a presence behind her. Logan's hand slid across the thin red fabric of the dress covering her belly. She felt his warm breath on her shoulder and he moved in gently, letting her feel the rise and fall of his chest against her shoulder blades.

She was upset. But she wasn't angry at his touch. Instead, it felt like a comfort blanket.

Two of the violinists lifted their instruments and the quintet started to play. It wasn't what she expected. Classical music—usually opera—was often heard in the piazza. But this was different. It was a modern song by a UK male singer, transformed and made beautiful by the strings. She could almost hear his words echoing about love and loss in her ears.

It was almost as if they knew exactly what to play.

She spun around, placing her hands flat on Logan's chest. He didn't say a word, just lifted one hand and let his finger trail down her cheek until it reached her shoulder, where he flicked her curls back.

He was watching her with those steady green eyes and she could see the hurt shimmering from him. He was trying so hard, but was finding this every bit as difficult as she was.

His other hand slid around her hips, halting at her lower spine.

They were locked together. Just the way they should be.

Her palms slid up the planes of his chest and rested on his shoulders. This was her Logan. No one else's. No one else could ever come close to the connection she felt with him.

His body started to sway, tiny movements from side to side. One hand stayed at the base of her spine and the other tangled through her hair.

Dancing. She hadn't danced since…

Since before she'd had Ariella Rose.

She and Logan had once danced all the time. Sometimes in the clubs of Florence, often at family events and sometimes in the privacy of their own home.

Most of all she'd just loved the feeling of being in his arms and the warm touch of his body next to hers.

As the melody moved past the introduction he reached up and captured her hand in his, leading her away from the stairs and onto the patterned floor of Piazza San Marco. Little lights glowed under their feet.

People were still walking past, stopping to listen to the music, with one other couple dancing nearby.

He turned her to face her, putting his hands on her hips. 'Ready to recapture the past, Lucia?' he whispered.

She reached up and put her hand on his chest again. She could feel his warm skin and beating heart underneath the fine Italian shirt.

All she could focus on was the way he was looking at her. It made her feel like the only girl on the planet.

She slid her hands around his neck and rested her head against his chest. 'Always,' she replied.

Their footsteps moved in perfect unison. The warmth of his body next to hers felt overwhelming.

They fitted so well together it almost felt like they'd never been apart. And Logan didn't just know how to sway to the music. He knew how to dance—how to really dance.

It was as if they could read each other's minds and knew exactly what the next steps should be. She moved her hand from his chest, sliding it along the length of his arm and letting their hands clasp.

She felt him stiffen against her and she lifted her head.

There was no doubt on his face. He released her from his grasp against him and spun her outwards. When she danced with Logan she always felt like she could fly.

He could lift and spin her as if she were as light as air. Her dress spun out, the ripples of red fabric twisting high from her thighs, the stiletto heels forgotten as she continued to follow his lead.

She could hear the murmurs around them as people stopped to stare. But all she could focus on was the beat of the music and the feel of Logan's hard muscles as they connected briefly through the parts of the music.

Logan knew how to lead. He knew how to steer her and how to whip her around, like a matador with a cape.

And she kept spinning. The lit arches of the Procuraties flashing past her line of vision. The evening was still warm and her body temperature was rising quickly.

She couldn't even begin to think straight. The only thing that counted was how right everything felt—how *connected* everything felt.

She dipped her head and spun under his arm three times as the crowd gasped. The momentum of the music was building. He caught her around the waist and dipped her backwards. It was one of their all-time favourite moves. The sensuality of the deep arch of her back, followed by her ever-so-slow stretch back up, ending up nose to nose with Logan.

He was breathing just as quickly as she was. A laugh escaped from her lips. Her hair fell over her face, some of her curls connecting with his skin. But he didn't brush them back, he just dipped his head further forward, allowing them both to be hidden beneath the veil of her hair.

'How are we doing?' he murmured. He ran one finger up her spine, sending shock waves everywhere, a thousand beautiful butterflies beating their wings against her skin.

It couldn't be more perfect than this.

Then he moved. The music was slowing, reaching a building crescendo. He spun her once more, letting her skirt billow around her and her hair stream outwards.

He caught her hips suddenly, stopping her in mid-pivot and pressing his head against hers. She didn't even have time to catch her breath before his lips were on hers.

There was no time to think about where they were or what they had been doing. There was no time to think about the audience or the scenery.

His hands skirted around her behind, her hips and up the sides of her waist, stopping as they tangled in her hair, and he anchored her head firmly in one hand.

She couldn't ever remember being kissed like this—even by Logan.

She couldn't get enough of him. His taste, his smell, the feel of his body beneath the palms of her hand. He was hers. He was all hers. And she didn't want this to stop.

He pulled his lips back from hers, staying close enough to let her feel his breath on her skin. 'It's you, Lucia. It's always been you.'

The music died around them, but she hardly noticed. Her heartbeat was roaring in her ears. The world around them was still spinning—just like her brain. It hadn't stopped. Not for a second.

Logan held her tightly to him. She could feel his knotted muscles, the tension as he held her. She had no doubt about the effects she had on his body.

Of the effects he had on hers.

It had been so long. She'd forgotten what passion like this felt like. Something had been ignited inside her. A tiny flame that had been dimmed for so long. Now the fire was burning so brightly she couldn't imagine putting it out again.

Logan's eyes fixed on hers. They were steady but had never seemed so determined—so heated.

He clasped one hand in his. 'Let's go.' He didn't wait for a response. He walked away briskly, pulling her behind him as he parted the crowd around them.

His long strides covered the expanse of Piazza San Marco easily, and she was running in her stilettos to keep up.

She was surprised to see the sleek, black gondola still waiting. He didn't wait for the chatting gondolier to pay attention, just turned and lifted her straight onto the swaying gondola, shouting an instruction to the gondolier.

With one tug the canopy was closed, leaving them in a pool of darkness, with only a few of Venice's lights flickering behind them.

A seed of doubt flashed through her brain. All the rational thoughts that she'd completely ignored for the last few hours started to take seed and let their roots unfurl. She couldn't stop the rapid thud-thud of her heart. Every inch of her skin was on fire, the tiny hairs on her arms standing on end.

Her eyes started to adjust to the dim light. Logan hadn't moved. It could only have been a few seconds, but it felt like so much longer. It felt as if his brain must be crowding with the same doubts that she was feeling. Her stomach clenched. Everything suddenly felt like a huge mistake.

Logan shifted his body towards hers, reaching up his hand towards her face. He ran one finger across her forehead. Her eyes automatically closed and the finger traced down over her eyelids, cheeks, across her lips then under her chin and to the tender skin of her décolletage.

He leaned closer, the heat from his body spreading towards hers.

And then he murmured those words again.

'It's you Lucia, it's always been you.'

Before, she'd been shocked. They'd been in the middle of Piazza San Marco with a crowd of onlookers. Here, it was entirely private. All she could hear was the movement of the gondola slipping through the waters of Venice.

She squeezed her eyes closed again for a few seconds. Her hand reached up towards him. She couldn't help it. She couldn't be this close to Logan and not touch him. It was all she could think about.

She felt him suck in a breath as she ran the palm of her hand along his now-stubbled jaw.

If she could suspend the past—suspend the memories—then everything about Logan was perfect.

Now, as he said the words it was just the two of them. Her heart wanted to melt. Her lips wanted to respond. She wanted to say it had only ever been him. She wanted to tell him that she'd never felt the same about anyone else—she *couldn't* feel the same about anyone else.

Without Logan she wasn't living. She was only existing.

She didn't want to just exist any more.

This time when he bent to kiss her she matched him move for move. She ran her hands through his dark hair and pulled him closer to her, pressing her breasts against his chest.

Logan knew how to kiss. He really knew how to kiss. There was a zing as their lips met. Teeth grazed her lips. Then his lips were firmly on hers. Tasting her, caressing her. Full sweet lips on hers, filling her with so much promise, so much expectation.

The zings didn't stop at her lips but carried on right around her body, like an army on rapid attack. She couldn't help her responses. She couldn't help but push harder against his body, her hands exploring his back and shoulders.

The kiss intensified with every passing second, sparking a whole host of memories throughout her body. It didn't matter that their eyes were closed. With this kiss Logan could see every part of her, burrow his way to the centre of her closed-over soul.

She'd always felt threatened by their closeness after the death of their daughter. Fear had pushed her into a position of retreat, because even though she'd told Logan she couldn't talk about things, once he'd kissed her she always felt at her most vulnerable. Her most open.

His earthy scent swam around her. His fingers stroked the back of her neck, giving her a promise of what was to come.

His kisses moved lower, along her cheek and down the delicate skin of her neck. For a moment she almost objected. She didn't want his lips to leave hers.

But Logan knew all her secret places. Knew the tiny spot at the back of her ear that made her gasp with pleasure and lose all rational thought. Before she'd even thought about it her head was arching backwards, opening up the more sensitive skin at the bottom of her throat.

And Logan didn't hesitate. He was on it in a flash. She wanted to move. Her dress was inching upwards, his hand brushing against her thighs. But space was cramped under the canopy, with nowhere really to go, and they both jumped apart as the gondola jerked suddenly as it scraped against wood.

She sat back in the love seat, trying to still her ragged breaths. There was another couple of bumps.

It had been deliberate. Of course it had. They'd reached their destination and their gondolier had enough experience to allow his guests a moment of warning.

Was this it? Was this where this evening ended?

Logan pulled back the canopy and stood up, straightening his rumpled jacket and shirt and then turning towards her. He didn't speak, just held out his hand towards her.

What happened next was up to her.

It was her apartment. Her space. She'd offered him somewhere to stay for the weekend, without even considering this as a possibility.

The sun had set now. The warm orange glow from earlier had disappeared.

But now Venice was alive with a million different lights brightening up the almost black sky. Logan was outlined like a film star on his final movie shot.

The backdrop was stunning with the beautiful architecture along the Grand Canal and silhouetted gondolas around them.

But all she could focus on was Logan.

Because she knew exactly how this night would end.

It was already written in the stars twinkling in the sky above their head.

She slid her hand into his and he pulled her towards him as the boat rocked on the water.

This was fate. It had to be.

And who was she to fight fate?

CHAPTER EIGHT

THE ROOM WAS bathed in the pale light of morning.

It wasn't what he expected—not at all. Last night he hadn't paid attention to anything around them. They'd barely managed to close the apartment door behind them before they'd stumbled through to her bedroom.

Lucia's room wasn't the stark white of the guest bedroom along the corridor. It was sumptuous and opulent, furnished in the colours she'd used to favour when painting. Purples and golds with a tiny flash of red. It suited the general feel of the apartment—the whole place still had the hint of a palace about it. And the beautiful décor and furnishings in the room were more personal—more Lucia—than the room he'd stayed in.

Lucia was still tangled in his arms, her head resting on his chest and her dark locks fanned out on the purple bedding. Her breathing was slow and steady. The early morning light and noise from the Grand Canal hadn't woken her yet.

He didn't want to move. Didn't want to breathe in case it disturbed her.

This was perfection. This was exactly the way things should be between them but he knew he would have to destroy it all.

It would be so easy. So easy to say nothing at all and ignore the huge elephant that sat in the corner of the room every time they were together. But Logan didn't want only part of Lucia. He wanted all of her. He'd waited this long. And if he couldn't have all of her...

His hand reached up and stroked her head. They would have to spend the next few months working together in Tuscany. They could flirt, laugh, love and sleep together and make a poor attempt at having a relationship.

But the truth was that any attempt would be futile until they'd spoken about Ariella Rose. They had to start from scratch. They could only build this relationship once they'd grieved together for their daughter. And he still didn't know if Lucia was capable of that.

His phone beeped on the table next to the bed. The noise stirred Lucia from her peaceful sleep and she woke gradually.

Her arm drifted across his chest. She was smiling as she woke, as if she were in the middle of some alluring dream.

Her eyelids flickered open, revealing her dark brown eyes surrounded by thick black lashes. All traces of last night's make-up had vanished. Lucia didn't need any. Her flawless skin and naturally red lips were enticing enough.

His stomach clenched as he waited for anything—any trace of regret about last night. 'Good morning, beautiful,' he said softly.

She smiled and closed her eyes again, pushing her naked body closer to his. Her fingers started tracing circles on his chest. 'Good morning, handsome,' she said sleepily.

Some of his tension dissipated. He could leave this. Say nothing. Stroke his fingers across her skin and pull her beneath the covers. It was the biggest temptation in the world right now.

And while it might offer some temporary sanctuary and pleasure it wouldn't take him to the place he ultimately wanted to be.

Somehow he knew it didn't matter how he phrased the question—he already knew how she would react.

It was horrible—knowing that the path they would have to tread would be a painful one. But he was ready for it. He'd been ready for it for the past twelve years.

'How are you feeling?'

She pushed her head up onto one hand as she lay facing him. Her face still had that relaxed, sleepy, dreamy quality about it. It was the most chilled he'd ever seen her.

'I'm fine.' She smiled. 'How are you?' There was a teasing tone to her voice—as if she wanted to take this to a whole other place.

His fingers wanted to reach out and touch her soft skin. It took all his will power not to move and instead to clench the purple sheet in his fist.

'We need to talk, Lucia. You know we need to talk.'

The muscles around her neck tensed. She turned her head away from him. 'No, we don't.'

It was an immediate, instinctual reaction. He knew that. He pushed himself further up the bed. The sheet moved with him, pulling from Lucia's skin. She made a grab for it. It was amazing how a few words could make you feel naked all over again.

He sighed. 'We have to work together, Lucia. We're going to be in Tuscany together. I don't want things to be awkward between us.'

Her head shot around. 'And this is how you stop it?' It was an accusatory tone. And he got that. He did. Lucia would much rather they never spoke about this at all.

He moved to the edge of the bed and picked up his discarded shirt from the floor, pulling it over his head. He shook his head. 'No, Lucia. This is how I start things. This is how we should start things. By talking.' He stood up. 'Now get dressed. We're going to go for breakfast together.'

He moved across the floor, finding his underwear, crumpled trousers and shoes. If he were a young man, concerned about his appearance, he might be cringing right now at the thought of going out in Venice in last night's clothes.

But he was a grown-up. An adult. And he had so much more to worry about.

Lucia was scowling at him. The beautiful red dress he'd bought her was bunched up in a little ball. He doubted it would ever look the same. 'I'm not coming.'

'Yes, you are.' He opened the door of her wardrobe, his eyes running rapidly over the colours, and pulled out a flowered dress, throwing it on the bed. 'Would you like me to select your underwear too?' He didn't mean to be cruel. But he wasn't prepared to take no for an answer. Not after all this time.

She pulled the sheet up under her chin. 'Stop it, Logan. You can't bully me into doing what you want. I'm not a child.'

He bent down next to her. 'I have never bullied you, Lucia. I never will. And you're right, you're not a child. You're a mother—just like I'm a father. Just because our child isn't here any more it doesn't change that.'

Her eyes widened. She was shocked. It was the last

thing she'd obviously expected to hear. And he wasn't quite sure where it had come from.

After a few seconds her fingers released on the sheet a little. He sensed the moment and opened the drawer next to her bed, pulling out matching white underwear. 'I'll give you a few minutes to get dressed,' he said, walking to the door and standing in the corridor.

Every part of him was on edge. He had no idea right now if he'd handled this right. He'd spent so long tiptoeing around Lucia that now it felt as if he'd just leapt in wearing a pair of clown-size shoes.

He held his breath, listening for any sign of movement. Any tiny noise.

After a few seconds he heard something. The gentle movement of a sheet. He leaned back against the wall. It didn't matter that she hated him right now. All that mattered was that they talk. That they *really* talked.

He walked through to the guest bedroom and quickly washed his face and hands, running his fingers through his hair and brushing his teeth. He had another shirt in his bag but it would probably be equally as rumpled. He hadn't planned on staying in Venice so clothes were definitely scarce.

It was too warm for a jacket so he walked through to the main room and waited for Lucia to appear.

It only took a few moments. She hadn't bothered with make-up and her hair was pulled back in a clasp. The yellow and pink flowered dress made her look much younger.

His heartbeat turned up a little notch. It was almost like turning back time. She had a white canvas bag in her hand and some flat sandals on her feet. But she'd never looked so beautiful.

He walked over to the main door and held it open. 'Let's go.'

There was a sinking feeling in his stomach. Almost as if he knew how this could turn out.

Lucia didn't even glance at him as she walked past. She had that determined edge to her chin.

But he could be equally determined. It was time to show her how much.

Talk about an awkward morning after. She couldn't believe she'd allowed herself to get into this position.

She knew so much better than this.

She was an adult and knew exactly what going for dinner and wine with Logan could lead to. The sexual chemistry between them had always been off the chart, but add into that the dress-buying and dancing and, well...what chance had she really had?

She held her head up proudly as she walked down the street towards her favourite café. This wasn't like doing a walk of shame the next day after a night-time encounter.

Logan had been the man she'd lived with. He'd been the man who'd cherished and treasured her. He'd been the man she'd loved with her whole heart.

She still did.

Her feet stumbled on the uneven street. Logan caught her elbow and she tugged it away. Where had that thought come from?

She squeezed her eyes closed for a second. This was because of last night. Memories of what had been and how good they had been together. She was being sentimental, nothing more. So why was her stomach permanently in knots?

She stopped at the tables on the street at her favourite café. Logan pulled out a chair for her. The waiter gave her a wave. 'Usual?'

She nodded. Logan caught his eye 'Make it two.'

Little parts of her were starting to unravel, even at those innocuous words. Logan knew that her usual would be coffee with steamed milk and a heated croissant with raspberry jam. He knew her that well and was happy to eat the same as her.

It was almost as if he were chipping away at the barriers she'd erected around herself all those years ago. The ones that had protected her. Stopped her from getting too close to anyone else and kept her safe from being hurt.

Logan folded his arms across his chest. He was sitting directly opposite her, his eyes watching her carefully.

He waited until the coffee appeared on the table and the waft of buttery croissants filled the air around them.

'It's been too long, Lucia,' he said quietly. 'I never wanted you to leave, but I understood you needed time and space.' He picked up his spoon and stirred his coffee. 'But it was never my intention to leave things this long.'

He had no idea what those few words could do to her.

The rest of Venice seemed completely at ease. People were laughing and strolling in the early Sunday morning light. Shopkeepers were just starting to roll up their shutters and open their doors. A street vendor wandered past, clutching buckets filled with beautiful flowers. The assorted scents started to mix with that of the breakfast croissants. It could be a beautiful day. So why did it feel like the worst?

Logan hadn't finished talking. 'I always hoped things would be different. I thought you would be married. I thought you would be a mother.'

He paused. 'I always hoped you would be.'

She felt tears spring to her eyes. It was almost as if he were twisting the knife that was currently piercing her heart. She knew that wasn't his intention. She knew he was trying his best to move things forward.

But Lucia had never moved forward. She could remember everything about Ariella Rose as if it had just happened yesterday. She could remember the sudden unexpected pain, the cramps, the awkward delivery. She could remember the tiny fragile bundle. Ariella had been so small she could fit in one hand, wrapped in a pink blanket made by Nonna.

The almost transparent skin. The tiny little blue veins underneath. She could remember how she'd had to gently ease up a tiny eyelid in order to see her baby's eyes. Eyes that would never see the world.

Lungs that would never fill with air.

She could remember all her hopes and dreams for the future evaporate with the silence in the air. The heavy, ominous silence of nothing.

Her horror had been so complete she'd only been able to shed a few tears. Tears of shock. It had been as if every emotion in her body had switched off. Gone into complete self-protection mode.

Now Logan was trying to open her all up to this again.

'Maybe I decided that wasn't what I wanted.' The words came out tight, almost angry, and Logan eyebrows arched slowly.

'You were made to be a mother, Lucia.' He held her

gaze as she tried to swallow. 'You would be the finest mother in the world.'

She was frozen. Couldn't breathe. Her mouth had never felt so dry, but the aroma of coffee was acrid to her now. The croissant mocked her.

Some modern career women would find his words insulting. But she didn't. Logan knew her better than anyone. He knew how much she'd relished being pregnant. He knew how much she'd planned for their daughter—they both had.

Although she was passionate about her career, she'd longed to raise their daughter.

She lifted her coffee cup with trembling hands. 'Things change.'

He shook his head and reached across the table towards her.

But she didn't want him to touch her. She couldn't take the feel of his skin on hers right now.

He leaned his elbows on the table and just kept talking. 'I've dreamt of being a father too. But it's never happened. It wasn't meant to happen—not with anyone but you.'

He said the words so easily. As if he'd contemplated them for a long time and had come to accept that this was his lot in life.

'I've met some wonderful women, but none that I wanted to marry, none that I wanted to raise children with. I only ever wanted to do that with you.'

She could feel the anger build in her chest. 'But we never planned Ariella Rose. You make it sound as if we had our future all written out.' She spat the words at him.

She couldn't understand how he could talk about any

of this so calmly. It felt as if he'd reached a fist into her chest and was squeezing all the blood from her pumping heart.

'My future was written the second I saw you, Lucia.' He hadn't raised his voice once. His words were calm and steady. He was so resolute.

She leaned across the table towards him. 'I can't talk about this,' she hissed.

It was the first time she saw a little spark in him. He gritted his teeth. 'Well, you have to. It's about time. You owe it to our daughter.'

She pulled back as if he'd wounded her. But Logan wasn't finished. 'You owe it to our daughter to talk about her and give her the love and respect she deserves.'

Her head was swimming. 'How dare you! You know I loved Ariella.'

'But you don't honour her memory.'

'What does that mean?'

Logan rubbed the palms of his hand on his trousers. It was obvious this was upsetting him just as much as it was upsetting her.

He took a deep breath. 'It means you walked away, Lucia. You walked away from the memory of our daughter and the memory of what we used to have. I think about her every single day. It doesn't matter that you're in Venice and she's in Tuscany. I visit her grave every month. You could too. But as far as I know you haven't been there since the day we buried her.'

Fury erupted inside her. Tears were brimming in her eyes but they just couldn't come any further— she hadn't been able to cry since the day they'd buried their daughter. From that point on everything had been locked inside.

'I can't go there. I can't visit.'

'Why?' He wouldn't stop. He wasn't going to let this go. It would have been better if they'd never seen each other again. The last thing she needed was stirring up the memories of Ariella Rose and any association with Logan did just that.

She wasn't able to separate the parts of him from their daughter. She couldn't just remember his kiss, his touch without remembering where it had led them. Couldn't block out all the pain it had caused.

'I just can't.'

'Then maybe that's what we should do.'

She felt herself bristle. 'Don't tell me what to do, Logan. We haven't known each other in a long time—you have no right.'

He stood up sharply, his chair screeching backwards, and she held her breath, wondering what would come next. The waiter stuck his head out of the door of the restaurant, watching carefully.

But Logan just shook his head, stretched out his back, then took a few steps towards her and knelt beside her chair.

She was still holding her breath as he slid his hand up and took hers. She hadn't realised it but her hands were cold and the warmth from him completely enveloped her.

His voice was quiet again, this time almost pleading. 'I have every right. We lost our daughter together. Who do you think I get to talk about Ariella Rose with? Who do I get to share the memories of our daughter with? I want to remember what we lost, Lucia. I loved her with every part of my heart—just as you did.' He sighed and looked up, meeting her gaze.

'This isn't just about you any more, Lucia. It was twelve years ago. I would have done anything to help you grieve, to comfort you after the loss of our daughter. But I've realised this is about me too. It wasn't enough just to make the arrangements. It wasn't enough to say a prayer. It wasn't about giving you the space you needed. I watched you fall apart right under my nose, I watched you shut yourself off from the world and bury yourself away. I thought I had no right to force you to talk. I thought I had to let you do this your own way. But twelve years on? I was wrong, Lucia. I was very wrong. For you, and for me.'

She squeezed her eyes closed again. She couldn't take his intense and sincere glance. This was exactly what she'd always tried to avoid.

It had been too much. Too much to think about. She couldn't bear it.

And now here was Logan—her strong, able Logan—telling her how much he'd been hurt too. He'd never worn his heart so much on his sleeve as he was doing now and it was tearing her apart.

She'd never even contemplated his hurt. His grief. She'd been too selfishly trying to cope with her own. Logan had appeared so composed, so strong. Now his face looked as if it had worn a river of grief across it. She could see her own pain reflected in his eyes, the tight grip of her hand telling her more than she wanted to know.

'You have to face this, Lucia. You're never going to get past this, *I'm* never going to get past this, if we can't talk together.'

Logan. Her handsome, strong Logan. She'd always hoped he would have married and had kids. He deserved to be a father. He deserved to spend his summer evenings playing in a garden, with his arms wrapped around the woman that he loved.

Twelve years ago she'd hoped that might be her.

He still wanted to save her. Even after all these years he wanted to patch her up and put her together again. But he couldn't do it then. And he couldn't do it now.

But things were different now. He'd realised how much *he* still hurt.

It didn't matter if Lucia wrapped her arms around his neck right now and told him she wanted to try and make things work again. It didn't matter that she might want a future with them together.

Now he'd realised exactly what he needed. For him. And for her.

He lifted his hand then ran his fingers through her hair at the side of her head. 'I loved Ariella Rose. I loved it that her eyes were so dark blue, though they probably would have turned brown—just like yours. I loved the fine downy hair we could see on her head. I loved that her fingers and toes were perfect. I dream about the person she could have become. And I wonder about the type of personality she would have had.'

He moved his fingers down her cheek. 'I wonder if she would have been like me, or if she would have been like you.'

He brought his hand down next to his other, clasping both of her hands in his. 'I love it that we made a little person. But I watch the calendar every year. Every year when it's her birthday I think about another year that we've lost. I think about the little girl who would have grown up and laughed and played and gone to school. I think she would be at an age right now where she would hate her overprotective dad. She would hate the fact I didn't want her to speak to boys or to wear clothes that made her look like a teenager. I would want to keep her all buttoned up in pink dresses and sandals.'

Lucia was shaking. And not just her hands. Every part of her body was shaking. It was as if his words were starting to penetrate her fortress-like exterior.

He could see the waiter casting anxious glances in their direction. But he didn't want to do anything that might distract her.

'Tell me how much you miss her, Lucia. Tell me what your hopes and dreams were for our daughter.'

He couldn't do anything to stop the shaking. He knew it was just her body's natural response. He just kept her ice-cold hands in his, hoping and praying she would finally start to open up.

Her voice was tight. Her fingers started to grip his hand more tightly. Almost as if she were clinging on for her life.

'I miss her every day.' The words came out in a rush. Then there was silence. Silence he was determined not to fill. It was the first time she'd ever said anything about their daughter.

Lucia finally started to talk again. 'I get so angry because I don't know whether she would have had dark hair, or blond hair like your sisters. I don't know whether she would have had curls or straight hair. I don't know whether she would have been a tomboy or a ballet dancer. Whether she would have wanted red shoes or pink or white.' She shook her head. 'There's so many things about my daughter that I don't know.

Will never know. And I feel cheated, completely and utterly cheated.'

His chest was tight. But tiny little parts of the tightness were giving away to relief. She was finally, finally starting to talk. Starting to talk about the life they had lost.

'Then I think about things that would never, ever have mattered. Not in the scale of things.' She looked upwards to the sky.

'What do you mean?' he prompted gently.

'I mean, would she have liked cats or dogs? Would she have been artistic? Would she have liked staying in Florence? How would she have got on at school? All the things that—if our daughter was actually here— we probably would have argued about and fussed over. But in the end, it doesn't mean anything.' Her eyes lowered and fixed on the canal next to the café. A few boats were puttering past. People going about their daily business.

No one else could know or imagine what was at stake at this table.

Logan took a deep breath. He had so much more to say. Even though he'd been much more able to talk about his grief than Lucia, there was something about it just being the two of them here that made it different.

No one else could really understand how they both felt—not unless they'd lost a child too.

He straightened up and sat back down in the chair opposite her again. But this time he pulled it closer, away from the table and round to the side so their legs were touching.

'I miss things,' he said softly. 'I miss us. I miss what

we used to have together. I didn't just lose a daughter, Lucia. I lost the love of my life too.'

He could see her swallow painfully. It wasn't just him that felt this way. But somehow Lucia didn't want to go there. It was as if, now she'd finally managed to say something about Ariella, she didn't know how to stop.

'Sometimes I think we were lucky. Sometimes I think that I'm selfish.'

His head shot up in surprise. 'What?'

She scrunched up her face. Her voice was sad. 'I look at other people who've lost children. You see them on the news all the time. They had a little person, a real little person with life and spark and personality, and it's just...' she shook her head '...ripped from their grasp. One day they have a little boy or girl in their room at home, talking, laughing, playing, then the next day because of disease or accidents or war their precious little person is stolen from them. Gone, in the blink of an eye.'

Her eyes fixed on the uneven ground beneath their feet. 'That's when I think that most of the time I don't know what I missed. I can pretend. I can build up all these thoughts of what Ariella Rose could have been like in my head.' She met his gaze. 'But the truth is, you and I will never know. Is it easier to lose a baby that you loved and hoped for than it is to lose an actual child you've spent years bringing up?' She shook her head again.

'I try to rationalise why I feel so empty. I try to make excuses about why I don't want to be around pregnant colleagues or friends.' She gave him a sad kind of smile. 'I have twelve years' worth of excuses, Logan, with reasons for not visiting new babies or friends playing happy families. It would surprise you how often I'm away with work.'

He could feel the tiny hairs standing up at the back of his neck. It just didn't feel quite right. He could feel her stepping back, detaching herself from the thoughts and feelings she'd been having a few moments ago. It was the slight change in the tone of her voice. The cool way she could look at him now.

For a few seconds her heart had been virtually on display. Her fears and hidden emotions had been coming to the surface. But even though she hadn't moved, was still sitting on the chair next to him, still letting their legs touch, she was pulling back again.

The only reason he could pick up on the tiny clues was because he knew her so well.

She straightened her spine in the chair. He could sense her sorting out her thoughts, finding a way to steal herself back from what she'd almost revealed.

He reached out to take her hand again. 'How would you feel about taking a visit to Florence again? How would you feel about us going together to Ariella Rose's grave?'

She pulled her hand back sharply from his, almost as if she'd been stung. It was too much. It was a step too far.

She wasn't ready to take it. She might never be ready to take it.

And with that realisation he felt the woman he'd always loved slip away from him once again.

Her face had turned into a mask. 'I don't want to do that, Logan. I don't think it's necessary.'

Her phone beeped in her bag and she bent forward, obviously glad of the distraction.

Their coffees and breakfast were virtually untouched, discarded.

A bit like how he felt right now.

She gave a false smile. 'It's work. With the computer program verifying Burano as the artist of the fresco, we can start to plan for the restoration now.'

She stood up quickly. It was almost as if their conversation had been forgotten.

For a few seconds he didn't move. He'd almost got there. *They'd* almost got there.

For him it was all or nothing. He knew that Lucia was the woman that he wanted, but he wasn't just prepared to accept a small part of her. And just when she'd started, just when she'd finally managed to talk about their daughter, it was almost as if he'd been able to see the shutters come down over her eyes, closing off the part of her that was most exposed, most vulnerable and cocooning it back in herself.

He had so many hidden hopes and plans for them. Last night had been wrong. Last night had made him think that there might just be hope for them. That this relationship could actually bloom and grow after all these years.

She didn't get it. She didn't get it that in his head they would grow old together. When they'd both lost their beauty, their youth and their health, they would still have each other. And that would be enough. That would always be enough.

Only it wasn't now. Not when he knew that the woman he loved with all his heart would never love him the same way. She couldn't. Part of her heart was permanently locked away. Had been for the last twelve years and it looked like it would stay that way for ever.

He stood up and put some notes on the table to cover breakfast. Lucia's whole face had changed. It was as if it had been replaced by a mask.

His stomach turned over. He could have played things so differently this morning. He could have ignored the past and just continued with the present, no matter how little of her he actually got.

But it would never have been enough. And even though his heart felt as though she'd ripped it in two, he knew this was right. For him at least.

He kept his voice as detached as he could. He would never make a scene. Never do anything to deliberately cause her embarrassment or upset.

'Shall we make travel plans back to Tuscany?'

Her shoulders dropped a little as he spoke. Was that relief that he saw? Relief that he'd finally let things go?

Her words came out rapidly and her footsteps matched his on the cobbles next to the narrow canal. 'I can arrange the return flights. We should be able to go back first thing tomorrow morning. The samples that I took earlier will be sent for automatic colour and pigment matching. I can only restore the fresco using products as close to the originals as possible. Thank goodness for modern technology.' She gave a wave of her hand and kept chattering as they crossed the bridge.

Logan felt numb. This was it. This was it for him and her.

He'd have to spend the next few months in Tuscany, working next to Lucia but keeping her at arm's length. Every glimpse whipped up a whole host of memories of the night before. He couldn't possibly be in her company and not think about what the two of them had lost and never recovered from.

There couldn't be a Logan and Lucia. Not if she still couldn't mourn their daughter.

It would be best for them both.

CHAPTER NINE

SHE FELT NUMB. It was the only way she could survive.

Last night had been a blur. They'd got up this morning just as the sun had been rising and made their way in a water taxi to the airport. Logan had spoken barely a word to her.

And that was what hurt most.

He'd been polite, of course, courteous even. But it had all been strained. Any time she'd caught a glimpse of his once gleaming green eyes all she'd been able to see was the blankness that had been pulled over them.

They stood patiently in the queue, checking in and filing through to Departures. As soon as they made their way through she made a feeble excuse that she needed to pick up some things.

Logan gave a nod of his head and said he was going for coffee and would meet her at the departure gate. He seemed almost as relieved as she was to get some space.

Lucia ducked into the nearest shop. She didn't even care which one it was—and started walking blankly through the aisles.

Lingerie. Just what she needed. She cringed as she passed a couple winking and nudging each other near the sexiest black and pink lingerie in the shop. She couldn't even remember the last time she'd spent money on matching lingerie. And she certainly wasn't going to need some any time soon. Not at these prices anyway. Who actually spent this kind of money on underwear?

Something inside her sparked a wave of fury. Her steps became quicker, more determined. She marched along the aisles until she saw something that caught her eye, something she might actually wear.

It was a pale pink satin nightdress trimmed with exquisite lace. It was not as short as she might usually wear, reaching down to at least her knees. She reached out and touched it. The heavy satin was silky to touch, pure of quality and luxury. She picked out her size and walked to the cashier's desk without a second thought.

The cashier folded and wrapped the nightdress in tissue paper and Lucia didn't even blink when she handed over her credit card.

Why shouldn't she buy herself something beautiful? As she pushed the package into her bag her mind flashed back to her bedroom and the beautiful red dress that Logan had bought her lying crumpled on the floor.

She hadn't even picked it up. She didn't need any reminder of the night they'd spent together. It was already ingrained in her brain.

She didn't need anything to remember the feel of his fingers on her skin, the feel of his lips on her neck and throat. The smell of his scent winding its way around her. The squeeze in her heart the next day when he'd told her they needed to talk.

And the look in his eyes when she'd finally stood up and walked away, pushing everything else back into a space she didn't have to deal with.

She'd been walking on eggshells ever since.

And not just around Logan. Around herself too.

For a few tiny seconds she allowed herself to think about Ariella Rose. She'd allowed herself to say a few words, to contemplate what might have been and what she'd lost.

But it had been too much. The wave of emotions that had swept over her had had to be quickly quelled. On that warm summer's day she'd never felt so cold. The tremors that had come over her body had been over-whelming.

It would have been so easy to bury her head in Lo-gan's shoulder and just hold on for grim life. But she was too scared. Scared that if she went there she might never come back.

The truth was that no adult should outlive their child. And only someone who'd been there could understand that. Her friends and family had no idea of the type of thoughts that had crept through her brain in the few days after her daughter's death. She'd never acknowl-edged them to anyone.

Instead, she'd kept things locked away—even from Logan. How did you tell the man you loved with your whole heart that you would rather be with your daugh-ter than him?

It had been too cruel. Even for her.

Her eyes scanned the coffee shop. Logan was sitting staring out of one of the windows, his hand stirring his cappuccino endlessly.

She dumped her bags in the chair next to him. It wouldn't be long until their flight was called. She walked over to the counter. 'Full-fat caramel latte with whipped cream and a strawberry frosted doughnut.'

A whole day's worth of calories about to be consumed in ten minutes. But she just felt like it. Sometimes days were just like that.

And from the look on Logan's face his day was entirely like that too.

It seemed the longest flight in history.

It was amazing the things you could think up to do rather than talk to the person sitting directly at your elbow.

Lucia was wearing a bright orange dress, and matching stilettos. She had a large brown leather bag—which looked as if it could carry the entire contents of her kitchen—slung over her shoulder.

Her wheeled suitcase looked bigger than his car. It was clear she was here to stay.

For a second he'd wondered if she was having second thoughts. She'd disappeared at the airport for a bit, then reappeared, eating a whole host of things that would never normally cross her lips.

Logan was far too wise to comment. Lucia hadn't been known for hormonal binges. But it had been twelve long years. Lots of things could have changed that he knew nothing about.

And, frankly, it wasn't his business any more.

As they landed at the private Tuscan airport and waited for their car, one of the signs at the newsstand caught his eye.

He gave her a nudge. *'When was the last time Prince Antonio saw his Cinderella bride?'*

For the first time since they'd left Venice the glazed expression left Lucia's face and her eyes widened. 'What on earth have we missed? We've only been gone a few days.'

He shook his head as the car pulled up in front of them. 'I have no idea. We'll need to talk to Louisa as soon as we reach the *palazzo*. I wonder if this will have implications for the wedding?'

He opened the door for Lucia and they climbed inside. After a few seconds she pulled out her laptop and started working. Logan sighed and leaned back, watching the green Tuscan hills roll by.

The journey from the airport took them back through the village and he took a few moments to study the surrounding architecture again. It was important that he keep the *palazzo* as in keeping with its surroundings as possible. Any kind of modern renovation would be disastrous. So, while modern fixtures and fittings could be included, they had to be sympathetic to the history of the house.

They pulled up outside the *palazzo*. It was a hive of activity. Monday mornings in the Italian building trade could notoriously start slowly. Not today.

Connor was in talks with someone outside the chapel building. It was obvious he was keeping on top of the security of the fresco.

A delivery of the special pink-coloured stone used in the *palazzo* was being unloaded. Some of the outer restoration work still needed to be completed. He could see his special stonemason signing for the delivery.

Louisa came walking out of the main entrance as Lucia grabbed her case. Louisa looked distracted, as if her mind were on a hundred other things. She hadn't even noticed their return.

'Louisa?' he said, trying to be heard above the building work around them. She was frowning and it marred her pretty face. Her hair was pulled back in a rumpled knot and her long tunic looked like yesterday's.

Her head flicked up. 'Logan.' Her eyes darted over to Lucia. 'Lucia. You're both back.' She walked over quickly. 'Do you have news?'

Lucia gave her a cautious smile. 'We do. The fresco *is* by Burano, he lived and worked in the Renaissance period and we have other examples of his work. He was both a painter and a sculptor. We're making arrangements to look at the sculpture on the fountain in the village. It could be another piece of his work.'

Louisa gave a smile and a quick nod. 'That's great. Really great. What happens next?'

Lucia glanced towards Logan. It was obvious that she was picking up the same vibes that he was. Louisa's body language was all over the place. She was saying the right words but her hands were continually knotting in front of her abdomen.

'Things will be fine. I'll begin the restoration work on the fresco. It could take a few months. All the costs will be covered by the Italian Heritage Board.'

'A few months?' Louisa looked shocked. 'But what about—?'

Logan stepped forward and took her arm, cutting her off. 'Are you okay? Don't worry about Lucia's work. It won't interfere with any of the plans here.' He nodded towards Lucia. 'We'll make sure of that.' He lowered his voice. 'Is this about the headlines? We saw them when we landed at the airport. Is the wedding still going ahead? Is there anything you need to tell us?'

Louisa's face tightened and she pressed her lips together. 'Of course the wedding is still going ahead. There's nothing to tell. Nothing to tell at all.'

It was clear by the tone of her voice that she wasn't willing to discuss anything.

She waved her hand towards the *palazzo*. 'Lucia, you're welcome to stay here, but…' she glanced at Lucia's stuffed suitcase '…you might need to make other arrangements while the wedding is taking place.'

Logan turned and stared at Lucia just as she turned and stared at him. Both of them had wide eyes. It was like a cartoon scene. It was something that hadn't occurred to either of them.

Of course Lucia would need somewhere to stay for the next few months. He'd invited her to stay with him in the farmhouse, but that had been when they'd been at the top of the campanile. It seemed like a million years ago. She'd promised to consider it and they hadn't discussed it again since.

He knew that he should say something here.

Logan's arrangement was different from everyone else's. He was staying in one of the old converted farmhouses on the estate. It was comfortable. It was private. And it was big enough for two people.

There were two reasonable-sized bedrooms. He had hardly set foot in the other one —even though he could have used it as his office. His computer and paperwork were currently spread over the dining-room table. Dining for one didn't really require the full use of the table.

He caught a glimpse of the expression on Louisa's face. She was caught in the middle, probably unable to fathom out what their relationship was. She waved her hand. 'I'll leave that to you two.' She walked away into the vineyards.

Lucia was watching her retreating back. 'Do you think she's okay?'

He shrugged. 'She certainly didn't want to be drawn into any gossip. She could be worried about how this could affect the prospects for the vineyard and the *palazzo*. I can only assume that the wedding costs are covering all the renovations around here. If they back out now...' He let his voice drift off. They both knew exactly what that could mean for Louisa.

Lucia gave a little nod and tugged at her case. 'In that case, I have things I need to do. I'm going back to chart some of the fresco and make an approximate estimate of how long the restoration work will take. I'll share the timetable with you when it's finished.'

Logan looked around. There was a mountain of work here for him too. A little gust of wind swept past and carried Lucia's rose-scented perfume towards him.

He cringed as it automatically evoked memories in his brain. Nights. Days. Passion. Love. And loss.

Avoiding Lucia in Palazzo di Comparino could be harder than he'd thought.

It could be nigh on impossible.

'See you later,' he said briskly as her eyes met his.

For the tiniest second he held his breath. There it was again, that connection. It sparked every time he looked into those deep brown eyes and reflected the pain and passion that had affected them both.

He dug his hands in his pockets and turned away.

It was best to break the connection.

Best for them both.

Lucia couldn't sleep. The windows in her bedroom were open wide and she could practically hear the music of the Tuscan hills calling to her. Every rustle of the vineyard leaves, every noise from the watering system, the tiny cranking noises of some of the mechanical systems were all being carried in the warm night air.

The bed was comfortable, but even wearing just her new satin nightdress and only having one sheet was proving too much. She couldn't settle. Every time she closed her eyes for a few seconds her brain started to replay the last few days with Logan.

And it was infuriating. Because it wasn't one tiny part—it was everything…almost told in parts like a TV series. Her nerves at speaking to him for the first time. That *whoosh* that had swept over her body when she'd set eyes on him again. The way her skin had prickled just from being near him. Feeling the heat from his body when he was in close proximity to her. The touch of his lips on hers, awakening all the old sensations. Being held in his arms as they'd danced at Piazza San Marco. And the feel of his skin against hers when they'd finally gone to bed together.

Being around Logan seemed to have set all of her five senses on fire. And now they'd been reawakened it seemed they didn't want to go back to sleep.

She sat up in bed for the twentieth time and slid her feet onto the floor. The tiles of the floor were cool and it took a few seconds to find her flat sandals.

She stood at the window for a moment, wondering if she should go outside. There was not a single person in sight. That wasn't unusual—it was the middle of the night. She glanced around her room.

There was somewhere she wanted to be. Was it worth getting changed? The chapel was only across the court-yard from the *palazzo*. Could she just sneak across the way she was?

She grimaced at the stuffed-full suitcase. Packing

when your mind was on other things wasn't exactly ideal. She hadn't brought a dressing gown. Or her running gear. Or a hairdryer.

She opened her door. It creaked loudly and she held her breath for a few seconds to see if anyone had noticed the noise.

The air in the corridor was still. Her sandals made barely a sound as she crept along and down the stairs. The front door of the *palazzo* wasn't even locked.

She slipped outside and her footsteps quickened as she crossed the courtyard, the warm air making her nightdress flutter around her. It didn't matter, there was nobody to see her. She couldn't explain it. Couldn't even think about it too much. But she was being drawn to the chapel like a magnet.

Except it wasn't really the chapel she wanted to see— it was the fresco.

The thick wooden door was heavy and she had to put her shoulder to it to finally push it open.

The slightly colder, stiller air of the chapel swept around her as soon as she stepped inside. Her footsteps stopped as the tiny hairs on her arms stood upright.

It was like walking into a scene from a scary movie. She was being ridiculous. Of course the chapel was slightly colder. The walls were thicker than the *palazzo*'s and the cooler air had probably helped with the preservation of the fresco.

It was pitch-black. Only a few strands of moonlight were sneaking through the stained-glass windows. Nothing was really visible. She hadn't thought to bring a candle with her.

She took a few small steps forward, hoping her eyes would adjust to the darkness around her. Her hand reached out to touch the cold wall. It was odd. This chapel must have hundreds of years' worth of history, hundreds of years' worth of stories to tell. Weddings, birth, funerals all held in here.

In a way it was nice the royal wedding was being held here. A piece of history was being brought back to life, back to its former glory. If they hadn't proposed to use this site, Burano's fresco might never have been discovered.

'Yaow!' She stubbed her foot on something—some kind of carpenter's toolbox—and bent to rub her bare toe. Her hand touched something on the floor. She fumbled for a second. A flashlight. Perfect. She flicked the switch and a thin beam of light cut through the darkness.

Now she could move more easily. She spun the torch around towards the fresco wall, the light hitting squarely on the Madonna's face. Lucia sucked in a breath. Her feet moved forward automatically. An invisible hand had reached into her chest and was squeezing at her heart.

This was it. This was what she'd needed to see. She moved the light a little downwards onto the face of baby Jesus, then back towards Mary. She drew up directly to the fresco, her hand shaking a little as Mary's face was illuminated in all its glory.

Every hint of colour, every hair on her head, every tiny line of her face—it was the expression that had been captured so beautifully. The expression that made her knees tremble.

She'd never seen it captured quite so perfectly. Even though it was paint that was centuries old she felt as if she could reach out and touch Mary. Stroke her cheek, feel the warmth of her skin, see the wonder in her eyes.

This was what she'd remembered. It was the thing that she'd pushed to the back of her head when she'd first seen the fresco. Now it was drawing her back.

Now she couldn't deny it. She couldn't ignore it.

This had all been in Burano's imagination. It felt as if he'd stepped back in time and caught that moment when a mother first looked at her child and was overcome by that huge wave of emotions and undeniable love. Baby Jesus was looking back at his mother with childlike wonder and awe. The look of love that only a child could give his mother—making the bond complete. The light behind the depiction of the Madonna and Child was almost ethereal. The glow around them was all-encompassing. All-consuming.

Her legs trembled. Her whole body was shaking.

And something, something from deep inside, was pushing its way out.

This was what she had missed. This was what she'd missed out on. This was what would never be hers. Never be shared between her and her daughter.

Her legs gave way, collapsing beneath her onto the dusty chapel floor as the sobs started to come out.

And twelve years' worth of suppressed grief started to flow.

Logan was pacing. He hadn't even made an attempt to go to bed. He'd heard rustling in the vineyard and had taken a restless walk to investigate. It had been fruitless. He'd found nothing. It had probably only been a fox.

But as he had been crossing back towards his farmhouse, something had caught his eye. At first he'd thought he had finally gone crazy and was imagining it. Then he'd looked again.

Lucia. Dressed in very little with bare legs, bare arms and a pale pink lace-trimmed nightdress fluttering around her in the warm breeze and clinging to every curve of her skin. Was she sleepwalking?

She seemed so focused, so light on her feet, that she almost floated across the courtyard, straight to the chapel entrance. He'd started to move in her direction but his footsteps had faltered as she'd paused at the chapel door, pushing it with her shoulder to lever it open.

Then she disappeared into the darkness.

Logan stopped. His heart was thudding in his chest. Should he follow, or should he leave?

Every part of his rational brain told him to step away. No matter how much he wanted to, he couldn't pursue a relationship with Lucia. Not like this. Not when they were both in different places.

But the protective element in him couldn't walk away. Couldn't leave her like this.

He walked quietly towards the chapel. A little beam of light appeared inside the chapel, cutting across the stained-glass windows. What was she doing?

He held his breath as he reached the doorway. Stepping inside the dark chapel was intimidating—and he was fully dressed. The thin beam of torchlight was focused on the fresco on the faraway wall.

He'd never seen it lit up like this before. He'd only ever really studied it in daylight. It looked entirely different under the concentrated light of a torch beam. The architect-minded part of him wondered how it must have looked hundreds of years ago in flickering candlelight.

Lucia had the beam directly on the Madonna's face. Under the artificial light her face was brightly illuminated. In a reach-out-and-touch kind of way.

The beam wobbled and he stepped forward. Part of his stomach was curled up in a ball. Lucia had come out to the chapel in the middle of the night. In the light reflected back off the fresco he could see her trembling, shuddering skin. Every muscle, every bone was shaking.

His response was automatic. He stepped forward just as she crumpled to the floor, her sobs cutting through the night air. The torch fell to the floor with a crash, the light sputtering out.

He was stunned. In twelve years he hadn't heard her cry. There had been a few tears just after the birth of their daughter—but none after that.

He wrapped his arms around her. Her skin was cold, chilled in the coolness of the chapel, so he pulled her against his chest and stroked her hair. He didn't care about the dust. He didn't care about the broken torch on the ground.

He just held her.

And she sobbed. Like no one he'd ever heard before. These weren't quiet, tiny sobs. These were loud and spluttering, echoing around the thick chapel walls. Her body was racked with them and he could feel her pain, feel her anguish. It was as if twelve years' worth of grief and sorrow had just erupted from her soul.

It was horrible to see the woman he loved like this. But he knew exactly how she felt. Only he could understand. So he waited and he held her, gently stroking her hair and whispering in her ear.

He had no idea how long they stayed that way. Eventually her sobs quietened, turning into little shudders instead of big outbursts. He changed position, pulling her up onto his knees, taking her bare legs away from the cold floor of the chapel.

His hands sneaked around her satin-covered waist and he pulled her against his chest. Her hands snaked up around his neck and her head tucked under his chin. He could feel her ragged breaths against his skin.

'I know, Lucia,' he said softly. 'I know how you feel. I loved her just as much as you did.'

She gave a little whimper and her fingers tightened around his neck. He waited a few seconds then gently lifted her head up. There was only a tiny bit of moonlight streaming through the stained-glass windows but he could see her tear-streaked face and he lifted both hands to caress it.

'Talk to me,' he whispered.

She shuddered, then nodded slowly.

It was odd. The strangest feeling in the world, but it was almost as if his body gave a little cry of relief.

'I miss her,' she said in shaky breaths. 'I miss her every day.'

His heart squeezed in his chest. He wanted to wrap his arms around her again and kiss her. But he needed to let her speak.

'I don't want to talk about her,' she said, her voice tinged with regret. 'If I don't talk about her, then none of it was real. None of it really happened.'

She shook her head as her voice rose in pain. 'Why, Logan? Why our baby? Why did we have to lose her? Do you know where we could be right now? Do you know what kind of life we could be leading?'

He nodded his head. 'Of course I do,' he whispered.

'But you were so calm, so controlled,' she said angrily. 'I couldn't be like that, I just couldn't. You did everything. You organised the flowers, the funeral, the casket. You spoke to the family.' She shook her head, her voice rising. 'How could you even do that? How could you even function? Our daughter was dead!'

'You think I didn't know that? You think I didn't hurt every bit as much as you? I hated that, Lucia. I hated every second of that. I hated the fact you wouldn't eat, you wouldn't sleep and you wouldn't talk to me. Organising was the only thing I *could* do. I wanted the world to know that Ariella Rose had existed. I wanted her to matter. I wanted to bury our daughter with the respect she deserved.' He hadn't realised this had been buried inside him. He hadn't realised he'd wanted to say all this to her.

'And I didn't?' She was crying again. 'You were so… capable. And I felt useless. I couldn't be the person I'd been. I couldn't be your other half. I couldn't look at you without thinking about her and what had been stolen from me!'

He clasped her head between his hands and leaned his forehead against hers. 'Stolen from *us*, Lucia,' he said quietly.

'I needed you. I needed you every second of the day. But I couldn't get to you. You locked yourself away from me and after a few weeks I realised that you needed to grieve differently from me. I didn't want to let you go. I never wanted to let you go. No matter how sorry I was, no matter how much I hurt, I still wanted you, Lucia. Every second of every day. You're the only person in this world for me. The only person I want to grow old with.' He traced a finger down her damp cheek. 'I just needed to see you cry. I just needed to know that you could acknowledge our daughter.'

She was still shuddering. He ran one hand down her

arm and could feel the tiny hairs on her arms standing on end.

'Why now? What's changed?'

She met his gaze with tear-filled eyes. 'You. I've avoided you for so long. Seeing you again, being together, remembering everything we've shared together, I couldn't hide away from it any more. It's just been bubbling underneath the surface the whole time. I couldn't keep it locked away any more. Not if I want to live.'

He gave his head a shake. 'But you wouldn't talk to me in Venice. You said you couldn't do it.'

She squeezed her eyes closed for a moment. 'I know.' Now she reached up and touched his face, his jaw. 'I think something just lined up for us, Logan.' She pointed towards the fresco. 'If you hadn't got this job, if this fresco hadn't been found, we probably wouldn't have met again.' She placed her hand over her heart. 'I *needed* this. I needed all this to happen.' She looked up towards the fresco. 'Hundreds of years ago Burano must have met someone, must have known a new mother, to capture the love and adoration in his painting. Because he's captured it so beautifully. When I first saw his fresco I wouldn't let the painting touch me. I wouldn't let it inside. I was jealous. I couldn't acknowledge the painting because *I* wanted to be that person. *I* wanted to be that mother who looks at her baby with such joy and pleasure, wondering what the world will hold for them.' The tears were falling freely down her face again.

All he wanted to do was comfort her. All he wanted to do was love her.

He sucked in a deep breath. 'Lucia, you can be that person. I want you to know that I love you. I want you— just the way you are. But if you want to try and have a family again then I'll be with you, every step of the way.' He stroked his thumb across her cheek. 'Likewise, if you just want to grow old and grey together and wander through the streets of Venice, or Florence, or even the Tuscan hills, I'll do that with you too. As long as I'm with you, I know I'll be happy.'

Her hands kept trembling as she wound them around his neck again, pressing her body against his and whispering in his ear. 'Can I be enough for you, Logan? Enough for you on my own? What if we weren't meant to have babies? What if that's never going to happen for us?'

He stood up, pulling her to her feet alongside him but keeping their bodies locked close together. He slid his hands along the satin slip covering her back and anchored her to him. He kissed one cheek and then the other. 'Then that's the way things are supposed to be. As long as I'm with you I can take whatever hand life deals us.'

He bent to meet her lips.

It was like the first kiss all over again.

This was the woman he'd fallen in love with all those years ago.

This was the woman he'd had to allow to walk away even though it had broken his heart.

This was the mother of his child.

This was his Lucia.

Her body was pressed against his and she responded to every touch, her fingers threading through his hair. Her rose scent wound around him, pulling him in in every way.

Her cold skin heated quickly, her lips matching every kiss.

For Logan, it was like coming home.

When Lucia finally pulled back he was shocked. She lifted a finger and placed it against his lips, keeping her body tight against his.

She took a deep breath. 'Logan, if this is going to work, there's something I need to do.'

His breath was caught somewhere in his throat. After twelve years there was finally a chance of a relationship again with Lucia. There wasn't anything he wouldn't agree to.

'What is it? What do you need to do? Because I don't want to lose you again. I don't want this chance to slip away from us.'

Her voice was trembling and her hand slid down his arm, interlocking their fingers. 'I was kind of hoping you would agree to do it with me.'

Her dark eyes met his gaze and he squeezed her hand tightly. 'Anything, Lucia,' he whispered. 'Anything for you.'

CHAPTER TEN

IT WAS A gorgeous summer's day with the sun high in the sky above them.

Logan was standing in front of her in his trademark cream suit and pale blue shirt. 'Ready?' he asked.

Her stomach was churning. Over and over. She would have tossed and turned last night if he hadn't held her safely in his arms. She'd even bought herself a new dress. Pale pink with tiny flowers. It was ridiculous. She didn't need it. But she'd wanted to wake up this morning and feel like everything was new.

More than anything, she wanted to be prepared.

Florence was alive. She'd forgotten how much she loved this city. Chattering voices were all around them, tourist parties bustling past and Italian voices mixing with a multitude of other languages.

She slid her hand into his, clutching her pink and lilac flowers in her hand. 'I'm ready,' she said with a certainty she hadn't known she possessed.

The walk through the streets took around fifteen minutes, the crowds lessening the further out they went. No one else was going where they were.

It was a pleasant walk with a few shopkeepers nodding at Logan as they passed by and him pointing out a few changes to the city since she'd left.

As the green archway of the cemetery came into view her footsteps faltered. Logan slipped his hand around her waist. As their bodies pressed against each other she fell into step with him. It felt natural and gave her the added reassurance to continue.

The cemetery was quiet, bathed in warm sunlight, with only a few people dotted around in quiet condolence.

Her throat was closing up as they walked along the white paved path. Like most cemeteries this one had a special section for children and babies. It was tucked away at the back, next to the white wall that separated the cemetery from the rest of the city.

There was a white bench in the middle, with lots of green grass and flower beds erupting with colour. Something inside her clenched. She hadn't allowed herself to think about this. She hadn't allowed herself to realise the beauty of the surroundings.

Within the cemetery walls she couldn't even hear the noise of the city outside. It was like their own private sanctuary.

She squeezed her eyes closed as they passed rows of little white headstones. So many little lives lost. So many other people who'd experienced the same pain that she had.

Had she maybe even met some of them? She'd been so immersed in her own grief that she hadn't stopped to think about anyone else's.

Their footsteps slowed. She'd only been here once and Logan had been numerous times but she still knew exactly where Ariella Rose was buried—it was imprinted in her brain.

They stopped and stood for a second, looking down at the little white headstone.

Beloved daughter.
Ariella Rose Cascini.
Born asleep.

Apart from the date, there was nothing else on the stone.

Lucia laid her head on his shoulder as silent tears fell down her cheeks. She needed this. She'd needed to do this for so long.

A dove swooped in the air above them, landing on the grass at their feet. Lucia gave a little nod of her head as it eyed her suspiciously then walked away. She put her pale pink and lilac flowers into the little white vase at the graveside then leaned over to touch the stone.

It was odd. Any marble headstone she'd ever touched before had been cold. But Ariella's wasn't. It was bathed in the bright light and warmed by the sun.

The horrible closed-in feeling that had been around her heart for so long was gone. The terrible weight and the dark cloud that had pressed on her shoulders for the last twelve years was finally gone.

Today she didn't feel despair all around her. Today she saw a beautiful memorial and resting place for her darling daughter. A place where she could come and sit sometimes if she needed to.

She'd been so afraid for so long. But with Logan by her side she didn't need to be.

'I love you, Ariella Rose,' she whispered. 'I'm sorry

I haven't been here and I promise to visit in the future.'
She stroked her hand along the stone and stood up,
taking the few steps to Logan and wrapping her arms
around his waist.

'Thank you,' she said quietly. 'Thank you for bringing me here.'

'Any time. Any time at all.'

He threaded his fingers back through hers. 'Do you
want to take some time? How do you feel?' His voice
was cautious.

She tilted her head up towards the sun and the face
of the man that she loved and adored. The man she
wanted to grow old with.

'I feel as if I've taken that step. The one that I've
needed to for so long. I'm ready now.'

He clasped both her hands in his. 'Ready for what?'

She met the gaze of his steady green eyes. 'Ready to
move forward. Now I can love the man I want to without feeling overcome with grief.' She smiled up at the
sun. 'Now I can look towards the future.'

There was a swell in her chest. A confidence she
hadn't felt in so long.

He reached up and slid his hand through her hair as
he pulled her to him.

'Then let's start now.'

And he kissed her.

And she kissed him right back.

She was laughing. She was running through the cobbled
streets of Monte Calanetti in her impossibly high heels.

He loved it. He loved every second of it. 'Watch out!'
he shouted. 'You'll break something!'

'Keep up, slowcoach!' she shouted over her shoulder as she made the final dash towards the fountain. He walked up behind her and slid his hands around her waist. He could feel her rapid breaths against his chest wall.

'Do you have them?' she asked.

He unfurled his fingers, revealing the shiny euro coins in his hand. He eyed the clamshell the nymph held above her head in the centre of the fountain. 'First time?' He was smiling. She'd tried this a hundred times before and had never managed to hit the mark—the clamshell that would make your wish come true.

Her deep brown eyes met his. 'First time,' she repeated. Her index finger moved the coins in the palm of his hand as if she was looking for just the right one. After a few seconds she smiled. 'This one,' she said, weighing the coin in her hand.

'That one? You're sure?'

'Oh, I'm sure.' She spun around to face the nymph. His hand was on her abdomen and she pressed her right hand over his, as she took a deep breath, pulled back her left hand and let the coin fly.

His eyes stayed on the coin as it caught the sunlight as it arced through the air, but his left hand was flicking something else into the fountain at their feet.

The coin was on a direct path and landed squarely in the middle of the clamshell. Lucia let out a shriek. 'I've done it! I've finally done it!' She spun around and flung her arms around his neck. 'I've finally done it.'

He picked her up and spun her around, her hair streaming out behind her. 'You've done it,' he cheered as he set her back down. 'Now, what did you wish for?'

For the first time his stomach wasn't in knots around Lucia. Slowly but surely she was turning back into the woman he loved. The dark shadows were going from her eyes. Her steps were lighter. She laughed more. She cried more. And she still loved to dance.

'Isn't the wish supposed to be a secret?' she said coyly.

He swallowed. He'd never felt more nervous, or surer about anything in his life. 'Look down,' he said quietly.

She blinked. It obviously wasn't what she had expected to hear. A frown creased her brow as she stared down, taking a few seconds to see the glint of gold under the clear water.

Her eyes widened and she bent down, putting her hand into the water and pulling out the ring.

'Logan?' she asked as a smile spread across her face.

It wasn't a traditional flashy engagement ring. He didn't want to waste any time. It was a gold wedding band studded with diamonds and rubies. It was a ring of promise. A ring of hope.

He didn't hesitate, just got down on one knee in front of the woman he loved. 'Lucia Moretti. You're the woman of my dreams. The woman I love with my whole heart. You are my perfect match. The person I want to laugh with, cry with, play with and grow old with. I believe this was meant to happen. I honestly believe we were meant to meet again and mourn our daughter together. I don't care where you want to make a life. I don't care if it's Venice, Florence, Rome or anywhere else. All that matters to me is that home is with you.' He pressed his hand against his heart. 'As long as I'm with you, I don't care where we are. You're the person I call home. You're all that I need. Will you make me the happiest man alive and marry me?'

She was still staring at the ring, watching the sun

glint off the little diamonds and rubies. The smile was permanently etched on her face.

She wrapped one arm around his neck and sat down on his knee. She didn't hesitate to slip the ring on her finger. 'How on earth could any woman refuse such a romantic proposal at Burano's fountain?' Her eyes were twinkling. She put her hand over his. 'There's no one else I ever want to be with. You're the only man for me.'

He pulled something out from behind his waist. 'I've brought you something else.'

She stared at the wrapped package. It wasn't big, small enough to tuck into his waistband. Plain canvas tied with string. She pulled the string and let the package unfurl. It was new paintbrushes and some oils. Her mouth fell open.

'How…how did you know?'

'That you'd want to take up painting again?'

She nodded as her eyes glistened with tears. 'Because we've come such a long way, Lucia. We've both moved on. You used to love painting and I know that you've found that little piece in your heart again that makes you ready to start again.'

She nodded her head slowly. 'You're right. I have. But I'd only just started to think about it.' She looked around. 'We're in such beautiful surroundings I can't help but feel inspired.'

He leaned forward to kiss her. 'Which leads me to my next question. Where do you want to live?'

She smiled and looked around. 'This might surprise you, but I've kind of grown fond of these Tuscan hills. I like the peace. I like the quiet. Maybe I'm not the city girl I thought.' She bit her bottom lip. 'How would you feel about finding somewhere to live around here?'

He stood and pulled her to her feet, holding her close. He ran his fingers through her hair. 'I think that this is a good place, a healing place. And I'm sure there's a Tuscan villa somewhere in these hills just waiting for us to renovate it. A villa where we can build you your own studio.'

She smiled again, 'All work and no play makes Logan a dull boy.'

She was teasing and he knew it. 'Who says anything about working?' he murmured.

She pressed a little kiss against his lips. 'Do you want to know what I wished for?'

'Are you going to tell me?'

She nodded. 'Someone must have been listening. When I threw that coin I wished for new beginnings.'

His eyebrows rose. 'You did?' It was perfect. It was as if everything was just meant to be.

'I did,' she said with confidence, and with that she rose up on her toes to kiss him. 'To new beginnings,' she whispered.

'New beginnings,' he murmured, and he kissed her right back.

* * * * *

THE BEST MAN &
THE WEDDING
PLANNER

TERESA CARPENTER

This book is dedicated to my editor Carly Byrne
for her patience, understanding, speed and good cheer.
I never see her sweat. Even when I do.
Thank you for everything.

CHAPTER ONE

"Now boarding, first-class passengers for Flight 510 to Florence."

Lindsay Reeves's ears perked up. She glanced at her watch; time had gotten away from her. She closed her tablet folio, tucked it into her satchel and then reached for the precious cargo she was personally escorting across the ocean. She hooked the garment bag holding the couture wedding dress for the future Queen of Halencia over her shoulder and began to move as the attendant made a second announcement. "First-class passengers now boarding."

"Welcome aboard." The attendant looked from the second ticket to Lindsay. "I'm sorry, both passengers will need to be present to board."

"We're both here. I bought a seat for this." She held up the garment bag.

The woman smiled but her eyes questioned Lindsay's sanity. "You bought a first-class ticket for your luggage?"

"Yes." She kept it at that, not wanting to draw any further attention. With the wedding only a month away, the world was alive with wedding dress fever.

"We have a storage closet in first class that can hold it if you want to refund the ticket before takeoff," the attendant offered.

"No, thank you." Lindsay pressed the second ticket into the woman's hand. "I'm not letting this bag out of my sight."

On the plane she passed a nice-looking older couple already seated in the first row and moved on to the last row where she spied her seats. She draped the garment bag over the aisle seat and frowned when it immediately slumped into a scrunched heap on the seat.

That wouldn't do. She pulled it back into place and tried to anchor it but when she let go, it drooped again. The weight of the dress, easily thirty pounds, made it too heavy to lie nicely. She needed something to hold it in place. After using her satchel to counter the weight temporarily, she slid past a young couple and their two children to speak to the flight attendant.

"We have a closet we can hang the dress in," the male attendant stated upon hearing her request.

"I've been paid not to let it out of my sight," she responded. True enough. Her reputation as a wedding planner to the rich and famous depended on her getting this dress to the wedding in pristine condition without anyone seeing it but her, the bride and her attendants.

"Hmm," the man—his name tag read Dan—tapped his lips while he thought.

"Welcome aboard, sir." Behind Lindsay another attendant, a blonde woman, greeted a fellow passenger.

Out of the corner of her eye Lindsay got the impression of a very tall, very broad, dark-haired man. She stepped into the galley to give them more room.

"You're the last of our first-class passengers," the attendant advised the man. "Once you're seated, please let me know if you need anything."

"Check," the man said in a deep, bass voice and moved down the aisle.

Goodness. Just the one word sent a tingle down Lindsay's spine. She sure hoped he intended to sleep during the long, red-eye flight. She wanted to get some work done and his voice might prove quite distracting.

"I've got it." Dan waved a triumphant hand. "We'll just put the seat in sleep mode and lay the bag across it."

He poured a glass of champagne and then another. "Will that work?"

"Yes, that will be perfect. Thank you."

"Seats aren't allowed to be reclined during takeoff. Once we reach cruising altitude I'll be along to put the seat down. And I'll look for something to secure it in case the flight gets bumpy."

"Great. You've been very helpful."

Lindsay headed back to her seat. Halfway through first class she caught sight of the newcomer and her breath caught in the back of her throat. He was beautiful. There was no other word for it. Long, lean features with high cheekbones, dark, slanted eyebrows and long, black eyelashes. Dark stubble decorated his square jaw.

Suddenly her eyes popped wide and she let out a shriek. "Get up!" she demanded. "Get up right now!"

He was sitting on the dress!

A frown furrowed his brow. He slowly opened lambent brown eyes so stunning she almost forgot why she was yelling. Almost.

"Are you talking to me?" he asked in a deep, rasping voice.

"Yes." She confronted the man, hands on hips. "You're in my seat. Sitting on my dress. Get up!"

"What's the problem here?" The other attendant appeared next to her.

"He's in my seat." She pointed an accusing finger. "Sitting on my garment bag. Make him move."

Behind her a young child began to cry. Lindsay cringed but held her ground.

The beading on this dress was intricate, all hand-sewn. If it had to be repaired it would cost a fortune. And she'd already paid a pretty penny to make sure nothing happened to it. How could someone sit on a garment bag without noticing it?

"Let's all calm down." The blonde attendant squeezed by Lindsay. "Sir, can I ask you to stand, please?"

The man slowly rose. He had to duck to the side to avoid hitting the overhead compartment. He must be six-four, maybe six-five; a long way to glare up from five feet four. She managed.

"I'm not sitting on anything." He gestured across the aisle. "I moved it there because it was in my seat."

Lindsay looked to her left. The garment bag rested in a heap on the seat with her heavy satchel dumped on top. She jumped on it, removing her bag and smoothing the fabric. It was all mushed as though it had been sat on.

"May I see your tickets, please?" Dan requested.

Lindsay pulled hers from the front pocket of her satchel and waited to be vindicated.

"Actually, you're both in wrong seats. My fault, I'm afraid. I'm used to a different plane. I do apologize. Ms. Reeves, you are on the left and, Mr. Sullivan, you need to move forward a row."

Lovely. She couldn't even blame the beast. Except she did.

At least he'd be in the row ahead of her so she wouldn't have to have him next to her the entire flight.

His brown gaze went to the toddlers in the row in front of the one the attendant indicated. "I'd prefer the back row." He pasted on a charming smile. "Is it possible to trade seats?"

No. No. No.

"Of course." The blonde gushed, swayed, no doubt, by his dimples. "There was a cancellation so no one else is boarding in first class. Is there anything I can get you before we continue boarding?"

"A pillow would be nice."

"My pleasure, Mr. Sullivan." She turned to Lindsay. "Anything for you, ma'am?"

Ma'am? Seriously? "I'd like a pillow. And a blanket, please."

"We'll do a full turndown service after the flight gets started." She gave Sullivan a smile and disappeared behind the curtain to the coach area.

Lindsay stared after her. Did that mean she didn't get a pillow or a blanket? This was her first time flying first-class. So far she had mixed feelings. She liked the extra room and the thought of stretching out for the long flight. But Blondie wasn't earning any points.

Lindsay draped the garment bag over the window seat as best she could until the seat could be reclined. Unfortunately that put her in the aisle seat directly across from Mr. Tall, Dark and Inconsiderate.

Nothing for it. She'd just have to ignore him and focus on her work. It would take the entire flight to configure the seating arrangement for the reception. She had the list of guests from the bride and the list of guests from the groom. And a three-page list of political notes from the palace of who couldn't be seated next to whom and who should be seated closer to the royal couple. What had started as a private country wedding had grown to include more than a hundred guests as political factors came into play.

It was a wedding planner's nightmare. But she took it as an opportunity to excel.

Before she knew it she was being pushed back in her chair as the plane lifted into the air. Soon after, Dan appeared to fold down the window seat. He carefully laid the heavy garment bag in place and secured it with the seat belt and a bungee cord. She thanked him as she resumed her seat.

She glanced out of the corner of her eye to see Sullivan had his pillow—a nice, big, fluffy one. Ignore him.

Easier thought than done. He smelled great; a spicy musk with a touch of soap.

Eyes back on her tablet, she shuffled some names into table seats and then started to run them against her lists to see if they were all compatible. Of course, they weren't. Two people needed to be moved forward and two people couldn't be seated together. That left four people at the table. She moved people to new tables and highlighted them as a reminder to check out the politics on them. And repeated the process.

A soft snore came from across the way—much less annoying than the shrill cry of one of the toddlers demanding a bandage for his boo-boo. Blondie rushed to the rescue and the boy settled down. Except for loud outbursts like that, the two boys were actually well behaved. There'd been no need for Sullivan to move seats.

"Would you care for a meal, Ms. Reeves?" Dan appeared beside her.

She glanced at the time on her tablet. Eight o'clock. They'd been in the air an hour. "Yes, please."

"You have a choice of chicken Cordon bleu or beef Stroganoff."

"I'll have the beef. With a cola."

He nodded and turned to the other side of the aisle. Before he could ask, Sullivan said he'd have the beef and water.

Her gaze collided with his. Brown eyes with specks of gold surveyed her, interest and appreciation sparkled in the whiskey-brown depths, warm and potent.

Heat flooded her, followed by a shiver.

"What's in the bag?" he asked, his voice even deeper and raspier from sleep. Way too sexy for her peace of mind.

"None of your business." She turned back to her table plan.

"Must be pretty important for you to get so upset. Let

me guess, a special dress for a special occasion?" He didn't give up.

"Yes. If you must know. And it's my job to protect it."

"Protect it? Interesting. So it's not your dress."

She rolled her eyes and sent him a droll stare. "I liked you better when you were snoring."

He grinned, making his dimples pop. "I deserve that. Listen, I'm sorry for my attitude earlier and for sitting on the dress. I had wine with dinner and wine always gives me a headache."

Lindsay glared at Sullivan. "So you did sit on the dress." She knew it. That had definitely been a butt print on the bag.

He blinked, all innocence. "I meant I'm sorry for dumping it over there."

"Uh-huh."

His grin never wavered.

"Why did you have wine with dinner if it gives you a headache?"

The smile faded. "Because dinner with my folks always goes better with a little wine. And I'm going to have a headache at the end either way."

"Okay, I get that." Lindsay adored her flighty, dependent mother but, yeah, dinners were easier with a little wine. Sometimes, like between husbands, a lot of wine was required.

A corner of his rather nice mouth kicked up. "You surprise me, Ms. Reeves. I'd have thought you'd be appalled."

"Parents aren't always easy." She closed her tablet to get ready for her meal. "It doesn't mean we don't love them."

"Amen. Respect is another matter."

That brought her attention around. He wore a grim expression and turmoil churned in his distracted gaze. The situation with his parents must be complicated. It was a sad day when you lost respect for the person you loved most in the world. She understood his pain only too well.

Thankfully, Dan arrived with a small cart, disrupting old memories. He activated a tray on the side of her seat and placed a covered plate in front of her along with a glass of soda. Real china, real crystal, real silverware. Nice. And then he lifted the cover and the luscious scent of braised meat and rich sauce reached her.

"Mmm." She hummed her approval. "This looks fantastic."

"I can promise you it is," Dan assured her. "Chef LaSalle is the pride of the skies."

She took her first bite as he served Sullivan and moaned again. She couldn't help it, the flavors burst in her mouth, seducing her taste buds.

"Careful, Ms. Reeves," Sullivan cautioned. "You sound like you're having a good time over there."

"Eat. You'll understand." She took a sip of her drink, watching him take a bite. "Or maybe not. After all, you've already eaten."

"I wasn't hungry earlier. Damn, this is good." He pointed to the video screen. "Shall we watch a movie with our meal?"

She was tempted. Surprising. After the disaster of last year, work had been her major consolation. She rarely took the time to relax with a movie. She was too busy handling events for the stars of those movies. A girl had to work hard to make the stars happy in Hollywood. And she had to work harder than the rest after allowing an old flame to distract her to the point of putting her career at risk. But she'd learned her lesson.

Luckily she'd already signed the contract for this gig. And she planned to make the royal wedding of the Crown Prince of Halencia, Antonio de l'Accardi, to the commoner, Christina Rose, the wedding of the century.

Thirty days from now no one would be able to question her dedication—which meant returning to the puzzle of the table seating.

"You go on," she told Sullivan. "I have to get back to my work."

"What are you doing over there? Those earlier moans weren't as pleasant as your dinner noises."

"It's a creative new form of torture called a seating arrangement."

"Ah. It sounds excruciating."

"Oh, believe me. It's for a political dinner and there are all these levels of protocols of who can sit with whom. And then there's the added element of personal likes and dislikes. It's two steps back for every one step forward. And it's a lot of manual double-checking…talk about a headache."

"Politics usually are." The grimness in his tone told her there was something more there. Before she had time to wonder about it, he went on. "The information isn't on spreadsheets?"

"It is, but there are more than a hundred names here. I have to seat a table and then check each name to see if they're compatible."

"You know you can set up a program that can look at the information and tell you whether the table mates are compatible at the time you put the name in."

She blinked at him. "That would be wonderful. How do I do that exactly?"

He laughed, a deep, friendly sound, then rattled off a string of commands that had her eyes glazing over. "The setup will take a few minutes but will likely save you hours overall."

"Yeah, but you lost me at the word 'algorithm.'" She wiped her mouth with the cloth napkin. "You really had my hopes up for a minute there."

"Sorry, tech talk. I own a company that provides software for cyber security. A program like this really isn't that difficult. Let me see your computer after dinner and I'll do it for you. It'll take me less than an hour."

This man was tempting her left and right. She weighed the hours she'd save against the confidentiality agreement she'd signed and sadly shook her head.

"Thank you for offering but I can't. This is a special event. I'm not allowed to share information with anyone except my staff, designated officials and pre-approved vendors."

"This is for the royal wedding of Prince Antonio of Halencia, right?"

Her eyes popped wide. How could he know that?

"Come on, it's not hard to guess. The wedding dress, the seating chart. We're on a flight to Florence. And I know they have an American event planner. Hang on, I'll take care of this."

He pulled out his cell phone and hit a couple of buttons.

"What?" she challenged. "You're calling the palace in Halencia? Uh, huh. I don't think so. You can hang up now."

"Hey, Tony." He raised a dark eyebrow as he spoke into the phone.

Tony? As in Antonio? Yeah, right.

"I got your text. Don't worry about it. I'm here for a month. I'll see you next week." He listened for a moment. "Yes, I had dinner with them. They were thrilled with the invitation. Hey, listen, the wedding planner is on my flight and she needs some programming to help her with the seating chart. She's bound by the confidentiality agreement from letting me help her. Can you give her authorization? Great, I'm going to put her on."

He held the phone out to Lindsay. "It's Prince Antonio."

CHAPTER TWO

LINDSAY ROLLED HER eyes at the man across the way, wondering how far he meant to take this joke and what he hoped to achieve.

"Hello?"

"*Buona sera*, Ms. Reeves. I hope you are having a nice flight."

"Uh, yes, I am." The voice was male, pleasant and slightly accented. And could be anyone. Except how had he known her name? Sullivan hadn't mentioned it.

"Christina is thrilled to have your services for the wedding. You have my full support to make this *il matrimonio dei suoi sogni*—the wedding of her dreams."

"I'll do my best." Could this actually be the prince?

"Duty demands my presence at the palace but I look forward to meeting you at the rehearsal. Zach is my best man. He will be my advocate in Monte Calanetti for the next month. He is available to assist you in any way necessary."

She turned to look at the man across the aisle and quirked a brow at his evil smirk. "Zach...Sullivan?"

"Yes. We went to college together. He's like a brother to me. If he can assist with the meal plan—"

"The seating chart." She squeezed her eyes closed. *OMG, I just interrupted the royal prince.*

"Of course. The seating chart. If Zach can help, you must allow him to be of service. He is quite handy with a computer."

"Yes. I will. Thank you."

"It is I who thanks you. You do us an honor by coming to Halencia. If I can be of further assistance, you have access to me through Zach. *Buona notte*, Ms. Reeves."

"Good night." Instead of giving the phone back to Sullivan she checked the call history and saw she'd spoken to Tony de l'Accardi. She slowly turned her head to meet chocolate-brown eyes. "You know the Prince of Halencia."

"I wouldn't take on the best man gig for anyone else."

The flight attendant appeared with the cart to collect his meal and sweetly inquire if he'd like dessert.

Lindsay rolled her eyes, barely completing the action before the blonde turned to her.

"Are you done, ma'am?"

Ma'am again? Lindsay's eyes narrowed in a bland stare. Her displeasure must have registered because the woman rushed on. "For dessert we have crème brûlée, strawberry cheesecake or a chocolate mousse."

Lindsay handed off her empty plate and, looking the woman straight in the eye, declared, "I'll have one of each."

"Of course, ma... Ms. Reeves." She hurriedly stashed the plate and rolled the cart away.

Lindsay slowly turned her head until Sullivan's intent regard came into view. Okay, first things first. "I'm only twenty-nine. Way too young to be ma'am."

He cocked his head.

She handed him his phone. "Why didn't you tell me you were the best man?"

He lifted one dark eyebrow. "Would you have believed me?"

She contemplated him. "Probably. I have a file on you."

His slanted eyebrow seemed to dip even further. "Then I'm surprised you didn't recognize me. You probably have profiles on the entire wedding party in that tablet of yours."

She lifted one shoulder in a half shrug of acknowledgment. "I've learned it's wise to know who I'll be working with. I didn't recognize you because it's out of context.

Plus, you don't have an eight-o'clock shadow in your company photo in which you're wearing glasses."

"Huh." He ran the backs of his fingers over his jaw. "I'll have to get that picture updated. I had Lasik eye surgery over a year ago. Regardless, I didn't know you were involved in the wedding until you started talking about the meal arrangements."

"Seating arrangements," she corrected automatically.

"Right."

The flight attendant arrived with dessert. She handed Zach a crystal dish of chocolate mousse and set a small tray with all three desserts artfully displayed in front of Lindsay.

"Enjoy," she said and retreated down the aisle.

"Mmm." Lindsay picked up a spoon and broke into the hard shell of crystalized sugar topping the crème brûlée. "Mmm." This time it was a moan. "Oh, that's good."

"Careful, Ms. Reeves, you're going to get me worked up if you continue." Zach gestured at her loaded tray with his spoon. "I see you like your sweets."

"It's a long night." She defended her stash.

"I guess you don't plan on sleeping."

"I have a lot of work." She gave her usual excuse then, for some unknown reason, confessed, "I don't sleep well on planes."

"It may help if you relaxed and watched the movie instead of working."

No doubt he was right. But work soothed her, usually. Over the past year she'd found it increasingly more difficult to believe in the magic of her process. She blamed her breakup with Kevin last year. But she hoped to change that soon. If a royal wedding couldn't bring back the magic in what she did, she needed to rethink her career path.

"Thank you for that insightful bit of advice. What don't you like about being best man? The role or the exposure?"

"Either. Both. Seems like I've been dodging the lime-light since I was two."

"Well, you did grow up in a political family." That brought his earlier comment and reaction into context. Her research revealed he was related to the political pow-erhouse Sullivans from Connecticut. "Never had any as-piration in that direction?"

The curse he uttered made her glance worriedly toward the toddlers. Luckily the lack of sound or movement in that direction indicated they were probably asleep.

"I'll take that as a no."

"I wished my father understood me so well."

She empathized with his pain. She felt the same way about her mother. Perhaps empathy was why she found him so easy to talk to. "I've found parents often see what they want to see. That addresses the exposure…what do you have against the role of best man?"

"I hate weddings. The fancier the event, the more I de-test them. There's something about the pomp and circum-stance that just screams fake to me." He licked his spoon and set the crystal dish aside. "No offense."

No offense? He'd just slammed everything she stood for. Why should she be offended?

And he wasn't done. "It's like the couple needs to dis-tract the crowd from the fact they're marrying for some-thing other than love."

"You don't believe in love?" It was one thing for her to question her belief in what she was doing and another for someone else to take shots at it.

"I believe in lust and companionship. Love is a myth best left to romance novels."

"Wow. That's harsh." And came way too close to how she felt these days.

The way his features hardened when he voiced his feel-ings told her strong emotion backed his comment. Kind of at odds with his family dynamic. The Sullivans were touted as one of the All-American families going back for generations. Long marriages and one or two kids who were all upstanding citizens. They ranked right up there with the Kennedys and Rockefellers.

The attendants came through the cabin collecting trash and dirty dishes. They offered turndown service, which Lindsay turned down. She still had work to do.

"Just let us know when you're ready."

Across the way Zach also delayed his bed service and got the same response. Once the attendants moved on, he leaned her way.

"Now you know you can trust me, are you ready for me to work on your spreadsheet? I'd like to do it before I start my movie."

"Oh. Sure." Could she trust him? Lindsay wondered as she pulled out her tablet. Just because she knew who he was didn't mean he was trustworthy. Too charming for her peace of mind. And a total flirt. "Do you want to do it on mine or should I send it to you?"

"Little Pixie, I'd like to do yours." His gaze ran over her, growing hotter as it rolled up her body. Her blood was steaming by the time his gaze met hers. "But since I have to work, you should send it to me."

"It'll do you no good to flirt with me." She tapped in her password and opened her spreadsheet. "What's your email?" She keyed in the address and sent it. "This wedding is too important to my career for me to risk getting involved with the best man."

"Oh, come on. The best man is harmless." Zach had his laptop open. "Got it. He's shackled for the whole event."

"The best man is a beast. His mind is all wrapped up in the bachelor party and strippers. He feels it's his duty to show the groom what he'll be giving up. And more than

half the time he's on the prowl for some action just to remind himself he's still free, whether he is or not."

Zach flinched. "Wow. That's harsh."

Oh, clever man. "With good cause. I have a strict 'no
fraternizing with the wedding party—including guests'—
policy for my company and the vendors I work with. But,
yeah, I've had to bolster a few bridesmaids who took it
too far and expected too much and went home alone. Or
refer them back to the bride or groom for contact info that
wasn't shared."

"That's a lot of blame heaped on the best man."

"Of course, it's not just the best man, but in my experience he can be a bad, bad boy."

"It's been a long time since I was bad."

"Define long."

He laughed.

"Seriously, I just want you to rewind the conversation a
few sentences and then say that again with a straight face."

His gaze shifted from his laptop to make another slow
stroll over her. Jacking up her pulse yet again.

He needed to stop doing that!

Unremorseful, he cocked an eyebrow. "I'm not saying I
don't go after what I want. But I'm always up front about
my intentions. No illusions, no damages."

Sounded like a bad boy to her.

"Well, you have fun, now. I'm here to work."

He shook his head as he went back to keying commands into his computer. "All work and no play makes
Ms. Reeves a dull girl."

"I'm not being paid to have fun." And that was the
problem right there—the one she'd been struggling with
for nearly a year.

Her work wasn't fun anymore.

And the cause wasn't just the disillusionment she suffered in her love life. Though that ranked high on the

motive list. She'd started feeling this way before Kevin had come back into her life. Instead of being excited by the creative endeavor, she'd gotten bogged down in the details.

Maybe it was Hollywood. Believing in the magic of happily-ever-after got a little harder to do with each repeat customer. Not to mention the three-peats. And the fact her mother was her best customer. Hopefully, husband number six would be the charm for her.

Seriously, Lindsay crossed her fingers in the folds of her skirt. She truly wished this marriage lasted. She liked Matt and he seemed to get her mom, who had the attention span and sense of responsibility of a fourteen-year-old. There was nothing mentally wrong with Darlene Reeves. She could do for herself. She just didn't want to. Darlene's dad had treated her like a princess, giving her most everything she wanted and taking care of all the little details in life. He'd died when she was seventeen and she'd been chasing his replacement all her life.

She'd had Lindsay when she was eighteen and then she learned to get the wedding ring on her finger before they lost interest. In between love interests, Lindsay was expected to pick up the slack.

She loved her mother dearly. But she loved her a little easier when she was in a committed relationship.

"Did you fall asleep on me over there?"

His question called her attention to his profile. Such strong features—square jaw dusted with stubble-defined cheekbones, straight nose. He really was beautiful in a totally masculine way. Too much temptation. Good thing her policy put him off limits.

"No. Just going over what I need to do."

"Perfect timing then." He swirled his finger and hit a single key. "Because I just sent your file back to you."

"So soon?" She reached for her tablet, excited to try the

new program. The file opened onto a picture of circles in the form of a rectangle. Each circle was numbered. She'd refine the shape once she viewed the venue. She ran her finger across the page and as it moved over a circle names popped up showing who was seated at the table.

"Cool. How do I see everybody?"

"You hit this icon here." He hung over his chair, reaching across the aisle to show her. He tried showing her the other features, but his actions were awkward. Being left-handed, he had to use his right hand to aid her because of the distance between the seats.

"This is ridiculous." Unsnapping her seat belt, she stood. "Do you mind if I come over there for a few minutes while we go over this?"

"Sure." He stood, as well, and stepped aside.

Standing next to him she came face to loosened tie with him. She bent her head back to see him and then bent it back again to meet his gaze. "My goodness. How tall are you?"

"Six-four."

"And the prince?"

"Six-one." Long fingers tugged on a short dark tendril. "Does this brain never stop working?"

"Not when I get a visual of a tall drink of water standing next to a shot glass."

"I'm not quite sure what that means, but I think there was a compliment in there somewhere."

"Don't start imagining things at fifty thousand feet, Sullivan. We're a long way from help." She tugged on his blue-pinstriped tie. "You can ditch this now. Was dinner a formal affair?"

The light went out of his eyes. He yanked the tie off and stuffed it in his pants' pocket. "It's always formal with my parents."

She patted his chest. "You did your duty, now move on."

"Good advice." He gestured for her to take the window seat.

She hesitated for a beat. Being trapped in the inside seat, surrounded by his potent masculinity, might be pushing her self-control a little thin. But his computer program blew her mind. From the tiny bit she'd seen, it had the potential to save her hours, if not days, of work.

"Ms. Reeves?" His breath wafted over her ear, sending a shiver racing down her spine. "Are you okay?"

"Of course." She realized he'd been talking while she fought off her panic attack. "Ah...hmm." She cleared her throat to give herself a moment to calm down. "Why do you keep calling me by my last name?"

"Because I don't know your first name," he stated simply.

Oh, right. The flight attendants had used their last names. The prince had given her Zach's name and then she'd read it on her spreadsheet.

"It's Lindsay."

A slow grin formed, crinkling the corners of his eyes. "Pretty. A pretty name for a pretty girl."

So obvious, yet the words still gave her a bit of a thrill. She pressed her lips together to hide her reaction. "You can't help yourself, can you?"

"What?" All innocence.

"Please. That line is so old I think I heard it in kindergarten."

She expected to see his dimple flash but got an intent stare instead. "It's not a line when it's true."

A little thrill chased goose bumps across her skin. Oh, my, he was good.

She almost believed him.

Shaking her head at him, at herself, she slid past him and dropped into the window seat.

He slid into his seat, his big body filling up the small

space. Thankfully they were in first class and a ten-inch
console separated their seats, giving her some breathing space. Until he flicked some buttons and the console
dropped down.

"That's better."

For who? She leaned away as he leaned closer. Just as
she feared, she felt pinned in, crowded. When he dropped
the tray down in front of her, the sense of being squeezed
from all sides grew stronger. Not by claustrophobia but
by awareness. His scent—man and chocolate—made her
mouth water.

"So is it easy for you?" He half laughed, going back to
their previous conversation. "To move on?"

"It's not, actually. My mom problems are probably just
as bad as or worse than your parent problems. Yet, here I
am, jetting off to Italy."

Mom's words, not hers. Darlene couldn't understand
how Lindsay could leave and be gone for a month when
Darlene's next wedding was fast approaching. It didn't
matter that Lindsay had booked this event well before
Darlene got engaged or that it was the wedding of the
year—perhaps the decade—and a huge honor for Lindsay to be asked to handle it.

"I doubt it."

"Really? My mother is my best customer."

"Oh-hh." He dragged the word out.

"Exactly. Soon I'll be walking her down the aisle to
husband number six."

"Ouch. Is she a glutton for punishment?"

"Quite the opposite. My mother loves to be in love. The
minute a marriage becomes work, it's the beginning of the
end. What I can't get her to understand is that you have to
work on your marriage from day one. Love needs to be
fostered and nourished through respect and compromise."

"Honesty, communication and loyalty are key."

"Yes!" She nudged him in the arm. "You get it. Maybe you won't be such a bad best man, after all."

He lifted one dark eyebrow. "Thanks."

"Anyway. I can waste a lot of time worrying about Mom or I can accept that it's her life to live. Just as my life is mine to live." She didn't know why she was sharing this with him. Her mother's love life wasn't a secret. Far from it. But Lindsay rarely talked about her mother. "Until the next time she comes crying on my shoulder, I choose the latter."

"At least she lets her suckers off the line."

"What does that mean?"

"Nothing." He ran a hand around the back of his neck, loosening tight muscles. "It's hard to let my parents just be when they keep harping on me to join the campaign trail."

"They want you to run for office?"

"Oh, yeah. I'm to stop messing around with my little hobby and turn my mind to upholding the family name by running for the next open seat in congress."

"Hobby? Didn't I read an article that your company just landed a hundred-million-dollar government contract to upgrade electronic security for the military?"

"You did." While he talked he opened the seating arrangement program. "And between that contract and Antonio selling me his share of the business, I've met a goal I set the day I opened my business."

Clearly, resignation overshadowed pride, so she ventured, "You exceeded your father's net worth?"

He shifted to study her. "So you're psychic as well as a wedding planner?"

"When you work with people as closely as I do, you get to know how they think."

"Hmm."

"It's an impressive accomplishment."

The Sullivans came from old money made from banking and transportation. Their political dynasty went back several generations. "Your parents must be proud of you."

"They didn't even mention it. Too focused on when I'd leave it all behind and fall in line with my family obligations." He tapped a few keys and her seating arrangement popped up on the screen. "Feels kind of hollow now."

"I'm sorry."

He didn't look up. "It doesn't matter."

"You mean it didn't matter to them."

He gave a negligent shrug. "I'm a big boy. I can handle it."

"Well, I officially call the parent battle a draw. I know it's not the same but…congratulations."

That earned her a half smile and a nod. Then he started to run her through the features of the computer program.

"This is fabulous." All she had to do was type a name into a seat slot and all the notes associated with that name appeared sorted by category and importance. "You have saved me hours of work."

His eyes gleamed as he went on to show her a few additional options. "And if you do this—" he punched a couple of keys "—it will auto-fill based on a selected category." He clicked social standing and then pressed Enter. Names popped into assigned seats.

She blinked. "Wow. What do the colors mean?" Many of the names were in red and blue.

"Blue means there's a conflict with someone else at the table. Red means there are two or more conflicts."

While he showed her how to access the conflicts, she impulsively pressed the button to call the attendant. The blonde appeared with impressive speed, her smile dimming slightly when she saw Lindsay seated with Zach.

"How can I help you?"

"We'd like two glasses of champagne, please. And some strawberries if you have them."

"I think I can find some. Be right back."

"Champagne?" He cocked his head. "You turned it down earlier."

"That was before. Now we have things to celebrate. I have this to help me finish my seating plan and you met a career-long goal."

The attendant arrived with a tray, setting it down between them. "*Buon appetito!* Ms. Reeves, would you like us to do your turndown service now?"

"Sure." Maybe the champagne would help her sleep. The woman turned away and Lindsay lifted a flute of bubbling gold wine. "To you. Congratulations and thank you."

Zach lifted his flute and tapped it against Lindsay's. "To you." A crystal chime rang out as pretty as the sound of her laughter. Her simple gesture almost undid the butcher job his parent's self-absorption had done to his pride. He didn't get them, probably never would. They couldn't spare the smallest show of affection. But this prickly little pixie put her animosity aside to toast his success.

She didn't know him except as a helpful jerk and a few dry facts on paper. Heck, she hugged the window in an attempt to maintain her distance yet she still celebrated his accomplishment.

It almost made him feel bad about sabotaging the wedding.

CHAPTER THREE

IT WAS A drastic plan. One Zach took no pleasure in. But he'd do whatever necessary to ensure his friend didn't suffer the frigid existence his parents called marriage. Antonio was already sacrificing his life for his country; selling off his business interests in America to Zach. He shouldn't have to give up all chance of happiness, too.

Zach reluctantly agreed to be best man. He didn't believe in big, lavish weddings. And he didn't approve of Tony's insane sacrifice. So why would he agree? Because Tony was the closest thing he had to a brother. Of course, he had to support him.

And of course he felt compelled to talk him out of throwing his future away.

Zach knew the circumstances of Antonio's marriage and it made him sick to think of his honorable, big-hearted friend locked into a miserable existence like his parents had shared.

He wasn't thinking of doing anything overt. Certainly nothing that would embarrass the royal family, especially his best friend. But he could cause a few delays. And earn enough time to talk his friend out of making the biggest mistake of his life.

Tony had a lot on his plate taking on the leadership of his country. Halencia had reached a state of crisis. Antonio's parents were gregarious, bigger-than-life characters madly in love with each other one moment and viciously in hate the next. There'd been public affairs and passionate reconciliations.

The country languished under their inattention. The

king and queen lived big and spent big, costing the country much-needed funds.

The citizens of Halencia loved the drama, hated the politics. Demands for a change had started years ago but had become more persistent in the past five years. Until a year ago when the king was threatened with a paternity suit. It turned out Antonio wasn't getting a new sibling. It was just a scare tactic gone wrong.

But it was the last straw for the citizens of Halencia.

The chancellor of the high counsel had gone to Antonio and demanded action be taken.

Antonio had flown home to advise his father the time had come. The king must abdicate and let Antonio rule or risk the monarchy being overthrown completely.

The citizens of Halencia cheered in the streets. Antonio was well loved in his home country. He lived and worked in California, but he took his duty as prince seriously. He returned home two or three times a year, maintaining a residence in Halencia and supporting many businesses and charities.

Everyone was happy. Except Tony, who had to leave everything he'd worked to achieve and go home to marry a woman he barely knew.

Zach knew the truth behind Tony's impromptu engagement four years ago. He was one of a handful of people who did. And though it was motivated by love, it wasn't for the woman he'd planned to marry.

Tony was a smart man. Zach just needed a little time to convince him that marriage was drastic and unnecessary.

Lindsay seemed like a nice person. She'd understand when this all played out. Surely she wouldn't want to bring together two people who were not meant to be a couple. Plus, she'd get paid either way. And have a nice trip to Italy for her troubles.

Once he was in Halencia and had access to Tony and

Christina, he'd subtly hound them until one or the other caved to the pressure. And maybe cause a snag or two along the way so the whole thing just seemed like a bad idea.

Of course he'd have to distract the pretty wedding planner with a faux flirtation to keep her from noticing his shenanigans. No hardship there. He was attracted enough to the feisty pixie to make it fun, but she was way too picket-fence for him so there was no danger of taking it too far.

He saw it as win, win, win. Especially for those not stuck in a loveless marriage.

She lifted her glass again. "And thanks again for this program."

"I hope you like puzzles, because there's still a lot of work there."

"Not near what there was." She picked up a strawberry, dipped it in her flute and sank dainty white teeth into the fruit. The ripe juice stained her lips red and he had the keenest urge to taste the sweetness left behind. "In fact, I may actually watch the movie."

"Excellent." He all but had her eating out of his hand with that act of kindness. And he'd needed something after stumbling onto the plane half blind with a migraine and sitting on the blasted dress. He'd popped some over-the-counter meds just before boarding. Thank the flight gods the headache had finally eased off.

He needed to stick close to her if this sabotage was going to work. He'd do his best to protect her as he went forward, but if it came down to a choice between her job and the happiness of the man who meant more to him than family, he'd choose Tony every time. No matter how pretty the wedding planner.

He'd revealed more about himself than he meant to, than he ever did really. But her attitude toward parental problems appealed to him: do what you can and move on. How refreshing to find someone who understood and accepted that not all parents were perfect. Many people didn't get along with their parents but most loved and respected them.

He tolerated his parents, but he wasn't willing to make a total break, which probably meant he harvested hope for a better relationship at some point. He couldn't imagine what might bring it about so he pretty much ignored them except when he was on the east coast or at a family function requiring his presence.

Next to him Lindsay sipped champagne and flipped through the movie choices. The dim lights caught the gold in her light brown hair. She had the thick mass rolled up and pinned in place but soft wisps had broken free to frame her face. He wondered how long the confined tresses would flow down her back. Her creamy complexion reminded him of the porcelain dolls his mother collected, complete with a touch of red in the cheeks though Lindsay's was compliments of the champagne.

She shot him a sideways glance, a question in her pretty baby blue eyes.

He realized she'd asked a question. "Sorry. I got lost in looking at you."

A flush added to the red in her cheeks and a hand pushed at the pins in her hair. "I asked if you preferred the comedy or the World War One drama." She turned back to the screen, fidgeted with the buttons. "But maybe I should just go back to my seat."

"No. Stay. This is my celebration, after all."

She glanced at him through lush lashes. "Okay, but you'll have to behave."

"I'll have you know my mother raised me to be a gentleman."

"Uh-huh." She made the decision for them with the push of a button. "That might be reassuring, except I doubt you've been under your mother's influence for quite some time."

He grinned and reached up to turn off the overhead light. "Very astute, Ms. Reeves."

Lindsay came awake to the rare sense of being wrapped in warm, male arms. She shot straight up in her seat, startling the man she cuddled against. His whiskey-brown eyes opened and blinked at her, the heat in his slumberous gaze rolling through her like liquid fire.

Escape. Now. The words were like a beeping alarm going off in her head.

"Can you let me out?" She pushed away from him, gaining a few inches and hopefully reinforcing the message to move. Now.

"Is the movie over?" He reined her in with an easy strength. His broad chest lifted under her as he inhaled a huge breath and then let it go in a yawn.

"Yes. This was fun." Too much fun. Time to get back to the real world. "But I need to get past you." He tucked a piece of her hair behind her ear instead of moving. The heat of his touch called for desperate measures. "I've got to pee."

He blinked. Then the corner of his mouth tipped up and he stood. "Me, too." He helped her up and gestured for her to go first.

"You go ahead," she urged him. "I want to grab a few things to freshen up with."

"Good idea." He opened the overhead compartment and grabbed a small bag. "Can I help you get anything?"

"Thank you, no." She waited until he wandered off to gather what she needed from her tote.

The attendants had performed her turndown service so both beds were down for the night. She automatically checked the garment bag holding the royal wedding dress.

It lay nicely in place, undisturbed since the last time she checked. She bent to retrieve her tote from under the seat in front of hers and decided to take the bag with her. Strap looped over her shoulder, she hurried down the aisle.

It was after one and the people she passed appeared to be out for the count. Even the attendants were strapped in and resting. Good. Lindsay intended to take her time. She wanted Zach to be back in his seat and sound asleep when she returned.

He was too charming, too hot, too available for her peace of mind. She hadn't needed to hear his views on marriage to know he was single. From her research she'd already gathered he had commitment issues. The only hint of an engagement had been back in his college days.

She'd found that snippet of information because she'd been researching his history with the prince. They'd both been going to Harvard's school of business but they'd met on the swim team. They both broke records for the school, Zach edging out Antonio with a few more wins. Antonio explained those extra wins came from Zach's longer reach. In the picture accompanying the article it was clear that Zach had at least three inches on all his teammates.

Tall, dark and handsome. Tick, tick, tick. The stereotype fit him to a tee, but did little to actually describe him. He was brilliant yet a terrible flirt. Could apologize when he was wrong and laugh at himself. But it was the touch of vulnerability surrounding his desire for his parents' approval that really got to her. She understood all too well the struggle between respect and love when it came to parents.

Bottom line: the man was dangerous. Way out of her league. And a distraction she couldn't afford. She may be headed for one of the most beautiful places on earth, but this was so not a vacation. She needed to stay sharp and focused to pull off the wedding of the century.

Face washed, teeth brushed, changed into yoga pants and a long-sleeved T-shirt, she glanced at her watch. Twenty minutes had passed. That should be enough time. She gathered her clothes and toiletries and tucked them neatly into her tote before making her way quietly back to her seat.

Zach lay sprawled on his bed. He was so tall he barely fit; in fact, one leg was off the bed braced against the floor. No doubt he had a restless night ahead of him. For once she'd sleep. Or pretend to. Because engaging in middle-of-the-night intimacies with Zach Sullivan could only result in trouble. Trouble she couldn't afford.

Climbing into her bed, she pulled the covers around her shoulders and determinedly closed her eyes.

She had this under control. She'd just ignore the man. If she needed something from the groom, she'd get it from the palace representative or Christina. There was no need for her to deal with Zach Sullivan at all. That suited her fine. She'd learned her lesson.

No more falling into the trap of self-delusion because a man paid a little attention to her. But more important—work and play did not go together.

"There must be some mistake." Lindsay advised the car-rental clerk. "I made my reservation over two months ago."

"*Scusa*. No mistake. My records show the reservation was canceled."

"That's impossible," Lindsay protested. Exhaustion tugged at her frayed nerves. This couldn't be happening. With everything she needed to do for the wedding, she absolutely required a vehicle to get around. "I had my assistant confirm all my reservations a week ago."

The clerk, a harried young man, glanced at the line behind her before asking with exaggerated patience, "Perhaps it is under a different name?"

"No, it is under my name." She gritted her teeth. "Please look again."

"Of course." He hit a few keys. "It says here the reservation was canceled last night."

"Last night? That doesn't make any sense at all. I was in the middle of a transatlantic flight." Enough. Arguing did her no good. She just wanted a car and to get on the road. "You know it doesn't matter. Let's just start over."

"*Scusa*, Ms. Reeves. We have no other vehicles available. Usually we would, but many have started to arrive for the royal wedding. The press especially. And they are keeping the vehicles. We have requested more autos from other sites but they won't be here for several days."

"There you are." A deep male voice sounded from behind her.

She glanced over her shoulder to find Zach towering over her. Dang, so much for losing him at the luggage carousel. Assuming her professional demeanor, she sent him a polite smile. "Have a good trip to Monte Calanetti. I'll keep you posted with updates on the arrangements. I'm going to be here for a bit." She smiled even brighter. "They've lost my car reservation."

"They didn't lose it. I canceled it."

"What?" All pretense of politeness dropped away. "Why would you do that?"

He held up a set of keys. "Because we're going to drive to Monte Calanetti together. Don't you remember? We talked about this during the movie last night."

She shook her head. She remembered him asking her what car-rental company she'd used and comparing their accommodation plans; he'd rented a villa while she had a room at a boutique hotel. Nowhere in her memory lurked a discussion about driving to Monte Calanetti together. There was no way she would have agreed to that. Not only did it go against her new decree to avoid him whenever possible, but she needed a vehicle to properly do her job.

"No," she declared, "I don't remember."

"Hmm. Must be champagne brain. No problem. I've got a Land Rover. Plenty of room for you, me and the dress." He grabbed up the garment bag, caught the handle of her larger suitcase and headed off. "Let's roll."

"Wait. No." Feeling panicked as the dress got further out of her reach, she glared at the clerk. "I want my reservation reinstated and as soon as a car is available, I want it delivered." She snatched up a card. "I'll call you with the address."

Dragging her smaller suitcase, Lindsay weaved her way through the crowd, following in Zach's wake. Luckily his height made him easy to spot. She was right on his heels when he exited the airport.

Humidity smacked her in the face as soon as she stepped outside; making her happy she'd paired her beige linen pants with a navy-and-beige asymmetrical short-sleeved tunic.

Champagne brain, her tush. What possible motive could he have for canceling her reservation if she hadn't agreed?

This just proved his potent appeal spelled danger.

Okay, no harm done. She handed him her smaller case and watched as he carefully placed the garment bag across the backseat. It should only take a couple of hours to reach Monte Calanetti. Then she could cut ties with the guy and concentrate on doing her job.

"How long to Monte Calanetti from here?" she asked as he held the door while she slid into the passenger seat.

"I've never driven it, but I can't imagine it's more than a few hours." He closed her in, rounded the front of the Land Rover and climbed into the driver's seat. A few minutes later they were in the thick of Florence traffic.

The old world elegance of the city charmed her, but the stop and go of the early evening traffic proclaimed work-force congestion was the same worldwide. She could admit, if only to herself, that she was glad not to be driving in it.

"Have you've been to Tuscany before?" she asked Zach.

"I've been several times. A couple of times with Antonio and once with my parents when I was twelve."

"So you know your way around?" She smothered a yawn.

"I do." He shot her an amused glance. "Enough to get us where we're going."

"I was just going to offer to navigate if you needed me to."

He stopped at a traffic light, taking the time to study her. "Thanks." He reached out and swept a thumb under her left eye in a soft caress. "You're tired. I guess relaxing didn't help you sleep."

She turned her head away from his touch. "I slept a little, off and on."

"Disrupted sleep can be less restful than staying awake." He sympathized. "Are you better at sleeping in a car?"

"Who can't sleep in a car? But I'm fine. I don't want to miss the sights. The city is so beautiful."

He drove with confidence and skill and a patience she lacked. He'd shaved on the plane; his sexy scruff gone when she woke this morning. The hard, square lines of his clean-cut jaw were just as compelling as the wicked shadow. The man couldn't look bad in a bag, not with a body like that.

Unlike her, he hadn't changed clothes, he still wore his black suit pants and white long-sleeved shirt, but the top two buttons were open and the sleeves were rolled up to his elbows. The suit jacket had been tossed onto the backseat.

"Florence is beautiful. The depth of history just draws me in. Halencia is the same. Since I'll be here for a month, I'm really hoping to get a chance to play tourist."

"Oh, absolutely. They have some really fantastic tours. I plan to stay after the wedding and take one. I'm torn between a chef and wine-tasting tour or a hiking tour."

"Wow, there's quite a difference there."

"I'm not going to lie to you. I'm leaning toward the pasta and wine tour. It goes to Venice. I've always wanted to go to Venice."

"Oh, yeah," he mocked, "it's all about Venice and nothing about the walking."

"Hey, I'm a walker. I love to hike. I'll share some of my brochures with you. There are some really great tours. If you like history, there's a Tuscan Renaissance tour that sounds wonderful."

"Sounds interesting. I'd like to see the brochures."

"Since technology is your thing, I'm surprised you're so into history."

"I minored in history. What can I say? I'm from New England. You can't throw a rock without hitting a historical marker. In my studies I was always amazed at how progressive our founding fathers were. Benjamin Franklin truly inspired me."

"You're kidding."

"I'm not." He sent her a chiding sidelong look. "I did my thesis on the sustainability of Franklin's inventions and observations in today's world. He was a brilliant man."

"And a great politician," she pointed out.

"I can't deny that, but he didn't let his political views define or confine him. I respect him for that. For him it wasn't about power but about proper representation."

"I feel that way about most of our founding fathers. So tell me something I probably don't know about big Ben."

"He was an avid swimmer."

"Like you and Antonio. Aha. No wonder you like him—" A huge yawn distorted the last word. "Oh." She smothered it behind a hand. "Sorry."

"No need to apologize." He squeezed her hand. "Don't feel you have to keep me company. Rest if you can. Jet lag can be a killer."

"Thanks." He'd just given her the perfect out from having to make conversation for the next hour. She'd snap the offer up if she weren't wide-eyed over the sights. Nothing in California rivaled the history and grandeur of the buildings still standing tall on virtually every street.

Zach turned a corner and the breath caught in the back of Lindsay's throat. Brunelleschi's Dome filled the skyline in all its Gothic glory. She truly was in Italy. Oh, she wanted to play tourist. But it would have to wait. Work first.

Riding across a beautiful, sculpted old bridge, she imagined the people who once crossed on foot. Soon rural views replaced urban views and in the distance clouds darkened the sky, creating a false twilight.

Lindsay shivered. She hoped they reached Monte Calanetti before the storm hit. She didn't care for storms, certainly didn't want to get caught out in one. The turbulence reminded her of anger, the thunder of shouting. As a kid, she'd hated them.

She didn't bury her head under the covers anymore. But there were times she wanted to.

Lightning flickered in the distance. Rather than watch the storm escalate, she closed her eyes as sleep claimed her. Her last thoughts were of Zach.

Lack of motion woke Lindsay. She opened her eyes to a dark car and an eerie silence. Zach was nowhere in view. Stretching, she turned around, looking for him. No sign. She squinted out the front windshield.

Good gracious, was the hood open?

She pushed her door open and stepped out, her feet crunching on gravel as a cool wind whipped around her. Hugging herself she walked to the front of the Land Rover. Zach was bent over the engine using a flashlight to ineffectually examine the vehicle innards. "What's going on?"

"A broken belt is my best guess." He straightened and directed the light toward the ground between them. "I've already called the rental company. They're sending a service truck."

She glanced around at the unrelenting darkness. Not a single light sparkled to show a sign of civilization. "Sending a truck where? We're in the middle of nowhere."

"They'll find us. The vehicle has a GPS."

Relief rushed through her. "Oh. That's good." She'd had visions of spending the night on the side of the road in a storm-tossed tin can. "Did they say how long before they got here? *Eee!*" She started and yelped when thunder boomed overhead. The accompanying flash of lightening had her biting back a whimper to the metallic taste of blood.

"As soon as they can." He took her elbow and escorted her to the passenger's-side door. "Let's stay in the car. The storm looks like it's about to break."

His big body blocked the wind, his closeness bringing warmth and rock-solid strength. For a moment she wanted to throw herself into his arms. Before she could give in to the urge, he helped her into her seat and slammed the door. A moment later he slid in next to her. He immediately turned the light off. She swallowed hard in a mouth suddenly dry.

"Can we keep the light on?" The question came out in a harsh rasp.

"I think we should conserve it, just in case."

"Just in case what?" It took a huge effort to keep any squeak out of her voice. "The truck doesn't come?"

"Just in case. Here —" He reached across the center console and took her hand, warming it in his. "You're shaking. Are you cold?" He dropped her hand to reach behind him. "Take my jacket."

She leaned forward and the heavy weight of his suit jacket wrapped around her shoulders. The satin lining slid coolly over her skin but quickly heated up. The scent of Zach clung to the material and she found it oddly comforting.

"Thank you. You won't be cold?"

She heard the rustle of movement and pictured him shrugging. "I'm okay right now. Hopefully the tow truck will get here before the cold seeps in. Worst case, we can move into the backseat and cuddle together under the jacket."

Okay, that option was way too tempting.

"Or you could get another one out of your luggage."

His chuckle preceded another crash of thunder. "Pixie girl, I don't know if my ego can survive you."

Maybe the dark wasn't so bad since he hadn't seen her flinch. Then his words struck her. "Pixie girl? That's the second time you called me that."

"Yes. Short and feisty. You remind me of a pixie."

"I am average," she stated with great dignity. "You're a giant."

"You barely reach my shoulder."

"Again, I refer you to the term 'giant.'" She checked her phone, welcoming the flare of light, but they were in the Italian version of Timbuktu so of course there was no service.

"Uh-huh. Feisty, pretty and short. Pixie it is."

Pretty? He'd called her that before, too. Pleasure bolstered her drooping spirits. She almost didn't care when the light faded again. Not that his admission changed her feelings toward him. He was a dangerous, charming man but she didn't have to like him just because he thought she was pretty. He was still off limits.

Hopefully he took her silence as disdain.

Right. On the positive side, the bit of vanity served to distract her for a few minutes. Long enough for headlights to appear on the horizon. No other vehicles had passed them in the twenty minutes she'd been awake so she said a little prayer that the approaching headlights belonged to their repair truck.

"Is the repair service coming from Monte Calanetti? How far away do you think we are?" She feared the thought of walking, but she didn't want to stay in the car all night, either.

"We're nowhere near Monte Calanetti," Zach announced. "By my guess we're about ten miles outside Caprese."

"Caprese?" Lindsay yelped in outrage. Caprese was the small village where the artist Michelangelo was born. "That's the other direction from Monte Calanetti from Florence. What are we doing here?"

"I told you last night. I have an errand to run for Antonio before I go to Monte Calanetti. It's just a quick stop to check on his groomsmen gifts and do a fitting."

"You so did not tell me."

"I'm pretty sure I did. You really can't hold your champagne, can you?"

"Stop saying 'champagne brain.' When did we have this conversation? Did I actually participate or was I sleeping?"

"You were talking, but I suppose you might have dozed off. You got quiet toward the end. I thought you were just involved in the movie. And then I fell asleep."

"Well, I don't remember half of what you've told me.

You should have reminded me of the plans we supposedly made this morning. I need to get to Monte Calanetti and I need my own car. I know you're trying to be helpful but..."

"But I got you stuck out in the middle of nowhere. And you're already tired from the flight. I'm sorry."

Lindsay clenched her teeth in frustration watching as the headlights slowly moved closer. Sorry didn't fix the situation. She appreciated the apology—many men wouldn't have bothered—but it didn't get her closer to Monte Calanetti. She had planned to hit the road running tomorrow with a visit to the wedding venue, the Palazzo di Comparino and restored chapel, before meeting with Christina in the afternoon.

Now she'd have to reschedule, move the interview back.

"Lindsay?" Zach prompted. "Are you okay?"

"I'm trying to rearrange my schedule in my head." She glanced at her watch, which she'd already adjusted to local time. Seven-fifteen. It felt much later. "What do you think our chances are of getting to Monte Calanetti tonight?"

"Slim. I doubt we'll find a mechanic willing to work on the Land Rover tonight. We'll probably have to stay over and head out tomorrow after it's fixed."

"If they have the necessary part."

"That will be a factor, yes. Here's our help." A small pickup honked as it drove past them then made a big U-turn and pulled up in front of them.

Zach hopped out to meet the driver.

Lindsay slid her arms into Zach's jacket and went to join them.

"Think it's the timing belt." Zach aimed his flashlight at the engine as he explained the problem to the man next to him. Their savior had gray-streaked black hair and wore blue coveralls. The name on his pocket read Luigi.

"Ciao, signora," the man greeted her.

She didn't bother to correct him, more eager to have

him locate the problem than worried about his assumption that she and Zach were married.

The driver carried a much bigger flashlight. The power of it allowed the men a much better view of the internal workings of the Land Rover. The man spoke pretty good English and he and Zach discussed the timing belt and a few other engine parts, none of which Lindsay followed but she understood clearly when he said he'd have to tow them into Caprese.

Wonderful.

Luigi invited her to sit in his truck while he got the Land Rover hooked up to be towed. She nodded and retrieved her purse. Zach walked her to the truck and held the door for her. The interior smelled like grease and cleanser, but it was neat and tidy.

"From what I remember from my research of Italy, small is a generous adjective when describing Caprese. At just over a thousand residents, 'tiny' would be more accurate. I'm not sure it has a hotel if we need to stay over."

"I'm sure there'll be someplace. I'll ask Luigi. It's starting to rain. I'm going to see if I can help him to make things go faster." He closed the door and darkness enveloped her.

The splat of rain on the windshield made her realize her ire at the situation had served to distract her from the looming storm. With its arrival, she forgot her schedule and just longed for sturdy shelter and a warm place to spend the night.

A few minutes later the men joined her. Squeezed between them on the small bench seat, she leaned toward Zach to give Luigi room to drive. The first right curve almost put her in Zach's lap.

"There's a bed-and-breakfast in town. Luigi's going to see about a room for us there." Zach spoke directly into her ear, his warm breath blowing over her skin.

She shivered. That moment couldn't come soon enough. The closer they got to town, the harder it rained. Obviously they were headed into the storm rather than away from it.

Fifteen minutes later they arrived at a small garage. Lindsay dashed through the rain to the door and then followed the men inside to an office that smelled like the truck and was just as tidy. Luigi immediately picked up the phone and dialed. He had a brief conversation in Italian before hanging up.

He beamed at Lindsay and Zach. "*Bene, bene,* my friends. The bed-and-breakfast is full with visitors. *Si,* the bad weather—they do not like to drive. But I have procured for you the last room. Is good, *si?*"

"*Si. Grazie,* Luigi." Zach expressed his appreciation then asked about the repairs.

For Lindsay only two words echoed through her head: one room.

CHAPTER FOUR

THE B AND B WAS a converted farmhouse with stone walls, long, narrow rooms and high ceilings. The furniture was sparse, solid and well worn.

Lindsay carried the heavy garment bag to the wardrobe and arranged it as best she could and then turned to face the room she'd share with Zach. Besides the oak wardrobe there was a queen bed with four posters, one nightstand, a dresser with a mirror above it and a hardback chair. Kindling rested in a fireplace with a simple wooden mantel, ready to be lit.

The bathroom was down the hall.

No sofa or chair to sleep on and below her feet was an unadorned hardwood floor. There was no recourse except to share the bed.

And the bedspread was a wedding ring quilt. Just perfect.

Her mother would say it was a sign. She'd actually have a lot more to say, as well, but Lindsay ruthlessly put a lock on those thoughts.

Lightening flashed outside the long, narrow window. Lindsay pulled the heavy drapes closed, grateful for the accommodation. She may have to share with a near stranger and the room may not be luxurious, but it was clean and authentic, and a strong, warm barrier against the elements.

Now why did that make her think of Zach?

The rain absorbed the humidity and dropped the temperature a good twenty degrees. The stone room was cool. Goose bumps chased across her skin.

She lit the kindling and once it caught added some wood. Warmth spread into the room. Unable to wait any longer, she made a quick trip down the hall. Zach was still gone when she got back. He'd dropped off her luggage and had gone back for his. She rolled the bigger case over next to the wardrobe. She didn't think she'd need anything out of it for one night.

The smaller one she set on the bed. She'd just unzipped it when a thud came at the door.

Zach surged into the room with three bags in tow.

"Oh, my goodness. You are soaked." She closed the door and rushed to the dresser. The towels were in the top drawer just as the innkeeper said.

Zach took it and scrubbed his face and head.

She tugged at his sopping jacket, glad now she'd thought to give it back to him. "Let's get this off you."

He allowed her to work it off. Under the jacket his shirt was so damp it clung to his skin in several places. He shivered and she led him over to the fireplace.

"Oh, yeah." He draped the towel around his neck and held his hands out to the heat.

"Take the shirt off, too," she urged him. She reached out with her free hand to help with the task, but when her fingers came skin to skin with his shoulder she decided it might be best if he handled the job himself.

To avoid looking at all the tanned, toned flesh revealed by the stripping off of his shirt, Lindsay held the dripping jacket aloft. What were they going to do with it? He handed her the shirt. With them?

A knock sounded at the door. Leaving Zach by the fire, Lindsay answered the knock. A plump woman in a purple jogging suit with more gray than black in her hair gave Lindsay a bright smile.

"Si, signora." She pointed to the dripping clothes, "I take?"

"Oh. Grazie." Lindsay handed the wet clothes through the door.

"And these, too." From behind the door Zach thrust his pants forward.

Okay, then. She just hoped he'd kept his underwear on.

"*Si, si.*" The woman's smile grew broader. She took the pants while craning her head to try to see behind Lindsay. She rolled off something in Italian. Lindsay just blinked at her.

"She said the owner was sending up some food for us."

As if on cue, Lindsay's stomach gurgled. The mention of food made her realize how hungry she was. It had been hours since they'd eaten on the plane. "*Si.*" She nodded. "*Grazie.*"

The woman nodded and, with one last glance into the room, turned and walked down the hall.

"You have a fan." Lindsay told Zach when she closed the door. "Oh, my good dog." The man had his back to her as he leaned over the bed rummaging through his luggage. All he wore was a pair of black knit boxer briefs that clung to his butt like a lover. The soft cloth left little to the imagination and there was a lot to admire.

No wonder the maid had been so enthralled.

And Lindsay had to sleep next to that tonight.

"What about a dog?" He turned those whiskey-brown eyes on her over one broad, bare shoulder.

Her knees went weak, nearly giving out on her. She sank into the hard chair by the fire.

"Dog? Huh? Nothing." Her mother had taught her to turn the word around so she didn't take the Lord's name in vain. After all these years, the habit stuck.

He tugged on a gray T-shirt.

Thank the merciful angels in heaven.

"I'm going to take a quick shower. Don't eat all the food."

"No promises."

He grinned. "Then I'll just have to hurry."

He disappeared out the door with his shaving kit under one arm and the towel tossed over his shoulder.

Finally Lindsay felt as though she could breathe again.

He took up so much space. A room that seemed spacious one moment shrank by three sizes when he crossed the threshold. Even with him gone the room smelled of him.

She patted her pocket. Where was her phone? She needed it now, needed to call the rental agency that very moment and demand a car be delivered to her. They should never have allowed a party outside the reservation to cancel. They owed her.

The hunt proved futile. Her phone wasn't in her purse, her tote or either suitcase. She thought back to the last time she'd used it. In the Land Rover, where it had been pitch-black. It must still be in the vehicle.

That was at the garage.

There'd be no getting her phone tonight. Dang it.

Stymied from making the call she wanted to, she took advantage of Zach's absence to gather her own toiletries and yoga pants and long-sleeved tee she'd worn on the plane. And a pair of socks. Yep, she'd wear gloves to bed if she had any with her. And if she had any luck at all, he'd wear a three-piece suit.

There'd be no skin-to-skin contact if she could help it.

Loosen up, Lindsay. Her mom's voice broke through her blockade. *You're young and single and about to share a bed with one prime specimen. You should be thinking of ways to rock the bed not bulletproof yourself against an accidental touch.*

How sad was it that her mother was more sexually aggressive than she was?

Her mom was forever pushing Lindsay to date more, to take chances on meeting people. She'd been thrilled when Lindsay had started seeing Kevin again. She'd welcomed him; more, she'd invited him to family events and made a point of showing her pride in Lindsay and her success.

Right, and look how that turned out.

To be fair, Mom had been almost as devastated as Lindsay when Kevin showed his true colors. She may be self-absorbed but Lindsay never doubted her mom's love. She wanted Lindsay to be happy and in her mind that equated to love and marriage. Because for her it was—at least during the first flush of love.

Lindsay wanted to believe in love and happily ever after, but it was getting harder to do as she planned her mother's sixth wedding. And, okay, yeah, Mom was right; Lindsay really didn't make an effort to meet men. But that wasn't the problem. She actually met lots of interesting men. While she was working, when it was totally inappropriate to pursue the connection.

The problem was she was too closed off when she did meet a nice guy. After stepfather number two, she'd started putting up shields to keep from being hurt when they left. She and Kevin had been friends before they were a couple and when they'd split up, her shields just grew higher.

She hadn't given up on love. She just didn't know if she was brave enough to reach for it.

You're in Italy for a month with a millionaire hunk at your beck and call. It's the perfect recipe for a spicy summer fling. Every relationship doesn't have to end with a commitment.

Mom didn't always practice what she preached.

The food hadn't arrived when Zach returned smelling of freshly washed male. He wore the same T-shirt but now his knit boxers were gray. She could only thank the good Lord—full-on prayer, here—that the T-shirt hung to his thighs, hiding temptation from view.

"Bathroom is free," he advised her.

Her stomach gurgled, but he looked so relaxed after his

shower and the storm had her so on edge she decided to get comfortable. Grabbing up the cache she'd collected, she headed for the door.

"Don't eat all the food," she told him.

"Hey, you get the same promise I did."

She stared at him a moment trying to determine if he was joking as she'd been. His features were impassive and he cocked a dark brow at her. Hmm. She better hurry just in case.

The bathroom was still steamy from his visit. As she pulled the shower curtain closed on the tiny tub she envisioned his hard body occupying this same space. His hard, wet, naked body. Covered in soap bubbles.

Oh. My. Dog.

She forced her mind to the nearly completed seating chart to remove him from her head. But that, too, reminded her of him so she switched to the flowers. Christina had yet to decide between roses and calla lilies or a mix of the two. Both were beautiful and traditional for weddings.

It may well depend on the availability. Christina wanted to use local vendors and merchants. She'd said it was for the people so should be of the people. Lindsay still puzzled over the comment. *It* was obviously the wedding, but what did she mean "it was for the people"?

Was the royal wedding not a love match?

Lindsay could ask Zach. He'd know.

No. She didn't want to know. It was none of her business and may change how she approached the wedding. Every bride deserved a fantasy wedding, one that celebrated the bond between her and the groom and the promise of a better future together. It was Lindsay's job to bring the fantasy to life. The reality of the relationship was not in her hands.

Her musings took her through the shower, a quick attempt at drying her hair, brushing her teeth and dressing. Fifteen minutes after she left the room, she returned to find

Zach seated on the bed, his back against the headboard, a tray of food sitting beside him.

The savory aroma almost brought her to her knees.

"Oh, that smells good." She dropped her things into her open case, flipped the top closed and set it on the floor before climbing onto the bed to bend over the tray and the two big bowls it held. She inhaled deeply, moaned softly. "Soup?"

"Stew."

"Even better. And bread." She looked at him. "You waited."

He lifted one shoulder and let it drop. "Not for long. It just got here. Besides, we're partners."

Her eyebrows shot up then lowered as she scowled at him. "We are so not partners." She handed him a bowl and a spoon. Tossed a napkin in his lap. Then settled cross-legged on her pillow and picked up her own bowl. "In fact, I think I should arrange for my own car tomorrow. I need to get to Monte Calanetti and you have to wait for the Land Rover to be repaired, which could take a couple of days."

"Getting a car here could take longer yet. You heard the rental clerk. All the vehicles are being taken up by the media presence here for the wedding."

"Oh, this is good." No point in arguing with him. She was an adult and a professional. She didn't require his permission to do anything.

"Mmm." He hummed his approval. "Are you okay with sharing?"

"The room?" She shrugged. "We don't really have a choice, do we?"

"The bed," he clarified and licked his spoon. She watched, fascinated. "I can sleep on the floor if you're uncomfortable sharing the bed."

"It's hardwood." She pulled her gaze away from him. "And there isn't any extra bedding."

"I can sleep near the fireplace. It won't be comfortable, but I'll survive. We're still getting to know each other, so I'll understand."

Crack!

Thunder boomed, making Lindsay jump and spill the bite of stew aimed for her mouth.

"Dang it." She grabbed her napkin and scrubbed at the stain on her breast. "Are you uncomfortable?"

"No." He took her bowl so she could use both hands. "But I'm a man."

Oh, yeah, she'd noticed.

"If something happened between us, I'd be a happy man in the morning. You, on the other hand, would be satisfied but regretful."

She glared at him. "Nothing is going to happen."

He held up his hands, the sign of surrender blemished by the bowls he held. "Of course not."

"So there's no reason not to share."

"None at all."

"It's settled then."

"Yep." He handed her bowl back. "Now you want to tell me what your deal is with storms?"

Zach watched the color leech from Lindsay's cheeks, confirmation that his suspicions were right that her reaction to the thunderstorm exceeded the norm.

She was nervous and jumpy, which was totally unlike her.

Sure she'd gone ballistic when he'd sat on the wedding dress, but considering the cost of the gown she could be forgiven for hyperventilating.

Generally he found her to be calm and collected, giving as good as she got but not overreacting or jumping to conclusions. Efficient but friendly. The storm had her shaken and he wanted to know why.

"Nothing." She carefully placed her bowl on the tray. "I'm fine."

"You're jumpy as hell. And it started before we got to the room so it isn't the sleeping arrangements. It has to be the storm."

"Maybe it's you." She tossed the words at him as she slid from the bed. "Did you consider that?"

"Nope." His gaze followed her actions as she put the suitcase back on the bed and began to organize the things she'd dumped in. "We're practically lovers."

Ice burned cold in the blue glare she sent him. "You are insane."

"Oh, come on." He taunted her. "You know it's going to happen. Not tonight, but definitely before the month is up."

"In your dreams. But I live in reality."

"Tell me about the storms."

"There's nothing to tell." The jerkiness of her movements told a different story.

"Okay. Have it your way." He relaxed back against the wall and laced his arms behind his head. "I like storms myself."

"You like storms?" The astonishment in her voice belied her indifference. "As I said, insane. I'm going to take the tray downstairs."

Zach grabbed the bread and wine from the tray and let her escape. Pressing her would only antagonize her.

He'd had nothing to do with the engine failure, but he approved of the results. If he were a man who believed in signs, he'd take it as karma's righteous nod.

He'd been playing with her when he'd alluded to them being lovers. Or so he thought. As soon as the words had left his mouth, he'd known the truth in them. He generally preferred leggy blondes. But something about the pixie appealed to him.

Her feistiness certainly. At the very least it was refreshing. With his position, family connections and money, people rarely questioned his authority and never dismissed him. She'd done both. And still was.

He had no doubt she'd try to make a break for it tomorrow.

He sipped at the last of his wine, enjoyed the warmth as it rolled down his throat. The fire had burned down to embers and he stirred himself to get up and feed it. The thick stone walls and bare wood floors kept the room cool so the fire gave nice warmth to the room. Plus, he imagined Lindsay would find it a comforting offset to the storm.

She was more pretty than beautiful, her delicate features overshadowed by that lush mouth. His gut tightened as heat ignited his blood just as flame flared over the fresh fuel.

Oh, yeah, he wanted a bite of that plump lower lip.

He'd have to wait. He'd put her off limits when he concocted the sabotage plan. He couldn't use her and seduce her, too. That would be too much. But she didn't need to know of his restraint. Just the thought of him making a move on her would keep her on edge, making it easier for him to cause a little chaos.

A glance at his watch showed the time at just after nine. Early for him to go to bed most nights but tonight, fatigue from travel, the time change and the concentration needed to drive an unfamiliar vehicle on unfamiliar roads weighed on him.

The room held no TV so it was sleep or talk.

He wouldn't mind getting to know his companion better but somehow he knew she'd choose the escape that came with sleep. Whether she actually slept or not. His feisty little pixie had a bit of the ostrich in her.

The door opened and she slipped inside.

"You're still up?" She avoided his gaze as she crossed to the bed and zipped the case that still sat on her side.

"Just feeding the fire."

She lifted the case and he stepped forward to take it from her.

"I can do it," she protested, independent as always.

"So can I." He notched his chin toward the bed. "You're falling asleep on your feet. Go to bed."

"What about you?" Caution filled her voice and expression.

"I'm going to tend the fire for a bit. I'll come to bed soon."

Relief filled her blue eyes and he knew she thought she'd gotten a reprieve; that she hoped to be asleep before he joined her in the far too small bed.

Truthfully, he hoped she fell asleep, too. No point in both of them lying awake thinking about the other.

Lindsay pretended to be asleep when Zach came to bed. His presence kept her senses on edge. Between him and the storm that still raged outside her nerves were balanced on a fine-edged sword.

She tried to relax, to keep her breathing even so as not to disturb Zach. The last thing she wanted was another discussion on why storms bothered her. It was a weakness she preferred to ignore. She usually plugged in her earphones and let her playlist tune out the noise.

Tonight there was nothing in the still house to disguise the violence of the weather outside the window. Everything in her longed to press back into the strong male body occupying the other half of the bed. Instead she clung to the edge of the mattress determined to stay on her side.

Thunder boomed and lightening strobed at the edges of the closed drapes. Lindsay flinched then held herself very still.

"Oh, for the love of dog, come here." Long, muscular arms wrapped around her and tugged her against the hard planes of a male chest.

Shocked by both action and words, Lindsay chose to focus on the latter. She glanced over her shoulder into dark eyes. "What did you say?"

"Woof, woof." And his lips settled softly on her cheek, a simple human-to-human contact that left her wanting more.

She sighed and made a belated attempt to wiggle away. Her body and nerves might welcome his touch but her head shouted, *Danger!* "I know it's silly. It's something my mom taught me when I was little. It kind of stuck."

"I think it's cute."

She went still. "I'm not cute. I'm not a pixie. And we're not going to be lovers. You need to let me go." One of them needed to be smart about this.

His arms tightened, pulled her back the few inches she'd gained. "Tell me about the storms."

"There's nothing to tell!"

His silence was a patient demand.

"What's to like about them? They're angry and destructive."

"A storm is cleansing. It can be loud, yes, but it takes the old and washes it clean."

She thought about that. "Destruction is not cleansing."

"It can be. If something is rotten or breaking, it's better to come down in a storm than under a person's weight. You might have to finish the cleanup but life is fresher once you're done."

"I doubt people who have lost their homes to a hurricane or tornado would agree with you."

"Hurricanes and tornadoes are different. This is a simple summer thunderstorm. Nothing to get so worked up over."

"I know." She lay with her cheek pressed against her hand. She should move away, put space and distance between them. But she didn't. Couldn't. Having strong arms surrounding her gave her a sense of belonging she hadn't experienced in way too long. It didn't even matter that it was all in her head. Her body had control right now. With a soft sigh she surrendered to his will and her body's demand.

"It's not even my phobia. It's my mother's that she passed on to me." She blamed the kiss for loosening her resolve. Hard to keep her wits about her with the heat of his kiss on her cheek.

"How'd she do that?"

"She hates storms. They don't scare her, though, they make her cry."

"Why?"

"She was only seventeen when she got pregnant with me. My dad tried to step up and they got married, even though he was barely eighteen. My mom is very high maintenance. Her dad always gave her everything she wanted. Took care of things for her. She expected my dad to do the same. She was too demanding and he finally left. It was during a storm that he took off and never came back. She was left pregnant and alone."

"So she cries when it rains."

"Yes." Lindsay had pieced the story together through the years. She loved her mother; she was fun and free-spirited. But Lindsay also recognized her faults; it had been a matter of self-preservation.

"Her dislike of storms comes from sadness."

She nodded, her hair brushing over his chin. She'd never talked to anyone about this.

"But your jumpiness suggests a fear-based reaction."

A shiver racked her body and she curled in on herself. Everything in her tightened, shutting down on a dark memory. She wanted to tell him it was none of his business, but then he might let her go and she wasn't ready to give up the cocoon of his embrace.

His arms tightened around her and his lips slid over her cheek, giving her the courage to answer.

"It's a lingering unease leftover from childhood. It's distressing to hear your mother cry and know there's nothing you can do to help."

"It seems the mother should be comforting the child, not the other way around."

"She's more sensitive than I am."

A tender touch tucked her hair behind her ear, softly trailed down the side of her neck. "Just because you're tough doesn't mean you don't need reassurance now and again."

She relaxed under the gentle attention. Though she rejected the truth in his words.

"This storm caught me when I was tired. I'm sorry I disturbed you. I usually put my earbuds in but I left my phone in the Land Rover."

"Ah, a sensible solution. I should have known." He shifted behind her, leaving her feeling chilled and alone. And then his weight settled against her again and earbuds entered her ears. "You're stuck with my playlist, but maybe it'll help you sleep."

She smiled and wrapped her hand around his. "Thank you."

His fingers squeezed hers.

She felt the tension drain away. Now she had the music, she'd be okay. She no longer needed the comfort of his arms.

Her eyes closed. In a minute she'd pull away. There was danger in staying too close to him. Already her body recognized his, which made it all too easy for him to hold sway over her. She needed to stay strong, to stay distant...

The last thing she knew was the feel of his lips on her cheek.

CHAPTER FIVE

LINDSAY WOKE JUST before eight with the earbuds still in her ears. The tunes had stopped. She felt around for the phone but came up with the end of the earbuds instead. Her hand hadn't encountered a hard male body, but the stillness of the room had already told her Zach was out and about.

She threw back the covers and her feet hit the floor, her toes curling in her socks against the chill of the hardwood. Padding to the window, she pushed back the drapes to a world awash in sunshine. The ground was still wet but the greenery and rock fences had a just-scrubbed brightness to them.

Or was that Zach's influence on her?

A peek down the hall showed the bathroom was free so she quickly grabbed her things and made a mad dash to claim it. Aware others may be in need of the facilities she kept it short and soon returned to the room to dress and put on her makeup.

Before going downstairs, she packed her things so she'd be ready to leave when a car arrived. In spite of Zach's comfort and kindness last night, or maybe because of it, she fully intended to make her break from him today.

The heavenly scent of coffee greeted her in the dining room. Some fellow occupants of the B and B were seated at the long wooden table, including Zach. Cheerful greetings came her way as she moved through the room.

"Breakfast is buffet style this morning as there're so many of us." A gray-haired gentleman pointed with his fork toward the buffet she'd passed.

"Henry, don't use your utensils to point." An equally

gray-haired woman pushed his hand down. "They'll think we have no manners." She smiled at Lindsay with a mouth full of crooked teeth. "That handsome husband of yours made you a cup of coffee he was about to take upstairs. I'm glad you could join us. I'm happy to meet up with some fellow Americans. We're Wes and Viv Graham from Iowa and the folks there on the end are Frank and Diane Murphy from Oregon."

"Nice to meet you all." She sent Zach a questioning look at the husband comment and received a shrug in reply. Right. She'd get him for that. Hopefully they wouldn't be there long enough for it to be an issue. She backtracked to the buffet.

Croissants, sausage, bacon, quartered oranges and some cappuccino. No eggs. She took a couple of pieces of bacon, one sausage and a few orange wedges.

"I was just about to come wake you." Zach appeared beside her and took her plate. "I've arranged for alternate transportation and it'll be here in about half an hour. How'd you sleep?"

Huh. If he was leaving in half an hour maybe she'd stick with him, after all. It would take her longer than that to get her phone. "I slept well, thank you." Truly thanks to him.

"You're going to want one of these." He placed a croissant on her plate. "It's called a *cornetto*. There's a wonderful jam inside."

He took off for his seat, leaving her to follow. Their audience watched with avid curiosity. At their end of the table, Lindsay smoothed her hand across his shoulders. "Thank you, sweetie." She kissed him softly, lingering over his taste for a beat longer than she intended to, then slid into the chair around the corner to his right.

She pressed her lips together. Okay, that bit of payback totally backfired. But playing it through to the end, she glanced shyly down the table. "I'm sorry. We don't mean to be rude. Newlyweds." She rolled her eyes as if that explained everything.

A pleased smile bloomed on Diane's face. "Oh, my dear, don't mind us old folks. Congratulations. You two enjoy yourselves." She turned to her husband. "Frank do you remember on our honeymoon when we—"

"Well done." Zach pushed her coffee toward her. "But that's the first and last time you ever call me sweetie."

She flashed him a provocative look. "We'll see."

Let him stew on that. He was the one to say they'd be lovers, after all.

"Be nice to me or I'll take your *cornetto*."

"I don't think so." She picked up the horn-shaped pastry and bit in. Chewed. Savored. "Oh, my dog."

"I told you so." Satisfaction stamped his features as he leaned back in his straight-backed chair.

"This is wonderful." She pointed at the jam-filled roll. "We have to have these at the wedding."

"We're a long way from Monte Calanetti."

"Oh, I'm aware." Censure met unrepentance. "Tell me again why we're in Caprese and not Monte Calanetti?"

"An errand for the prince."

She waited for more. It didn't come.

"I took care of it this morning. I'm ready to go when the new transportation gets here."

That was a relief. She finished the last of her *cornetto* with a regretful sigh and a swipe of her tongue over her thumb. "Maybe not these exact rolls but definitely *cornettos*."

"I'm all for it, but I suggest you discuss that with Christina."

She nodded, eyeing him speculatively through another bite. "How well do you know Christina?"

"Not well." He glanced down, snagged one of her orange wedges. "I met her once. Theirs has been a long-distance relationship."

"She seems really nice. And she showed a lot of enthusiasm when we first started planning, but she's cooled off lately."

"Really?" That brought his head up. "Do you think she's having second thoughts?"

Lindsay gave a half shrug. "Very few brides make it to the altar without suffering a few nerves along the way. It's probably nothing. Or nothing to do with the wedding, anyway."

"Tony's been off, too. He got me to come all this way a month in advance of the wedding, but now it feels like he's avoiding me."

"I'm sure they both have a lot on their plates right now." So much for the reassurances she'd been hoping for. The fact Zach had noticed something off, too, gave her some concerns. "I'll know more after my appointment with Christina, which was supposed to be this afternoon. I'll have to reschedule. Oh, that reminds me. I need to get my phone out of the Land Rover."

"Sorry, I forgot." Zach reached around and pulled something from his back pocket. He set her phone on the table. "I had Luigi bring it by this morning."

"Thanks." She picked it up, felt the warmth of the glass and metal against her flesh and tried to disengage from the fact it had absorbed the heat from his hot bum.

A loud whopping sound overhead steadily got louder. Everyone looked up. Then, in an unchoreographed move, they all stood and rushed to the back terrace. Lindsay, with Zach on her heels, brought up the rear.

As she stepped out onto the cobblestone patio, a helicopter carefully maneuvered in the air, preparing to land in the large farmyard.

Zach watched Lindsay's face as the big bird neared the

ground, knew by the pop of her eyes exactly when she spied the royal insignia on the door. She turned to stare at him as the inn occupants wandered forward to examine the helicopter and talk to the pilot.

Zach surveyed the royal conveyance with a smirk. "Our new transportation."

"You have got to be kidding me."

He liked the look of awe in her eyes. Much better than the fear she'd tried so hard to hide the night before. There was something more to her dislike of storms than a left-over agitation from her mother's distress. Something she wasn't willing to share, or maybe something she didn't fully remember.

He wished he could have done more than just lend her his earbuds.

"It's good to have friends in high places. When I told Tony you were concerned about missing your appointment with Christina, he insisted on putting the helicopter at my disposal in assisting you for the duration."

Actually, Zach had suggested it; still Tony jumped at the chance to accommodate Christina. Forget bending over backward, Tony was doing flips to give Christina the wedding of her dreams. Because he knew their lives were going to suck.

For Zach's part, he figured the sooner he got to Christina, the sooner he could talk sense into her. They'd only met once, but Tony lauded her with being a sensible, caring person. Surely she saw the error in what they were about to do.

He could only hope she'd listen to reason and end things now. Then he and the wedding planner could spend the next month exploring the wonders of Tuscany.

Shock had her staring wide-eyed at the big machine. "I have a helicopter for the next month?"

"I have a helicopter until after the wedding. The pilot takes his orders from me."

"Ah. But you're here to help me." She rubbed her hands together. "So, I have my very own helicopter for the next month. Oh, this is going to make things so much easier."

"I'm glad you're happy." And glad he'd be able to keep tabs on her. Things were falling nicely into place. "I told him I had designs on his wedding planner and I needed something to impress her."

All wonder dropped away in a heartbeat.

His little pixie turned fierce, getting right up in his space.

"Listen to me, Mr. Sullivan." Her blue-diamond eyes pinned him to the spot. "You may not think much of what I do, but it's very important to me, to your friends and, in the case of this wedding, to this country. I was starting to like you, but mess with my business and you won't like me."

Dog, she was beautiful. She may be tiny but she worked that chin and those eyes. He'd never wanted to kiss a woman more in his life. Defensive, yes, but not just for herself. She honestly cared about Tony and Christina. And the blasted country.

He did like her. More than he should. He'd have to be careful not to damage her in his rescue mission.

"Tony is why I'm here. Ms. Reeves. I promise you, I'm going to do everything in my power to make sure this turns out right for him."

"Okay, then." Her posture relaxed slightly. "As long as we understand each other."

"Understand this." He wrapped his hands around her elbows, lifted her to her toes and slanted his mouth over hers.

She stiffened against him for the briefest moment, in the next all her luscious softness melted into him. She

opened her mouth to his and the world dropped away.
The sparkling-clean farmyard, chattering Midwest tourists and his majesty's royal helicopter disappeared from
his radar.

He'd meant the kiss to be a distraction, to focus her
on his mythical seduction and away from his actual plan
to change Tony's mind about marrying Christina. And
vice versa.

But all he knew in that moment, all he wanted to know,
was the heated touch of the pixie coming apart in his arms.
He wrapped her close, angling the kiss to a new depth.
She tasted of berry jam and spicy woman. Her essence
called to him, addled his senses until he craved nothing
more than to sweep her into his arms and carry her up
to their room.

Her arms were linked around his neck and he'd dragged
her up his body so they were pressed together mouth to
mouth, chest to chest, loins to loins. It wasn't enough. It
was too much.

Someone patted him on the arm. "You young ones need
to take that upstairs."

The world came crashing back. Zach slowly broke off
the kiss. He lifted his head, opened his eyes. Passion-
drenched pools of blue looked back at him. Her gaze
moved to his mouth. A heavy sigh shifted her breasts
against his chest. She looked back at him and blinked.

"You should put me down now."

Yes, he should. The kiss had gotten way out of control
and he needed to rein it in. "I don't want to. Christina will
understand if we're an hour late."

What was he saying? *Get a grip, Sullivan.*

"I won't." She pushed against him. "This was a mistake. And it won't happen again."

"Why not?" he demanded because that's what he'd
want to know if he were seriously pursuing her, which

he wasn't. She was too sweet, too genuine for him. He needed someone who knew the rules of non-commitment.

Still, when he set her on her feet, he took satisfaction in the fact he had to steady her for a moment.

"Because I'm a professional. Because you are the best man."

"And you have a policy. You're the boss, you can change policy."

"Not a good idea." She straightened her shirt, smoothing the fabric over her hips. "I have the policy for a reason. I'm the wedding planner. I'm not here to have fun. I'm here to work. You—" she swept him with a glance "—would be a distraction when I need all my wits about me."

"Signor..." The pilot approached. "If you desire to stick to your flight plan, we should leave within the next fifteen minutes."

"Thank you."

"May I assist with the luggage?"

Glad to have this scene wrapping to a close, Zach met her gaze. "Are you ready?"

"I am." She stepped back, composed herself. "I just need to grab my luggage and the wedding dress." She headed into the house. "Do you think they'd mind if I took a few *cornettos* to go?"

Grinning, he followed her inside. He best be careful or this woman was going to turn him inside out.

Lindsay loved traveling by helicopter. She'd been a little nervous to start out with, afraid the heights might get to her. Nope. Whizzing through the air above the scenic vista gave her a thrill.

The helicopter flew over a meadow that looked like gold velvet. She pointed. "It's beautiful. What crop is that?"

"No crop, *signorina*." The pilot's voice came over her headphones. "Sunflowers."

"Sunflowers," she breathed. She'd never seen a whole field of the big, cheerful flowers.

Zach tapped the pilot on the shoulder and he took them down and did a wide loop so she actually saw the flowers. She'd told Zach she wasn't there to have fun, but, oh, she was.

That didn't mean she could throw caution to the wind and jump into a summer fling. Her blood still thrummed from his embrace. It would have been so easy to let him seduce her. Except she couldn't. She needed to grow a spine, put him in his place. The problem was she melted as soon as he touched her.

If she was honest, the physical attraction wasn't what worried her. She liked him. Way too much for her peace of mind. That made the physical all the more tempting. She wanted love in her life but this was the wrong time, wrong place, wrong man.

Restraint came at a cost, but she wouldn't jeopardize everything she'd built on an overload of hormones. She just needed to resist him for a few weeks and then she'd be back in Hollywood and he'd be back in Silicon Valley.

Zach pointed out the palace as they flew over Voti, Halencia's capital city and Christina's home. The big, yellow palace presented a majestic silhouette with its square shape and the round battlement towers at the corners. The notched alternate crenels screamed castle. The building had a strong, regal presence set on a shallow cliff side overlooking the sea on one side and the sprawling city of Voti on the other.

One of the towers had been converted into a heliport.

"Are we landing at the palace?" She spoke into the microphone attached to the headphones.

"Yes." Zach nodded.

"So I'll get a chance to meet Prince Antonio?"

Now he shook his head. "Sorry, he's in meetings all day. We'll be going straight down and out to a car waiting for us. We'll be just in time for your one-thirty appointment with Christina."

The helicopter made a wide turn then started its descent. Lindsay experienced her first anxious moments, seeing the land rush up to meet her. Without thinking, she reached out and grabbed Zach's hand.

His warm grip wrapped around her fingers and gave a squeeze. She instantly relaxed, feeling grounded. Putting her stringent, no-fraternizing policy aside for a moment, she smiled at him. He'd been gentle and kind last night and was supportive now. No doubt he'd hate the description, but he was a genuinely good guy.

Even though she was essentially a stranger to him, Zach had gone over and beyond the call of duty.

She longed to see some of the interior of the palace, but a palace attendant met them and a very modern elevator took them straight down to the ground level. The attendant led them through a ten-foot portico, which he explained was the width of the castle walls.

Wow, Lindsay mouthed. Seriously, she felt like a little girl at Disneyland. She was so busy trying to see everything at once she nearly tripped over her own feet.

Zach grasped her elbow. Steadied her. "Careful, Tinkerbell."

Caught gawking. But she couldn't care. This was amazing. "We're in a castle. Couldn't I be Cinderella?"

He released her to tug on her straight ponytail. "No changing up now. Tinkerbell is a pixie, right?"

"She's a fairy. And you need to stop. I'm not that short."

"You're a little bitty thing. With lots of spunk. Nothing bad about that."

She rolled her eyes. "If you say so." They exited onto

a round driveway where a car and driver waited. She grabbed Zach's arm to stop him. "Listen, you don't need to come to my appointment with Christina. I can promise you'll be monumentally bored. If you stay here, you may get a few minutes to visit with Antonio."

"I want to come. It'll be good to see Christina again and to let her know Antonio isn't shirking his groom duties." He waved the driver off and held the door open for her himself. "Besides, I'm not hanging around hours just to get a few minutes of Tony's time. We'll connect soon enough."

She should go through her notes on the ride through Voti to be prepared for the appointment. Should, but wouldn't. The city was so charming, not a high-rise to be seen, and the buildings were bunched closely together, creating narrow lanes. The warmth of the earth tones and red-tiled roofs was like an architectural hug. She loved the bursts of color in hanging planters. And the odd little plazas they'd drive through that all had lovely little fountains.

Christina worked not far from the palace. All too soon the car pulled to a stop in front of a three-story building. Lovely, black, wrought-iron gates opened into a cobblestoned courtyard.

"Zach, Ms. Reeves, welcome." The driver must have called ahead because Christina stepped forward to greet them.

She was tall—Lindsay's notes read five nine and her subtle heels added a few inches to that—and stunning with creamy, olive skin and thick reddish-brown hair sleeked back in a French twist. She wore a fitted suit in cobalt blue.

Standing between her and Zach, Lindsay did feel short.

"Christina." Zach wrapped her hand in both of his. "You haven't changed a bit in four years."

"You flatter me," she said in perfect English, her accent charming. She led them through the courtyard and up a curving wrought-iron staircase to an office on the second floor. "We both know that's not true. Thank goodness. I was barely out of school and quite shy."

"And soon you'll be the Queen of Halencia."

Christina's eyelashes flickered and she looked down as she waved them into seats. "I prefer to focus on one thing at a time. First there is the wedding."

"Of course."

"Thank you, Ms. Reeves, for coming so early to assist in the preparations. I originally intended to continue with the foundation on a part-time basis in their offices here in Halencia, but the prince's advisors have convinced me I'll be quite busy. It would be unfair to the foundation to hold a position and not be here to help. It is such a worthy endeavor. I would not want to hamper it in any way."

"It's important work. I'm sure, as the queen, your interest will be quite beneficial, so you'll still be of help."

"That's kind of you to say." Christina inclined her head.

A regal gesture if Lindsay had ever seen one. Maybe she'd been practicing.

Lindsay waved toward the open window. "You have a lovely view of the palace from here. It must be amazing to sit here and see your future beckoning for you."

Christina's smile slipped a little. "Yes. Quite amazing."

"It's a lot to think about, isn't it?" Zach spoke softly. "All that you're giving up. All that you're taking on?"

Appalled at the questions that were sure to rattle the most confident of brides let alone one showing a slight nervousness, Lindsay sent him a quelling glance.

"I am at your disposal to assist in any way I can," she advised her bride.

"You have been wonderful. My mind is just everywhere these days. I hope you do not mind taking on the bulk of the arrangements?"

"Of course. If we can just make some final decisions, I

can take care of everything. Your attendants are all set, the dresses have been received and a first fitting completed. I just need to know your final thoughts on the flowers, the total head count and whether you want to do indoors or outdoors for the reception. I have some sketches for you to look at." She passed a slim portfolio across the desk. "The palace wants to use the royal photographer, but I know some truly gifted wedding photographers if you decide you want a specialist."

"I am sure the royal photographer will be fine. These are marvelous drawings, Ms. Reeves. Any of these settings will be wonderful."

"Lindsay." She gently corrected the soon-to-be princess, who seemed near tears as she looked at the reception scenes. Lindsay could tell she wasn't going to get much more from the woman. "Every wedding should be special. What can I do to make your day special?"

"You have done so much already. I like the outdoors. I remember playing in the palazzo courtyard, pretending it was a palace. It seems appropriate."

"Outdoors is a lovely choice. Regarding flowers, we passed a meadow of sunflowers on our way here today. Gold is one of the royal colors you listed. I wondered—"

"Sunflowers! Yes, I would love that. And roses, I think. You seem to know what I want better than I do."

"I've done this for a long time. I'll get the final head count from the palace contact. We've covered almost everything. But we never addressed if they do the traditional 'something old, something new, something borrowed, something blue' here in Halencia or if you even want to play along?"

"What is this tradition?" A frown furrowed her delicate brow.

"It's just a fun tradition that originated in England. It

represents continuity, promise of the future, borrowed happiness and love, purity and fidelity."

"It sounds quite lovely. But I do not have any of these things."

"The fun is in getting them. In America the items are often offered by friends and family. If you share you're doing this, you'll get everything you need and it will all have special meaning for you."

"I know of something old." She tapped a finger against her desk. "Yes, I would like to have it for the wedding. It is a brooch that has been in my father's family for many years. It is said that those who wore the brooch at their wedding enjoyed many happy years together. Yes. I must have the brooch."

"Sounds perfect." Pleased to get a positive reaction and some enthusiasm from the bride, Lindsay made a note in her tablet.

"But I do not know where the brooch is." Sadness drained the brief spark of light. "The women of my generation have not chosen to go with the old tradition. Do you think you can help me find it?" Christine's eyes pleaded with Lindsay. "My grandmother or Aunt Pia might know who had it last."

Goodness, Lindsay never liked to say no to a bride, but she couldn't see how her schedule would accommodate hours on the phone tracking down a lost family jewel.

"Sure, we'll be happy to locate it for you."

Zach stole her opportunity to respond. But, sure, it was a good way to keep him occupied and out of her hair.

"We're talking a few phone calls, right?"

Christina shook her head. "The older generation of women in my family are very traditional. They will not talk of such things to a stranger over the phone. And they will not talk to you alone, Zach." She reached for a pen and paper. "I will write a letter you can take with you. *Grazie*, both of you."

Oh, Zach, what had he got them into? The hope in Christina's eyes prevented Lindsay from protesting time constraints.

"I wish I could give you more time but with learning the workings of the palace, I am a bit overwhelmed." Christina handed Lindsay the letter she'd written. "With the two of you helping, I feel so much better."

"I'm glad." Lindsay tucked the letter into her tote.

"Lindsay, do you mind if I have a moment alone with Christina?" Zach made the quiet demand and tension instantly radiated from his companion.

"Of course." Lindsay stood and offered her hand to Christina. "I'll keep you apprised of the arrangements."

"Thank you." Christina used both hands to convey her urgency. "And the progress in locating the brooch."

"Absolutely." Lindsay smiled and turned away. With her back to Christina, Lindsay narrowed her eyes at him and mouthed the words, "Do not upset the bride."

He maintained an impassive demeanor. "I'll be along in a moment."

Though Christina watched him expectantly, he waited for the distinct click of the door closing before he addressed her.

"I hope you'll forgive my concern, but I noticed you seem unsettled."

"I have much on my mind."

"I understand. But I also know the circumstances of your…relationship with Antonio." The situation warranted discretion on so many levels. "And I wonder if you're having second thoughts?"

Her chin lifted in a defensive gesture. "No."

"Perhaps you should."

Surprise showed before she composed her features

into a calm facade. "I can assure you I have considered the matter thoroughly. Did Antonio send you here to test me?"

"No. Tony has asked me to be his advocate in all things wedding related. I take my responsibilities seriously and when I look at this situation, I have to wonder what the two of you are thinking. Marriage is a binding, hopefully lifelong, commitment. The two of you barely know each other. No one would blame you if you changed your mind. Least of all Tony. He knows how much you've already sacrificed for your country."

Her shoulders went back. "Has he changed his mind?"

It would be so easy to lie. To destroy the engagement with a bit of misdirection that resulted in an endless loop of he said, she said. But he had some honor. The decision to end it must be hers, Antonio's or theirs together.

"No. He's determined to see this through. He's very grateful to you."

She nodded as if his words affirmed something for her. "Thank you for your concern. There is much to adjust to, but I will honor my promise. In little over a month, I will marry Prince Antonio."

CHAPTER SIX

LINDSAY WAS STILL puzzling over what Zach felt compelled to talk to Christina about in private as she climbed to her room on the third floor of Hotel de la Calanetti, a lovely boutique hotel situated on a hillside overlooking Monte Calanetti's central courtyard.

Considering his opinion of lavish weddings and how unsettled Christina came across, leaving them alone together made Lindsay's left eyebrow tick. He better not have caused trouble.

In retrospect she wished she'd waited to say goodbye to Christina until after he'd spoken to her. Then Lindsay might have learned what the discussion had been about. Or maybe not. The other woman's natural poise hid a lot. Lindsay had been unable to tell if the woman was upset when she'd walked them out.

Holding the garment bag draped over her arm, Lindsay stepped aside so the hotel manager's teenage son, Mario, could unlock the door.

"Signorina." He ducked his head in a shy move and gestured for her to precede him.

She stepped in to a comfortable, refined room furnished with nice 1800s furniture. Thankfully there was a private bathroom. One large window allowed sunshine to flow in and provided a delightful view of the village and town center.

But it was tiny; smaller than the room at the farmhouse. Though this room included a desk, which she was happy to see, and a comfortable chair, she barely had space to walk around the double bed.

She tipped Mario—who'd lugged her suitcases up the three flights—with some change and a smile.

"Grazie, signorina." He rewarded her with a bashful grin and raced away.

The garment bag took up the entire closet to the point she had to bump it shut with her hip. She'd hoped to leave the dress with Christina, but the bride had nixed that plan. The queen had made a reservation with a favorite *modiste* in Milan and Christina had asked Lindsay to hold on to the dress and bring it to the fitting.

So of course that was what she'd do. And apparently everything else.

When Christina had walked them out, she'd given Lindsay a brief hug and whispered, "I trust you to finish it. Please make the prince proud."

Lindsay got the message. She was on her own for the final push. Luckily her assistant would be arriving in a few days.

Hands on her hips Lindsay surveyed her room. It was lovely. And if she were here on vacation it would be perfect. But where was she going to work?

The desk for computer work was the least of her needs. She'd shipped five boxes of pre-wedding paraphernalia to the hotel. Upon check-in, Signora Eva had eagerly informed Lindsay the boxes had arrived and she'd be sending them up shortly.

Lindsay puffed out a breath that lifted her bangs. She thought longingly of the hillside villa Zach had pointed out as they'd flown over it. He had the whole place to himself. He probably had a room he could donate to the cause. Unfortunately he'd constantly be around. Talking to her. Distracting her. Tempting her.

Better to avoid that trap if she could.

She lifted her suitcase onto the bed and started unpacking. When she finished, she'd walk down to the town cen-

ter to get a feel for the small city. She may have to find
office space; possibly something off the town courtyard
would be pleasant and close. In the meantime, she'd ask
Signora Eva to hold on to the boxes.

Dressed in beige linen shorts and a cream, sleeveless tunic,
Lindsay strolled down the hill. There was no sidewalk,
just the ancient cobblestoned street. Charming but not the
easiest to walk on.

A young man zipped by her on a scooter, followed
closely by his female companion. Lindsay watched them
until they turned a corner and vanished from view. She
hadn't heard from the car-rental company yet. Monte Calanetti was a lovely little city, but not small enough she could
do all her business by foot.

The zippy little scooter looked promising. It wouldn't
hold anything, but she could have things delivered. But
where? Not the hotel. She'd get claustrophobic after a day.

She reached the city center; not a courtyard, but a plaza.
Oh, it was lovely. In the center an old fountain bubbled
merrily, drawing Lindsay forward. Businesses ringed the
plaza, many with hanging pots of flowers. It was bright
and colorful and had probably looked much the same a
hundred or even five hundred years ago.

Well, minus the cars, of course.

History in Tuscany wasn't something that needed to be
brought to mind. The past surrounded you wherever you
went, influenced your very thoughts. Already Lindsay was
contemplating how she could make it a part of the wedding.

"Buon giorno, signorina," a male voice greeted her.
"May I assist you in finding your way?"

She swung around to confront a large, barrel-chested
man with a full head of black hair dusted gray on the sides.
His bushy mustache was more gray than black. Friendly
brown eyes waited patiently for her assessment.

"Hello." She smiled. "I'm just wandering." She waved her hand around. "I'm spellbound by the beauty of Monte Calanetti. You must be so proud the royal wedding will be performed here."

"Indeed we are. I am Alonso Costa, mayor of this fair city. I can assure you we have much to offer those who stay here. Amatucci's is one of the best boutique vineyards in the world, and Mancini's restaurant is superb. I fully expect Raffaele to earn an Italian Good Food Award this year. What is your interest, *signorina*? I will direct you to the best."

Oh, she was sure he could. She liked him instantly. He'd be a great source to help her.

"It's nice to meet you, Alonso, I'm Lindsay Reeves and I'd like to learn more about your beautiful city. Would you like to join me for coffee?"

White teeth flashed under the heavy bush of his mustache. "I would be most delighted, *signorina*. The café has a lovely cappuccino."

"Sounds wonderful." She allowed him to escort her across the plaza to an outdoor table at the café. He went inside and returned with two cappuccinos and some biscotti. She began to wonder if they had a gym in town. All this wonderful food, she'd be needing one soon.

She introduced herself more fully to the mayor and he proved a font of information. As she'd expected the media, both print and electronic, had already landed heavily in Monte Calanetti.

Alonso rubbed his chin when she asked after office space. "I will ask around. But I must warn you most available space has already been rented or reserved. The wedding has proved quite prosperous for the townspeople. Many have rented out spare rooms to house the paparazzi or provide work space as you have requested."

He named a figure a family had asked for the rental of their one-car garage and her mouth dropped open.

"Si," He nodded at her reaction. "It is crazy. But the press, they bid against each other to get the space."

"Well, it's more than I can afford. I'll have to figure out something else."

The empty chair next to Lindsay scraped back and Zach joined them at the table. He laid one arm along the back of her chair while holding his other hand out to Alonso. "Zach Sullivan. I've rented the De Luca villa."

"Ah, the best man." Alonso shook hands. "A palace representative provided a list of VIPs who would be visiting the area for the wedding. Your name is on the top."

Zach grinned. "It's good to know Tony has his priorities straight."

The casual reference to the prince impressed the mayor. He puffed up a bit as he gave Zach the same rundown about the town he'd given her. Except he offered to arrange a tour of the vineyard and make reservations at the restaurant. With great effort she restrained an eye roll.

"Tell me about the fountain," she asked to redirect the conversation.

Alonso gave her a bright smile. "The legend is that if you toss a coin and it lands in the clamshell you will get your wish. We recently learned that the sculptor of the nymph was Alberto Burano. The fact that the nymph wore a cloak caught the attention of an art historian. She recognized Burano's style and researched the fountain and Burano until she linked the two."

"That's amazing. And brings more value to the fountain and the city. Do you know anything more about the legend?"

"Actually, Lucia's search inspired me to do one of my own and I found that nymphs are known to be sensual creatures of nature, capricious in spirit living among humans but distant from them so when one presents an offering, such as the clamshell, it means the nymph has found true love and the offering is a gift of equal love."

"It's a lovely legend of unselfishness and love." The romance of it appealed to Lindsay.

"But does it work?" Zach questioned.

"Before I did the research I would have said half the time. Now, when I think back to the stories I've heard, success always involved matters of the heart. I believe when the coin lands in the clamshell it activates the gift and the wish is granted when true love is involved."

Zach quirked one dark eyebrow. "You're a romantic, Mr. Mayor."

Alonso smiled and shrugged in a very Italian gesture. "This is what I have observed. Does it make me a romantic to believe in the legend? Maybe so. But the tourists like it."

"I'm sure they do," Lindsay agreed. "Who doesn't like the thought of true love? Wouldn't it be cool to have a replica of the fountain at the reception?"

"*Si.* There is a mason in town that makes small replicas he sells to tourists. I'll give you his number. He might be able to make something bigger."

"That would be great. Thanks."

The mayor's cell phone rang. "Excuse me." He checked the display. "I must take this call. It has been a pleasure to meet you both. *Il caffè* is my treat today."

"Oh, no," Lindsay protested. "I invited you."

"And I am pleased you did. Allow me to welcome you both to Monte Calanetti with this small offering. You can reward me by thinking of local resources when planning this illustrious wedding."

"I already planned to do so."

"Ah—" he made a show of bowing over her hand "—a woman who is both beautiful and clever. You are obviously the right person for the job."

"You flatter me, Alonso. But I must be truthful. The bride insists that I use local goods and people whenever I can."

"Molto bene." He nodded, his expression proud. "Already our princess looks after the people. But I think maybe you would do this anyway, *si*?"

"I've found that local talent is often the best."

"Si, si. As I say, a clever woman. *Buona giornata.* Good day to you both. Ms. Reeves, I will get back to you with a referral. *Ciao.*" He made his exit, stopping to yell something inside the café. Then with a salute the mayor hurried across the square.

"I thought the French were supposed to be the flirts of Europe," Zach mused.

"I liked him."

"Of course. He was practically drooling over you. Clever woman."

She laughed and batted her lashes. "Don't forget beautiful."

His eyes locked on hers, the whiskey depths lit with heat. "How can I when you're sitting right next to me?"

Held captive by his gaze, by a quick and wicked fantasy, it took a beat to compose herself. She cleared her throat as she chased the tail of the topic. Oh, yeah, the mayor. "You can tell he cares about his town and his people. I respect that. Excuse me."

She grabbed her purse and made her escape. Whew, the man was potent.

"Where are we going?" He slid into stride next to her.

And apparently hard to shake.

"We are not going anywhere." She reached the fountain and began to circle the stone feature, making the second answer unnecessary.

"I thought I made it clear, I'm here to assist you."

She flashed him a "yeah, right" glance.

"I appreciate the offer, but my assistant will be arriving at the end of the week." She continued circling.

"What are you doing?"

"I'm checking out the fountain, choosing the best place to throw a coin." The fountain was round, about twelve feet wide with a rock formation rising from slightly off center to a height between seven and eight feet. The cloaked nymph, reclined across two rocks from which the water flowed, reached forward, displaying one nude breast as she offered the clamshell to the side of the rushing water so some of it ran over the stone dish. If you threw too far to the left, the flow of water would wash your chance away, too far to the right and an over-cropping of rock would block the coin.

"You're going to make a wish? For true love? I thought your schedule didn't allow for such things."

"It doesn't." He was right about that. "It's not for me."

"For who then? Your mother?"

"Now there's a thought. But...no." Unfortunately she didn't know if her mother would recognize true love if she found it. She was so focused on the high, she rarely made it past the first few bumps. Even true love required an effort to make it work. "I'm making a wish for Antonio and Christina."

He stopped following her and planted his hands on his hips. "Why? They're already headed for the altar. They don't need the nymph's help."

"Really?" she challenged him. "You're that sure of them?"

His expression remained set. "I think fate should be allowed to take its course."

"And I think it needs a little help." She dug out her coin purse. Hopefully American coins worked as well as euros. Choosing a spot a little to the left because she was right-handed, she tossed her coin. Too light. It fell well short of the clamshell. She tried again. This one went over the top. A third got swept away by the water. "Dang it. That one was in."

"You're not going to make it in. It's set up to defeat you."

"Hey, no advice from the galley." Maybe a nickel? Oh, yeah, that had a nice heft. "What did you talk to Christina about earlier?"

"If I'd wanted you to know, I wouldn't have asked you to leave."

"Tell me anyway." The nickel bounced off the rock.

"No. Try a little twist at the end."

"I'd share with you," she pointed out as she tossed her last nickel. And missed.

"It's none of your business."

She fisted the dime she was about to throw and faced him. "Wrong. I'm here to plan the royal wedding, which makes the bride very much my business. She was already unsettled. And I know you're not a big fan of lavish weddings. I need to know if you upset her."

"I didn't upset her," he said too easily.

"Good. Great. So, tell me, what did you talk about?"

He just lifted a dark eyebrow at her.

"Seriously, I need to know. Just because she didn't look upset doesn't mean she wasn't."

"You're being a nutcase."

"And it'll all go away if you just tell me."

"Okay." He shoved his hands into his pockets. "I picked up on her uneasiness, as well. I asked her if she was having second thoughts."

"Zach!"

"What? This is my best friend. If she's going to bolt, now would be the time to speak up. Not when he's standing at the altar."

"I told you, all brides go through a bit of nerves. Unless you're the M-O-B, pointing out their shakiness only makes it worse. Even then it can be iffy."

His features went blank. "M-O-B?"

"Mother of the bride."

"Oh. She's probably the last person Christina would confide in."

"Why do you say that?"

"My impression is the two aren't particularly close."

"Hmm. Good to know." Lindsay had already noted Christina's reluctance to include her mother in the planning.

Mrs. Rose made her displeasure quite well known, which brought Mr. Rose out to play. Lucky for Lindsay the palace official had taken over dealing with the Roses.

"All the more reason to show Christina support rather than undermine her confidence," Lindsay advised Zach.

"Rest easy. She assured me she would be marrying Tony."

"Okay." She read his eyes and nodded. "Good. Thanks." She turned back to the fountain. "My last coin. What kind of twist?"

"You're still going to make a wish? I just told you Christina's fine."

"I want more than fine. I want true love."

"You do know most political marriages aren't based on love." Something in his tone had her swinging back to him. The late-afternoon sun slanted across his face, casting his grim features into light and shadow.

"Yes," she said softly, "but is that what you want for your friend?"

He moved closer, brushing her ponytail behind her shoulder. "So what is your wish?"

"I'm wishing for true love and happiness for the bride and groom." With the words, she pulled her arm back. As it moved forward Zach cupped her hand and, as she released the coin, gave it a little twist.

The dime flew through the air and plopped with a splash right in the middle of the clamshell.

"We did it!" Lindsay clapped her hands then threw her arms around Zach's neck and kissed his cheek. "Thank you."

He claimed a quick kiss then set her aside. "Don't celebrate yet. We still need to see if it works. Which should only take—what?—the next fifty years."

"Nope." Flustered from the kiss, Lindsay stepped back shifting her attention from him to the fountain. What had he said? Oh, yeah. How did it work? "Now we have faith."

The first attempt to find the brooch was a bust.

Lindsay tried insisting she could handle finding the brooch herself. It was something she could do while she waited for her assistant to arrive and figured out her work space situation. And she needed a break from Zach, especially after the kiss at the fountain. His casual caresses were becoming too common and were definitely too distracting for her peace of mind.

A little distance between them would be a good thing.

Unfortunately, as he pointed out, Christina's grandmother lived in a tiny house in a village halfway between Monte Calanetti and Voti, and Lindsay didn't have transportation without him. A new rental hadn't showed up and the helicopter flew at his discretion. Plus, he'd offered to interpret for her. Since Mona didn't speak much English and Lindsay didn't speak much Italian, she was stuck.

Mona Rose was small with white hair, glasses and lots of pip. She greeted them warmly as Christina had called to say they would be coming. Lindsay sat on a floral-print couch with crocheted lace doilies on the arms while Zach lounged in a matching rocking chair.

Mona served them hibiscus tea and lemon cake while she chatted with Zach.

Lindsay smiled and sipped. After a few minutes of listening, she discreetly kicked Zach in the foot.

He promptly got the clue. "She's very pleased Christina wishes to wear the brooch. She wore the brooch for her wedding and had many happy years with her Benito. Her daughter, Cira, chose not to wear the brooch and now she's divorced with two children."

"I'm sorry to hear that." Lindsay accepted a plate of cake. "Does she know where the brooch is?"

Zach conveyed the question.

Mona tapped her chin as she stared out the window. After a moment she took a sip of her tea and spoke. "Sophia, my youngest sister, I think was last to wear *le broccia*." She shook her head and switched to Italian.

Zach translated. "Pia is her older sister. Her daughter was the last to get married. She didn't wear the brooch, either, but Mona thinks Pia may have it."

"Grazie." Lindsay directed her comments to Mona, smiling to hide her disappointment. She was hoping this chore could be done.

"Would you be willing to do a quick look through your things while we're here? Just to be on the safe side."

Zach translated both the question and Mona's answer.

"*Si.* I will look. Christina is a good girl. And Antonio, he is good for Halencia. But they will both need much luck."

The next morning Lindsay struggled to get ready while shuffling around five large boxes. When she'd returned to the hotel last night, all five boxes had been delivered to her room. As predicted, she'd had a hard time getting around the bed. She'd actually had to climb over it to get to the bathroom.

When she'd asked about it at the front desk, Signora Eva apologized but explained a delivery of provisions had forced her to reclaim the space she'd been using to store Lindsay's boxes. That had meant the boxes needed to be delivered to Lindsay's room. This morning she'd managed to arrange them so she had a small aisle around the bed, but she had to suck in a breath to get through.

The thought of unpacking everything in this limited space made her cringe. She'd be tripping over her samples every time she turned around.

Frustrated, she left the room for some breakfast. Later she wanted to view the palazzo and chapel where the wedding and reception would take place. But she hoped to rent a scooter before making the trip to the other side of town.

If any were still available.

The press truly had descended. On her way to breakfast she fended off two requests for exclusive shots of the wedding dress. She informed them the dress was under lock and key at the palace and suffered no remorse for her lie.

When Signora Eva came by to refill her coffee, Lindsay asked if she knew of any place she might rent for a work space and received much the same response as she'd gotten from the mayor.

She was processing that news when her cell rang.

With a sinking heart she listened to her assistant advise her she wouldn't be joining her in Halencia, after all. While Mary gushed on about the part she'd landed in a situation comedy all Lindsay could think about was how she'd manage without an assistant.

Lindsay needed to be out in the field a lot. She counted on her assistant to keep track of all the details of a wedding, do follow up and advise Lindsay of any problems. She'd quickly become bogged down if she had to take on the extra work.

Because she cared about Mary, Lindsay mustered the enthusiasm to wish her well. But as soon as she hung up she had a mini meltdown. Stomping over to the sideboard, she plopped an oversize muffin onto her plate and returned to her seat, her mind churning over her lack of options...

As Lindsay made the hike up the hill to Zach's villa she contemplated the obvious answer to her space problem. Much as she preferred to avoid Zach, after two short days she seriously considered asking him for help.

Her hesitation wasn't worry over his answer. He'd been ordered to assist her and he genuinely seemed to take his duty seriously.

The problem would be in dealing with him.

From the air, the villa had looked vast enough to provide a small corner for her without causing her to trip over him at every turn. But she wouldn't know until she saw the inside, which is what had prompted this little trip.

She wiped her brow with the back of her hand. Only eight in the morning and already the day had some heat to it. The blue, cloudless sky offered little relief from the relentless sun. But it also meant no humidity.

"Good morning, partner." Zach's voice floated on the air.

She paused and shaded her eyes to seek him out. He stood on a terrace of his rented villa. The big, stone building rested right up against the old protective wall that ringed the city. From this vantage point it looked huge. Three stories high, the bottom floor created the terrace where Zach stood. The top floor was a pergola with windows on all sides.

"Good morning." She waved.

"You missed the street." He gestured for her to backtrack a bit. "It's a narrow drive right by the pink house."

She followed his directions, turning at the pink house, and there he was coming to greet her. He wore khaki shorts and a blue cotton shirt untucked. The sleeves were rolled to expose his muscular forearms. He looked cool, calm and competent.

How she envied him.

The trees thinned as they neared the villa. He took her

hand and led her down a steep set of steps and a walkway along the side of the house. When they rounded the corner, her breath caught in her throat.

The small city spread out below them, a backdrop to the green lawn that covered the hillside. Oak, olive and pine trees provided shade and privacy. To her right a table and chairs sat under a covered patio, the ivy-covered trellis lending it a grotto effect while a stone path led to a gazebo housing white wicker furniture.

To the far side rosebushes lined a path leading to an infinity pool.

Forget the palazzo. This would make a beautiful setting for a wedding. Well, if you weren't a royal prince.

She took pride in the large, lavish weddings she'd planned for hip and rising celebrities, but she took joy in putting together weddings that were cozy gatherings. Yup, give her intimate and tranquil over pomp and circumstance any day of the week.

"Come up with me." A spiral wrought-iron staircase took them to the terrace he'd been standing on when he'd hailed her. She followed his tight butt up the steps.

Good dog, he was fine. His body rivaled any sight she'd seen today. Even the view from the terrace that provided a panoramic vista of everything she'd seen.

"Impressed yet?" Zach asked behind her left ear.

"I passed impressed before I reached the pool."

"I had my coffee out here this morning. I don't think I've ever spent a more peaceful moment."

"I'm jealous." She stepped away from the heat of his body. She needed her wits about her when she presented her proposition. His assertion they'd be lovers haunted her thoughts. And dreams.

Oh, she was a weak, weak woman in her dreams.

As heat flooded her cheeks she focused on the view

rather than his features. "I'm afraid I'm about to disrupt your peace."

"Pixie, just looking at you disrupts my peace. In the best possible way." He punctuated the remark by tracing the armhole of her sleeveless peach-and-white polka dot shirt, the backs of his fingers feathering over sensitive flesh.

She shivered, shaking a finger at him as she created distance between them. "No touching."

He grinned, again unrepentant. "What brings you by today?"

"I wondered if you wanted to go to the cake tasting with me." She tossed out her excuse for the spy mission. Men liked cake, right?

As soon as the words left her mouth, she thought better of her desperate plan. If she worked here, it would be more of his charming flirtation and subtle caresses until she gave in and let him have his wicked way with her. Or she stopped the madness by seducing him on the double lounge down by the pool. Enticing as both scenarios were, neither was acceptable.

"You know…never mind. I've already taken advantage of your generosity. Enjoy your peace. I can handle this on my own." She turned for the stairs. "I'll catch you later."

The chemistry between them nearly struck sparks in the air. The force of the pull buzzed over her skin like a low-level electrical current. She had it banked at the moment, but the right word or look and it would flare to life in a heartbeat.

Her best bet was to walk away and find another solution to her problem. One that didn't tempt her to break her sensible rules and put her company at risk. She purposely brought Kevin to mind, remembered the pain and humiliation of his betrayal and recalled the looks of pity and disapproval on the faces of her friends and colleagues.

She'd never willingly put herself in that position ever again.

"Cake." Zach caught her gently by the elbow. "You can't tease me with cake and then walk away. It's one of the few chores regarding this wedding gig I'd actually enjoy."

She studied him for a moment before replying. He met her stare straight-on, no hint of flirting in his steady regard. She appreciated his sincerity but still she hesitated.

"Okay. You're in. But we have to go now. I have an appointment to view the palazzo this afternoon. Has the rental company replaced your car yet?"

"No. I have my assistant following up on it. Do we need the helicopter?"

She shook her head. "The bakery is in town." She supposed she'd have to follow up on her own rental now. Pulling out her phone, she made a note. "But it's hot out. My plan is to rent a scooter."

A big grin brought out a boyishness in his features. "You don't have to rent a scooter. There are a couple downstairs in the garage along with something else you might find useful."

"What?"

"Come see." He strode over to a French door and stepped inside.

Trailing behind him, she admired the interior almost as much as the exterior. The bedroom they moved through displayed the comfort and luxury of a five-star hotel. Downstairs it became apparent the villa had gone through a modern update. The lounge, dining room and gourmet kitchen opened onto each other via large archways, creating an open-concept format while exposed beams and stone floors retained the old world charm of a Tuscan villa.

Oh, yeah, she could work here. Too bad it was a no-go.

Off the kitchen Zach opened a door and went down a

half flight of stairs to the garage. He flipped a light and
she grinned at what she saw. A sporty black golf cart with
a large cargo box in the back filled half the space. On the
far side were two red scooters.

"Sweet. This will work nicely."

"Dibs on the cart."

She lifted her eyebrows at him. "What are you, ten?"

"No, I'm six-four. I'd look foolish trying to ride the
scooter."

Running her gaze over the full length of him, she admired the subtle muscles and sheer brawn of his wide
shoulders. She saw his point. He'd look as though he were
riding a child's toy.

He grunted. "Work with me here, Lindsay. You can't
tell me no touching and then look at me like that."

"Sorry," she muttered. She claimed the passenger seat.
Caught.

Turned out wedding planning could be quite tasty. Zach
finished the last bite of his sample of the white amaretto
cake with the vanilla bean buttercream icing. And way
more complicated than it needed to be.

The baker, a reed-thin woman with a big smile and
tired eyes, had six samples set out for them when they'd
arrived at the quaint little shop on a cobblestoned street
just off the plaza. She'd dusted her hands on her pink ruf-
fled apron and explained what each sample was.

Lindsay explained Christina had already chosen the
style and colors for the cake; their job was to pick out the
flavors for the three different layers. It took him five minutes to pick his three favorites. Lindsay agreed with two
but not the third. He was happy to let her have her preference, but…no. The baker brought out six more samples,
which were all acceptable.

The fact was they couldn't go wrong whatever choice

they made. There was no reason this appointment needed to be an hour long. But Lindsay insisted the flavors be compatible.

They were finally done and he was finishing off the samples of his favorites while Lindsay completed the order with the baker up at the counter.

He'd be taking a back seat on the hands-on stuff from now on. He was a stickler for attention to detail, but efficiency had its place, too.

The little bell over the door rang as two men strolled in, one tall and bald, the other round and brown-haired. They eyed the goods on display and Zach heard a British slant to their accent.

He knew immediately when they realized who Lindsay was. They closed in on her, obviously trying to see the plans for the cake. Their interest marked them as two of the media horde invading the town.

Lindsay politely asked them to step back.

Baldy moved back a few inches but Brownie made no move to honor her request.

Zach's gaze narrowed on the two, waiting to see how Lindsay handled herself. His little pixie had a feisty side. She wouldn't appreciate his interference. And this may well blow over. All press weren't bad, but he knew money could make people do things they'd never usually contemplate.

Ignoring the looming goons, Lindsay wrapped up her business and turned toward him. The media brigade blocked her exit, demanding details about the cake, pestering her for pictures. She tried to push past them but they went shoulder to shoulder, hemming her in.

In an instant Zach crossed the room.

"You're going to want to let her by."

"Wait your turn." Brownie dismissed him. "Come on, sweetcakes, show us something."

Sweetcakes?

"It's always my turn." Zach placed a hand on either man's shoulder and shoved them apart.

They whirled on him like a mismatched tag team.

"Back up," Brownie snarled at Zach's chest. And then he slowly lifted his gaze to Zach's. Even Baldy had to look up.

Zach rolled his thick shoulders. That's all it usually took. Sure enough, both men took a large step back.

"Ms. Reeves is with me." He infused the quiet words with a bite of menace. "I won't be pleased if I see you bothering her again."

"Hey, no disrespect." Baldy quickly made his exit. Brownie clenched his jaw and slowly followed.

"Thank you." Lindsay appeared at his side. "Those two were more aggressive than most."

"Are you okay?" He pulled her into his arms. "Do you put up with that often?" He couldn't tolerate the thought of her being hassled by those media thugs on her own.

"All the time." For a moment she stood stiffly, but with a sigh she melted against him. "One of the guys at my hotel offered me a hundred-thousand dollars for a picture of the wedding dress, which means the tabloids are probably willing to pay a million for it."

"That explains why you've lugged it halfway across the world."

"I said it was locked up at the palace. But for a million dollars, I don't doubt someone might try to check out my room anyway."

That did it. He may not support this wedding, but he had his limits. He wouldn't put his plan, or Tony's happiness, before Lindsay's safety. The thought of her vulnerable on her own at the hotel and someone forcing their way into her room sent a primitive wave of rage blasting through him. He had to fix this.

"You should give up your room at the hotel and stay with me at the villa. It would be safer for you."

CHAPTER SEVEN

"UH, NO." LINDSAY pushed away from the safety of his arms. Yes, she'd been spooked by the menacing media jerks, but was Zach totally insane? "That is not an option." She even thought better of asking for work space at the villa. "This—" she waved between the two of them, indicating the chemistry they shared "—makes it a bad idea."

"Even I'm picking up on what a big deal this is for the press." He led her back to their table. "It didn't really strike me at first. I'm used to photographers hanging around hawking at Antonio for a picture. Some of them can be unscrupulous in their bid for a shot." He sat back crossing his arms over his chest his gaze intent, focused on her, on the problem. She had a sudden, clear vision of what he'd look like sitting at his desk. "It's the only solution that makes sense."

She sent him a droll stare. "You're just saying that to get in my pants."

"Not so."

The bite in the denial sent embarrassed heat rushing through her.

"Yes, I want in your pants, but not at the expense of your safety."

She blinked at him, her emotions taking a moment to catch up with her hearing. Obviously she'd touched a nerve.

"Okay."

"Excellent." Satisfied, he leaned forward in his chair. "It's settled. You'll move into the villa. We'll find a secure spot for the dress and you can choose a room for yourself and one of the spare rooms for your office. Or you can use the sunroom if you prefer."

"No. Wait." Panicked, she made a sharp cut-off gesture with her hand. "I was acknowledging your comment not agreeing to move in. We need to talk about this."

"We just did."

"Yes, and I appreciate your putting my safety ahead of your libido, but what does that mean? I've told you how I feel about maintaining a professional distance with all members of the wedding party, especially the best man."

A raised eyebrow mocked her. "I remember."

She gritted her teeth. "Well, you're a touchy-feely guy and I can't deal with that in a professional relationship."

A stunned expression flashed across his well-defined features but was quickly replaced with a contemplative mask.

"You have my promise I'll try to keep my hands to myself."

"The problem with that sentence is the word *try*."

He ran a hand over the back of his neck, kneading the muscles and nerves as if to relieve tension, studying her the whole time. Then he flexed his shoulders and faced her.

"Here's the deal. I'm not a touchy-feely guy. Not normally. I go after what I want, but I respect boundaries and I can handle being told no."

Yeah, like that happened.

"For some reason it's different with you. I like my hands on you, like the touch and taste of you to the degree it's instinctive to seek it."

OMD. That is so hot.

"So, yes. I promise to *try*."

She gulped. "Okay."

His eyes flashed dark fire. "Is that okay you'll stay or—"

"Yes. Okay, I'll move in." It may be insane to move in

with him, but she would feel safer. Plus, it solved her work problem. "But I'm keeping my room at the hotel. Space is already at a premium here in Monte Calanetti and I need a place I can retr—uh…go to if things don't work out."

"Fair enough. And as a gesture of my commitment, I'll pay for the room since you won't be using it."

"That's not necessary."

"It is to me. I'll feel better with you at the villa, and I want you to know you can trust me."

She slowly nodded. "Okay. I'll go pack."

"I had your boxes delivered up here, but if you choose this space, you'll need a proper desk. It has a bar and a billiard table, but that's it."

"I don't need anything new," Lindsay protested.

"I doubt the owners will object to us leaving behind an extra piece of furniture."

"That's not the point." He'd warned her that the space lacked a desk or table for her laptop. But, seriously, she didn't see the problem; she sat with it in her lap half the time.

"Pixie." He stopped in the upper hallway and swung to face her. His hand lifted to touch but he caught himself and curled the fingers into a fist that he let drop to his side. "Didn't you look at the numbers? The government contract will lift me to billionaire status. I can afford a desk."

He opened a door she'd thought was a linen closet. It revealed a staircase of stone steps. His hand gestured for her go ahead of him.

"First of all—" she paused in front of him "—congratulations."

A pleased smile lit his eyes. The simple expression of joy made her glad she'd put that first.

She got the feeling he received very little positive reinforcement in his personal life. The business world recognized and respected his genius, and his employees obviously appreciated his success and most likely his work ethic. But as an only child whose parents ignored his personal business interests in favor of their own agenda for him to join his father in politics, who did he have that mattered to tell him job well done?

She shook the thought away. He was not a poor, unfortunate child, but an intelligent, successful man.

And he'd hate her pity.

"Second—" she started up the stairs "—it's not for you to buy me a desk."

"The duties of a best man are unlimited. But you could be right. Do you want me to call Tony and ask him? Because I can pretty much guarantee his response will be, 'If the wedding planner needs a desk then buy her a desk. And don't bother me with such trivial things.'"

Aggrieved, she rolled her eyes, making sure he saw as she rounded the bend in the stairs. "Please, even if he blew off the request that easily, he wouldn't add that last bit."

"Not only would he say it, Pixie, that was the clean version. Tony doesn't have a whole lot of patience these days."

"He must be dealing with a lot—oh, I love, love, *love* this."

She strolled into the middle of the bright room and did a slow turn. The room was a long octagon. Three walls were made of glass and windows, two others were of stone and one held a fireplace. The last was half stone, the other half was a stained-glass mural of a Tuscan hillside; a bar with brown-cushioned stools ran almost the full length of the wall. At the far end there was a door. She checked it out and found it opened onto another spiral staircase that led to the terrace below.

"A separate entrance."

"Yes, I'll give you a set of keys. When your assistant gets here, she can still have access if we're gone."

"That'd be great but my assistant won't be coming."

"What happened?"

"My practical, poised, ever-efficient assistant finally landed a part in a sitcom."

"Ah, the joy of proprietorship in Hollywood."

Still feeling deserted, Lindsay nodded. "It's the third time it's happened to me. Of course, I'm thrilled for her. But seriously? Worst timing ever."

"Hey, listen. I'm the first to admit this wedding stuff is not my thing, but I'll help where I can."

"Thanks, but you've done enough by offering me this space. I'll finally be able to put up my wedding board. And the help I need involves a hundred little things, well below your pay grade." She really couldn't see him playing secretary. And she may appreciate the space and assistance, but the last thing she needed was to have him constantly underfoot.

"There's no help for it. I'll have to hire someone local. Maybe Alonso knows someone he can recommend. On the plus side, it will be good to have someone who knows the area and the people, who speaks the language and knows the cost of things."

"Alonso will know someone. In the meantime, I'm sticking with you. I'll get a locksmith in to reinforce the locks on all the doors."

She wanted to protest the need for him to shadow her. Instead she nodded, knowing he was reacting out of concern for her. And she was happy to have the extra security for the dress. It might seem a bother for something they'd only have for another week, but she'd be more comfortable knowing the villa was secure.

She strolled further into the room. In soft beige and sage green, the furniture looked sturdy and comfortable. A U-shaped couch invited her to sit and enjoy the amazing view. The billiard table Zach had mentioned was on the right and her boxes were stacked on the green felt. Past it was the fireplace wall with a bookshelf that offered a wide selection of reading material. Another door hid a bathroom.

The ceiling was high, the beams exposed, and a large fan circulated the air in the room.

There were only two low-slung tables. One in front of the large couch and one between the swivel chairs near the fireplace.

"Oh, yeah, I can work here. No hardship at all."

She'd totally make do.

Hands on his hips, Zach surveyed the room. "You'll need a desk." He repeated his earlier decree. "And you mentioned a wedding board. Is that a whiteboard?"

"A whiteboard would be nice, too. My wedding board is usually a corkboard. I need to be able to tack things to it."

He had his phone in his hands and was making notes. She sighed, knowing there'd be no shaking him until she hired an assistant. In one sense it was reassuring to know she wasn't on her own, but it made her plan to avoid him a no-go. It was almost as if fate were working against her.

"I guess we have our shopping list, then. What do you want to do now? Unpack your boxes? You said earlier that you wanted to check out the palazzo."

"Yes. The boxes can wait." Better to have the boards when she went to do that, anyway. "But, honestly, there's no need for you to accompany me. Stay. Enjoy your day."

"I'm coming with you."

Of course he was. At this point, it was easier to agree than to argue. "Fine. Let me call Louisa and remind her I'm coming then we can go."

"Who's Louisa?"

"The owner of the palazzo. We've spoken a couple of times. She seems nice. Did you hear they discovered a fresco when they were restoring the chapel?"

"No. That's quite a discovery. It has to add to the property value."

"You are such a guy."

"Pixie, were you in any doubt?"

"Hello, Louisa, it's so nice to finally meet you. Thank you for allowing us to tour the property today." Lindsay greeted the owner of the palazzo.

It surprised Zach to see Louisa was an American. The two women were close to the same age but dissimilar in every other way. Louisa topped Lindsay by four or five inches and wore her white-blond hair in a messy knot on top of her head. Her willowy frame and restrained posture gave her a brittle appearance.

Funny, she held no attraction for him because she fit his type to a tee: long, lithe, and blond. Sure he recognized she was a beautiful woman, but she appeared almost fragile next Lindsay's vibrancy.

"Louisa, I have to say I'm a little concerned. I thought the renovation would be further along." Lindsay swept her hand out to indicate the overgrown vegetation and construction paraphernalia strewed through the courtyard and surrounding grounds.

"I can see why you'd be confused." Louisa's smile was composed. "But we're actually right on schedule. They've just completed the interior restoration. The construction crew will be back today to finish clearing out their equipment and trash. The next step is the landscapers, but I was actually thinking of hiring some men from town first, to just clear all this out."

"That might be a good idea," Lindsay agreed. "Just level it and start fresh."

"Exactly. I can see some rosebushes, lavender and a few wild sunflowers. But it's so overgrown it's hard to know if they'd be worth saving if we took the time and effort to clear the weeds around them."

Lindsay nodded as the other woman talked. "I think you have the right idea."

Zach enjoyed watching them interact. He liked how Lindsay's ponytail bobbed as she talked and the way the sunshine picked up golden highlights in her hair.

He almost forgot his purpose in shadowing her every move.

Mostly because it was against his nature to be covert, to be less than helpful. Case in point: this morning. When he saw Lindsay being intimidated by the press, he jumped right into fix-it mode and invited her to move into the spacious villa. And he'd provided her with a prime workspace. Hell, he fully intended to get her a desk.

All of which went against his prime objective of keeping Antonio from a life of misery. With that thought Zach took out his phone and texted his friend, tagging him for a meeting time.

Right now his biggest problem was the blurring line between his mock flirtation with Lindsay and his honest reactions. There'd been too much truth in his arguments to get her to stay at the villa. She was too comfortable to be around, too soft to the touch, too easy to imagine in his bed.

And too dangerous to succumb to.

He hadn't felt this way about a woman since…ever. And he wasn't going there.

From here on out he was back on his game.

"Thanks for talking it through with me." Louisa folded her arms in front of her. "I'm very grateful to the monarchy for doing the renovation of the palazzo and chapel. I certainly couldn't have afforded anything this elaborate all at once. Probably never, come to that. But it's been a pretty intense process. It's good to have someone to discuss a decision with."

"I bet." Lindsay grinned. "Call on me anytime. I'm great at discussion."

"I can see you are." A friendly sparkle entered Louisa's light blue eyes. "And probably pretty good at decisions, too."

Lindsay rocked on her heals. "Yeah, it's kind of part of the job description."

The composed smile held a little more warmth as Louisa gestured to the chapel. "Shall we do a walk-through? I'm afraid we'll have to make this fairly quick. I have an appointment in Florence tomorrow. I'm driving over tonight so I'll be there in the morning. I've booked passage on the two o'clock ferry."

"That's fine. Today I just want to get a feel for the place and take some pictures so I know what I'm working with. And—oh, this is beautiful." Lindsay surveyed the interior of the chapel with a mix of wonder and calculation on her face. "So charming with the arched windows and the dark wood pews. I can come back on another day to get actual measurements and check out the lighting. I love how the jewel colors flow over the stone tiles from the stained-glass windows. Christina has chosen an afternoon wedding and evening reception. She wants to have it outdoors, so the landscaping will be important."

"I won't be able to hire the workers to clear the grounds until I return from Florence," Louisa informed her, "but I'll make it a priority when I get back."

"Why don't I handle that for you?" Zach offered, seeing an opportunity to cause a few days' delay. He'd simply tell the workers to be careful to preserve any original flowers. "I'll talk to the mayor to get some referrals."

"Thank you. I appreciate it. They did a wonderful job with the restoration," Louisa stated. "It was quite a mess in here. Stones were missing, the stained-glass windows were broken and some of the walls had wood covering them. Here's the fresco that was uncovered." Louisa moved to a shallow alcove and Zach followed Lindsay over.

He understood her gasp. The ancient painting of Madonna and child took his breath away. The colors were vibrant, the detail exquisite. It was almost magnetic—the pull of the fresco, from the pinky tones of Jesus's skin and the color of Mary's dark blue robe, to the white and yellow of the brilliant beam of light encasing them and the greens of the surrounding countryside bright with orange and red flowers. The details were so exact, every brush stroke so evident, it seemed it could have been painted a week ago rather than five hundred years.

"Look at the love on their faces." Lindsay breathed. "The artist caught the perfect expression of Mary's unconditional love for her child and Baby Jesus's childlike wonder and awe for his mother. It shows the full bond between mother and child. This will certainly add to the ambience of the wedding."

With the beauty and love inherent in the fresco, Zach could see how she'd think so. But with his friend's future and happiness at risk, he couldn't take that chance.

Zach surprised Lindsay with his patience and insight the next day as they toured four nurseries. She had a whole list of requirements from bouquets and boutonnieres to centerpieces and garlands and more.

Lindsay planned to use roses for the groomsmen, sunflowers over linen chair covers for the reception and a combination of the two for everything else.

To bring about a sense of intimacy in the courtyard and to define the separate areas for eating and dancing, she planned to have rustic scaffolding erected. Lights, flowers and silk drapery would blend rustic with elegance to create a sense of old and new. She actually appreciated Zach's male point of view and his logistical input.

The helicopter came in handy as they buzzed around the countryside. Deciding on the second vendor she spoke with, Lindsay asked to return to the nursery to put in her order. Zach made no argument. He simply directed the pilot and helped her aboard.

Zach waited patiently in an anteroom of the magnificent palace. He stood at the terrace doors overlooking a section of the rose garden. Curved benches spaced several feet apart created a circle around a marble fountain of a Roman goddess.

Lindsay would love it. He had to hand it to her, that woman worked. He could practically hear her discourse on what a lovely venue the rose garden would be for a wedding, how the circle represented the ring and the ring represented the commitment made between bride and groom, who once joined together there became no beginning and no end, just the unity of their bond.

"Yeah, right."

"Talking to yourself, *amico mio*?" a gruff voice said before a hand clapped on his shoulder.

"Just keeping myself company waiting for you."

"I'm glad you came." Tony pulled Zach into the hug he'd learned to endure through the years. Tony was a demonstrative man, how could he not be with such passionate parents?

"Yeah, well, it became clear if I wanted to see you, I'd have to come to you."

"I only have thirty minutes. I wish I had more time to give you. Hell, I wish we were at Clancy's eating wings, drinking beer and catching a game."

"We could be there in fourteen hours," Zach said, hoping it would be that easy.

Tony laughed. "I'm tempted." He opened the terrace door and stepped outside. To the left stood a table with comfortable chairs. And a bucket of beers on ice.

"What, no chicken wings?"

"They are on the way."

Zach sat across from his friend and leaned back in his chair. Tony looked tired. And harassed. Zach knew Tony had to be busy for him to put Zach off. They were as close as brothers, too close for the other man to brush him aside.

"How are things going with the wedding?" Tony asked.

"Let's just say I could tell you in excruciating detail and leave it at that."

Tony grinned. "Thanks, bro. I mean that."

"Only for you," Zach assured him. "How are things going here?"

"Slowly." Tony grabbed a beer and opened it. "Everyone has a different opinion of how the monarchy should be run."

"And you have to learn the worst-case scenario for each before you'll make a determination," Zach stated, knowing that's how his friend operated. In working security protocols he liked to work backward to make sure the worst never happened.

"It doesn't help that I constantly have to address some question or concern about the wedding or coronation. It's a lot to juggle."

"So maybe you should put the wedding off." Zach took the opportunity presented to him. "Get the monarchy stabilized first and then revisit the idea of marriage when you can choose someone for yourself."

"Are you kidding me?" Tony laughed again. "Instead of cheering me, the people would be rioting in the streets. I think they want this wedding more than anything else."

"Because it's a Cinderella story?"

Tony shrugged. "Because I've made them wait so long."

"Because you never intended to marry Christina."

"Shush." Tony glanced around the terrace. "We won't speak of that here."

"Someone needs to speak of it before it's too late to stop it."

"That time is long gone, my friend. Christina will make a good queen. The people love her."

"They don't know her any better than you do. She's been off in Africa."

"Taking care of sick children. It plays well. Ah, the chicken wings. *Grazie*, Edmondo."

The servant bowed and retreated.

Zach quirked a brow at his friend. Tony shrugged and they both reached for a chicken wing.

After a moment Tony sighed. "Man, I needed this." He upended his beer, drinking the last. "I don't know anything about running a country, Zach."

"You know plenty. You've been training for this your whole life. Even while living in California," Zach reminded him.

"That's different. I always planned to hand over control to a republic, but I'm not sure that's what the people want. They are all behind this wedding and I can't let them down. I just need to do the opposite of what my dad would do and I'll be doing a better job than has been done."

"A little harsh, don't you think?"

"No." Tony shook his head and reached for another beer. "I love my parents, but their relationship is messed up. I don't ever want to love anyone so much it messes with my head. Better a business arrangement than a volatile, emotional mess."

Zach plucked a bottle of beer from the bucket, knowing he'd gotten as far as he was going to get tonight. He reached out and clicked bottles with Tony. "To the monarchy."

Tony's statement about a business arrangement only made Zach more determined to see him freed from a loveless marriage. Because his friend was wrong. At least a volatile, emotional mess inferred someone cared. You didn't get that guarantee with a business arrangement. What you got was a cold, lonely life.

CHAPTER EIGHT

WHAT A DIFFERENCE a week made. As she flew through the air on the way to Milan, Lindsay thought about all she'd accomplished since her last flight in the helicopter. She had her wedding board up and she'd made contact with all the local vendors she'd lined up before coming to Halencia, confirming plans and reevaluating as necessary.

She'd talked to the landscapers and she had an appointment at the end of the week to meet at the palazzo to go over her needs for the wedding and reception. On the mayor's recommendation, Zach had hired a crew to clean up the palazzo and chapel grounds. They should be well done by the time she met with the landscapers.

Yesterday she'd hired an assistant. Serena was twenty-two, fresh out of university and eager to assist in any way she could with the royal wedding. Lindsay worried a little over the girl's age, knowing she'd have to be strong enough to say no to outrageous offers for inside information about the wedding, and mature enough to know when she was being played. But Serena was Mayor Alonso's daughter and she had his glib tongue and a no-nonsense attitude that convinced Lindsay she could handle the job.

Plus, she just plain liked the young woman.

She'd gone a little googly-eyed over Zach but, seriously, who wouldn't? It was a fact of life she'd have to put up with.

"We are coming up on Milano," the pilot announced.

Lindsay leaned forward to get a view of the northern city. Two prominent pieces of architecture caught the eye. A very modern building of glass and metal that twisted well into the air and an ancient cathedral dramatically topped with a forest of spires. Both buildings were stunningly impressive.

She glanced at Zach and found his gaze on her. Smiling, she gestured at the view. "It's spectacular."

"It is, indeed," he agreed without looking away from her.

She turned her attention back to the view, pretending his focus on her didn't send the blood rushing through her veins.

He'd kept to his promise not to touch her. Well, mostly. He didn't play with her hair or take her hand, but he stayed bumping-elbows close wherever they went. And he still liked to put his hand in the small of her back whenever he directed her into or out of a building or room.

Serena had asked if they were together, so Lindsay knew the townspeople were speculating about their relationship. She'd given Serena a firm no in response and hoped the word got out about the true state of things.

They landed at a heliport on a mid-rise building not far from the Duomo di Milano. Downstairs a car was waiting to take them to a shop along Via Monte Napoleone. Lindsay checked her tablet to give Zach the address.

She looked forward to handing the dress over to Christina and the queen's seamstress. Providing security for the gown had proved more stressful than she'd anticipated. Having it off her shoulders would allow her to focus on the many other elements of the wedding demanding her attention.

"There it is. Signora Russo's. Christina and the queen are meeting us there. I already spoke to Signora Russo about the damage to the beading. She said she's a master seamstress and she would fix it."

"I'm glad to hear it."

A valet took the car and she and Zach were escorted inside. An attendant took the garment bag and led them to a plush fitting suite. A large, round couch in a soft ivory with a high back topped by an extravagant flower arrangement graced the middle of the room.

The bride and queen stood speaking with a petite, ageless woman in a stylish black suit. Lindsay walked across the room with Zach to join them.

Christina made the introductions. It might have been Lindsay's imagination, but the other woman seemed quite relieved to see them.

"Zachary!" exclaimed Her Royal Highness Valentina de l'Accardi, Queen of Halencia when she saw Zach. "As handsome as ever." She glided forward and kissed him on both cheeks. "*Mio caro*, thank you for helping Antonio. He is so busy. Many, many meetings. We do not even see him at the palace."

"Valentina." Zach bent over her hand. "You are ever youthful. I thought for a moment Elena was here."

"Zachary!" Valentina swatted his forearm and giggled. Yes, the matriarch of Halencia giggled. And flushed a pretty rose. "Such a charming boy. Be careful, Ms. Reeves, this one knows what a woman wants to hear, be alert that he does not steal your heart."

"Yes. I've noticed he's a bit of a flirt."

"*Si*, a flirt." Warm brown eyes met hers with a seriousness her lighthearted greeting belied. The woman clasped her hand and patted it. "I am so pleased you were able to come to Halencia to plan Antonio and Christina's wedding. I wanted only the best for them."

"Now, you flatter me." Lindsay squeezed the queen's hand before releasing her and stepping back. "It is I who is privileged to be here. And to be here in Signora Russo's shop. I may have to steal a moment to shop for my own dress for the wedding."

"Oh, you must. My friend will take the best care of you. Giana, Ms. Reeves needs a dress. Charge it to my account. It shall be my treat for all her hard work."

Appalled, Lindsay protested. "Your Highness, I cannot—"

"I insist." The queen waved her objection aside. "I only wish I could stay and help you shop. And see Christina in her gown!" She sighed with much drama. "Regretfully, I must leave. One of Antonio's many meetings draws me away. Christina—" Valentina moved to the bride's side and Christina bowed to receive a kiss on the cheek. "Worry not. Giana has made many women look like a princess. She will do her *magia* and make you a *bella* bride."

For an instant Christina seemed to freeze, but in a blink it passed and she bowed her head. "*Grazie*, Your Highness."

"But you, Christina, will be a real princess. And that demands something special from a woman. The reward is something special in return." She picked up an ornate, medium-size box from the couch and slowly lifted the lid. A glimmering tiara rested on a bed of white velvet.

Christina put a hand to her throat. "Valentina."

"I wore this when I married Antonio's father. It must stay in my family, but you would honor me if you wore it when you marry my son."

Tears glistened in Christina's eyes. "It's beautiful." Diamonds and sapphires swirled together in gradually bigger scrolls until they overlapped in the front, creating a heart. "It's too much."

"Nonsense. A princess needs a tiara," Valentina insisted. "It would please me very much."

Christina sent Lindsay a pleading look. What should she do?

Lindsay gave a small shrug. "It's something borrowed and something blue."

"Oh, my." Christina gave a small laugh. "You said the items would come."

"I must go." Valentina handed the box to Christina.

"Try it on with your dress and veil, you will see. A security officer will stay behind to collect it until the wedding."

"Valentina." Christina gripped the other woman's hand. *"Grazie."*

"Ciao, my dears." With a wave of her fingers, the queen breezed out the door.

Immediately the room felt as if a switch had been flipped and the energy turned off.

Giana Russo excused herself and followed behind Valentina.

Christina sighed, her gaze clinging to Zach. "And I'm supposed to follow that?"

Lindsay's gut tightened. She'd soothed many a nervous bride. But a nervous queen-to-be? That was out of her league. She sent Zach a pleading look.

He didn't hesitate. He went to Christina and wrapped her in a warm hug. "She's a force of nature, no denying that. Everyone likes Valentina. She's fun and vivacious." He stepped back at the perfect moment. "But what Halencia needs now is warm and constant. And that's you."

"Grazie, Zach." Christina's shoulders relaxed with his words. "I am glad you came today."

"Of course. Hey, listen. I'm sorry for sitting on your dress. I'll pay for all the repairs and alterations."

"You sat on my dress?" Christina's surprise showed on her face. "Lindsay said some beading came loose during the travel."

"With a little help from my butt." He glanced at Lindsay over his shoulder, gratitude warming his whiskey eyes. "She seems to think Signora Russo can do *magia* and fix it."

"Si, si. I can fix." Giana blew back into the room. An attendant followed behind and carried Christina's beautiful gown into one of the dressing rooms. "I have looked

at the damage. It is not so bad. A little re-stitching will solve everything."

"Nonna!" A little girl ran into the room. Adorable, with big brown eyes and a cap of short, wild curls, she clutched a bright pink stuffed dog under arm. She came to a stop when she spotted three strangers with her grandmother.

"Ah, Lucette. *Scusa il bambina*." Giana tried to pick up the toddler but she squealed and ducked behind Christina. "My apologies. We had a small emergency and I was recruited to babysit. My daughter should be here shortly to get her. Lucette, come to Nonna."

"Oh, she's no trouble. *Ciao*, Lucette." Christina bent at the knees so she was on the same level as the little girl, who stared at her with big, beautiful eyes. "What's your doggy's name?"

Lucette giggled and held out the dog. She jabbered a mouthful of words that made no sense to Lindsay at all. She looked at Zach but he shook his head, indicating he didn't understand the words, either.

"What a lovely name." Christina apparently made the dog's name out or pretended to. She chatted with the child for another few minutes, making the girl laugh. From her ease with the little one, it was obvious Christina loved children. Her gentleness and genuine interest delighted Giana's granddaughter until a harried assistant hurried into the room and swept the girl up.

"Scusa." The young assistant bobbed her head and left with the little girl.

Giana sighed. "Such excitement today. Are you ready, Signorina Rose, to try on your dress?"

Christina nodded. She and Giana disappeared into one of the dressing rooms.

Lindsay and Zach looked at each other.

"Do we stay or go?" Zach asked.

"I'm going to stay until she comes out." Lindsay sat

facing the occupied dressing room. "She may want company for the whole appointment. You can go if you want. I'm sure she'd understand."

"I'll wait to see how long you're going to be." He settled next to her. Way too close. His scent reached her, sensual and male, distracting her so she almost missed his question. "Have you ever come close to being the bride?"

"Not really." She smoothed the crease in her pale beige pants. "The one time I even contemplated it, I found out the relationship existed more in my imagination than in reality."

Interest sparked behind his intelligent gaze.

"How about you?" She tried to sidetrack him.

"Once," he admitted. "How do you get to marriage in your imagination? You're too levelheaded to make up what's not there."

"Thanks for that." She uncrossed and then re-crossed her legs, creating distance between them on the couch though her new position had her facing him. "He was my high school sweetheart. We got split up during our senior year when his parents moved away."

"That's tough."

She chanced a quick peek at him through her lashes to see if he truly understood or was simply saying what he thought she wanted to hear. The intensity in his regard showed an avid interest, encouraging her to go on.

"It was tough. We just understood each other. I lost my best friend as well as my boyfriend." The crease on her right leg got the same smoothing action as her left. "I always felt he was the one who got away."

"But you reconnected."

"We did. When the royal wedding was announced last year, he saw a piece where it mentioned I was the event planner, so he looked me up in Hollywood."

"And you had fonder memories of him than he had for you?"

"You could say that." The gentle way he delivered the comment made it safe to look at him as she answered. "I was so surprised and happy to see him. My mom, too. She's always on me to find a man. At first it was as though Kevin and I'd never been apart." Because of their past connection, he'd skipped right under her shields. "We were having lots of fun just hanging out and catching up. But I was so busy. Especially after word I'd been chosen to handle Antonio's wedding started to get around.

"Kevin was a freelance writer, so his schedule was flexible and he offered to help. I didn't want to take advantage, but I wanted to be with him. I let him tend bar at a few of the smaller events. That went well, so he started pushing to work the weddings."

"This is where the but comes in?"

Lindsay nodded, went back to plucking at her crease.

Zach's hand settled over hers, stilling the nervous motion.

She calmed under his touch. Under the sympathy in his eyes.

It still hurt to recall what a fool she'd been.

"First I got a warning from one of my vendors. He didn't know we were involved and he said I should keep an eye on the new bartender. He'd seen him outside with one of the guests."

"Bastard."

"It gets worse. And it's my own fault."

"How is it your fault when he's the one cheating?"

Good question. Too bad she didn't have a good answer.

"Because I let him charm me. When I asked him about what the vendor had seen, he didn't get defensive or act guilty. He had a story ready that the woman told him she was feeling sick so he'd walked her outside, hoping fresh air would help. I had no reason not to believe him. It explained what the vendor saw and…Kevin could be very solicitous."

"But it happened again."

Her head bobbed; perfect representation for the bobble-head she'd been.

"He tried to explain that one away, too. But I was starting to wise up. I should have ended it then." But that ideal from the past lingered in her heart, overriding the urging of her head. "Before things started going south, I'd been invited to a big wedding of a studio head and asked Kevin to go with me. I didn't want to go alone and I wasn't working so I thought it would be okay." She blinked back tears. "I should have known what he wanted. The clues were there."

"He was using you."

"Oh, yeah. He always wanted to know who everyone was. I thought he was just starstruck by the movers and shakers of Hollywood. The truth was he had a script he was shopping. I found him messing around with a well-known producer."

"Male or female?"

That surprised a bark of laughter from her; the moment of levity easing her rising tension. "Female. But thanks for that perspective. I guess it could have been worse."

"Bad enough. He hurt you."

"Yes. But only because I saw what I wanted to see."

"The possibility of a wedding for the wedding planner?"

"How is it you can see me so clearly?" she demanded.

It was uncanny how he saw straight to her soul. She hadn't been half as sad at losing Kevin as she had been to lose a boyfriend with marriage potential. She wanted what she gave to all her clients. A lovely wedding, in a spectacular venue, with friends and family surrounding her as she pledged her love. She longed for it with all her heart.

Kevin had stolen that from her. He'd given her hope, dangled the reality within her reach, only to yank it away. He was a user with no real affection or respect for her.

He'd seduced her for her contacts. And, yeah, that hurt. Her pride had taken a huge hit and the experience had left her more relationship-shy than ever. But it had taken less than a week for her to recognize it was more work-related than personal. He could have damaged her reputation. She'd worked twice as hard since the breakup to make sure it didn't happen again.

And she shored up her defenses to keep from letting anyone close enough to use her again. Or hurt her.

"Because it's all right here." Zach responded to the question about seeing her so clearly by stroking his thumb over her cheek. "There's no deception in you, Lindsay. You're open and giving and articulate."

"You're saying I'm an open book. How flattering." Not.

"I'm saying there's no artifice in you. When you interact with someone, they know they're getting the real you—straightforward good or bad. Do you know what a gift that is? To know you can trust what's being presented to you without having to weigh it for possible loopholes and hidden agendas?"

"Politics," she said dismissively.

"School. Business. Friends. Dates." He ran down a list. Then, too restless to sit, he rose to pace. "For as far back as I can remember I've known not to take anything at face value. My nannies used to praise me for being a good kid then lie about my behavior to get a raise."

"That's terrible." What a sad lesson for a child to learn. "You said you almost got close to a wedding. What happened? Is it what put you off big, fancy weddings?"

"It never got that far." He fell silent and fingered a wisp of lace edging a floor-length veil. Then he moved to one glittering with diamonds and, finally, to one of lace and the opalescence of pearls.

As the silence lengthened, she knew an answer wasn't coming. And then he surprised her.

"Luckily I learned before it was too late that it wasn't me she wanted but the Sullivan name." The lack of emotion in his reply spoke volumes.

He didn't add more. He didn't have to. After a childhood of indifference, he'd fallen for a woman only to learn she had more interest in his family name than in the man who carried that name.

Lindsay felt his pain. Shockingly so. Meaning he was getting under her skin. That shouldn't be happening; her shields were firmly in place. Zach just refused to acknowledge them. And he was getting to her.

She wanted to know more, to ask what happened, but she'd been wrong to get so personal. They weren't on a date. They were working. She had no right to dig into his past when she insisted theirs was a professional relationship.

Yet she was disappointed. She rarely talked about herself, never exposed her heart like that. And he'd responded, obviously reluctant to share but reciprocating just the same. How unfair that life should send her this man when all her attention needed to be focused on her job.

He lifted the lace-and-pearl veil and carried it to her.

"What are you doing?" she breathed.

Pulling her to her feet, he turned her and carefully inserted the combs of the veil in her hair. The exquisite lace flowed around her, making her feel like a bride even in a sleeveless beige-linen pant suit.

"Imaging you as a bride." His breath whispered over her temple. "What would you choose for yourself, Lindsay?"

"I'm like you," she said as he led her toward a three-way mirror. Why was she letting him do this? "I want small, intimate."

"But with all the trimmings?"

"Of course. Oh, my." The pearls on the lace gave it a glow. He'd placed the veil just under her upswept bun. The lace caressed her arms as it fell down her back in an elegant waterfall of tulle and lace and pearls. It had such presence it made her beige pantsuit appear bridal.

The picture in the mirror stole her breath. Made her longing for what eluded her come rushing back.

She'd hoped coming to Tuscany, managing the royal wedding, would help her get her wedding mojo back. Peering into the mirror she realized that would only happen when she opened herself to love again. Sweat broke out on her upper lip at the very notion of being that vulnerable.

"I love the pearls against your sunshine-brown hair." Zach brushed the veil behind her shoulder and met her gaze in the mirror. "You're going to make a beautiful bride."

With him standing beside her in his dress shirt and black pants the reflection came too close to that of a bride and groom. Her heels brought her up to his shoulder. They actually looked quite stunning together.

She swallowed hard and took a giant step backward, reaching up at the same time to remove the veil. She was in so much trouble.

"I'm the planner, not the bride," she declared. "I don't have time to play make-believe." Handing him the veil, she retreated to the couch and her purse. Time to put fanciful thoughts aside and call Christina's aunt to set up an appointment on their way home.

Because she'd liked the image in the mirror way too much for her peace of mind.

Just Lindsay's luck. Christina's aunt Pia couldn't meet with them until five in the evening. She ran through her current to-do list in her head, looking for something she could check off.

"Oh, no, you don't." Zach tugged on her ponytail. "You've worked nonstop this past week. We are due some rest and relaxation. We're in the lovely city of Milan. I say we play tourist."

Okay, there were worse ways to spend the afternoon than wandering the streets with a handsome man on her arm.

Lunch at an open café on the Naviglio Grande—a narrow canal with origins in the 1100s used to transport the heavy marble to the middle of the city where the Duomo di Milano was being built—was a true delight. As was strolling along the canal afterward and checking out the antique stores and open-air vendors.

A lovely candleholder at a glassblower's stall caught her eye. How perfect for the reception tables. They had a flat bottom and five-inch glass petals spiked all the way around to create a floral look. The piece had presence but was short enough to converse over without being in the way. And she loved that it came in so many colors. She wanted the one with spiking gold petals. It reminded her of sunflowers.

"I'd like to order two hundred, but I need them within two weeks. Can you do that?" The young artist's eyes popped wide.

"Si. Si," he eagerly assured her. "I have ready."

"Why so many?" Zach asked. "And don't you already have candleholders with the royal crest on them?"

"Yes, but I think the clear glass bowls etched with the royal crest will sit nicely right in the middle of these and be absolutely gorgeous with a candle inside. A win-win." She got a beautiful, unique presentation that was both fragile and bold, and the palace got their staid, boring candleholders used.

"That's pretty genius." He applauded her.

"It's my job to mix the styles and needs of the bride and groom into a beautiful event that's appealing to them individually and as a couple."

"I'm learning there's more to this wedding planning stuff than I ever would have believed."

"Yeah. I'll convert you yet."

"Now, that's just crazy talk."

She sent him a chiding glance. "I want two hundred because I want plenty for my reception tables, but I also think the candleholders will make good gifts for the guests. What do you think, best man? Christina has pretty much left the decisions up to me and you're Antonio's stand-in. Do you think this would make a good gift for the guests to take away?"

He blinked at her for a moment, clearly surprised to have his opinion sought. He rubbed his chin as he contemplated the candleholder she held. "It's a pretty sophisticated crowd, but, yeah. Each piece is unique. That will appeal to the guests while the piece will also act as a reminder of the event."

"Then it will have served its purpose."

She turned back to the vendor. "In two weeks," she repeated, needing to know his excitement wasn't overriding his capabilities.

"*Si, si…due* weeks. I work night and day."

Given he would be working with heat and glass, she wasn't sure that was a good idea. She made a note in her tablet to check on his progress in a week. If he wasn't going to make it, she'd adjust her order to cover the tables only. And just give the royal crest candleholders away as a gift. But she really hoped he could pull it off.

She gave him her card with her email, asked him to send her a purchase order and advised him he'd have to sign a confidentiality agreement. His hand shook as he took the card, but he nodded frantically and handed Zach the package containing the sample she'd bought.

Zach made the next purchase. A Ferrari California T convertible. She thought they were just window shopping when he dragged her to the dealership. There was no denying the cars were sexy beasts. And it seemed the height of luxury to have the showroom on the fifth floor.

Even when Zach started talking stats and amenities, she blew it off. Nobody walked into a Ferrari dealership and walked out with a car. Or they shouldn't. It was a serious investment and required serious thought.

But Zach stood, hands on hips, surveying the slick car and nodding his head to whatever the salesman was saying. The portly man spoke English with such a thick accent she didn't know how Zach understood him.

"What color?" Zach asked her.

Her turn to blink at him in surprise at having her opinion sought. "What?"

"What color do you like better? The red or the black?"

"Are you insane? You can't just walk in here and buy a car."

"I'm pretty sure I can."

"But—"

"I've been thinking of buying one," he confessed. "I'm stoked at the idea of buying it here in Italy, from the original dealership. And it'll be nice to have a car since the rental company hasn't replaced the Land Rover yet."

She eyed the beautiful, sleek cars. "They'll probably have it replaced before they can deliver one of these."

"Pixie, they could have a car ready in an hour. But they have one downstairs with all the amenities I want. I could drive it back to Monte Calanetti if I wanted."

"Oh, my dog. You're serious about this."

He grinned, flashing his dimple and looking younger and as satisfied as a teenaged boy getting his first car.

"It's the California T series. I have to have one, right? I deserve something for closing the government deal. What color?" he demanded again.

Okay, she got it. He sought a physical treat for recent accomplishments because he wasn't getting any emotional accolades. Who could blame him? Not her.

"Indeed you do." Adjusting her mood to his, she glanced around the show room. "You don't want red or black. Too cliché."

"I'd use the word classic."

"I like that pretty blue. It reminds me of the sea around Halencia. If you're taking a souvenir home, it should represent where you've been."

"The blue." His inclined his head, his brown eyes reflecting his appreciation of her comeback. "Hmm." He strolled over to look it over better. "I'm not really looking for pretty."

"Is rockin' a better adjective? More masculine? We can use that if you prefer, because it's a rockin' pretty blue."

"I like rockin'."

"But do you like the blue?"

"I do. Though the classics are nice, too."

"They're cliché for a reason."

"Signora." The salesman flinched, unable to stay silent any longer. *"Per favore,* not say cliché."

"Scusa," she apologized, sending Zach an unrepentant smirk.

He said something in Italian to the salesman, who nodded and stepped away.

"I have to do this," he said, lifting her chin on his finger and lowering his mouth to cover hers as if he couldn't wait another moment to taste her.

CHAPTER NINE

THE FLAVOR OF him filled her senses. Oh. Just, oh.

She should protest, step away, remind him of their professional status. She did none of those things. Instead she melted against him, lifting her arms around his neck.

How she'd missed his touch. She thrilled at his hands on her waist pulling her closer, at his body pressed to hers from mouth to knees, the two of them fitting together like cogs and grooves. This was more dangerous than watching their reflection in the mirror at Signora Russo's. By far.

Didn't matter. She sank into sensation as she opened to him. More than she should in a Ferrari dealership. Or maybe not. They were hot cars, after all.

A throat clearing loudly announced the return of the salesman.

Zach lifted his head, nipped her lower lip.

"Hold on." She ducked her head against him, turning away from the salesman.

"What are you doing?" He spoke gently and cradled her head. Perfect.

"Saving you some money. Tell our friend over there that you're sorry, but I'm totally embarrassed and want to leave."

He rattled off a few words of Italian. Predictably the salesman protested.

She pushed at Zach, making a show of wanting to leave. "Tell him you'll have to buy the car when you get back to the States because we're leaving Milan tonight and probably won't make it back here."

While he conveyed her message, she grabbed his hand

and began pulling him toward the exit, carefully avoiding the salesman's gaze.

The salesman responded in a conciliatory tone, his voice growing closer as he spoke.

"He just dropped the price by ten thousand dollars," Zach advised her.

She frantically shook her head and, holding his hand in both of hers, she bracketed his arm and buried her face in his shoulder. "Let's see if we can get him to twenty. Shake your head sadly, put your arm around me and head for the elevator."

"You know I can afford the car."

"So not the point."

"What was the point again?"

"Trust me. He's not going to let you walk away."

He sighed, then she felt the movement of his head and his arm came around her. She leaned into him as they walked toward the elevator.

"I can't believe I'm leaving here without a car."

"You can always order it online and have them deliver it. If he lets you walk away."

"You owe me dinner for this."

They got all the way to the elevator before the salesman hailed Zach. He rushed over, all jovial and solicitous, giving his spiel as he approached. The elevator doors opened just as he arrived next to them. The man opened his arms wide in a gesture that welcomed Zach to consider what a good deal was being offered.

Zach nodded. *"Si, avete un affare."*

"You took the offer?"

"I have. And you're invited to visit the gift shop and pick out a gift while I finalize things here."

"Oh. Nice touch. Okay, you can buy the car." She stepped into the elevator. "Don't be long."

Thirty minutes later he collected her from the gift shop

and they headed out. On the street he pulled her into his arms and gave her a long, hard kiss. Then he draped his arm around her shoulders and started walking.

"That's the most fun I've had in a long time."

"How much?"

"For twenty-five thousand less than quoted."

"Aha! So you owe me dinner."

"You have skills, Pixie."

"I have a few tricks. I'm always working with a budget whether it's five hundred dollars or five million, so I've learned to negotiate for my job. I enjoy the challenge. You have money. You're used to buying what you want without worrying about the cost."

"I've negotiated for my business."

"But that's different, isn't it? You're on the sales side then, demanding value for services. When it comes to buying—"

"I want the best regardless of price. It's how I was raised."

"You were fortunate." As soon as the words left her mouth she remembered what he'd said about people in his life always having an agenda even when he was a young child and how his parents brushed aside his success to make demands of him. Money didn't make up for everything. She quickly changed the subject.

"So, are you driving home? Am I visiting Christina's aunt on my own?"

"I'm going with you. I went with the blue car, which needed modified for some of the upgrades I wanted. They'll be delivering the car in a couple of days. We have an hour before we need to meet the helicopter. Do you want to go see the cathedral?"

He was right. Today had been fun. She couldn't remember when she'd last let go and played for a day. She liked playing tourist. Wanted it to continue.

She sighed, knowing she needed to rein them in. A bell kept pinging in her brain, warning her to stop the foolishness, reminding her of the danger of surrendering to his charm. Hadn't she already rehashed all this with herself at the fitting?

Yes, and she knew what she risked if she continued to let her emotions rule her actions.

Yet she still reached up and tangled her fingers with his at her shoulder.

"It'll be rushed, but it sounds like fun."

"Okay, let's go." He stepped to the curb and waved down a taxi. "At least we'll get to see it. And if we really want to see more, we can plan a day when we can come back and do a full tour."

Her heart soared at the way he linked them into the future.

She deserved this time. Work always came first and because the nature of it was so party central she experienced a faux sense of having an active social life. For too long she'd suppressed her loneliness. Just this once she'd let loose and enjoy the history and charm of an ancient city in the company of a gorgeous man totally focused on her.

Sliding into the back of the cab, she smiled when Zach linked their hands. And sighed when he leaned in for a kiss.

Tomorrow could take care of itself.

Zach in a Speedo was a piece of art.

He swam once or twice a day. She remembered from her research that he'd met Antonio on the Harvard swim team. Obviously he still enjoyed the water. And she enjoyed him.

Funny how his swims always seemed to coincide with her need for a break. Uh-huh, a girl was allowed her illusions.

And she could look as long as she didn't touch.

The man was grace in motion. Watching that long, tanned, toned body move through the water gave her a jolt that rivaled caffeine. It was one fine view in a villa full of spectacular views and it made Lindsay's mouth water with want.

Now that she knew how it felt to brush up against that fine body, she longed for more. But she was back in the real world so she turned away from the sight of Zach striding confident and wet from the pool.

She took a sip from her soda, needing the wet and the cool. And drained it before she was through. Leaving the empty can on the bar she joined her assistant at the lovely oak table Zach had purchased for her use.

She pulled up her email and sent Christina a message to let her know they were still on the hunt for the brooch. As Christina had warned her Aunt Pia had been leery about talking to them, but with Christina's note she'd finally softened. She'd given the brooch to her daughter, but the younger woman hadn't worn it for her wedding, either. Pia had called her daughter while they were there and she couldn't recall what had happened to the brooch. Pia suggested Sophia might know.

Lindsay would be meeting with Sophia tomorrow, two weeks from the wedding.

"Serena, can you call and remind Louisa that Zach and I will be meeting the landscapers at the palazzo this morning."

The two of them were set to leave in a few minutes and she needed work to help her get the visual of his nearly nude body out of her head.

"Already done. And I sent the information to the glassblower as you requested. He already confirmed delivery for a week before the wedding."

"Excellent."

Serena turned out to be a godsend. She looked cool and competent in blue jeans and a crisp white tee, her long black hair slicked back in a ponytail that nearly reached her waist. And she was every bit as efficient as she appeared.

"Let's put it on the calendar to check with him in a few days to be sure he's on schedule. If I have to find another gift, I'd rather know sooner than later."

"*Si*, I put a note on your calendar."

"Perfect."

They went over a few other items, scratching off two on the to-do list and adding three. "The palace rep is supposed to take care of ordering the table and chairs, but can you call to make sure they have and confirm what they've ordered."

Her brown eyes rounded. "You want me to check the palace's work?"

"Yes. There's no room for misunderstandings. I need to know every detail is covered."

The girl nodded. "*Si*, I will call them."

"Good. I know this may be a hard concept for you, Serena, but until this wedding is over, your first loyalty is to me. It's my job to give the prince and Christina a beautiful wedding that will represent the house of L'Accardi well. You have no idea how many errors I've found by following up on details handled by other people. Some have been innocent mistakes, but others were outright sabotage."

"That's terrible!"

Lindsay nodded. "If I hadn't caught the mistakes, intentional or otherwise, not only would the bride and groom have been disappointed and possibly embarrassed, but my reputation would have suffered badly."

"*Si*. I will check every detail."

"*Grazie.* And don't forget to find a nice, understated dress for the occasion. Something in light blue."

Serena's brown eyes rounded even bigger than before. "I am to attend the royal wedding?" It was a near squeak.

"You'll be working it with me, yes."

"Oh, my goodness! I have to shop!"

Lindsay smiled. "After you check on the table and chairs."

"*Si.*" Serena nodded, her eagerness offset by a desperate look in her eyes.

"And bring me the receipt. It's a work expense."

Relief flooded the girl's features. *"Grazie."*

"Are you ready to go?" A deep male voice filled the room.

Zach stood in the doorway to the house, thankfully fully dressed in jeans and a brown T-shirt that matched his eyes.

"Ready." Lindsay grabbed her purse and dropped her tablet inside. "Let's go."

The wind whipped through her hair as Zach drove them across town in the golf cart. He pulled straight into the drive.

Two things struck her right away. Louisa was in the middle of a heated discussion on her doorstep. Her opponent towered over her smaller frame. He had dark hair, broad shoulders and a wicked-fine profile.

And second, construction paraphernalia had been cleared away but the grounds were only a quarter cleared.

"What the heck, Zach?" Lindsay demanded as she climbed out of the golf cart. "I thought you hired someone to clean this all out."

"I did and I take full responsibility for the mess-up. I hired the crew the mayor recommended and I told them to clear out all the weeds but to save the original plants."

"No, no, no. Everything was supposed to be cleared out."

He grimaced. "I'm hearing that now, at the time I was answering a text from my office. I got it wrong. I'm sorry."

"They didn't even do what you asked." She stomped forward, scanning the dry brush and overgrown ground cover. "The landscaping team is going to be here any minute. The construction team is scheduled to start the day after they're done. This needed to be done already."

This couldn't be happening. She'd had everything planned down to the last minute. There were acres to clear. The whole property needed to be in shape, not just the area around the chapel and palazzo.

"Lindsay, I'm sorry."

Lindsay swung around to Louisa. The other woman stood huddled into herself, the tall man she'd been arguing with at her side.

"This is my fault," Louisa said. "I've been distracted the past few days. I should have noticed the grounds weren't being cleared out like they should be."

"No. It's mine. I should have been checking on the progress." Follow up on every detail. Hadn't she just pressed that fact home with Serena? She'd been the one to drop the ball.

"Placing blame does no good." Zach refused to play the role of dunce. He'd made this mess. It was up to him to clean it up. "We need to focus on a solution."

"He's right." Hands on his hips, the tall man Louisa had been arguing with surveyed the grounds. "You must be Lindsay Reeves, the wedding planner. Nico Amatucci." He held out his hand as he introduced himself. "I own the vineyard next door."

"Right." She shook his hand, appreciated the firm grip. "We're serving your wine at the reception. I've sampled some. It's very good."

"Zach Sullivan, best man." Zach inserted his hand between the two of them, not caring for the admiration in

Amatucci's gaze as it ran over Lindsay. Some distance between the two suited Zach fine.

No way was Zach letting the other man play hero while he chafed under the restraint of his plan. It didn't help that his gut roiled with guilt at seeing Lindsay so upset.

He was making her work harder than she needed to on the most important event of her career. Watching her blame herself for something he'd done didn't sit well, no matter how well-intentioned his plan had been.

Especially when he had nothing to show for it.

Neither Tony nor Christina showed any signs of backing out of the wedding. The two of them had managed to distance themselves from what went on in Monte Calanetti so any delays Lindsay suffered were mere blips on their radars.

Zach had only managed one meeting with Tony, but whenever he broached the topic on their hurried calls, Tony shut him down. Christina did the same when Zach got a few minutes alone with her at the fitting, though he had to give her points for being much more polite about it.

"I'm not sure how this happened." Zach gritted his teeth as he played his part for his audience of three. "I was telling Lindsay I hired the crew Mayor Alonso recommended. He mentioned the owner had just broken up with his girl, but I didn't figure that signified."

"Are you talking about Fabio?" Nico ran his hand through his dark hair. "He gets *molto* messed up when he and Terre are fighting, and he is no good for anything."

"I need to call him, get him out here." Lindsay took out her tablet. "This needs to be finished today. If he can't get it done, I need to get someone who can."

"Let me talk to him, *signorina*," Nico offered, his tone grim. "His girl is *incinta*. Fabio needs the work. I will make sure it gets done."

Lindsay hesitated then slowly nodded.

Seeing the despair in her indomitable blue eyes shredded Zach. He decided right then to stop messing with her. Why should she suffer for Tony and Christine's stubbornness?

She shouldn't.

No more than he should be forced to play the fool.

The trip to Milan rated as one of the best days of his life. He'd enjoyed spending time with Lindsay, more than anyone he could remember in a long time. She was smart and fun, and too restrained, which challenged him to loosen her up. And she constantly surprised him. He marveled at her performance at the Ferrari dealership.

Her ex had given her enough grief. Zach wouldn't add to it.

He'd still try talking sense into the couple. For all the good it would do him. But no more messing with the wedding.

"Fabio's going to need help getting this all done," Zach announced, feeling the need to fix the problem. "Who else can we get to help?"

"I can call my men over to lend a hand for a few hours," Nico offered.

"Thanks, that's a start. I'm going to call the mayor."

"I'll help," Louisa stated. "It'll feel good to get outside and do some physical labor for a change."

Zach lifted his brow at that. The temperature topped eighty and the palazzo was in a valley. There was little in the way of a breeze to offset the mugginess from the clouds overhead.

"It is too hot for you," Nico told her bluntly. "You will stay inside."

Wrong move, buddy. Zach watched the storm brew in the palazzo owner's light blue eyes. She was almost guaranteed to work harder and longer than she would have if the other man had kept his mouth shut. But her offer gave him an idea.

"No," Louisa informed Nico, her chin notched up, "I will not. I'm partially responsible for this situation and I want to help."

"Me, too," Lindsay piped in. "Louisa, do you have an extra pair of gloves? We can get started while Nico contacts Fabio."

"I do. I have a scarf, too. You'll want to put your hair up."

The women wandered off. Nico glared after them. "She never listens."

Zach cleared his throat and clapped Nico on the shoulder. "My man, let me give you some advice. Rather than order a woman about, it's better to make her think it's her idea to start with."

Nico grimaced. "I know this. But she drives me… *pazzo.*"

"Crazy? I know the feeling. Perhaps when she starts to weary you can casually mention how thirsty the workers look and she'll go inside to provide refreshments."

"You misunderstand. There is nothing between us," Nico clarified with more emphasis than necessary. "As there is between you and Ms. Reeves."

"If you asked her, she would say there is nothing between us, either."

Nico scowled.

Zach laughed. "You should call me Zach, as we'll be working together." And they got to work.

The whole town came out to help. Or so it seemed. The mayor arrived shortly after a remorseful Fabio. Alonso didn't ask what needed to be done. He wore khaki pants and an old denim shirt with the sleeves rolled up to his elbows. He picked up a shovel and got to work.

Lindsay called Serena and she showed up with a few

friends, four of Nico's men arrived in a pickup, including his brother Angelo. Eva's son, Mario, and a pack of early teens pitched in. The barber closed his shop to help. And on and on it went. Even the landscaping crew joined in, helping to haul debris and refuse away.

Everyone was happy and laughing.

At some point Lindsay was introduced to Vincenzo Alberti, the director of tourism. When she expressed her gratitude, he explained that the whole town was proud the royal wedding was happening there. That they wanted their city to be represented well and that they were all excited to be a part of it in some way.

Lindsay wiped at the sweat on forehead with a towel she'd tucked into her waistband and surveyed their progress. Another hour should see it done. A good thing as it would be dark not long after.

She was hot and sticky, tired and sore. And hungry.

She imagined everyone else was, too. But no one was leaving. They all meant to see it finished. Nico and Louisa had put their animosity aside to coordinate the workers' efforts.

"Almost done." Zach appeared beside her, his tanned and muscular chest on full display. As had many of the men, he'd ditched his shirt somewhere along the way.

She resisted the urge to run her palm down his sweaty abs. More than once she'd caught herself admiring the flex and flow of muscle and tendon under smooth flesh. Dark and tanned, he fit right in with the Halencians. Fit and toned, he matched the laborers pace for pace.

He was poetry in motion and she had a hard time keeping her attention fixed on her chore. Especially with him standing in front of her.

"I'm amazed by the support we got from everyone." Rather than look at him she watched the landscapers fill

their truck with bags of weeds. "I wish there was something we could do for them."

"I was thinking the same thing." He took her towel
and wiped the back of her neck, sending tingles down her
spine where his fingers trailed over her skin. "I thought
about hosting a party at the villa, but I prefer to reward
everyone now, so I asked Alonso for a suggestion. He
mentioned Mancini's. I called and talked to the owner.
Raffaele Mancini said he'd open up the patio for us and
put a nice meal together."

"'Nice' is the operative word there, champ. Mancini's
is catering the wedding. Eva also told me about Mancini's as an option for an upscale meal. I'm not sure I can
afford that."

"I'm covering it."

"You don't have to do that."

"I insist. I feel this is mostly my fault. Paying for dinner
is a small enough thing to do. Plus, Mancini heard about
what happened and apologized for not making it over here
to help out. So he's giving us a discount."

The spirit of this town just kept amazing her.

"Shall we start passing the word? Mancini's at eight.
That'll give Raffaele time to cook. And the rest of us time
to clean up."

Dinner turned into a party. When Lindsay stepped inside, assisted by Zach's hand at the small of her back,
she got pulled into a big hug by the maître d', who was
a curvy blonde with bright gray eyes and a smile so big
she beamed.

"Hello. Welcome to Mancini's." Surprisingly the bubbly blonde was American. Then she announced why she
was so excited, "Winner of the Italian Good Food Award!"

"Wow." Lindsay knew the award was on par with the

Michelin Star in France. "Congratulations. That's fantastic."

Zach echoed her. "Raffaele didn't mention it when I spoke to him earlier."

"We just heard an hour ago. You must be Lindsay Reeves and Zach Sullivan, the wedding planner and best man. I'm Daniella, Rafe's fiancée. We have the patio all set up for you. Some people have already started to arrive. You'll have to excuse us if we're a little giddy tonight. We're over the top about the award."

"As you should be," Zach said easily. "I hope you, Raffaele and the staff can join us later for a congratulatory toast."

That smile flashed again. "I'm sure that can be arranged. I'll tell Rafe."

The patio was enclosed but the large windows were wide open, letting in the cool evening air. Wine bottles hung from the overhead beams along with green ivy. Red-checked tablecloths covered two large picnic tables that seated twenty each and three round tables at the far end.

A couple of extra chairs were needed, but everyone shuffled around so everyone got seated. Alonso arranged it so he and Vincenzo sat with Lindsay and Zach along with Nico and Louisa.

Raffaele had "thrown together" a steak Florentine for them that melted in Lindsay's mouth. She was definitely putting it on the wedding menu.

She wondered if Raffaele knew how to make *cornettos*.

"I'm exhausted," Louisa told Lindsay toward the end of the delicious meal when they had the table to themselves. "But it's a good tired."

"It's the same for me." Lindsay sipped her wine. "We accomplished a lot today. The landscapers will start tomorrow and the owner assured me they would make up the lost time."

"That's great. I'm glad we were able to get it done for you."

"I'm so impressed with the townspeople. How they rallied together to help out and were so cheerful even working in the heat and mugginess."

"Well, they're all enjoying dinner. This was a nice gesture."

"Zach's the one to thank. But we were happy to do it. Everyone worked so hard. I can tell you I've decided to order some big fans for the wedding and reception. I want the guests to be comfortable."

Louisa clinked her wineglass against Lindsay's. "I like the way you think. I'm sorry I dropped the ball."

"Don't sweat it. You worked as hard as anyone today." Lindsay eyed Zach talking with Nico, Alonso and a couple of other men near the bar. "And I know how easy it is to get distracted."

"Are the two of you involved?" Louisa asked.

Lindsay's gaze whipped back to her fellow American.

"There's a...tension between the two of you," the woman explained.

"He'd like there to be." Lindsay rolled the stem of her wineglass between her fingers, watched the liquid swirl as her thoughts ran over the past two weeks. "But I need to stay focused on the job. As today clearly proved."

"He can't take his eyes off you."

"And Nico keeps you in his sights. Is there something between the two of you? You seemed to be arguing this morning."

"We're always arguing." Louisa's gaze flicked over the man in question. Her expression remained as composed as always, but there was no hiding the yearning in her pale eyes. "That is why it's good there's nothing between us."

A loud cheer went through the patio. Lindsay glanced around to see Rafe and Danielle had joined the party. Another round of cheers sounded as waiters flowed through the room with trays of champagne glasses.

Alonso grabbed a flute and held it high. "*Primo*, a huge *grazie* to Raffaele and Mancini's for hosting us tonight on such short notice. And for the wonderful meal he provided." More cheers. "*Secondo*, we are all excited to be here to share in the joyous news of Mancini's receiving the Good Food Award!" He held his glass high. "We had no doubts, *amico mio*, none at all. *Complimenti!*"

"*Complimenti!*" The crowd clapped and cheered, lifting their glasses and sipping.

Rafe stood on a chair. "*Grazie, grazie.* I am happy so many of my friends could be here to share this with me tonight. Business picked up when Mancini's was chosen to feed the royal wedding guests. Now, we have the Good Food Award the tourists will come even more. Monte Calanetti is on the map!"

A roar of approval rose to the roof.

"Nice touch, sharing his success with the citizens." Zach slid into his seat. "Classy."

"Raffaele is good people," Louisa affirmed. "I'm going to congratulate him on my way out. Good night. Zach, thank you for dinner."

"My pleasure."

Louisa walked away, leaving Lindsay and Zach alone together. He picked up her hand. "You look tired."

"I am." Too tired to fight over possession of her hand. She really needed to tell him the day in Milan had been a mistake and they needed to regroup to where they'd been before the trip. But every touch weakened her resolve.

"I'm sorry I messed up." There was a quality to his voice she couldn't quite pinpoint. She dismissed it as fatigue and the fact he probably didn't have to apologize for his work effort very often. Like never.

"You thought you were hiring the best crew," she reminded him. "And, you know, I really enjoyed today, getting to know more of the local people, seeing how they all rallied around each other to help. It was an inspiring experience. As you said before, too often people are all about their own agendas. Today reinforced my view of humanity."

"Sometimes those agendas can be well-meaning." Again his tone was off.

"You mean like Fabio obsessing over his girl and their baby? I get that, but look at how many lives he impacted by not honoring his contract. Yes, I enjoyed the day, but the landscaper is still going to have to make up lost time, and I lost a whole day. Life is so much easier when people are up front with each other."

He brought her hand to his mouth and kissed her knuckles. "Let's go home and soak our aches away in the Jacuzzi."

Oh, goodness, that sounded wonderful.

And dangerous.

She'd promised herself she'd get her head on straight today, put her infatuation aside and focus on the job. It was the smart thing to do. All he wanted was a summer fling. She had only to recall how he'd clammed up after she'd shared her humiliating history with Kevin to realize his interest was strictly physical.

And still she tangled her fingers with his. "Let's go."

CHAPTER TEN

AFTER THE INTENSE heat of the day, the balmy softness of the night air caressed Lindsay's shoulders with the perfect touch of cool. The rest of her, submerged in the hot, roiling water of the spa, thanked her for her foolish decision.

"I really did need this." She rolled her neck, stretching the tendons.

Strong hands turned her and began to work at the tightness in her shoulders. "So much stress."

The low timbre of Zach's voice made her whole body clench in need. She tried to shift away, but he easily held her in place.

"I never would have thought a wedding would be so much work."

She bit her bottom lip to suppress a moan, not wanting to encourage him. "Why, because it's just a big party? It's more than that, you know. It's two people creating a life together. That requires the meshing of many moving parts. The bride and groom, family members, attendants and, in this case, palace representatives and dignitaries. And that's just on the day. Before that there's flowers, food, wine, cake, photographers, seating in the chapel, setting up for the reception. Seating arrangements. Thank you, once again, for your help with that. I got the final approval from the palace today."

"My pleasure."

There was that tone again. She glanced at him over her shoulder. "You stopped listening after family members, didn't you?"

"You caught me." He let her float away a bit before turning her so she faced him.

"What's up with you?" She brushed the damp hair off his furrowed brow. "You've been slightly off all night."

"Today was my fault."

So that was it. Zach was so laid-back with her she sometimes forgot he ran a multibillion-dollar company. He was used to being in control and being right.

"We already talked about this. Stop feeling guilty."

"You know how I feel about large weddings."

"So what? You deliberately hired someone you knew couldn't do the job? You're just feeling bad because you're a problem solver and today it took a lot of people to fix the problem. It's okay. You repaid them all with a very nice dinner. And they all got to celebrate Mancini's award with Raffaele. I didn't hear a single gripe from anyone today, so cut yourself some slack."

"It's not that. I can't help but think Tony and Christina are making a mistake."

"So you subconsciously sabotaged the cleanup?"

He looked away, staring out at the lights of Monte Calanetti. "Something like that. They barely know each other."

"They've been engaged for four years."

"And he's lived in America the whole time."

This was really tearing him up. So often since they'd met he'd been there for her when she'd needed him. She wished she had the magic words that would ease his concerns.

"They have no business getting married."

"Zach—" she rubbed his arm, hoping to soothe "—that's not for you to say."

"They're going to end up hating each other." The vehemence in his voice reinforced his distress. "I watched it happen to my parents. I can't stand to watch it happen to a man I think of as my brother."

She cupped his cheek, made him look at her. "No matter how much we love someone, we can't make their decisions for them. We wouldn't welcome them doing so for us and we owe them the same respect."

He sighed then pulled her into his lap, nuzzling the hair behind her ear. She wrapped her arms around him and hugged him tight. His arms enfolded her and they sat there for a while just enjoying the closeness of each other.

"She threw me over for my father."

Lindsay went still. "Who?"

"The woman I once got close to marrying."

"Oh, Zach." She tightened her grip on him and turning her head slightly, kissing him on the hard pec she rested against. "I'm so sorry."

"We met in college. My name didn't intimidate her, which was a real turn-on. It seemed all the girls I met were supplicants or too afraid to talk to me. Julia was a political science major. She said that was to appease her parents, that her real love was her minor, which were arts and humanities."

"She targeted you."

"Oh, yeah, she played me. Right from the beginning." He suddenly rose with her in his arms. "It's time to get out."

"I suppose we should." Her arms ringed his neck as he climbed out. She longed to hear more but had the sense if she pushed, he'd close down on her. So she kept it light-hearted. "I'm starting to prune."

He claimed her lips in a desperate kiss, holding her high against him as he devoured her mouth. His passion seduced her body just as his vulnerability touched her heart.

He carried her to the cabana where they'd left their towels. He released her legs and let her slide down his body. In her bare feet he towered over her, a dark shadow silhouetted by the nearly full moon. It took him a mere second to bridge the distance before his mouth was on hers again, hot and unsettling.

The right touch and she'd be lost to reason. From the reaction of his body to hers she knew he felt the same.

But he'd started his story and if she let this moment slip away, she may never hear the full tale.

She pulled back, leaning her brow on his damp chest while she caught her breath. "Tell me."

His hands tightened on her and then his chest lifted in a deep breath. He reached for her towel and wrapped it around her before grabbing his own.

She slid onto the double lounge and patted the cushion beside her. He joined her and pulled her into his arms so her back was to his front and the vista of Monte Calanetti spread out before them.

"She showed disinterest to catch my attention. And when I finally got her to go out with me, we just clicked so smoothly. We enjoyed all the same things. Had some of the same friends. She made me feel like she saw me, Zach Sullivan, as more than the son of William Sullivan. I reached the point where I was contemplating marriage. So I took her home to meet the parents. She was so excited. For the first time she asked me why I wasn't studying political science."

"With your family background, you'd think she'd ask that fairly early in the relationship."

"Yes, you'd think. I explained that I wanted nothing to do with politics. That technology was my passion. And I told her what she could expect with my parents. How they married to connect two politically powerful families and how they spent more time with others than with each other."

"And she went after your father."

"She barely spoke to me for the rest of the flight. I thought she was mulling it over, feared I'd put her off."

"You just gave her a new target." She held him tighter.

"She assumed because I grew up surrounded by politics

that I didn't need to study it. And when I let her know I had no interest in it, and revealed my father liked to play discreetly, she went for the big guns. I caught them kissing in his study."

"I'm so sorry. I know how debilitating it is to walk in on a scene like that. The shock, the embarrassment, the betrayal. But I can't imagine how much worse it must hurt for her to be with your father."

With a double betrayal of this magnitude in his past, she kind of got why he didn't like big weddings. And why he was concerned for his friend.

"I just wanted out of there. My dad stopped me and said she'd be the one leaving. She'd come on to him, surprised him with the kiss. He wasn't interested. After she stormed off, he told me he may not be the best husband, but he'd never put a woman before his son."

"Well, that was good, to know he didn't betray you. Still, it's not something you can unsee."

He rested his head against hers, letting her know he sympathized with her, too. "It meant a lot. It's the single incident in my life I can look back on and know he put me first."

Wow, how sad was that? And yet when she looked at her own life, she couldn't find one instance that stood out like that. The difference was that her mom may put herself first, but Lindsay knew her mother loved her. From what Zach described, his folks rarely displayed affection.

She rolled her head against his chest, letting him know she understood his pain.

"So you've never gotten close to marriage since?"

"No. I've never met a woman I could see myself with five years from now let alone fifty. I don't ever want to end up like my folks. I want someone who will knock me off my feet."

"Good for you. That's what you should want. Hearing you say that about five years down the line, I realize I didn't have that with Kevin, either. I could see myself in a nice house with a couple of kids, but Kevin wasn't in the picture."

"I can see you in my future."

Her heart raced at his words and she had to swallow twice before she could answer. "Do you now?"

"Yes, all the way to tomorrow. I got a call from the dealership. The Ferrari will be here by nine. I thought we could drive to Sophia's."

She bit her lip, waffling a tad because she'd lost so much time today it was hard to justify the drive when the helicopter did the job so fast. Still she didn't want to make him feel even guiltier about today's events.

And, truly, how often did she get the chance to drive through the Halencia countryside in a Ferrari convertible with a handsome billionaire by her side?

This was probably a once-in-a-lifetime adventure. So why not stop fighting the inevitable and let the billionaire seduce her? She only had him for another couple of weeks. Less, really. She didn't want to look back and regret not knowing him fully.

Because she was very much afraid she'd be looking back a lot.

"Do I get to drive?"

"A little pixie like you? I don't think so." He laughed, his body shaking with the sound. The good cheer was wonderful to hear after his earlier despair.

"Come on. We both know it's not the size that matters, but what you do with it." His laughter shook her some more. "I feel I earned the opportunity to drive it at least once."

"We'll see."

"Oh, I'm driving." She snuggled into him. "I can tell it's going to be a lucky day."

"Yeah? How?"

"Well, if you're going to get lucky tonight, it seems only fair I get lucky tomorrow."

He picked her up as if she was no bigger than the pixie he called her and set her in his lap. Using the edge of his hand he tipped her face up to his and kissed her softly.

"Am I getting lucky? What about your strict policies?"

She brushed his hair back, enjoying the feel of the silky strands running through her fingers. "I should stay strong, but you are just too tempting, Mr. Sullivan."

He leaned forward and nipped her bottom lip. "I like the sound of that, Ms. Reeves. Shall we start with a bath in the claw-foot tub?"

How did he know she'd been dying to soak in that tub? It was a modern version of the old classic and could easily hold the two of them. She'd just been waiting for him to be gone long enough to slip into the master bathroom.

Something was still off with him. Why else suggest walking back to the house and risk her coming to her senses? Seated as she was in his lap, there was no doubting his desire for her. Maybe his attempts at humor hadn't quite rid him of his funk in talking about his near miss with wedded bliss.

Unwilling to risk him coming to his senses, she leaned into him, looped her arms around his neck and pressed her lips to his. "Why don't we start here?"

He needed no other prompting. He rolled her so she lay under him. Her head was cradled in one big hand holding her in place for his kiss that belied the fierceness of his embrace by being tender. He cherished her with his mouth; seducing her with soft thrusts and gentle licks until she melted in his arms.

He pulled back, his face unreadable in the darkness of the cabana. A finger traced slowly down the line of her jaw.

"I don't want to hurt you," he said, his breath warm against her skin.

"Then don't," she responded and pulled him back to her.

There were no more words after that, her mind too absorbed with sensation to put coherent thoughts together. The balmy night and towels served to dry them for the most part but she found a few stray drops of water on his side and he shivered when she traced her fingers through the drops, trailing the wet across his smooth skin.

It thrilled her to know her touch affected him as strongly as his did her. He stirred her with his gentleness, but he ignited her when his mouth became more insistent, his touch more demanding. She arched into him, seeking all he had to give.

He grinned against her mouth, assuring her he'd take care of her. A moment later her bikini top slipped away and he lavished attention on the exposed flesh. Her nipple puckered from the rush of heat on damp skin. And the agile use of his tongue.

Wanting nothing between them, she wiggled out of the rest of her suit and pushed at his. Despite her efforts, the damp cloth clung to him.

"Off." She panted against his mouth.

He pushed it down and off without leaving her side. She admired his efficiency almost as much as she admired his form. He was so beautiful she would have liked to see him but he felt too good in her arms for her to regret anything.

Especially when his mouth and fingers did such wicked things to her.

She felt more alive, more energized, more female than any other time in her life.

Being outside made it a hedonistic experience. The night breeze caressed heated skin, while the scent of roses perfumed the air. The rush of emotion compelled her to reach for the moon that hung so heavy in the sky.

Her senses reeled from an overload of sensation. He made her want, made her sizzle, made her mind spin.

When he joined them with an urgency that revealed he was as engaged as she was, she was excited to know she moved him, too. It made her bolder, braver, more determined to drive him insane with pleasure. She loved when he hissed through his teeth, when he kissed her as if he'd never get enough.

When he lost control.

When the connection they shared took her to a whole new level.

Never had she felt so close to another person, in body, in spirit, in heart. He lifted her higher, higher until together they soared through the stars and she shattered in the glow of the moon.

And later, after they roused and he led her to the house for a warm soak in the claw-foot tub and then landed in the comfort of his bed for a repeat performance, she knew for her this was more than two bodies seeking each other in the night.

Somewhere along the way, she'd fallen in love with the best man.

Lindsay stared out the window of the passenger seat in the Ferrari, brooding to the point where the beautiful countryside flew by unnoticed.

She'd had such a lovely morning with Zach. Waking snuggled in his arms, she'd waited for the regret to hit. But no remorse surfaced. She loved Zach. Being in his arms is where she wanted to be.

That would change when she had to walk away. In the meantime she'd make the most of every moment with him.

Watching him put the new Ferrari through its paces on

the trip to Aunt Sophia's pleased her on a visceral level. Seeing his joy, absorbing his laughter, listening to him explain what made his new toy so special. His happiness made her happy, too.

The return trip was much more subdued, with Zach as quiet as she was.

Christina's aunt Sophia was a lovely woman, but a bit unorganized. Pia had called her, so she knew why they were there. She was so happy Christina wanted to wear the pin. Sophia had worn the brooch and she and her husband were still happily married after thirty-nine years.

Lindsay got her hopes up because Sophia seemed certain she had the brooch somewhere, but she'd already looked through her personal jewelry so she thought she must have stored it in the attic with other family heirlooms. Bad knees kept her from doing the search herself so she'd invited Lindsay and Zach to look all they'd like.

Luckily the attic was clean. And airy, once Zach opened the windows. But there was a lot to look through. She found a standing jewelry hutch and thought for sure the brooch would be there. Unfortunately not. Nor was it in any of the boxes or trunks they'd searched. In the end they'd left empty-handed.

"You okay?" Zach reached over and claimed her hand. "You did everything you could to find the brooch."

"I know." She summoned a wan smile, grateful for his support. "I just hate to disappoint the bride. Especially Christina. I've never had a bride disassociate herself so completely from the process so close to the wedding. It's almost as if she's afraid to invest too much of herself into the wedding."

"She's dealing with a lot."

"I get that. That is why I really wanted to find the brooch." With a sigh she turned back to the window. "It's the one thing she seemed to latch onto. It kills me not to be able to find it for her."

The car slowed and then he pulled to the side of the road. She looked at him. "What's wrong? Is it something to do with the car?"

"I needed to do this."

He cupped her face in his hands and kissed her softly. Then not so softly. Slightly breathless she blinked at him when he lifted his head.

"Much better." He slicked his thumb over her bottom lip.

He surprised her by getting out of the car and walking around the hood. He opened her door and helped her out. She looked around and saw nothing but green rolling hills for miles.

"What are we doing?"

"Well, I'm going to be riding. And you are going to be driving."

"Really?" Squealing in excitement she threw herself into his arms. "Thank you. Thank you. Thank you." She peppered his face with kisses between each word.

"Wait." He caught her around the waist when she would have run for the driver's seat. "You do know how to drive a stick, right?"

"I do, yes." This time she pulled his head down to kiss him with all the love in her heart. She knew he was doing this to distract her from her funk, which made the gesture all the more special because he'd categorically refused to let her drive earlier. "I'll take care with your new baby."

He groaned but released her.

She practically danced her way to the driver's seat. Of course she had to have the roof down. That took all of fourteen seconds. Too cool. He took her through where everything was and she pushed the ignition.

Grinning, she said, "Put your seat belt on, lover."
And she put the car in gear.

Grave misgivings hounded Zach as he stared down at the
crystal bauble in his hand. Two hearts entwined side by
side. Christina's lucky brooch. He'd given up on finding
it, given up on sabotaging the wedding, but he'd opened
a small tapestry box in one of the trunks in Sophia's attic
and there it was. Tarnished, with a few crystals missing,
but unmistakable nonetheless.

He'd had no plan when he'd taken it, but for one bright
moment he saw a light at the end of the tunnel of Tony's
train-wreck plan to marry a woman he didn't love. Without the brooch might Christina back out of the wedding?

With no more thought than that he'd pocketed the trin-
ket.

Now as he clutched it, he realized what he'd done.
Christina wasn't backing out. Tony wasn't listening to
Zach's appeals to rethink the madness. And Lindsay would
freak if she ever learned he'd taken it. On every level professional, friends, lovers, she'd see it as a betrayal.

How could she not when that's what it felt like to him?

He wished he'd never seen it. Never taken it. Never
risked everything he'd come to care so much about. Hell,
he'd invested so much time in this wedding, even he cared
about it being a success.

If only Tony wasn't the victim in all this.

It killed Zach to stand aside while his best friend set
himself up for such a big fail. But there was no going back
now. It didn't matter that the brooch was not wearable.
Didn't matter that he had regrets. The damage was done.

He thought back to the conversation they'd had in the
car on the way back from Sophia's. With the brooch burning a hole in his pocket he'd voiced his concerns for Tony
and Lindsay had warned him interference never paid off.

"Do you know how many weddings there are where someone doesn't think it's a good idea for some reason?" she'd asked him. "The timing's not right, someone's too young, someone's too old, their ages are too far apart. They don't know what they're doing. She's all wrong for him. He's too good for her. Every one. Show me a wedding and there will be a dissenter in the crowd somewhere."

"They couldn't all be wrong."

"Oh, yeah. Some of them were spot-on. But has it ever worked out well when they try to intervene? No. Because it's not their decision to make. The heart wants what the heart wants."

"What if it isn't love?" he'd demanded.

"Then the situation that brought them together wants what it wants. If the couple is consenting adults, then it's their decision to make."

He heard the message. Understood that a marriage was between the man and woman involved. Still, it was hard to swallow when he knew this was a wedding that was never meant to be.

Glancing around, he looked for a place to stash the piece. Spying a likely spot, he buried it deep. After the wedding, he'd find a way to return the brooch to the Rose family.

In the meantime it was time he got on board and supported his friend.

"Hey," Lindsay called out to Zach where he still sat sipping coffee on the terrace. "I'm doing laundry today. I'm going to grab your stuff."

She went into his walk-in closet and gathered up the items in the hamper. There wasn't that much and she could easily handle it with her things. Something thumped to the floor as Zach filled the doorway.

A crystal brooch, two hearts entwined side-by-side, lay on the brown-and-rust rug.

Heart racing, she blinked once then again, hoping—no, praying—the view would change. Of course it didn't. Christina's brooch lay on the floor at her feet.

It had been hidden in Zach's dirty laundry. Because it was his dirty secret.

Pain bigger than anything she'd ever suffered tore through her heart.

"Lindsay." He stepped into the room that had seemed so big a moment ago but was now tiny and airless.

"You found the brooch." As if it might bite, she backed away from it. A heavy ball of dread lodged in her gut.

"Let me explain." He reached for her.

She pulled away from him.

"What's to explain? You kept it from me. Hid it." Rather than look at him, she stared down at the crystal pin. The silver was tarnished, a few crystals were missing; a beautiful piece ravished by time. It would need to be repaired before it could be worn again.

She lifted anguished eyes to his. "You lied to me."

"I didn't lie," he denied. "I just didn't reveal I'd found it."

"How is that not lying when our whole purpose for being there was to find the brooch?"

"You have to understand, I just want the two of them to stop and think about what they're doing. A lucky pin is a joke." He bent and picked it up. "This is a bandage at the best and a crutch at the very least."

"I understand perfectly." Her stomach roiled as nausea hit. She circled to the left, wanting out of the closet without touching him. "You haven't been helping me at all. You've been using your position as best man to spy on the wedding preparations. Oh, oh." As realization dawned, she retreated from him. When her back hit the wall she sank and wrapped her arms around her knees.

"It was your fault. I thought you were confessing because you felt bad. But it was your fault. You knew exactly what you were doing when you hired Fabio—or had a good idea, anyway. It was all you."

He went down on his haunches in front of her. She shrank away from him.

"Lindsay, this wasn't about you. You were never meant to get hurt."

She closed her eyes to block him out. "Go away."

"You have to listen to me."

"I can't believe anything you say."

"Antonio is a good guy. Always thinking of others. He's kept up with his duties while working in America. He's invested in a lot of businesses here, supported charities. Now he's giving up his life to be king, devoting his life to his country. He deserves to be happy. He has the right to choose his own wife."

"It's his life, Zach. He made his decision. He trusted you." She swallowed around the lump in her throat. "I trusted you."

"You don't understand." He rolled forward onto his knees. And still he loomed over her. "There's more at play here."

"I don't want to understand. I just want you to go away."

"I can't." He sounded as if he had a mouth full of glass shards. "Not until I fix this."

"You can't fix this." She shook her head sadly. These past few days with him had been so perfect; a paradise of working and living together. Finding time to escape for a drive or some loving.

But it had been a fool's paradise.

"There's no undoing what's been done."

"There has to be." He reached for her.

She flinched from him.

His hand curled into a fist and fell to his side. "After the deal with the palazzo grounds I stopped. I saw how upset you were and I couldn't be responsible for that. You were never meant to get hurt."

"Stop saying that. What did you expect to happen when a wedding I was planning fell apart at the seams?" How could he possibly believe she'd come out of the situation unscathed if the prince called off the wedding? She was right in the middle of it. Especially with all the little things that had gone wrong. Starting with him sitting on the wedding gown.

Oh, God.

Had he sat on the dress on purpose? Had he known even then who she was and planned to use her all along?

"No, of course not," he responded, revealing she'd spoken aloud. "I had this idea before I left home." He rubbed the back of his head in frustration. "I didn't know who you were when I boarded the plane. This wasn't about you. It was about saving Tony from a lifetime of misery. The wedding planner got paid either way. But I got the opportunity to save him."

Fury drove her to her feet. "You think I'm worried about getting paid? Damn you." She stormed from the closet, not stopping until she reached her room. Yanking her suitcase from where she'd stored it, she opened it on the bed and began dumping in clothes.

Of course he followed her. For such a smart man, he knew how to do stupid real well.

"Do you think I work for a paycheck? Is that all your work is to you? I bet not." She emptied the drawers into the case and went for her shoes. "I take pride in my work."

The shoes didn't fit. She forced herself to stop and fold. She would not come back here. She went into the bathroom and grabbed what toiletries she'd left down here. She clenched her teeth when she thought of the items now occupying space in the master bathroom. He could have them. No way was she going back in that room.

He still stood in the doorway when she returned to her room. His shoulders drooped and his features were haggard. He looked as though he'd lost something precious.

Good. He'd pulled her heart from her chest and stomped on it. Let him suffer.

"I take satisfaction in giving the bride and groom something special, a day they can look back on with pride and happiness."

She closed the suitcase, pushed on the lid a couple of times to mash it down and then started zipping.

"There's more involved than arranging the flowers and cuing the music." With her suitcase closed, she yanked it from the bed and pulled up the handle. Finally she lifted her chin and faced Zach. "But then, I know you don't put much value in what I do. I really should have listened when you said you hate big weddings."

"Lindsay, no—"

"What did you say?" She talked right over his protest. "Oh, yeah, the couple needs to distract the crowd because they're marrying for something other than love."

"Don't do this. Don't leave. I didn't mean you."

"Oh, and let's not forget, love is a myth best left to romance novels."

He groaned.

"No, it's good this happened. Foolish me. I believed I was falling in love. It's so good to know it's just a myth. In a couple of days I'm sure I'll be fine."

She passed him in the doorway, making certain not to touch him. "But you should know there's nothing fake about what I do. I put my heart and soul into my weddings. And the couple doesn't walk away empty-handed. I make memories, Zach. I intend to give Antonio and Christina a spectacular wedding to look back on."

She turned her back on him and walked out. "Stay out of my way."

CHAPTER ELEVEN

AFTER SEVERAL DAYS of brooding, of waffling between righteous indignation and hating himself for the pain he'd caused Lindsay, Zach finally came to the conclusion the first was really no justification for the second.

She still used the sunroom as her workshop, but mostly Serena worked there and when Lindsay did come by, she kept the doors locked; a clear signal for him to stay out.

As he had for the past two evenings, he sat in the shadows of the patio, waiting to catch her when she left for the day. Hoping today she'd talk to him. He hadn't seen her at all yesterday and his chest ached with missing her.

In such a short time she'd burrowed her way into his affections. Watching her work fascinated him; the way she gathered a few odd items together and made something beautiful. Her expression when she concentrated was so fierce it was almost a scowl. Many times he'd wanted to run his thumb over the bow between her brows to see if her creative thoughts might transmit to him and show him what had her so enthralled.

He missed her wit, her laughter, the way she gave him a bad time.

Steps sounded on the spiral staircase and he surged to his feet, meeting her as she reached the patio level. The sun was setting behind her, casting her in a golden glow. Strands of her hair shimmered as a light breeze tossed them playfully around. In juxtaposition her blue eyes were guarded and the skin was pulled taut across her cheeks.

She made to walk by him and he caught her elbow in a light hold.

"Won't you talk to me for a minute?"

She didn't look at him. But she didn't pull away, either.

"There's nothing more to say between us."

"There is." He ran his thumb over the delicate skin of her inner elbow. Touching her fed something that had been deprived the past few days. Still, he forced himself to release her. "I tried to explain, but I failed to apologize. I'm sorry, Lindsay. I didn't think hard enough about how this would affect you. I never meant to devalue what you do."

Her shoulders squared and she half turned toward him. "But you don't value it. You've seen the effort involved, you can respect that. But you don't see the value in a beautiful wedding because you see it as the prelude to a flawed marriage."

"In this case, yes."

She sighed. "Zach, I've heard you talk about your parents enough to know what growing up with them must have been like. And I know you love Antonio, that he's probably closer to you than anyone. Mix that with your dislike of big, fancy weddings, and I'm sure this has been hell for you."

"I meant well," he avowed, grateful she saw what motivated him. "I can't stand the thought of him making this mistake, of him being miserable for the rest of his life. But Tony isn't rational when it comes to Halencia."

"Why? Because he refuses to see things your way?" She shook her head, the disappointment in her eyes almost harder to take than the hurt it replaced. "I think that's a good thing. I think a king should be willing to sacrifice for his country. Considering what his parents have put this country through, I think that's exactly what Halencia needs right now. And I think as his friend and best man, you should start showing him some support."

Hearing it broken down like that made him pause and rethink. Hadn't he had the same thought just days ago?

She took the opportunity to walk away. "I understand

why you want to save Antonio. What I can't forgive is your willingness to sacrifice me to get it."

Unable to take anymore, Zack texted Tony.

Need to see you. I've messed up bad. You may want a new best man.

After sending the message, Tony wandered down to the pool to wait for the helicopter to arrive on the wide lawn they'd been using as a landing area. It would be at least an hour, but he had no desire to sit in the house so full of memories.

He stared at the pool and remembered the night he made love to Lindsay.

He couldn't regret it. Wouldn't.

Having her come alive in his arms was one of the high points in his life. He'd connected with her more closely than with any other woman he could recall. Her honest reactions and giving nature seduced him every bit as much as the silky feel of her skin and hair, the sweet taste of her mouth, the soft moans of her desire.

The few days he'd had her by his side had given him a brief glimpse into what the future could hold.

He wanted to scoff at the notion. To discount it as an indicator he'd been on one wild trip to Tuscany. But the truth was he could all too easily see her in his life. Not just here in Halencia but back in the States, as well.

And it scared the hell out of him.

The only thing that scared him more was the thought of losing her from his life altogether.

He knew the biggest betrayal for her was the intimacy they'd shared while she believed he'd been using her. But that's not what happened. He'd wanted Lindsay before he'd known she was the wedding planner. His attraction for her was completely disassociated from what she did.

Or so he'd thought.

Now he knew better. What she did was a part of who she was. She'd spoken of being disillusioned with her job. Her impassioned speech calling him to task for thinking a paycheck would suffice if the wedding fell apart proved she wasn't as lost as she'd feared. She'd been shaken because she let herself get caught up with Kevin and he'd used her.

It sickened Zach to realize he'd done the same thing.

Time to make it right.

The whoop, whoop, whoop of the helicopter sounded in the distance and grew louder. Finally. In another hour or so he'd see Tony, apologize for the mess he'd made of everything and put this whole fiasco behind him.

Being so close to Lindsay but parted from her drove him insane. He wanted to stay and fix it, but she needed to be here. He didn't. Hell, Tony probably wouldn't want him here when he learned what Zach had done.

He'd go back to the States and wait for her to come home. Then he'd find her and apologize again. No justifications, just a straight-up apology.

Ready to have this done, he strolled toward the helicopter. As he got closer he was surprised to see the pilot headed toward him. And then he knew.

"Tony." He broadened his stride and met his friend in a hug. "You came."

"*Si, amico mio.*" Unselfconscious in showing emotion, Tony gave Zach a hard squeeze then stepped back to clap him on the arm. "Your text sounded serious."

"I've messed up."

"So you said. We must fix whatever you have done. I do not care to have anyone else for my best man."

"You haven't heard what I've done yet."

Tony had given up so much to support his country, would he be able to forgive Zach for messing in his affairs?

He couldn't lose both Lindsay and Antonio. Why hadn't he thought with his head instead of his heart?

"This sounds ominous." By mutual consent they headed toward the house. "You are my brother, Zach. You have seen how far I will go for my sibling. There is nothing you can do that will change my love for you. I need someone I can trust at my back during this wedding."

Zach walked at his friend's side. They were passing near the pool when Tony stopped. He looked longingly at the pool.

"Ah, the water looks good. I have not been swimming since I got to Halencia."

"You want to swim?" Zach grabbed his shirt at the back of the neck and pulled it off over his head. "It's as good a place to talk as any."

He stripped down and dove in. As soon as the water embraced him, he struck out, arm overhead, legs kicking, arm overhead, kick, again and again. He needed the physical exertion to empty his mind of everything but the tracking of laps and the knowledge Tony matched him pace for pace.

Tony tapped his shoulder when they reached fifty. "Let's hit the spa."

Zach slicked a hand over his face and hair and nodded.

In one big surge, he propelled himself up and out of the pool. He walked to the controls for the spa and flicked the switch to generate the jets. After grabbing a couple of towels from a storage ottoman and tossing them on the end of a lounger near the spa, he hit the mini fridge for a couple sodas and joined his friend, sighing as the hot water engulfed him.

"Grazie." Tony took a big swig and closed his blue eyes on a groan as he let his head fall back. "You don't know how good this feels. Hey, I know you're working with the

palace liaison on the bachelor party but can we do it here? Keep it tight and quiet."

"Sure. How about poker, cigars and a nice, aged whiskey?"

"Perfect." Tony laughed. "Now, tell me what's up."

Zach did, he laid it all out, not bothering to spare himself. "The good news is you'll still have a beautiful wedding, but I think I should go."

"It's not like you to run, Zach."

He barked a harsh laugh. "None of this is like me."

"True. You actually let her drive your new car?"

Zach eyed his friend still laying back and letting the jets pound him with bubbles. "Focus, dude. I almost wrecked your wedding."

"But you didn't." Tony straightened and spread his arms along the edge of the spa. He nailed Zach with an intent stare. "You messed up your life instead. You care about Ms. Reeves."

He got a little sick every time he thought about never seeing her again. But that wasn't something he was willing to share.

"She's a good person. And she's really worked hard to give you and Christina an event to be proud of. She found these cool candleholders that merge your two styles—"

"Stop." Tony held up a dripping hand. "I'm going to stop you right there. Dude, you're spouting wedding drivel. Obviously you're in love."

"Shut up." Zach cursed and threw his empty soda can at his friend's head. "You know I don't do love."

"I know you have a big heart or you wouldn't care so much about my future. You deserve to be happy, my friend, and I think the wedding planner makes you happy."

How easily Tony read him. Zach had been happier here in Halencia than as far back as he could remember.

But he'd ruined any chance of finishing the trip in the same vein.

"You deserve happiness, too. That's all I really wanted when I started this mess."

"I appreciate that you want me to be happy. But this is something I have to do. To be honest, the thought of a love match would terrify me. Watching the roller coaster that has been my parents' marriage cured me of that. I will be happy to have a peaceful arrangement with a woman I can admire and respect who will stand by my side and represent my country. Like your Lindsay, Christina is a good woman. We will find our way. You need to do the same."

His Lindsay. That sounded good.

"My being here hurts her. It's best if I leave and let her do her job."

"You mean it's easier. Well, forget it. You're my best man and I'm not letting you off the hook. Relationships take work, Zach."

That's what Lindsay said when she was talking about her mother's many marriages.

"If you care for this woman, and it appears you do, you need to fight for her. Apologize."

"I did. She didn't want to hear it."

Tony cocked a sardonic eyebrow. "Apologize again."

Zach nodded. "Right."

"Tell her you love her."

Love. Zach held his friend's gaze for a long moment, letting unfamiliar emotions—confusion, fear, sadness, exhilaration, joy, hope—rush through him. And finally he nodded. "Right."

A knock sounded at Lindsay's door. She ignored it. Now she was back at the hotel she was fair game for the press who thought nothing about knocking on her door at all hours. So pushy.

Another bang on the door.

She kept her attention on her schedule for the next week. Circled in red at the end of the week was *the* day. The wedding.

The rehearsal was in two days, four days in advance of the actual event because it was the only day everyone could get together. She'd have to see Zach, deal with him. As long as he didn't start apologizing again, she'd be fine.

She knew he'd meant well, that he loved Antonio like a brother. She even admired how far he was willing to go to ensure his friend's happiness.

But she couldn't tolerate the fact that she was acceptable collateral damage.

Why did men find her so dispensable?

She was fairly smart, had a good sense of humor. She worked hard; if anything, too hard. She was honest, kind, punctual. Okay, she wasn't model beautiful, but she wasn't hideous, either.

So what made her so unlovable?

More knocking. Ugh, these guys were relentless.

"Signorina? Signorina?" Mario called out. "Are you there? Mama says you should come."

Oh, gosh. She'd left the poor kid standing out there. Lindsay set her tablet aside and rushed to the door.

"Signorina." Mario greeted her anxiously. "Someone is here to see you. Mama says you must come."

Lindsay gritted her teeth. Zach. Why couldn't he leave her be? "Can you tell him I'm busy?"

His eyes grew big and he frantically shook his head. "No, *signorina.* You must come."

She'd never seen the boy so agitated. Fine, she'd just go tell Zach, once more, to leave her alone. Mario led her downstairs to a room she hadn't seen before. A man stood looking out on the rose garden.

"Zach you need to stop— Oh, sorry." She came to an

abrupt halt when the man turned. Not Zach. "Oh, goodness. Prince Antonio. Your Highness."

Should she curtsy? Why hadn't she practiced curtsying?

"Ms. Reeves, thank you for seeing me." He spoke in
slightly accented English and had the bluest eyes she'd
ever seen. They twinkled as he took her hand and bowed
over it in a gesture only the European did well. "I hope you
are not thinking of curtsying. It is entirely unnecessary."

His charm and humor put her instantly at ease. That
ability, along with his dark, good looks and the sharp intelligence in those incredible eyes, would serve him well
as King of Halencia. She wondered if they'd approached
him about running for president.

"You're here to plead his case, aren't you?" Why else
would the prince seek her out? He'd showed little to no
interest in the wedding plans, even through his advocate.

Anger heated her blood. How dare Zach put her in this
position? What could the prince think but that she allowed
her personal business to interfere with his wedding preparations? Showing no interest and having none were two
different things.

This whole situation just got worse and worse.

"I am." Prince Antonio indicated she should sit.

She perched on the edge of a beige sofa. The prince sat
adjacent to her in a matching recliner.

"Your Highness, I can assure you the plans for the
wedding are on schedule. And, of course, I will continue
to work with Zach as your representative, but anything
beyond working together is over. He should not have involved you."

"Please, call me Tony."

Yeah, that wasn't going to happen.

"You are obviously important to Zach and he is important to me, so we should be friendly, *si*?"

She meant to nod; a silent, polite gesture to indicate she heard him. But her head shook back and forth, the denial too instinctive.

"He does not know I am here."

That got her attention. "He didn't send you?"

"No. In fact he planned to leave Halencia, to concede the field to you, as it were. He wanted to make it easier on you."

"Oh." What did she make of that? He was supposed to be best man. Of course he'd have to tell the prince if he planned to leave. Had he already left? Was that why Antonio was here, to tell her she'd be working with a new best man?

Her heart clenched at the thought of never seeing Zach again. The sense of loss cut through the anger and hurt like a sword through butter.

"But he is my best friend. I do not want another for my best man."

"Oh." Huge relief lifted the word up. The feeling of being reprieved was totally inappropriate. He'd used and betrayed her. That hadn't changed. Just as her foolish love for him hadn't changed. It was those softer feelings that tried to sway her now.

Too bad she'd learned she couldn't trust those feelings.

"I have never seen Zach so enamored of a woman. Is it true he let you drive his car?"

She nodded. And she knew why. In piecing things together she figured that must be the trip where Zach had found the pin. She'd been brooding on the trip back and he'd felt guilty.

As he should.

The prince laughed, drawing her attention.

"He really does have it bad. I wish I could have been here to watch this courtship."

"There's been no courtship, Your Highness. Far from

it." She'd stayed strong for two weeks. Why, oh, why had she let his vulnerability get to her? Because she'd fallen for him. Her mom was fond of saying you couldn't control who you fell in love with. Lindsay always considered that a tad convenient.

Turned out it wasn't convenient at all.

"Antonio," he insisted. "I am hoping I can persuade you to cut him some slack. I am quite annoyed with him myself, but I understand what drove him. Zach is not used to having people in his life that matter to him. He is a numbers man. He would have calculated the risk factors and figured those associated with you were tolerable. If the wedding was called off, you would still get paid."

"So he said, but there's more than a paycheck involved here. There's my reputation, as well."

"Which would not suffer if I or Christina called off the wedding."

"It would if it was due to a jinxed wedding, which I can only speculate is what he hoped to achieve."

"Was it such a bad thing he did? Fighting for my happiness?"

"That's not fair." She chided him with her gaze but had to look away as tears welled. She had to clear her throat before speaking. "People don't use the people that matter to them."

Something close to sadness came and went in his blue eyes. "Yes, we do. We are just more up front about it. Zach told me you have the brooch."

It took a second for her brain to switch gears "Yes. It's in my room. It's damaged so I haven't mentioned we found it to Christina yet."

"This is good. If you please, I'd like to take it with me to see if I can get it repaired in time for the wedding."

"Of course. I'll go get it." She quickly made the trip

to her room and returned to hand him the antique piece. "It's really a lovely design."

"Yes, two hearts entwined side by side." Expression thoughtful, he ran his thumb over the crystals. "You can see why it represents true love and longevity."

"Indeed. I hope you are able to get it repaired in time. More, I hope it brings you and Christina much happiness."

"*Grazie*, Ms. Reeves. I can see why Zach has fallen for you. I think you will be good for him."

She sighed on a helpless shrug. "Your Highness."

"Antonio." He bent and kissed her cheek. "As you think about his sins, I wish for you to consider something, as well."

Cautious, she asked, "What's that?"

"Zach does not let anyone drive his cars."

She opened her mouth on a protest.

He stopped her with a raised hand. "Not even me."

She blinked at him as his words sank in, biting her tongue to hold back another ineffective "Oh."

He nodded. "Zach told you of Julia?"

She inclined her head in acknowledgment.

"Ah. Another sign of his affection for you. He does not talk about himself easily. He does not speak of Julia at all. He thought he should have known, that he should have seen through her avarice to her true motives. He's never been as open or as giving since. Until now."

Antonio stepped to the door. "Please do not tell Christina of the brooch. I do not want her to be disappointed if it is not ready in time." With a bow of his head, he took his leave.

Lindsay continued to look at where he'd been. She wrapped her arms around herself, needing to hold on to something. Because everything she believed had just been shaken up.

The Prince of Halencia had come to see her, to plead

Zach's case after he'd tried to sabotage Antonio's wedding. How mixed up was that? If Antonio could overlook Zach's craziness, could—should—Lindsay?

Hurt and anger gripped her in unrelenting talons, digging deep, tearing holes in her soul. She wanted to think this would let up after a couple of weeks of nursing the hurt as it had with Kevin, but this went deeper, stung harder.

What she felt for Kevin had been make-believe; more in her head than anything else. What she felt for Zach came from the heart. And it hadn't stopped just because he'd hurt her. The wrenching sickness in her gut when Antonio'd said Zach planned to leave proved that.

Seeking fresh air, she slipped out of the house and into the dark garden. Lights from the house showed her the way to a path that led to the back of the garden where a bench sat beside a tinkling fountain.

The earthy scent of imminent rain hung in the air. Lindsay looked up. No stars confirmed clouds were overhead.

Great. A storm. Just what she needed.

But it wasn't fear or an uneasiness that took control of her head. Memories of being stuck in Zach's car and staying with him at the farmhouse B and B in Caprese bombarded her.

He'd held her, a stranger, because she was afraid. He'd listened to her sad tale of being scared because her mother always cried during storms. The truth was her father left during a storm and deep down in her child's psyche, she'd feared her mother would leave, too, and Lindsay would be all alone.

Antonio had asked if Zach's fighting for his happiness was such a bad thing.

And the answer was no. She understood Zach's motivation. He'd grown up a victim of his parents' political alliance and the trip to see them en route to Halencia probably triggered the need to intervene on Antonio's behalf.

If this were just the summer fling she'd convinced herself she could handle, she'd forgive him and move on.

But she loved him.

She dipped her fingers in the fountain and swirled the water around. It was still warm from the heat of the day.

She missed the villa. Missed sharing coffee with Zach in the morning seated out on the terrace watching the city come alive down below. She missed his sharp mind and dry humor and his total ignorance of all things wedding-related.

But most of all she missed the way he held her, as if she were the most precious thing in his world.

And that's what she couldn't forgive.

He'd made her believe she mattered. And it had all been a lie.

She'd never been put first before.

Her dad had walked out before she even knew him. And her mother loved her. But Lindsay had always known her mother's wants and needs came first. Even when it was just Lindsay, work came first.

For a few magical days Zach had made her feel as if she was his everything. It showed in the way he'd touched her and by the heat in his eyes. It was in the deference and care he'd demonstrated, the affection and tenderness.

Maybe it was a facade he assumed and that's how he treated all the women in his life—the thought sliced through her brain like shards of broken glass—but it felt real to her. And she couldn't—wouldn't—accept less just to finish out a summer fling.

No more settling. She'd done that with Kevin and learned her lesson. She'd been willing to settle for a fling with Zach because she'd sensed how good it would be between them. And she'd been right. But she loved him, and a fling was no longer enough. She needed honesty, respect and a willingness to put your partner first.

How often had she watched her mother's relationships fall apart because a little work was involved? Her mom was so used to being the center of her world she didn't see that sometimes she needed to make her husband feel he was the center of her world.

Antonio inferred Zach cared for her. He made it sound as if Zach had planned to leave to make things easier for her. More likely he'd wanted out of this whole gig. But there was the bit about letting her drive his car when he never let anyone drive his cars, not even the man he thought of as his brother.

No. Just stop. She pushed the wistful thinking aside as she headed inside. His actions told the story. He didn't love her. He'd proved that when he'd put his friend before her.

Zach had said he liked storms, for him they washed things clean, made them shiny and new, allowing new growth. A good metaphor for him. He was the storm that allowed her to put the horror of Kevin's betrayal behind her. But would her heart survived the tsunami Zach had left in his wake?

CHAPTER TWELVE

TWO DAYS LATER Lindsay walked with Serena toward the Palazzo di Comparino chapel. The rehearsal started in twenty minutes. Nothing was going right today. She should be totally focused on damage control and all she could think about was the fact she'd be seeing Zach in a few minutes.

Her mind and heart played a mad game of table tennis over him. One moment she was strong and resolute in holding out for what she deserved. The next she was sure she deserved him, that his actions proved he cared deeply for the people in his life and she wanted to be one of those people.

"You just got an email from Christina confirming she will not make it to the rehearsal." Serena jogged to keep up.

Lindsay came to a full stop, causing Serena to backtrack. "What about Antonio?"

"He is still delayed at the palace, but he is trying to get here."

"Okay, we're talking a good two hours. Let me call Raffaele to see if he can move dinner up." Before the big blowup between them, she'd suggested to Zach that he host the rehearsal dinner at the villa. With her taking care of the details, he'd been happy to agree.

It was a no-brainer to put Mancini's in charge of the food. Still moving dinner up an hour would be a challenge. But so worth it if it allowed if at least one of the bridal couple to make it to the rehearsal.

"The prince's email said we should start without him."

"Wonderful. Zach will have to act as the groom and can you play the part of Christina?"

"Oh, Lindsay, I am sorry, but I cannot."

"Sure you can. I know these are high-profile people, but all you have to do is walk slowly down the aisle. No biggie."

"No, remember, Papa and I are meeting the glassblower to pick up the last delivery of candleholders. I have to leave in half an hour."

"Oh, yeah, that's tonight. Well, of course. Why should anything workout tonight?"

"Perhaps Papa can go on his own?" Serena made the offer hesitantly. Generous of her since Lindsay knew the two were looking forward to the road trip. A little father-daughter time before Serena went back to school.

"No, you go. I know this trip means a lot to you. I'll work something out."

"You could play the bride," Serena suggested.

"Uh, no. Thanks, but I have to keep things moving." So not a good idea. The very notion of walking down the aisle to Zach in groom mode messed with her head.

And her heart.

The elderly priest had other ideas. He looked like a monk of days gone by and he held her hand and patted the back ever so gently. He spoke softly, listened carefully, and totally took over the rehearsal. Everything must be just so.

He explained what was going to happen, who was going to go where, who stood, who sat, who would leave first and who would follow. He was quite thorough.

Because she found her gaze repeatedly finding Zach, who looked gorgeous in a white shirt and dark sports jacket, Lindsay ran her gaze over the participants. Everyone listened respectfully. Even Queen Valentina and the king, who sat holding hands. Apparently they were in an "on again" phase of their relationship.

The chapel looked lovely. A rainbow of colors fell through the stained-glass windows and standing candle-holders in white wrought-iron lined the walls from the back to the front and across the altar, illuminating the small interior. For the wedding they would be connected with garlands of sunflowers and roses.

And from what she observed, the palace photographer seemed to be doing a good job. He was the only extra person in the room. Serena had quietly made her departure during the priest's soliloquy.

"Come, come." The priest raised his cupped hands as if lifting a baby high. "Let us all take our places. You, young man—" he patted Zach on the shoulder "—will play the part of the groom. And you, *signorina*—" he looked at Lindsay "—will be our bride today."

No, no, no.

Pasting on a serene smile, she politely refused. "I'm sorry, Father, I really need to observe and take notes to ensure a smooth ceremony the day of the wedding."

"*Si, si.* You will observe as the bride. Come, stand here." He motioned to his right.

Zach stood tall and broad on the priest's left.

She swallowed hard and shook her head. She couldn't do it. She couldn't pretend to be Zach's bride when she longed for the truth of the position with all her broken heart.

"Perhaps Elena can play the bride?" she suggested. Hoped.

"Oh, no. Elena has her own role to play as the maid of honor. You are needed, *signorina*. Come."

There was no protesting after that. Plus, others would begin to make note if she made any more of a scene. Clenching her teeth together, she moved forward, holding her tablet in front of her like a shield, looking every-where but at Zach.

She was fine while the priest directed the action from the altar, but when he stepped away to help people find their spots, Zach narrowed the distance between them by a step then two.

"Please don't start anything here," she implored.

"I'm not." He put his hands in his pockets and rocked on his heels. "How have you been?"

"We should listen to the Father."

"I've missed you."

"Zach, I can't do this here."

"You have to give me something, Lindsay. You asked me to stay away and I have."

She narrowed her eyes at him. "You've texted me several times every day." Crazy things, thoughtful things, odd facts about himself. She'd wanted to delete them without reading them, but she'd read every one, came to look forward to them, especially those that revealed something about him.

"I needed some link to you. I'm afraid I'm addicted."

"You're not going to charm me, Zach." She frantically searched out the priest. When was this show going to get on the road? When she looked back, Zach was closer still.

He bent over her. "You smell so good. Do you miss me at all?"

"Every minute of every day." Her hand went to her mouth. Oh, my dog. Did she just say that out loud?

"Lindsay—"

"The priest is calling me." Heart racing, she escaped to the back of the chapel where the wedding party congregated. The priest nodded when she appeared, as if he'd been waiting for her.

"*Si, si.* We will start with the procession. Just as I described. *Signorina*, you will be last with Signor Rose."

Lindsay took her place by the robust man who made no

effort to disguise his disapproval of Christina's absence. She wasn't Lindsay's favorite person at the moment, either.

Oh, gosh, instead of settling, her heart raced harder. Zach stood at the altar waiting for her to come to him. It felt too real. And, sweet merciful heavens, she wished it were real.

It mattered what he'd done. Yes, he'd meant well. And no, he hadn't known her when he initiated his plan. But it mattered.

The procession began to move. She closed her eyes and stepped forward. Her foot slipped on the uneven ground, so, okay, that wasn't going to work. She opened her eyes and concentrated on the smooth stones of the chapel floor.

He had apologized. And he'd honored her request to stay away. But he hadn't let her forget him, or the time they'd spent together.

Had that been him fighting for her? Or was that wishful thinking?

Suddenly, Mr. Rose stopped and Zach's strong, tanned hand came into view. She fought the urge to put her hands behind her back. All eyes were on her, on them, but this was for Antonio and Christina's wedding. Nobody cared about her or Zach; they didn't care that touching him would be a huge mistake.

She hated how her hand shook as she placed it in his.

He set her hand on his arm and led her to stand in front of the priest. And then he covered her hand with his warm hold and leaned close to whisper, "No need to be nervous. I'm right here by your side."

For some odd reason she actually found his promise reassuring. Facing the priest, not so much.

"Well done, well done." He motioned for the wedding party to be seated. "Lindsay, Zach, if you will face each other. Next I will begin the ceremony. I'll share a few words and then we'll go through the exit procession."

Lindsay turned to face Zach and he took both her hands in each of his. It was the most surreal moment of her life.

The priest began. "Today is a glorious day which the Lord hath made, as today both of you are blessed with God's greatest of all gifts, the gift of abiding love and devotion between a man and woman. All present here today, and those here in heart, wish both of you all the joy, happiness and success the world has to offer—"

"Stop. I can't do this." Lindsay tried to pull away. This hurt too much.

"Lindsay, it's okay." Zach's voice was calm and steady. His hold remained sure and strong as he moved to shield her from the audience. "Father, may we have a moment?"

"Of course, my son." The priest bowed and moved away.

"Breathe, Lindsay. It's going to be okay." Zach leaned over her. "I felt it, too. How right those words were between you and me."

Lindsay clutched at Zach's hands, clinging to him as emotions raged through her heart and head.

"I can't do this. I'm sorry." Aware her behavior embarrassed both her and him, she lifted bleak eyes to meet his gaze. What she saw made the breath catch in her throat.

His eyes were unshielded and in the dark, whiskey depths shone a love so big and so deep it seemed to go on forever. She felt surrounded in a cushion of caring, lifted on a throne of adoration.

"Zach," she breathed.

"I love you, Lindsay." The words echoed everything his eyes already revealed.

Hope slowly swelled through her as her love surged to the surface eager for all his gaze offered. Already weakened, her self-preservation instincts began to crumble as unleashed longing filled her heart.

"I hurt you and I'm more sorry than I can say that I let the fears of my childhood control my common sense when it came to Tony's wedding. You opened my eyes to what I was doing and he hammered it home. But even when I finally accepted the truth and apologized, something still nagged at me, a sense of wrongness that grew rather than diminished."

Behind him she was aware of movement and whispers, reminding her they were not alone. But all she heard, all she saw, was Zach and the raw pain filling eyes that had been overflowing with love just moments ago.

"And then the truth came to me. I couldn't get past how my actions hurt you. I wronged you, not just by disrespecting what you do and by making you work harder, but by putting Tony's needs before yours. That's when I knew the happiness I take in your company and the joy that consumes me when I touch you is actually love."

Now his hands were tight on hers. She ran her thumbs softly over the whites of his knuckles. Everything he'd said was just what she'd longed to hear. She let the last of her concerns melt away.

"Zach." She squeezed his hands. "I love you, too."

Relief flooded his features and he rested his forehead against hers. "Thank God. Because this is bigger and more terrifying than anything I've ever known."

A laugh trilled out of her. "Yes. I'm glad to know I'm not alone."

"You'll never be alone again." He raised his head and his love rained down on her. "Watching you walk down that aisle to me felt more right than anything else in my life. I love you, Lindsay Reeves. Will you marry me?"

"Yes." No hesitation, no need to think. Her misery had come from that same sense of rightness. She longed to spend the rest of her life with this man. "I would love to marry you."

"Right now?" His brown gaze danced with love and mischief.

She blinked at him. "What?"

"Will you marry me right now, in this beautiful chapel we refashioned together?"

Her mind slowly grasped what he wanted, and then her heart soared with excited anticipation. Still, she couldn't get married without her mother. "What about our friends and family?"

"We can have a lavish ceremony back in the States. As big as you want. But I don't want to wait to claim you as mine. So I made sure everyone who truly matters is here."

He stepped back to reveal the chapel filled with people. She saw Louisa sandwiched between Nico and Vincenzo. Raffaele and Daniella sat next to Eva and Mario. Alonso and Serena were here instead of on the road. And many more of the townspeople she'd met and worked with over the past month filled the pews, including the King and Queen of Halencia.

And standing with the grinning priest was Prince Antonio and...her mother.

"Mom?"

"I knew you'd want her here." Zach's hand rested warm and familiar in the small of her back.

"You must have been planning this for days."

"It's the only thing that's kept me sane." He lifted her chin, his mouth settling on hers in restrained urgency. When he raised his head, his eyes gleamed with the heat of desire, the steadfastness of love. "Shall we do this?"

She nodded slowly. "Yes."

Her answer ignited a flurry of activity. Antonio stepped forward while her mother grabbed her hand and hustled her back down the aisle and out the door. In an instant she was in her mom's arms being hugged hard.

"I'm so happy for you, baby. Zach is a force of nature.

If he loves you anywhere near as much as his actions indicate, you will have a long and joyous marriage." She sighed. "For all my marriages, I've never had anyone look at me with so much love."

Lindsay was too excited to have her mother here to care that her special day had circled around to focus on her mom's feelings.

"I'm so glad you're here. You look beautiful." Her mom wore a lovely, pale green silk suit that went well with her upswept brown hair and green eyes. "And you're wrong. Matt looks at you like that. You've just been too focused on yourself to notice."

"Lindsay!" her mother protested, but a speculative glint entered her eyes. "I'll let that slide. We need to get you ready."

"I think I'm as ready as we have time for." Lindsay glanced down at her flowing ivory dress that came to just below her knees in the front and to her ankles in the back and knew she'd been set up. Serena had insisted the dress was perfect for today; business moving into party mode. Of everything she owned this would have been her choice for an impromptu wedding gown.

"Oh, we have time for a few special touches." Darlene pulled Lindsay around the side of the chapel where a full-length, gold-framed mirror leaned against the side of the building, next to it was a garment rack with a flow of tulle over one end and a stack of shelves hanging from the other.

"Something old." From the shelves her mother lifted out a set of pearl-and-sapphire earrings.

"Grandma's earrings." Darlene had worn them for her first wedding and Lindsay recalled saying wistfully she'd wear them at her wedding someday. Her mother had remembered. Her hands shook a little as she put them on.

"Something new." A beaded belt and matching shoes adorned in pearls and crystals shimmered in the late-afternoon sun. While Lindsay traded her sandals for the high-heeled pumps, Darlene stepped behind her and clipped it into place at her waist. They both fit perfectly.

"Something borrowed." Mom smiled. "I saved this because you loved it so much." The tulle turned out to be a full-length veil scalloped on the edges in delicate pearl-infused embroidery. "Close your eyes and face the mirror."

Lindsay's heart expanded; she hadn't realized her mother had been paying such close attention to her reactions through the years. She closed her eyes against a well of tears while Darlene fussed with the veil and the lovely floral hair clip that went with it.

Next she felt a rouge brush dust over her cheeks and some gloss being dabbed on her lips. A tissue caught an escaping tear.

"You can open your eyes."

Lindsay did and was amazed to find a beautiful bride staring back at her. "Mom."

"You're stunning, baby."

Lindsay nodded. She felt stunning and ready to begin her life with Zach.

"Let's go. Your man is waiting."

Rounding the corner of the chapel, she spied the replica of the fountain from the plaza and thought of the wish she'd made with Zach. The wish for true love had been meant for Antonio and Christina. Lindsay supposed she'd been pushing it to make a wish for another couple, but she couldn't be disappointed that fate had chosen to grant true love to her and Zach.

This time when she walked down the aisle her mother escorted her and Lindsay's heart swelled with joy as her gaze locked with Zach's. He'd changed into the suit he'd been wearing when they'd met and she loved the symbolism of the gesture. He knew her so well.

There was no shaking as she placed her hand in his,

just a surety of purpose, a promise to always be there for him. The warmth and steadiness of his grip was the same as it had been earlier and she recognized he'd always be her rock. She suddenly realized something she'd missed when taking in the surprise he'd given her.

"What about your parents?" she whispered.

"They couldn't make it."

"I'm sorry." And angry. His parents didn't deserve him.

"Pixie—" he cupped her cheek "—you're all the family I need."

Her throat closed on a swell of emotion. She swallowed and pledged. "I love you."

"I can't wait for you to be my wife."

"Ahem." Antonio placed his hand on Zach's shoulder. "The priest is waiting."

"Right." Love and anticipation bright in his gaze, he gave the nod. "We're ready, Father."

"We are gathered together on this glorious day which the Lord hath made, to witness the joining of Zachary Sullivan and Lindsay Reeves, who have been blessed with God's greatest of all gifts, the gift of abiding love and devotion between a man and woman..."

* * * * *

LET'S TALK
Romance

For exclusive extracts, competitions
and special offers, find us online: